Praise for

Love & Secrets

AT CASSFIELD MANOR

"*Love and Secrets at Cassfield Manor* by debut author Sarah L. McConkie is a charming Regency romance with plenty of intrigue. Christine Harrison is a dutiful young lady who is on the path of securing a proper marriage. She surrounds herself with friends and acquaintances who will bring out the best in life. But when Christine discovers that things aren't always as they seem, and everyone has a secret, she realizes that her perfect plan of life isn't what's truly important. Readers will love the twists and turns of an intriguing plot, and the gentle romance will make your heart sigh."

—HEATHER B. MOORE, *USA Today* best-selling author of
Heart of the Ocean and *Love Is Come*

"A fun story with plenty of twists, turns, and, of course, romance."

—E. B. WHEELER, award-winning author of
Born to Treason and *Yours, Dorothy*

"*Love and Secrets at Cassfield Manor* is the perfect step into the Regency era. Full of fun, witty, and often mysterious characters, it's a book you won't want to put down!"

—ASHTYN NEWBOLD, author of *Road to Rosewood*

"*Love and Secrets at Cassfield Manor* is a charming Regency romance with a sweet and sometimes sassy heroine matched with a mysterious, yet dashing, suitor. Their story has just enough twists and turns mixed with a bit of intrigue that readers will be eagerly turning pages to see if there will be a happily ever after. Sarah McConkie has woven a swoon-worthy story that will have you closing the book with a smile."

—JULIE COULTER BELLON, author of *A Highlander's Hidden Heart*

Love & Secrets

AT CASSFIELD MANOR

SARAH L. MCCONKIE

SWEETWATER
BOOKS

An imprint of Cedar Fort, Inc.
Springville, Utah

ISBN 13: 978-1-4621-2212-7

Published by Sweetwater Books, an imprint of Cedar Fort, Inc.
2373 W. 700 S., Springville, UT 84663
Distributed by Cedar Fort, Inc., www.cedarfort.com

LIBRARY OF CONGRESS CATALOGING-IN-PUBLICATION DATA

Names: McConkie, Sarah L., 1987- author.
Title: Love and secrets at Cassfield Manor / Sarah L. McConkie.
Description: Springville, UT : Sweetwater Books, An imprint of Cedar Fort,
   Inc., [2018]
Identifiers: LCCN 2018006668 (print) | LCCN 2018010951 (ebook) | ISBN
   9781462129188 (epub, pdf, mobi) | ISBN 9781462122127 (perfect bound : alk.
   paper)
Subjects: LCSH: Man-woman relationships--Fiction. | GSAFD: Regency fiction. |
   LCGFT: Romance fiction.
Classification: LCC PS3613.C3814 (ebook) | LCC PS3613.C3814 L68 2018 (print)
   | DDC 813/.6--dc23
LC record available at https://lccn.loc.gov/2018006668

Cover design by Priscilla Chaves and Shawnda T. Craig
Cover design © 2018 Cedar Fort, Inc.
Edited by Valene Wood and Nicole Terry
Typeset by Kaitlin Barwick

Printed in the United States of America

10 9 8 7 6 5 4 3 2 1

Printed on acid-free paper

To Daniel—
the man who outshines Mr. Darcy or Mr. Knightley any day.

Thank you for having the perfect solution to every problem
and for being a better ending than any book.

CHAPTER 1

The first morning after their arrival at Cassfield Manor always began at sunrise, at least for the Harrison sisters. After spending a long winter in Rothershire, the two sisters could hardly wait for the salty air and the sound of crashing waves.

Christine and her sister, Lizzy, walked arm in arm toward the water's edge. The rising sun warmed their faces as they walked through the rocky, grass-lined plateau toward where the sand met the water.

"Do you think Meg and Ivory will join us soon?" Lizzy asked, her bright-blonde hair disheveled and falling into her face. A few freckles dotted her nose, which wrinkled just slightly when she smiled. Christine pushed her own slightly darker hair away from her eyes and gathered her skirts around her slight figure, the wind having just switched directions. This morning they had not called their maids. The sea at the sunrise held more allure than perfecting their appearance, especially since any male suitors would not call for several days.

"I cannot say," Christine replied with a smile. "You know how Ivory likes her sleep. She and Meg arrived very late last night, and I am sure they are much wearied from the journey."

"Ah, but how could one not come right to the water's edge with the sound of the waves ascending to our windows?" Lizzy exclaimed, throwing her arms wide and spinning.

Christine walked on, passing a few shells and moss-covered gray boulders, considering more practical matters. "You know, Lizzy, I must pride myself on even convincing Ivory Rusket to come all the way from London to our manor. I still have great hopes that her friendship will provide us many advantages." Christine gazed back at the stone house rising above the grasses with its large latticed windows. They continued to walk alone. "I would even go so far as to suggest that she would never have started visiting Meg so often had it not been for our connection."

Lizzy stopped. "You really think so, sister? Meg and Ivory are cousins. It is so very natural for them to visit each other!"

"Ah, Lizzy." Christine took her sister under her arm like a mother bird. "Your sweetness would assume so. But you know Rothershire is far from London, and Ivory connects herself with others to serve her advantage. Meg's circumstances would not have been so reduced if her mother had not married for love. And the consequence is that the Allensbys will never have a tenth of the income of Ivory's family. So it is beneficial to Meg to have rich friends like us, and it is beneficial for Ivory to have high society to enjoy when she comes to the north country. And"—Christine's voice lowered—"it *was* my plan, before Mr. Davenport came to Rothershire, to marry one of Ivory's connections. But hopefully I have secured an admirable catch for myself, so *you* ought now to invest in meeting some young acquaintance of Ivory's circle."

Lizzy smiled. "I do not think I shall ever marry a man with half as many credentials as you have found. I know so little of men and the world! Just think," Lizzy said, her ever-hopeful air showing itself, "this shall be our last summer before you become my *married* sister."

Christine puffed herself up a little. "Yes, Mr. Davenport will arrive in a few days, and I do hope to receive an offer of marriage from him soon. But it will not happen yet, to be sure. I have not quite won his heart. These things take time."

Lizzy, being only sixteen, nodded in agreement, like she did with most things Christine declared, but added, "Say what you want, sister, but I have seen the way he looks at you."

Christine smiled and sighed to herself as she thought of the rich young beau from Cheshire. Two months ago he arrived at dinner with the Grenvilles, boasting a handsome figure, piercing eyes, and six thousand a year. And when Christine learned of his recent purchase of a second estate, increasing his per annum by two thousand, she declared him almost perfect.

As the sun crept just above the ocean's edge, Christine recalled why she loved their days at Cassfield Manor. The beauty and serenity of the scene stood without compare, the cool blue-green of the ocean extending westward as far as the eye could see.

Christine had given up wading a year ago, proclaiming herself too old. And although Christine allowed herself now only the seaside stroll—for it was time to give up childish things and become a lady—this morning, convinced by Lizzy, she walked through the sand, searching for shells.

The sisters shared years of memories at Cassfield. Years ago when their older brother tormented them with splashing and shaking wiggling crabs in their faces. Then as he married and moved away, years of just Christine and Lizzy, pretending to be mermaids washed up on some foreign land with people who had legs, searching for seashells, playing in the sun and disregarding the multitude of warnings from their mother. "You will ruin your complexion!" "Girls, you will look like peasants by the time we return home!" The summer Christine found a shell with a hole in it and wore it on a necklace until it broke. The summer Christine and Lizzy first decided to invite Meg. And then last summer when Christine found it imperative that they invite Meg's cousin, Miss Ivory Rusket, to join them. The dynamic of the group would never again be the same.

Less than a half hour later, Christine and Lizzy spotted Ivory and Meg making their way to the sea wall. Christine saw Ivory first, looking almost the same as the year before but perhaps slightly more beautiful, if that were possible. Her figure, still slight, had more alluring curves than a year before, and her stunning full lips and large bright eyes seemed even more striking. Her shorter cousin Meg ran behind, her dark hair bobbing up and down in a disheveled bun as the two came toward the Harrison sisters.

As soon as she reached earshot, Ivory exclaimed, "I am so very glad to see you both in your day dresses with unkempt hair. I daresay we will see no one. Meg seemed quite anxious to join you for a morning stroll, even though both of us could benefit from some attention to our appearance."

Meg gave a half-smile toward her taller, slender cousin but said nothing, for she always spoke the least of the four. The girls then began to walk along the water's edge, the companions bursting into raptures, relating a year's worth of chatter all at once. It was Ivory's speech, true to form, which prevailed over her peers.

"Ladies," Ivory said, her round, green-hazel eyes opening wide, "I have so much to tell you from London!"

Christine sighed and carefully concealed her eye roll, wondering how her friend had waited so very long to begin such an address, for Ivory believed all she had to say to be quite important.

"Do tell!" Lizzy answered, eager for any news, especially from London.

Ivory looked at them all and began. "At one of the first balls of the season, I was introduced to someone, and I am very taken with him. And . . ." Ivory paused, "I daresay he is *very* taken with me."

Christine and Meg, both older than their esteemed friend and cousin, exchanged a dubious side-eyed smirk as Ivory looked more intently at Lizzy, who received her raptures without hesitation. "You would have loved it, Lizzy! And I know you would all approve of him!"

"What are his credentials?" Christine asked, skeptical of such open praise. Someone of Ivory's status ought to list his holdings and social status before all else.

"To be candid," Ivory replied, "I own I do not know! But we had a delightful time together. His name is Mr. Henry Robertson. He was introduced in a very high circle and he has scores of friends and acquaintances, so he must be respectable, I daresay! He carries himself so well, and he presents himself just as a gentleman ought. At *that* very ball, he asked me to dance his first dance, and I saw him later at a few others. We have since danced several more times—and dined together more than once!"

Ivory linked her thin arm through her cousin's and cocked her beautiful mouth to the side. Meg smiled as Ivory continued, "I even invited him to visit us at Cassfield this spring."

Christine's eyes widened as she processed such a comment. Her walk halted for a moment.

"You invited a complete stranger to my parents' manor? Do you know what my father and mother will think? We do not know anything of his character! He has not been properly introduced!"

"I told Mr. Robertson of our plans, and he said he might be stopping by Broughington Lake on business. I mentioned to him that we would be near there at Cassfield! So, naturally, he promised to come visit us for a few days!"

Christine's mind filled with quizzical incarnations of Ivory's beau as she repressed several additional comments on such a scheme. A businessman? Surely one did not first describe a man of character by his business dealings. What of his holdings, his status, and procurements? Was he to inherit anything more than a business ledger? Why would Ivory condescend to associate with someone so much below her—and then presume to bring him to Cassfield? And above all else, what if his stay interrupted Mr. Davenport's visit? Nothing could get in the way of making every moment of Mr. Davenport's time perfect at Cassfield Manor.

These were the questions that so eagerly presented themselves before Christine's mind. She was doubtful, however, if Ivory had as of yet entertained such analytical thoughts toward this man—or any man, for that matter.

And Christine had made sure to inform Ivory of Mr. Davenport and Mr. Grenville's visit very clearly. How could Ivory invite an unknown gentleman to her family's manor? It was not Ivory's place to do so, nor did Christine want any of Ivory's male guests usurping the spotlight and prominence of the men Christine's father had already invited. Christine sighed, studying Ivory's perfect figure and beautiful, inviting mouth. Of course this Mr. Robertson would chase her all the way to Cassfield, regardless of social implication or connections.

They had started walking again, and at last, Christine contented herself by saying, "I must have you know that I do not approve and I do not like the sound of such impropriety. A true gentleman would wait until the head of the house invited him to stay, as our guests Mr. Davenport and Mr. Grenville have done. I am not sure your invitation will stand at Cassfield, Ivory. You will have to be the one to tell my father about it. I could never have the audacity to propose such an activity."

And I will not have it interfere with my time with Mr. Davenport, Christine added silently to herself. She would not allow Ivory to upstage her.

"I am happy to tell your father of my proposal," Ivory said. "Mr. Harrison will *not* mind. And after all of you have the pleasure of making Mr. Robertson's acquaintance, you will be glad for his company. You will surely approve of him, I know it."

Christine exhaled audibly and then begrudged a smile, reflecting that her father, Mr. Harrison, was among the happiest, most obliging of men and would in fact most likely concede to Ivory's request. He never wanted to displease anyone.

Christine turned her head and said no more. Her eyes followed the curve of the shore, gazing at the long grasses and silty path before her. She breathed in deeply, the fresh, crisp smell of ocean filling her nose.

Every past spring, she had felt safe at Cassfield. It was her sanctuary, devoid of gentlemen and social protocols. But this spring would be different and hopefully occupied with a new kind of amusement. Christine had pressed her father to invite Mr. Davenport and his friend Mr. Grenville to visit. She wanted to use this time at Cassfield to further her relationship with Mr. Davenport—and now Ivory came with her own agenda, trying to outshine Christine.

Christine then gave way to a tug of emotions. Mr. Davenport excited her. He met or exceeded most of her requirements for a husband. But she knew life would never be the same if her future continued with him. Her days of female enjoyment and camaraderie would be exchanged for the illustrious position of mistress of the house with servants and carriages at her disposal.

It was a fine prospect, but how she sometimes still resisted change.

But Christine desired marriage more than anything else and knew it must be her pursuit. She was of age and the eldest daughter of a rich gentleman and knew she ought to make the best of her situation before she grew too old. She had carefully preened herself over the last year for such obligations and opportunities. Mr. Davenport showed the most promise and the handsomest face, not to mention he seemed quite taken with her.

Christine listened again as Meg began her part next. Meg looked radiant in the morning sun, always becoming, yet much less ostentatious than her cousin. Her quiet, grounded personality contributed most to her overall prettiness. Her pale skin turned rosy, and her blue eyes twinkled while she described to her friends the many seascapes she hoped to portray in her artwork. She would paint Cassfield Manor, the ocean and its various lights and stages, and—if they would allow her—each one of her dear friends amongst her masterpieces.

Lizzy agreed and encouraged all speeches, while Christine stayed unusually silent, lost in reflections. The chatter eventually subsided, and having walked a long distance, the girls turned back.

Lizzy, Meg, and Ivory returned to dress for the day, but Christine chose to remain near the water's edge a little longer, slipping off her shoes, abandoning custom now that she sat alone. To Christine, the blue of the ocean, with its crisp wet bubbles kissing her bare feet, shone as a metaphor for the changes before her. This summer could bring much excitement and improvement—if Ivory and her beau did not disrupt Christine's plans with Mr. Davenport.

Mr. Oliver Davenport

Mr. Davenport took the letter from the tray hastily, perplexed by the feminine hand of the address, which seemed a bit messy for Miss Christine Harrison. Mr. Davenport knew Christine always wrote with a decided, accomplished design. He would travel to this lovely Miss Harrison in a few days, and perhaps she wrote the address quickly to assure its arrival before he left to her.

But upon opening the letter, he stopped. His eyes narrowed, every muscle in his body tightened, and he released hold of the single sheet of paper, its unfolded edges landing on the table. It seemed to burn his palm like a fire. He peered warily as he read its contents.

Mr. Davenport,

I am sure you did not suspect my pen to write this letter, but alas, I must do my father's bidding. He wishes to inform you that the last shipment you directed has been properly placed and the deposit of funds has entered your London bank account.

As for myself, I hope that when you return to London, I might have the good fortune of seeing you again.

Sincerely,
Miss Estelle Braxton

Having understood both the success of the shipment and the sentiment of the writer, he hastily crumpled the paper and threw it directly into the hearth, full of disgust.

Why must she write the letter? He would not see her again. She ought to know he still felt the same today as he had a year ago—resolute in his refusal of her. And now he stood even more determined to never think of Miss Braxton again. He had decided to marry Miss Harrison, and within the next few months, he would ask for her hand.

He would send no reply.

Thrusting the unexpected note from his thoughts, Mr. Davenport tried for the rest of the evening to think of ways to promote his relationship with Christine. He felt drawn to her open smiles and witty comments. He reflected on her hair, full of loose curls, and her pleasing figure. He felt grateful for his friend Mr. Grenville for presenting such a favorable option to him. Mr. Davenport had known of her person and family for years, but now he believed her mutually interested, and his holdings had increased enough to win her. Their temperaments suited each other well, humor and intellect among them. She seemed drawn to his alluring charm, and he thought her dazzling and quite well bred.

Eventually, the advantage of Christine Harrison displaced his unpleasant thoughts of the letter and his former love. He slept soundly that night, recalling Christine's beautiful dark-blonde curls, her blue-green eyes, and the sum of fifteen thousand pounds upon her marriage to him.

CHAPTER 2

"Mr. Harrison," Miss Rusket began the next morning, her large eyes full of triumph. She looked over her breakfast plate and turned with authority to the head of the table. "I have an acquaintance from London that might be passing through Broughington Lake within the week. Might he visit here?"

There was a hint of a pause, and then Mr. Harrison clapped his hands together. "Of course!" he replied. He turned his shoulder opposite the direction of Ivory and slightly shook his head, so that only Christine could see his expression, which she met with her own incredulous glance. Christine knew exactly how to interpret his face. Requests without regard to societal norms were not altogether unexpected from Ivory. Mr. Harrison did not fall prey to such schemes, and yet Christine's father granted the request because of his generosity, regardless of the imposition. This characteristic of her father endeared him to her and Christine could not help but accept his generous kindness, notwithstanding Miss Rusket's untoward request.

The talked-of Mr. Robertson arrived at Cassfield just before dinner. Ivory had insisted that the girls wait inside that day, and the friends now stood huddled around an upper-story window, carefully out of sight, watching the stranger step from his carriage. They heard the butler usher him in.

"Mr. Harrison, I presume," said a hearty, confident voice a moment later, a bit muffled as it carried up from downstairs. "I must apologize for arriving without being formally introduced. My name is Henry Robertson. I would like to thank you for allowing me to visit."

Christine harrumphed grudgingly. At least *he* had the sense of propriety and decorum to officially point his arrival at Christine's father. From the rest of the conversation, Christine could tell that Mr. Harrison liked him straightaway and, upon hearing Mr. Robertson planned to stay at an inn, immediately insisted he stay at Cassfield instead. Mr. Robertson heartily accepted. At Ivory's urging, Christine consented to the four of them descending downstairs for dinner.

Just before they started the stairs, Christine inspected him, though she did not have a perfect angle from above. She could see his hair, the color of bleached sand, curled over his forehead. He had a strong nose, but not too large. He had broad shoulders, and his quite tall form stood adorned in the jacket of a gentleman, though it was still to be seen if he deserved such a title. Christine tried hard to stifle her resentment toward Ivory. How dare her beau arrive even before Christine's planned guests?

Supper was served promptly after the girls came down, as receiving Mr. Robertson over food seemed only appropriate in the Harrison home. Mrs. Harrison entered and joined her husband's side, and the rest of young ladies curtsied toward the new visitor.

"Allow me to introduce my dear wife, Mrs. Harrison, whose scrupulous eye attended to every detail of this evening, including most of all the menu. And then we have my eldest daughter, Miss Harrison; my youngest, Miss Elizabeth; and, of course, our dear friends Miss Allensby and Miss Rusket, whom you know, of course."

Mr. Robertson bowed to each, smiling amiably. "It is a pleasure to meet the esteemed acquaintances of Miss Rusket." He walked toward Christine. "May I have the honor of escorting you?"

Christine stifled a sigh. He was trying to win her over with his gallantry. It was his *duty* to escort her, as the eldest of the household. She took his arm anyway, determined to be unimpressed as they filed into the dining room.

Hosting meals was a matter of pride for Christine's mother. They kept an excellent cook with the budget to complement her. The dining room matched the finesse of Cook Cooper's abilities, done up in the newest style, a lush green brocade upholstering the dark wood chairs. Beautiful Italian pictures hung on the wall, and every piece of etched china and crystal perfectly coordinated. Mounted candlesticks show-cased the long rectangular table, providing a welcoming glow to the abundant surroundings.

After everyone took their places, they were served soup, which Mr. Robertson greeted with an excitement not usually given to an opening course. In truth, Mr. Robertson seemed thrilled with just about every-thing. He sat in between Christine and Miss Rusket, whose elated face said much concerning her feelings toward the evening. As he compli-mented Miss Rusket on her appearance, Christine took a moment to inspect him, sipping discreetly from her bowl to hide her scrutiny. He was tall—even when seated—and his hair, light blond and slightly curly, waved perfectly across his brow. It could be said that his bright-blue eyes were his best feature, and he was fairly handsome, but it was the way his eyes wrinkled and his wide smile opened that drew a person to him. One might conclude, after even a few minutes in his presence, that he was amiable, perhaps even slightly charming. As the meal carried on, Christine found that he asked interesting questions, laughed a great deal, and carried the conversation with finesse.

After a half hour, Christine begrudgingly thought to herself, *Well done, Ivory,* contrary to all previous misgivings. Christine had not yet made out his character, but he seemed like a fine man—presenting himself admirably on many fronts. He was not quite as well established or attractive as Mr. Davenport, but Ivory seemed quite taken with him, and if she really did not care about his income or standing, he might just do the job credibly.

A few minutes later, Mr. Robertson said, "Mr. Harrison, why is it that you enjoy fishing so much?" Mr. Harrison had earlier extended an invitation to Henry Robertson to accompany him on his boat the next morning. Because Mr. Harrison had since reiterated the invite three times, such a conversation proved a sure success.

"I admit that I like fishing," Mr. Harrison said, "only for the sport of it. Truthfully, I love being on the water, enjoying something other than my estate ledger. If I could have it my way, I would spend a few hours outdoors each day rather than showing myself as the head of the household. But alas, 'tis my duty." Mr. Harrison smiled. "Sometimes I think I would have been a better sailor than a gentleman."

"I think I know how you feel," Mr. Robertson reflected toward the group. It was truly remarkable how he carried himself with so much ease. Christine, however, was not sure he *did* know how her father felt, for how could he possibly know the constraints of a gentleman if he himself was not one?

Christine watched Henry smile, turning deliberately toward her mother. "And Mrs. Harrison," Mr. Robertson said, "this meat is delicious. Please give my compliments to your cook."

Mrs. Harrison smiled, "Why thank you, Mr. Robertson. We do our best to have only the finest meat and freshest seafood here at Cassfield Manor—only the best for our guests."

"Yes, I like to believe we employ the best cook in the county!" Mr. Harrison said. "Cook Cooper was a lucky find," he added, squeezing his wife's hand.

Christine knew this to be true, for her mother thought so highly of their cook that she traveled between Cassfield Manor and Wellington Estate, in Rothershire. Christine also understood that such dinners held exceptional pleasure for her parents especially when feeding eligible male visitors.

The rest of the meal passed pleasantly, each in their turn questioning Mr. Robertson. As the young women then went through to the drawing room, Miss Rusket wanted to know all her friends' thoughts on her beau.

"He is quite charming," Lizzy complimented.

"Yes, and quite tall, with rather captivating manners," Meg added. Ivory beamed.

Christine nodded, but gave no other reassurance to her friend.

A few minutes later, as the men came into the drawing room, Mr. Robertson brought news of London, which Christine deemed rather interesting.

"Miss Rusket," he said, "I understand your father, Lord Molliard, sits in the House of Lords in Parliament?"

"Yes he does, Mr. Robertson," Ivory said, for once glowing about one of her parents.

"What do you think of their deliberations this season?" he asked.

Ivory shifted her eyes a bit and replied, "I do not actually know, Mr. Robertson. My father hardly ever talks of what occurs at Parliament, and I admit, I do not have a mind for it! Seems to me like a bunch of arguing Whigs!"

"Ah, of course," Mr. Robertson replied with a good-natured laugh. Christine perceived, however, that he sought a more thoughtful answer from Ivory.

The excitement of the evening reached a zenith when Mr. Robertson robustly declared, "And to you all, I would like to formally invite you to a ball held by my aunt in London the first week of June. I seem to have many gentlemen from university and business who will attend, and I now can promise them there will be a few kind young ladies willing and able to dance with them, if you will oblige. This will be the last large ball of the Season in London, and you all must be in attendance!"

Christine nodded, Lizzy smiled, and Meg slightly clasped her hands together, while the outspoken Ivory proclaimed, "We would be delighted!"

She turned to the other three, throwing her arms out wide and declared, "And you must all stay with me. What a great way to repay you for my visits to Cassfield! What a splendid time we shall have!"

Christine guarded her grin. An invite to London during the Season with Ivory as her guide would prove quite diverting. Sometimes Ivory did run away with her tongue, but her associations made her loquacity much more tolerable.

It then seemed the perfect time to interrogate their handsome guest.

"May I ask you how old you are?" Lizzy queried. "For we ought to know how old your friends will be at your aunt's ball."

"Twenty-six," he replied. "And I can assure you there will be many gentlemen of similar age and temperament enough to please you all." He flashed a smile in all directions. Mr. Robertson had no trouble holding his own amidst four young ladies. Christine hoped the dialogue would turn toward Mr. Robertson's particulars, and Meg ventured there next.

"And do you have any sisters or brothers?" Meg asked him, finding a way to enter the conversation. Of course Meg would ask about his family. *If only there were some way to ask about his per annum sum,* thought Christine. For once, she wished for town gossip at her disposal, but there was none to be had on this Mr. Robertson.

"I have several sisters. Four, to be exact, all older than me and married. I therefore have several nieces and nephews, as you might expect with four married sisters, but only one brother."

"And where do you live most of the year?" Lizzy interjected, each girl wanting to know everything about him.

"In London, although I travel to Scotland often, and I have recently returned from Asia on business."

On this point Christine found her segue. "Traveling to Asia!" she exclaimed, interested but wanting more to ascertain his standing as a "man of trade." Poor Ivory was having trouble getting in any conversation with each of her companions dominating Mr. Robertson's answers, but Henry seemed not to mind.

"Do tell us of this adventure," Christine continued, hoping her voice rang with attention and not skeptical curiosity, which sentiment hailed closer to her true feelings.

"It takes many months to travel there, so I began my journey eighteen months ago. My brother and I spent a few months traveling deep into their main trade cities, looking for fabric suppliers. We hope to gain an edge on the market in England in the ways of silk, brocade, and other less-common textiles. It takes quite a bit of luck and determination to make connections enough to import such items from so far away."

He shot a quick glance toward Ivory, pretending to not notice her put-out expression. She had already heard each of these particulars.

"I returned this winter, but my brother has not yet arrived. He stayed behind to finish some dealings and see the shipment through. He should be back within a fortnight or sennight if I am lucky."

This piece of information produced a flood of further questions from each of the young ladies, who directed inquiries at him with almost no rhyme or reason. He continued answering all queries, with Ivory now gaining the floor by asking the most questions about his business that she had not yet learned. This seemed a defensive stance, based on the tightening of Ivory's jaw, and Christine was sure Ivory felt relieved to remember that there would be *other* men at Mr. Robertson's ball.

Through all of this, Christine could not help but notice that Mr. Robertson seemed excessively genuine and very attentive to all around him. He acted like a gentleman but talked liked a businessman. Ivory did not seem to concern herself with his rank, but Christine still wondered about his status. *And yet many gentlemen needed a business savvy head on their shoulders*, thought Christine, *to maintain one's estate and holdings*. Her Mr. Davenport had done credibly in this regard, even increasing his land.

The Harrison daughters had listened to many a diatribe from their father over dinner of men who were "squandering away their inheritances as soon as they became of eligible age, not reinvesting their money properly to ensure the future of the family holdings." Their father loved repeating adages of his own creation that reflected his sentiment. Often, after the aforementioned, well-worn sentence, he would add this warm piece of advice: "You can marry more money in a half-hour than a man can earn in a lifetime."

Christine understood exactly the advantage of a wealthy match.

And so, after listening to Mr. Robertson, Christine believed his business to be an upstanding kind of business, and she commended him for that, but she wondered just how much money he obtained through it and what degree of status it provided him.

The next morning, neither Ivory nor Christine saw Mr. Robertson. He had dressed earlier than the women of the house and joined Mr. Harrison fishing before anyone had a chance to waylay him. Such an action suited Mr. Harrison, who always desired a first mate.

That afternoon, Mr. Robertson was not seen until dinner, but the evening intensified when Mr. Robertson alluded to the book Ivory held. All of the young ladies retired to the drawing room, and this time he asked Miss Rusket about the volume of Aristotle's works. Christine witnessed quite the scene as she looked over her own book. Clearly, Mr. Robertson spoke as one very well versed, and Ivory was not his equal, knowing very little of the tome she currently clutched. She was one of the most enjoyable creatures to be around but had no penchant for analytical conversations.

"And what, Miss Rusket, do you think about Aristotle? Or do you prefer Plato?"

"I must admit I do not have the mind for philosophy. I much prefer something a bit lighter." Ivory brushed her hand across the cover of her unopened volume.

"Shall we discuss Shakespeare, then?" he asked.

"Yes, of course. I have read *A Midsummer's Night Dream*," she began, fiddling with her hands.

The conversation, however, did not go much further when she could not quite remember if Hermia or Helena loved Lysander. Such observations proved to her companions, if not to Ivory herself, that the two resided on different planes. Mr. Robertson clearly loved literature, and Ivory was not much of a reader. Ivory preferred talking of people and the trends of the day. To his credit, Mr. Robertson had attempted to ask a woman's opinion of politics, which Christine thought quite remarkable. To Christine, it seemed an evidence of his pleasing—although unconventional—demeanor. To Mr. Robertson, no one was his superior. Ivory, however, did not find his political and literary questions a rare virtue, and the conversation had become strained at best. After a few minutes, Christine realized there was some silence between Ivory and Mr. Robertson, so she interjected, "Should Lizzy play for us tonight? We did not hear her on the pianoforte yesterday."

Both people previously involved in the tête-à-tête jumped at the idea.

"What a nice diversion! I do love music!" Ivory said.

Christine played after Lizzy, and the evening was spared any further tense conversation. Mr. Robertson seemed to enjoy the evening but did not appear overly interested in Miss Rusket by the time everyone retired to sleep.

The next morning, Christine's maid finished her hair and dress first, and Christine walked down the corridor to check on the progress of her friends. Hearing Ivory's voice, more intimate than usual, Christine stopped just behind the door, which stood barely ajar, unsure whether she ought to enter.

"How I wished I would have read more of the books my tutor had suggested, for then my conversation would have been much more interesting with Mr. Robertson last night."

Christine could see the back of Meg's head, her curls already pinned, as Meg said, "Do not fret about last night. You looked beautiful, and Mr. Robertson is still quite taken with you." She placed a soft hand on Ivory's looking glass. "But tell me, how is it having your own tutor? It sounds tiresome. I have only ever had a few painting instructors years ago."

Christine, not wanting to seem like she was eavesdropping, gently slid into the doorway.

"Good morning," Ivory said, and then she hastily went back into her conversation, including Christine in her hushed whispers. "Have I never told you of her before? Miss O'Rourke is not tiresome in the least!" Ivory's animated hands moved briskly, not bothering to explain the beginning of the story. "I always thought her *quite* wonderful. She is so knowledgeable. She helped me with mathematics, language, literature, and was the most pleasant person to be around—or at least I thought. But her discharge from our household has become quite a scandalous piece of hushed-up gossip," she said, her eyes widening. "A few months ago, she was dismissed by my mother, who claimed she found my tutor alone with a man who had just come to court me." Ivory looked up toward Christine at the moment, reading her face. "And she found her kissing him in the female servants' quarters. My mother does not stand for any such impropriety and dismissed her on the spot, refusing any character recommendations in the future. It is really *quite* tragic. I have not heard from her since. But I loved her advice and her company, and I do so hope she is well."

"That is rather shocking," Meg replied. "I can see why your mother kept the whole affair so secret."

"I have to admit, I would never have thought Miss O'Rourke to do such a thing," Ivory said defensively.

"I am sure she is a good person, Ivory," Meg said, always sweet and not wanting to pass judgment. "Perhaps your mother exaggerated the offense."

Ivory nodded, touching a few pieces of her hair.

Christine knew then just how comfortable Ivory felt with her and Meg. She had no sisters and had chosen to confide in them such a sad tale. Ivory looked to Christine as though she wished they would change the subject.

"Well," Christine said cheerfully after a moment's pause, "I trust you slept well?"

"Indeed," Ivory responded, bustling about as if she had not just divulged such information.

"And so what shall we do with Mr. Robertson today, Ivory? Or do you have plans to keep him all to yourself?" Christine asked, trying too late to stifle an edge to her jest.

"Oh no, I daresay we shall see nothing of him, at least this morning. He went into Broughington Lake to check on business!" For visiting Ivory, he seemed *quite* busy occupying his time in other ways.

"I see," Christine said, who felt a bit relieved by his absence but also wanted more time to discern his character. "I hope he returns before dinner."

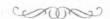

Mr. Robertson did return from Broughington Lake by the midafternoon. Christine, seeking to learn more of Mr. Robertson's background, proposed they all take a stroll on the water's edge. Mr. Robertson agreed heartily, and the four girls and one gentleman made their way to the shore. The thin grass waved only slightly, and the tall, mossy stones stood as sentinels in the bright sun. Christine left Lizzy and Meg and caught up with Ivory and Mr. Robertson, who walked arm in arm. Upon seeing Christine, Mr. Robertson graciously offered his other arm. She took it, using this moment to unearth his rank in society.

"Mr. Robertson, tell us more of your family. You said you live most of the year in London? What part?"

Mr. Robertson smiled. "Currently, my brother and I live with my cousin, and it is his aunt who will be hosting the ball. They live a few blocks from Grosvenor Square. It is through him that I met Miss Rusket."

Such a report made his cousin's status seem reputable. But she could not stop there.

"I see," she said. "And how long have you and your brother owned your business?" She tried to muffle her disdain.

"We started four years ago, after moving to London. My family is Scottish, Miss Harrison, and only in the last few years have we lived in London. But we quite enjoy town and plan to remain there."

"Oh, you are Scottish, then," Christine replied with a lofty tone. "I had been trying to place your mannerisms and the slight accent, and now I understand fully," she stated and then, teasing him a little, added, "I suppose we will not hold that against you."

Miss Rusket then tried to pull Mr. Robertson into some discussion of the fashions of London, and Christine noticed him answering with a quite uninterested tenor. During this one-sided conversation, Christine mulled over Mr. Robertson's comments. He had, by the relation of his cousin, quite respectable connections in London. He came from Scotland, but surely his Scottish lineage must have also been of the gentry.

Christine pretended, quite often in those first few days, to be put off by Mr. Robertson, but she actually believed he would prove to be a wonderful friend. They could, she hoped, become the best allies: him introducing favorable connections to her, and she introducing him to many other rich and beautiful women, if and when Miss Rusket blew by.

The morning following, Christine passed by her father's study on the way to breakfast.

"Christine," he said, beckoning to her, "Mr. Robertson is a great man! I am very pleased for Miss Rusket. I hope he has some friends that you will be able to make advantageous connections with." He then lowered his voice a bit and continued, "But it would be best, I assure you, to make connections with his acquaintances quickly, for your mother declares that Mr. Robertson does not enjoy Miss Rusket at all, and she believes their interaction will soon wane, thus ending your connection."

"Why is that?"

"She believes they are not matched well. But Miss Rusket is beautiful, and terribly well connected, and I tried to remind your mother that "matching" is not always a prerequisite for an engagement. She often does not realize how lucky she had it to marry me." He grinned at Christine, and she returned the smile.

"At any rate, I do hope you enjoy yourself at his ball later this Season. You need to savor these events, my dear. Enjoy yourself! You ought to align yourself with Mr. Robertson and his associates." Christine mused at this thought, because heretofore, her father had been quite partial to Mr. Davenport.

"Perhaps you are right." A faint smile crossed her lips as she turned. "I will try."

That evening, Christine sat in front of a large mirror as her maid rearranged a few curls. Lizzy sat on the bed across the room with her gown laid out, just waiting for her own maid to arrive from downstairs. The girls chose to share this large suite, with its two feather beds, ample furniture, and natural light, so they could exchange confidences each evening and see the ocean out one window and spy on the entry gates from the other. Christine had just applied a bit of perfume when her maid's head turned toward the large, latticed-paned window and she declared, "Look miss, a carriage comes up the park."

"Really?" Christine turned her half-pinned head toward the window. "We were not expecting anyone until tomorrow." Lizzy sprang from her bed and joined her sister, looking over her vanity to spy the carriage.

Christine watched as a pair of sable horses came to a stop and two gentlemen began to descend from a coach just below her window. Christine knew instantly it was her Mr. Davenport, identifying his carriage and remembering just how Mr. Davenport carried himself, with his friend Mr. Grenville trailing behind. She looked at herself in the mirror, remembered half her hair still cascaded down her shoulder and determined she could not go downstairs to greet him presently. She returned her glance out her window, this time seeing the tall, blond Mr. Robertson hurry from the front door, gathering his coat around him. Though walking quickly, he stopped completely upon meeting Mr. Davenport's gaze. Both men straightened, and they seemed to exchange a few words but each did not move toward the other. Christine thought she saw Mr. Davenport stand a little taller, his shoulders tense. Mr. Robertson waved his hand, and Christine thought she heard some excuse as he mounted the horse brought up for him.

Christine turned to Lizzy and said, "How curious. What a strange meeting."

She then addressed her maid, "And if you do not mind, I would like to finish as soon as possible." The maid nodded and began working quickly.

No more than two minutes later, Ivory barged in Christine's room. She looked practically on fire, with Meg trailing behind obligatorily.

"I have just received the most awful news!"

Ivory thrust an unfolded piece of paper between Lizzy and Christine, who hastily read its contents.

Mr. Harrison and the young ladies of the house,

I regret to inform you that I must leave immediately. Please give my apologies to Mrs. Harrison, as I will not be able to dine with you. I will have to explain in more detail when I see you all in a few weeks at the ball. I have left the date and address enclosed for that meeting.

Best regards,
Mr. Henry Robertson

"He cannot be serious," Ivory declared, her tone agitated and quiet. Christine answered, "We hardly just met him."

"Why is his leaving so abrupt?" Lizzy asked. "Did he tell you his trip might be shorter?"

"No, he did not. I have no idea what has caused his departure. This letter was given to your father, and he had it sent directly to me." Ivory turned toward the window, tightening her jaw. Mr. Robertson was already out of sight.

Ivory sprawled dejectedly across Christine's bed and began immediately conjecturing what news could have made him leave so suddenly. Meg and Lizzy joined in straightaway, fabricating schemes that provided more comfort than truth to Ivory. Christine mused that one of the great condolences of young female acquaintance lies in sharing improbable suppositions regarding young men. If not accurate, at least they provided Ivory some excuse at such a time as this.

But Christine, hair now complete, was anxious to welcome their new visitors.

"I am sure he has a very good explanation, which we shall ask him at his aunt's ball. But as he left, I did see Mr. Davenport and Mr. Grenville arrive. I am sure they have made their introduction to my father. Shall we go down and welcome them now?"

Mr. Henry Robertson

Two Years Previous

Henry Robertson sat apprehensively next to the bed, wishing he had more time. His father lay dying, sick with a hot fever that could not be controlled. Henry's large, strong hands held his father's, and he looked into the same crystal-blue eyes as his own.

"There is something I have yet to explain," the older man said, struggling for breath. "As I have not time nor strength to give the details now, you must go to your grandfather and ask him to explain." He looked deeper into his son's countenance and drew in again. "Trust me, it is for the best. This is how it must be. I am sorry I have not spoken of it sooner." He took a deep breath in as though he were going to add more, but instead exhaled. He gasped and then, after a few more strained moments, closed his eyes. The room suddenly felt cold and dark as Henry rested his head on the bed beside his father, his eyes filling with tears. It was only one week ago that his father's health had made a turn for the worse. No one was expecting such an sudden passing of this robust man.

And yet his grandfather, though aging, still stood so clear in mind and able-bodied, even now outliving his son. Henry loved his father, and always had. One could not have wished for a better example nor, in his older years, a better confidant and friend. Why did he have to leave them now? There was so much Henry still wanted to learn from him, to ask him.

But what had his father meant in his last words? What secret had his father and his grandfather kept all this time? It was not like his father to hold back. He almost always spoke his strong opinion openly; one always knew his beliefs.

Perhaps William will have some idea when he arrives, Henry thought.

William, Henry's brother, rode an express coach through the night and arrived the next morning. The brothers talked through the matter-of-fact details of the funeral, neither brother discussing any memory or thought that did not pertain to the task immediately ahead. But after a few hours, Henry finally told William of his last moments with their father.

"Do you know what he spoke of?" Henry asked.

William knit his brow and ran his hand over his forehead.

"I have no idea, brother. I am just as surprised as you." William heaved a great sigh. "But there will be time to find out. For now, the most important thing is that the family comes together to mourn and also to celebrate the life of our father."

And so, though painful, Henry and William prepared a few remarks to celebrate the greatness of their father, Lewis Robertson. A scholar by profession and a gentleman, he had touched many lives through his teaching and his large circle of acquaintances. His wife had died many years prior, and his daughters all successfully married and now had families of their own. But his two sons remained his faithful and loving friends until his death and were the ones now charged with all of the familial responsibilities.

At the services, Henry and his brother gave a few words, followed by their grandfather, who spoke last. Then, in true Scottish fashion, the bagpipes sounded as the gathering ended and the party marched to the gravesite. Finally, when all was finished and the attendees had all made their respects to Henry and William, the finality of the situation struck the brothers. Since their mother's death, their father had always been their strength.

As the last of the guests filed out, Henry and his brother returned to the Robertsons' great stone manor and collapsed exhausted just inside the front study. A hand fell on each of their shoulders. Their tall, smiling grandfather, complete with his firm grasp and angled jaw, stood behind them.

"It has been a good day, lads. Your father has been honored just as he ought to be honored. He would be proud of what has transpired today." He paused, smiling but holding back a tear, and then continued, "And I am sure he mentioned something of this to you, Henry." He held a thick, sealed letter. "The two of you must open it together. He has herein written his instructions and wishes. I am sorry he left us so quickly. I know he wanted to speak to both of you of this matter before your twenty-fourth birthday."

Henry and his brother paused and looked up at their grandfather. Henry thought he might ask him for more explanation but then decided against it, peering at the wax-sealed envelope now laying on the table. These were the last words and wishes of their father. Glancing back into his grandfather's eyes and then at William, Henry noticed each fighting the urge to let a tear slip out. Grandfather again patted them both on their shoulders.

"I realize he left us just a few days shy of this day. But alas, this is God's timing, not our own."

The two brothers stood and turned toward their grandfather as he pulled them both into a hug and then walked away, a slight limp pulling on his massive form.

Henry and William looked down at the letter before them.

Henry found his face wet with tears as he embraced his brother a moment longer than usual. His brother clasped Henry's shoulder as he pulled away, their eyes meeting, William's face also creased with tears. Henry hastily wiped his cheeks on his sleeve. Grasping the envelope, he slowly broke the seal and handed the letter to William, as both brothers sat in the large wooden chairs that surrounded the study. With a look of apprehension, William unfolded the paper, revealing the lengthy letter inside.

CHAPTER 3

It took but a moment for Christine to convince Meg to come downstairs, and Lizzy willingly followed, knowing her sister and her friend's interests stood in the drawing room below. Ivory took a little more coercion, but she finally gathered herself, smoothed her hair, and acquiesced.

As Christine led them down the stairs, her heart fluttered when she saw Mr. Davenport, wearing a green waistcoat that drew out the color of his eyes with sharp brown riding boots and a perfectly matching striped vest. She stood proud that *her* esteemed visitor would now occupy their time. He gallantly whisked off his top hat and bowed low. Mr. Grenville, shorter and broader in form than Mr. Davenport, tugged on his cravat and shifted his weight. He seemed more out of place upon seeing Meg again—he stumbled over himself when she entered, his eyes tracking her movements as she walked in after Christine. He was clearly much less in command but mustered his manners and bowed slightly toward them all.

"Welcome to Cassfield, Mr. Davenport," Christine said with a long curtsy. "I hope you are not disappointed."

"I am already impressed by what I have seen, but the sight of you is no less striking," Mr. Davenport said as he stood, a smile widening across his lips.

Christine blushed, looking at Mr. Davenport through full lashes. Their recent acquaintance, starting a few months ago, had been quite promising. Here at Cassfield, Christine hoped it would blossom into full courtship.

Christine introduced Mr. Davenport and Mr. Grenville to Ivory, and the familiar part of the group exchanged pleasantries since their last dinner together.

"What timely arrival you have made," Christine said, thinking inwardly that she avoided an afternoon of Ivory recounting the one hundred things that could have happened to Mr. Robertson. "Perhaps we might call for some tea on the patio. I am sure you are both in need of refreshment."

"Yes, we did not expect to arrive so early this afternoon. And the idea of tea sounds splendid, Miss Harrison," said Mr. Davenport, who gallantly extended his arm and led the way. Christine continued to bestow ample smiles in Mr. Davenport's direction, angling herself toward him as she poured each cup, waiting for him to engage her in more conversation.

But Mr. Grenville spoke first. "Miss Allensby," he said as he lifted his saucer, "you seem quite at ease here at Cassfield. Is it your first trip?"

Christine understood that Mr. Grenville knew the answer, but he eagerly wanted to begin the conversation. Christine watched Meg bolster the courage to respond, seeming grateful for the direct question.

"No, Mr. Grenville, I have traveled here three times, each during the spring," Meg replied as she offered a shy smile.

Christine mused as Mr. Grenville, with an almost giddy grin, played his uninformed guise well, monopolizing Meg for the remaining hour. Christine reflected that the Harrisons had spent many dinners and balls in the company of the Grenvilles, growing up in the same parish, and the mothers of each family were the closest of friends. The young Mr. Grenville had thought that one day he might court Lizzy, not having quite enough of an inheritance for Christine. But upon meeting Meg a few months ago, his intentions moved clearly toward her. And now, more than ever, Mr. Grenville's forthright gestures shone clear.

After they dispensed with the tea, Meg took out her sketchbook and tried to capture the view from the front of the house toward the water. It made Christine smile, knowing that many of the questions Mr. Grenville asked Meg he already knew the answer to, having been well apprised by his mother or Christine. These were the innocent kinds of misrepresentations that were often employed when trying to form a relationship, and Christine did not hold it against him.

Christine had such time to reflect on Meg's situation because her handsome Mr. Davenport employed himself by asking questions of Ivory across the small table set for their party. He was smiling, as he always did, and Christine did not know whether questions were said in earnest with simple courtesy or, as Christine feared, with too much flirtation.

"What is it, Miss Rusket, that brings you to Cassfield?" he asked with a warm and inviting tone.

"What brings me? I can assure you, Mr. Davenport," she began with her usual coquettish way, "that I would not miss a trip to Cassfield with my dear cousin and friends when presented to me." Christine noticed how quickly Ivory forgot Mr. Robertson's absence.

"And will you quit this place when your Season becomes more engaging?"

"I daresay I *will* be quite busy next year, perhaps too busy to visit, so I fully plan on making this year memorable."

He smiled and nodded, asking a few more questions about London. Christine lamented silently that Ivory always had London to speak about.

But Mr. Davenport knew how to engage multiple people and finally turned to Christine. "And now, Miss Harrison, may I ask what is new since our last dinner together?"

Christine searched for something stirring to say, relieved that the conversation had moved away from Ivory and on to herself.

"We have not much to report, excepting this trip and the ball that we plan to hold for Lizzy this winter at Wellington Estate."

"And, pray tell, is this your means of suggesting an invitation to myself?" He angled toward her with a roguish grin.

"Indeed, Mr. Davenport, how well you have guessed my ploy," Christine teased back.

Christine mulled over this short exchange, adding some conclusions to her understanding of his character. Mr. Davenport's words were often concise and pointed. He was amiable and very sincere with those he cared about. He was also endowed with the graces of intelligence and self-awareness, especially in conversation. If one were put to choosing sides, one would nine times to ten choose Mr. Davenport, for his persuasion coupled with charisma was a fearsome *tour de force*. Even now, he ensnared Christine, Ivory, and Lizzy all at once as they each clung to his every word.

"And a ball for you, Miss Elizabeth! How wonderful. What is the occasion?" asked Mr. Davenport.

"My seventeenth birthday. People say it is time I make an official entrance into society," Lizzy answered with a sweet smile.

"Right they are, for you are as lovely as Miss Harrison, I daresay." He bestowed his eyes on Christine as he spoke. Christine was just about to ask another question when Ivory superseded her.

"Mr. Davenport," she said as his handsome face whipped toward her, "do tell us of your travels here. Did you have a pleasant trip?"

Mr. Davenport flashed a smile toward Ivory and then began a stirring retelling of their journey from Rothershire.

As he spoke, Christine reflected on his aptitude of conversation. A true chameleon, Mr. Davenport left most people pleased to have met such a jovial and sharp character—believing that he had accepted them and enjoyed every moment together.

Such was the case with Miss Rusket, who bestowed her high praise of Mr. Davenport later that evening.

"His manner of speaking does him credit, Christine. I am quite impressed with your acquaintances. Mr. Grenville seems a fine man as well."

"Why thank you," Christine responded quickly, hoping her friend would not try to become too intimate an acquaintance with Mr. Davenport. Christine had not entered in to full courtship with Mr. Davenport, and she worried if her rich and beautiful friend seemed too alluring, Mr. Davenport might change his mind. Ivory seemed to possess a magnetic power over any male she came in contact with.

Luckily, Christine knew of the complicated side of Mr. Davenport's personality. He had expressed to Christine more than once in the last few months that he often developed a faceted opinion of those he met, and it was not always one full of approbation. He wore the guise of a happy disposition—always smiling—though not always thoroughly impressed. Christine watched every move Mr. Davenport made, mildly hoping that this would be the case toward Ivory.

In the next few days, the party dined together, walked the shores several times, and even took a day trip into Broughington Lake to see the town and visit the shops. Mr. Davenport and especially Mr. Grenville seemed willing to do whatever the ladies thought enjoyable, and the group spent almost all of every day together, except when Mr. Harrison convinced the men to go fishing with him.

This evening, the charming Mr. Davenport had chosen to position himself across from Christine on the settee.

"Now tell me," Mr. Davenport began in his formal yet inviting tone, "what you have lately read. I know you love your books."

Christine leaned forward, grateful for a question directed only to her.

"*King Lear*, sir. Although such a tale as that I think hardly worth reporting. Sometimes I wonder who deemed Shakespeare so marvelous. Not all of his works were created equal, do you not agree? It is a bizarre tale."

"Yes, quite. But you like *Romeo and Juliet*, I am sure. Is there a lady who does not enjoy that story?" He looked into her eyes, his green irises ensnaring her.

Christine blushed slightly upon such a romantic suggestion. Still unsure of his motive or direction, Christine replied, "Such a story of true love would be well liked by anyone, I should think."

He raised his eyebrows toward her as his head tilted up, as if to say "*touché*."

She thought of adding something more witty and flirtatious, but was interrupted by Ivory.

"Mr. Davenport," Ivory crooned from across the room, "I am in dire need of a Loo partner against our Paris aficionados. Meg and Mr. Grenville keep whispering in French and plan to conspire against me. Would you be so kind?"

"I do enjoy a game of Loo, Miss Rusket," he said as he rose.

He obliged so quickly that Christine decided to make herself exceedingly busy, pretending her novel to be full of intrigue. What did Mr. Davenport really think of Ivory? Christine wished she knew. As the night continued, their game seemed painstakingly long. The happy tones of Ivory and Mr. Davenport frustrated her to no end, and she finally convinced herself to have the self-control to stop counting the many smiles Mr. Davenport bestowed on Ivory. Only once did his eyes catch Christine's, and they locked their gaze for a moment, but then he swiftly turned back to his partner.

Christine breathed a sigh of relief when Lizzy asked her to join her for a piano duet. Lizzy had been stitching a fine piece of embroidery for most of the evening, but upon looking up, she seemed to read Christine's distressed face perfectly. Lizzy always did come to her rescue.

The four others of the party finished their game and listened contently to the Harrisons' performance. Mr. Davenport complimented Christine directly after their first piece, but Christine's jealousy rose again as she saw Ivory position herself closest to Mr. Davenport. Upon noticing a few yawns, and quite tired of the evening's course of events, Christine suggested they all turn in, and the party agreed.

The next morning at breakfast, Christine's determination to engage Mr. Davenport was even stronger.

"And what shall we do today, Mr. Davenport? I believe it is your turn to choose." Christine said with an open smile and wide eyes. He returned the glance, looking as though he would say something charming, when Mr. Grenville interrupted.

"Excuse me, but I thought perhaps we might spend the afternoon in the garden with you ladies. Miss Allensby, you did say you wished to paint the landscape?"

It was rather unlike Mr. Grenville to overshadow his powerful friend, but his drive to do just as Meg wished was clearly becoming stronger every day.

"Surely, and perhaps a few of us should pose for Miss Allensby," replied Mr. Davenport good-naturedly, and he turned this time to Christine. "I understand Miss Allensby is quite the artist."

When breakfast concluded, the party set out for the grounds, Mr. Grenville and Meg pulling in front of the group. Lizzy, thankfully, took Ivory's arm in hers and exclaimed, "You must sit for Meg. I would so love to see your likeness!"

This left Mr. Davenport to Christine, and he offered his arm, which Christine took quite willingly.

"Mr. Grenville seems to be very taken with Miss Allensby this trip," she let out, hoping he would have more insight about his friend.

"Yes, quite. I do not often see Mr. Grenville overly excited about anything, but Miss Allensby has won his favor."

"She is so very likeable: sweet, calm, amiable, and a good listener." She paused, sending coquettish glances toward him. "Some of us do not possess quite so many virtues."

"Surely you must not be talking of yourself, Miss Harrison." Mr. Davenport tilted his head and smiled down at her. Christine thought he meant this honestly, but his ability to tease stirred high, and she was not quite sure of his intention.

"Yes, sir. I meant myself and most of us in this party." Her eyes twinkled a bit and her mouth turned upward as she added, "Well, at least myself and my current walking partner."

She had found something witty to say, and she could tell he liked it.

"Would you not include Lizzy and Ivory as well?"

"Lizzy is every bit as sweet as Meg, of course, but I might put Miss Rusket more into our category," Christine said, just as Ivory turned around and linked her arm through Davenport's other side.

"Yes, you know that neither of us are as sweet as those two." Ivory gestured to Meg and Lizzy ahead of her. Ivory had listened to their whole interaction.

During the rest of the afternoon, Christine enjoyed a few conversations with Mr. Davenport, until Meg begged Christine to sit for her portrait, and Ivory monopolized Mr. Davenport as they walked through the garden together.

And then Ivory declared she must go inside, having too much wind, and Lizzy consented to go with her. Christine had just finished her portrait and stood now hearing Mr. Grenville reciting something—in French—to Meg's utter delight.

Mr. Davenport seemed to wait deliberately for Christine. He began by offering a few smiles in her direction and then extended his arm to escort Christine toward the house. Christine could smell the flowers flanking them on both sides as they walked through the hedges leading out of the garden. Mr. Davenport proceeded, in their confidence, to speak. "Miss Harrison, I realize I have not been very forthright in my conversations here." He paused momentarily and resumed, quite altered in tone, his green eyes softening in the setting sun, a half-smile creasing his mouth. "I must tell you that I admire you greatly. Since we met a few months ago at the Grenvilles', I have been impressed with your intellect and your wit. And of course, there has always been your beauty." Christine's hand rested on his arm as they walked, and now Mr. Davenport placed his free hand on hers. He looked into her eyes for a moment, and his eyes wrinkled in a soft smile toward her. Christine blushed and ran her free hand over her curls.

He continued, "And now, seeing you here at Cassfield, I have been nothing but impressed with the care you take toward others. The way you cheer Miss Allensby on with Mr. Grenville! She needs it. And the way you watch out for Lizzy. And the way you enjoy Miss Rusket when one might be envious of the attention paid to her."

This speech, especially the last sentence, gave almost too accurate a read on her true feelings. *How well he understands me*, Christine thought.

"And so," he said more hushed, "I have not known your feelings toward me, and thus may seem guarded or only generally amiable. But please know this is a flaw of my nature. My feelings and intentions for you run quite deep."

Perhaps her worry of Ivory's dominance had overshadowed her feelings for Mr. Davenport. She examined herself now, a bubbling warmth rising within her. He did care for her! His ability to befriend everyone stemmed from good manners, not a lack of interest on his part. Now, here he was, paying her attention in the most sincere of methods.

Her eyes met his as he continued. "I would like to tell you that I admire you and do hope that we can become better acquainted when you leave Cassfield and return to Rothershire and Wellington in a few weeks."

Christine knew she often showed her emotions with too much transparency. She looked down, full of smiles. She had wanted to secure his affections while here at Cassfield, and now he finally communicated them clearly, when she least expected it. She gripped the side of her skirt and walked calmly forward, trying to tame her excitement as she thought of what to say.

She often feared saying too much, or coming on too strong too soon, especially with a gentleman such as Mr. Davenport. She had never had a conversation like this with any man before. Then she thought of her father's counsel to enjoy herself. So rather than mask the true feelings that rose to the surface, she stated, "I thank you for your forthright conversation, Mr. Davenport. I wish I could be so eloquent and descriptive in the way I feel." She faced him fully and opened a wider smile than she was generally comfortable to give. "You have quite intrigued me, and I am honored by your sentiment. I would be pleased to know you better as well."

And then, because she detected the glint of a triumphant smile behind Mr. Davenport's eyes, she added brazenly, "You have done a fair job so far, but I wish you luck in your attempt to know me. It might be a harder task than you are willing to accept."

Mr. Davenport tilted his head to the side, stepping away from Christine and folded his arms across his chest. They had stopped walking just before the back doors of Cassfield Manor, a large stone wall enclosing them more intimately for a moment. He leaned his shoulders against the barrier, grinning. Christine stopped near the entrance of the garden, gripping the edge of a bench to stop her hands from fiddling with the bow of her dress.

"I will gladly take that challenge and test my luck, Miss Harrison." He smiled confidently and pushed off the edge of the wall. Christine looked down at the gravel below her feet. She bit her lip and then raised her gaze to meet his. He stood there, quite handsome and more assured, and extended his arm once again. She took it with a contented sigh as they walked toward the back doors.

Upon entering the house, the green-eyed chameleon turned to Lizzy and Ivory and took up conversation. Christine stood somewhere between vexed and intrigued, going mad as he once again treated everyone as equals, reminding herself it was simply good manners. And twice he sent glances her way, which this time seemed to hold more meaning, and Christine conceded that such deliberate actions must prove his statements to her true.

The next morning, Mr. Grenville walked toward Ivory and, pointing to the hallway, asked in a hushed tone, "May I ask you a few particulars about London?"

She quickly placed her arm on his and led him to the next room, as she whispered, "I know you really want to know more about Miss Allensby, and I am happy to inform you . . ."

As the two walked out of earshot, Christine, understanding the scheme, speedily suggested that Meg, Lizzy, and Mr. Davenport move into the drawing room.

Once there, Mr. Davenport took advantage of the smaller group of only females, at ease once again. With his usual charm, he began, "I have been meaning to ask, but it slipped my mind until now. How do you know the Mr. Robertson I saw leaving as I arrived at Cassfield?"

Christine, wanting the situation understood, immediately answered, "Mr. Robertson is a recent acquaintance of Miss Rusket, and his business brought him near Cassfield, so she invited him to visit." It must be made clear that he came for Ivory, not herself.

"Ah, it is a good thing I asked now, while she is gone," Mr. Davenport said, and he looked around, more serious than usual. "I would be afraid to align myself with him."

"Why is that, Mr. Davenport?" Christine asked, alarmed.

His mouth tightened at the corners a bit and he continued, "You see, he and I attended university together. He is one of those fellows who often operates with an underlying scheme at hand, while seeming to be the most upright and pleasant sort of gentleman."

"Oh really?" Meg interjected. "What kind of scheme?" Meg was never the one to start gossip but had a very good mind for remembering it once she heard it.

He nodded at Meg and then turned his gaze directly at Christine. "He needs to get married. Quickly. And to someone with connections, monetary endowment, as it were. If Mr. Robertson started courting someone in your position, Miss Harrison, or Miss Rusket's financial state, I would think twice about an engagement."

Christine leaned forward. "Why quickly? And a marriage according to connections is not unusual. If there is attachment there, what is the harm of Miss Rusket and Mr. Robertson marrying? Surely people have married for much baser reasons, have they not, Mr. Davenport?"

She wished Mr. Davenport to believe Ivory was already spoken for.

"Well, yes, I suppose if it were an advantageous marriage on his part, that would not be something to warn against. But it is also because of his family's antics about inheritance. He is a twin. The rumor is that the twin who marries first or best will win the family estate. And therefore, it is a race to marry, and I daresay he will take anyone—especially if she has as much money as Miss Rusket! I believe he came back from traveling on business early to secure a relationship of this kind. Family estates are not to be won but distributed properly, as I am sure you all agree! He simply cannot be trusted. I would be afraid to align myself with him or his family. It is so distasteful, especially how he moves through society—so many high friends and acquaintances, when he himself is unknown and from Scotland. His family pays no heed to following societal and class rules. No one knows just how much their estate is worth."

"Not even you, Mr. Davenport?" Christine pressed him, her interest piqued.

"No, surely not me. I have told you all I know about him. We were never great acquaintances."

Christine then recalled the cold greeting she had witnessed between them from her window a few days previous.

"How strange!" Christine said. "Miss Rusket, with her sum and her free nature would be a good candidate to secure an estate then."

Meg turned and looked down the hallway. "I will be sure to let her know," she replied, more determined than usual.

Christine stood and walked toward the window. Mr. Davenport followed, coming behind her saying in a whisper, "I am glad to know he is not *your* acquaintance, Miss Harrison. I suspected you had better judgment than Miss Rusket, and now I am certain."

Christine stood still for a moment. She then folded her arms across herself and replied, "Why thank you, Mr. Davenport," barely above a whisper. She turned her face half toward him, wondering if he saw her blush. He bestowed on her an accepting smile, his green eyes dancing as he met her gaze, and she felt that finally she knew he did not care for Miss Rusket. He had his heart set on her.

Christine retired that night with two thoughts filling her mind. First, her pulse quickened as she reviewed the inclinations of Mr. Davenport. The picture of his face as they stood by the window flashed before her eyes. She felt confident in his regard once again. He meant to continue their friendship—and move toward courtship. He seemed quite set on that fact, and it filled her with hope and anticipation. What would the next few months bring? How much time would pass before he would ask for her hand?

And then, he had felt comfortable enough to warn them of Mr. Robertson. The girls had been so impressed by Mr. Robertson a week ago: his manners, the way he carried himself, and his ease with people. Could it all be an act? He *had* left abruptly from Cassfield, which seemed very strange. Perhaps it had to do with his lack of interest in Ivory? But if he needed to marry quickly, why leave her without more commitment? Christine could not account for such behavior, but it did not matter. Christine knew Mr. Davenport esteemed her judgment and wanted to court her, and she need not concern herself with Mr. Robertson.

CHAPTER 4

The next morning, Christine woke up early, wanting some time to think before embracing the day. She wanted to revel in all Mr. Davenport had said in the last few days. The business of constant company wore on her, and she craved time to be completely alone, with only her thoughts. This morning she wanted silence.

Christine dressed quickly, choosing her simple light-blue muslin. She descended the stairs, entering the drawing room, which overlooked the ocean. She glanced across the room to the large bay windows and the exposed patio. There she positioned herself to enjoy the sea breeze. She opened the window silently when she heard, "Hello, Miss Harrison."

Stepping backward, alarmed, and a little put off that her quiet spot was taken, Christine stumbled over herself. Mr. Davenport stood, having just risen from his seat on the patio. He bowed and acknowledged Christine, who quickly composed herself and tried to not look angry.

"May I sit here?" she asked, pointing at a bench near him, attempting to regain control of herself.

"I would be delighted," he said. His green eyes seemed more like glinting emerald than she remembered. His short dark hair glistened in the sun, and Christine watched him clench his jaw. Something about his look drew her in, but at the same time left her confused. Christine marveled at just how handsome he had become since the first time she saw him. Pulling herself from her reverie, she realized she was not moving. Before sitting on the tufted bench that backed the patio edge, she adjusted the windowed doors, careful to leave them open so that they were not *completely* secluded.

"What are you doing here, Mr. Davenport?" Christine asked, trying to sound casual.

"Can not one enjoy the cool ocean breeze in peace?" he replied, smiling, seemingly to acknowledge that he had just stolen her breeze and her peace.

Christine half-smiled and said, "Surely, for that was exactly what I was coming to do."

"Then I am glad I caught you here."

How did he know this is where she would come?

He continued with a more serious tone. "I am just here bemoaning my fate for the next day of traveling. I do not enjoy riding all day, and I mourn leaving the company of you all. Things are much quieter and much more serious back in Rothershire."

"That is true," Christine agreed. "And that is why I love it at Cassfield. It is as though one can forget about obligations and expectations. It is easier to be close to nature and in tune to what is really important."

She stopped herself, surprised by the free speech that just left her lips. Mr. Davenport seemed to have a power over her in that moment to elicit her true feelings.

"Cassfield has led you to become more forthright, Miss Harrison," he said softly, inviting her to say more.

Christine suddenly wished she had not let her tongue run away with her thoughts. Yesterday's comments and now this. She said nothing.

He spoke again, but with a complete change of tone. "I agree with your insight. I do hope we can have more open conversations like these when we have both returned to Rothershire." He turned his head and met her eyes as they locked on his for several moments. She had no problem becoming lost in his gaze once again. When he finally looked away, he continued, "I had better make sure my bags are packed and ready. I will leave you to your quiet and your breeze."

And with that he rose, bowed, and left. This was typical Davenport fashion, so engaging and then so short. Christine felt the impact of every word he said.

"Goodbye, and I wish you a safe journey," she called out behind him.

Christine, unable to think of anything else to say, sat still and watched the tails of his coat disappear behind the door and wished then that their conversation had not yet ended. She reflected on her short time with Mr. Davenport. Was this the way courting happened? Small conversations here and there, which actually meant a great deal? She had known Mr. Davenport for a few months, and this last week changed their relationship. Now more than ever, he seemed to have a vested interest in Christine. She could honestly declare that she believed him to desire pursuing their relationship and developing it into something more substantial, for they had passed the stage of mere acquaintances.

As she sat lost in thought, Christine realized how much of her mind Mr. Davenport had occupied in the last few weeks. She thought about his inviting face and tall stature. He was a respectable young man with good connections. From what she understood, he had just invested in a large amount of property. She smiled. He was strikingly handsome, rich, witty, and well liked. She relished his attentions. Christine could not hope for a better match for herself.

But then Christine stopped her thoughts, not wanting to assume too much. A lurking suspicion crept in that he might not yet be convinced. The only thing to do was wait until she returned to Wellington, where decisions and obligations could become real again.

With the gentlemen gone from Cassfield, Christine and her companions found themselves with a now-exhausted guest list of eligible young men and nothing to do. The days rolled on toward the end of May with little consequence. More readily than in years past, the girls prepared to return home. Those last days at Cassfield naturally filled with conjecture and discussion, as one could imagine with four young females contemplating and ruminating over gentlemen they had come to know and enjoy. No matter the location—walking on the beach, assembling for dinner, or enjoying the breeze of the ocean—at least one of the young ladies, though more commonly most of them, could be found talking about one of the absent gentlemen.

No one ever came to a solid conclusion on what had caused Mr. Robertson to go away. The facts stood that Mr. Robertson had left a letter, he left suddenly, and, although none admitted it, everyone knew that Mr. Robertson and Ivory probably did not have a future together.

"Should we still attend his aunt's ball?" Ivory asked the day before leaving Cassfield. Mr. Robertson, wonderful as they all thought he was, seemed to be quite an overworked subject in Christine's mind. Ivory was trying to convince herself that everything would be just the same between them when she returned to London.

"Well, I do not see why not," Lizzy began. "I think that he invited us and his invite still stands. After all, he could have left suddenly and *not* given the particulars about the ball. And I am sure that there will be many new people there! I would guess even a hundred people. Surely he has invited half of London, and we should be in that half!" Lizzy always loved parties, and had not yet attended many balls—let alone in London—and the prospect thrilled her.

"I think you are right," Ivory said, happy for the reassurance. "We surely must go. It would most likely cause more gossip or suspicion if I were not to attend."

"On one of our walks, Mr. Robertson did tell me he had many eligible young men he thought we would like to meet," Christine began. "Although, Meg, you should just come for the entertainment. We know you have your heart set on someone else already." Christine cast a slight smile toward Meg, who returned the gesture shyly. Christine was artfully trying to throw the attention from herself—she did not wish to address her own growing attachment for Mr. Davenport, not having any concrete engagement to speak of yet.

"It is settled then!" Ivory sounded triumphant. "We will go! And you will all be there with me in case it is an awkward meeting for any of our party. Besides, I am so excited for you to visit London again. The weather is exceptional this time of year."

The next day the party quite willingly left Cassfield. Christine's father rode his horse, Mrs. Harrison's carriage and the daughters' carriage trailing behind. That last carriage was mostly silent, each girl tangled in her own thoughts. But for once it seemed that instead of sadness, the prospect of what was ahead held the greater excitement. In just a few weeks, these young women had changed—men had infiltrated their foursome and each assented to the alteration.

The first morning at Wellington Estate, Christine eagerly expected a call from Mr. Davenport and Mr. Grenville. Or perhaps an invitation to dine with Meg, with the hope that perhaps the men would be invited there as well.

As she grew more and more impatient, Christine decided to walk to Allensby House and seek Meg's company. Christine was let into the drawing room with only Meg sitting by herself reworking a bonnet.

"Meg, do you have a moment to spare?" Christine looked around, grateful for an empty room. "I came to talk to you about Ivory."

"Yes, of course. What is it?" Meg whispered, slightly alarmed.

"Did you ever chance to mention to Ivory what Mr. Davenport said about Mr. Robertson?" Christine looked intently at Meg and only then noticed a pair of new pearl-drop earrings.

"But first, where did you get your earrings? Are those new?"

Meg blushed for a moment. "I knew you would notice. You always do. Mr. Grenville left them for me. They are in town on business, did you know? Mr. Davenport as well. These were a little present here when we arrived home. I thought it was ever so attentive of Mr. Grenville. He wrote that they were for my birthday! And they are such a beautiful shade of pink."

"Yes, they truly are," Christine answered. Apparently, Meg knew more about the men than she did. She realized the men had left before they returned home, but why did Mr. Davenport not at least leave a note? She had been their hostess, after all, and he had made it sound as though they would begin serious courtship. Meg had received plenty of attention. Christine shook her head slightly and tried not to become too flustered.

Christine stood a bit taller and tried to get back to the reason for her visit. "But what about your conversations with Ivory?"

Meg came out of her reverie. "Right." Christine tried to ignore her friend's enamored aura. Meg's tone tightened a little, and she said, "I could not get up the courage to tell her about him. After all, Mr. Davenport made him seem so vile, but somehow Mr. Robertson just did not seem that divisive to me. And I was not sure Ivory and Mr. Robertson's attachment would be growing any deeper, so I thought it might be best to not make matters worse, so to speak."

Christine reflected on Meg's speech. "I guess you are right to consider her feelings, but perhaps if they continue to show attachment at the ball we should warn her?"

"Yes, an appropriate course of action to be sure," Meg said, as though a weight lifted from her.

They continued to spend the rest of the evening together, and Lizzy eventually joined them for dinner. Mr. Robertson was not spoken of again, but Christine still felt uneasy about his relationship with Ivory. She told herself to be patient and see what the natural course of time would bring. Perhaps Mr. Robertson would pose no harm.

Lizzy asked several questions of Meg and Christine, excited for not only a ball, but one in London. Every detail mattered: what to wear and how to fix their hair, just exactly what fashions were in style, how many dances there would be, and most importantly, who would be there.

Perhaps, thought Christine, *if Mr. Davenport were still in London, he would be invited to the ball through some connected party.* She could only hope such a coincidence might occur.

"I brought both my white gown and my lavender taffeta. Which do you think I should wear?" Meg asked Christine as they traveled the two-day journey south to Ivory's house. Mr. Harrison had journeyed with them through the first night and then sent them on for the last day of travel.

"I wondered the same thing," Christine replied. "Although I daresay that this will not be a white party. Surely this ball is only standard fare in London, and we do not want to appear in our whites while no one else would be wearing theirs."

"I cannot tell you how many dresses I packed," Lizzy responded. "I did not know what kinds of occasions I would need to be prepared for!"

Ivory received them late that evening, and almost the entire morning and afternoon the next day was spent in preparations for the ball.

Christine chose to wear her green taffeta with her hair in a low, curly bun, letting the natural volume of the curls magnify themselves to their wispiest ability. She also counseled Lizzy, who vacillated on which dress to wear, and helped her decide on a light teal matelassé with lace edging and short butterfly sleeves. Lizzy's light-blonde hair employed a few more braids and plaits than usual, with her soft ringlets framing her face.

Meg's gown flattered her full figure, and she had Ivory's maid pile her chocolate hair high on her head in an elegant bun. As a final touch to her ensemble, she wore her new pearl-drop earrings, a token of her allegiance to a certain Mr. Grenville.

As they made their final preparations, Ivory stated, "Dear friends, I have learned what caused Mr. Robertson to leave Cassfield so early."

Christine's interest piqued, remembering all of the suspicion that surrounded Mr. Robertson's sudden departure.

"Yes, Ivory, tell us all. And, of course, how you feel about him presently. I am sure we all wish to know." Christine looked at Lizzy and Meg, who nodded in unison.

"Well first, I was quite put out that he did not come and call directly as soon as I arrived home," Ivory said, employing her usual full animation, hands characteristically on her hips with her mouth drawn tight. "However, we were both invited to a dinner of a mutual friend, and he explained himself there." She waved her hand. "As it stands, I am sure we have no future together, but he was all kindness and civility. He explained his brother had been severely wounded in a horse accident while on business in the Orient. Apparently, Mr. Robertson is his brother's closest family, and the letter was from his business steward saying he was needed immediately."

This explanation satisfied Christine, absolving Mr. Robertson of any suspicion she had toward him. She knew he must have had a good reason for his swift and unexpected leaving. Ivory seemed not quite as forgiving, but she had several more interests already, so Mr. Robertson became a mere friend once again and was no great loss to her in the long run. Christine found such an explanation to be just the sort of thing to suit Mr. Robertson and felt glad that the invitation to the ball still stood, regardless of Ivory's affections toward him. Mr. Robertson's connections, if they proved to be as good as he said, would surely widen the Harrisons' circle and hopefully benefit Lizzy. Christine decided that she liked Mr. Robertson much more when he was not directly overshadowing her Mr. Davenport.

The excitement of the evening clung to the warm summer air. Now, as each girl looked in the mirror, all stood pleased with each appearance. Christine tried to feel confident and beautiful, which she believed was the best way to approach a ball full of rich and powerful people, especially when some of them would be eligible and male. But Christine had to admit that she did feel a little apprehensive—and she suspected Lizzy and Meg felt the same way—about the unknown and palatial circumstances they were about to experience. Ivory, she knew, felt no trepidation about the evening before her.

Ivory had a new dress ordered for the occasion. It was a beautiful soft coral, the entire gown employing an overlay of imported French lace that came up and down in scalloped gathers. She wore a white peony in her hair to accent the corresponding pattern on the dress and wore a necklace of pearls and crystals. She stood even more striking than her usual self. Christine knew that Miss Ivory Rusket would be the epitome of London fashion—and gossip—that night.

Just before leaving, Christine looked wistfully out the window, nerves starting to enter her body. Would Mr. Davenport be invited? She longed for him to be in attendance, knowing his presence would bring her the confidence she so desired. She almost feared the ball, being removed from her comfortable circle of acquaintances. She hoped Mr. Robertson possessed many friends who were willing to dance. She dreaded the feeling of being overlooked and having nothing to report but a strikingly low number of partners and much time standing to the side like a disregarded painting.

Mr. Oliver Davenport

That same night, at almost the same hour as the young ladies entered their carriage, Mr. Davenport headed toward the door.

"Do not expect me home early, Grenville," Mr. Davenport said as he threw on his overcoat.

Mr. Grenville sat in the parlor of Mr. Davenport's small London house, much too engaged in the letter he wrote to Meg to notice that his friend seemed underdressed for an evening event. Mr. Grenville was used to his friend often coming and going, especially in London.

As Mr. Davenport reached the street, he turned left, heading toward Cheapside by foot. He then continued toward the docks of London, meeting a large wagon at the edge of Bridge Road. Mr. Davenport recognized the small painted *B* in the corner, hastily mounting the box.

"We meet again, old friends," Mr. Davenport stated as he shook hands with the two men who were seated there.

The older man and the younger man shared the same complexion and face, excepting the older possessed more gray hairs than brown and had many more wrinkles in his olive complexion. The latter, twenty-five years his junior, pushed his thick, brown, unkempt locks away from his eyes and said, "Hold your breath, Davenport. Shall we get right down to it?"

"By all means, Mr. Braxton," Mr. Davenport replied with ice.

The younger Mr. Braxton began unfolding his plan. "You see behind us six crates, each filled with bolts of fabric just unloaded at the docks. It was my job to procure them, and now I rely on you to find buyers. The owners of the shipment believe it discarded in customs due to diseased rat infestation, so they have cost us nothing. Make the price at which you sell them to the buyers believable but lower than their costs by a bit, and we shall each have a handsome profit." The younger Mr. Braxton wielded an evil, confident glare. "Are we agreed?"

An eerie smile spread across Mr. Davenport's face. "Of course. Let us take the shipment back to my flat. I have already discussed with buyers. You or one of your men could drive it north?"

"Yes, my son shall," said the older Mr. Braxton. "Although it was a pity you were not here earlier. Our dear Estelle watched your shipment the first half of the day."

Mr. Davenport did not wish to discuss Mr. Braxton's daughter then or ever. He changed the subject to something the Braxtons would not resist. "I daresay we ought to have a drink before leaving, if you will allow me to take the bill."

The young Mr. Braxton smiled for the first time that evening at such a suggestion, and the wagon headed toward their customary pub. An hour later, both Braxtons, having consumed much on Davenport's ticket, begged for a rendezvous with the crates the next day instead, unable to make it there presently in such a state.

Mr. Davenport had suspected as much and prepared to walk home, knowing to not over-drink in his accomplices' presence. As he walked out of the arched door, a woman intercepted him from the shadow of the nearby alley.

"Going by foot, are you?" said the lady with nut-brown hair. Her deep purple taffeta shimmered in the moonlight.

"Excuse me, miss, but I think a woman of your standing ought not to be out alone at such an hour. Have you lost your way?"

"On the contrary, Mr. Davenport, I was waiting for you. I wanted to ask you to join me for dinner tomorrow evening," she said as she stepped into the light.

Mr. Davenport staggered backward a few paces and then regained his composure with a slight bow. "Este—Miss Braxton—you should not be here. Tomorrow I travel back to Rothershire. And now," he said, exhaling, "I must be going at once."

"Then, sir, I merely wish to say that it is a pleasure to see you in London again. I have missed you."

Mr. Davenport looked warily from side to side, attempting to forgo eye contact.

"You are too kind," he finally replied, moving one step toward her and stopping. "But I must insist on taking my leave."

She then raised her palm, cutting him off so that he grasped her hand to kiss it, surprised she already stood so close to him. He turned quickly and did not look back for at least two blocks, relieved by that time he saw no traces of shimmering taffeta.

CHAPTER 5

The young ladies rode in Ivory's finest carriage. Two cream horses and two coachmen deposited them at Lady Fowler's estate that evening at eight. The scene did not disappoint. Each pair of eyes beheld the opulent splendor: tasseled curtains made of mauve velvet lined the walls, floors laid in marble welcomed them, and two full-sized statues of Hercules and Aphrodite greeted each visitor that passed, with several liveried servants lining the entry way.

Christine marveled at the signs of lavishness at every turn. The ballroom sparkled with several hundred candles, flickering on the periphery as the last glow of sun extinguished, its colorful setting displayed by the great west windows. The room held at least one hundred and fifty people gathered in small groups scattered throughout. Every table bore a vase overflowing with dazzling flowers, causing the room to fill with a soft fragrance, which invited Christine and her party in further. In the back of the room, in front of the windows, stood Mr. Robertson, almost a head taller than the man he was talking to and at least a foot above the two ladies who stood in his circle.

Ivory led the party forward. Christine was grateful to not enter first—the transparent awe on her face would surely embarrass her. She managed to gain composure as Mr. Robertson spotted them and hurriedly excused himself from his group, as though he had been watching and waiting for them every moment. He moved toward them with purpose. Christine sighed in relief, for it felt more appropriate to have a male figure introduce them rather than Ivory. His greeting began unaffected and inviting.

"Miss Rusket, Miss Harrison, Miss Elizabeth, and Miss Allensby. I was sure you would come! And indeed you have! It is so very agreeable to see you all again. I must apologize once more for leaving Cassfield so early. I am sure Miss Rusket informed you of my reason. Please come in and make yourselves comfortable. It would be my honor to introduce you to some of my closest friends." With that he turned to wink at the Harrison sisters, reminding them of his promise that his friends consisted of many fine, eligible bachelors.

He motioned toward the back left of the room, and the ladies followed. Christine studied Ivory, whose expression told Christine that she seemed pleased with this reception. Christine surmised Ivory must have forgiven Mr. Robertson of any grievance, on account of the sumptuous ball and ample young men she saw around them. And so far, no matter how hard she looked, Christine could not cast suspicion or blame on him. Yet she esteemed Mr. Davenport and his opinion, so something must be suspicious with Mr. Robertson—she just did not know what yet.

Christine followed the others to the back of the ballroom, replaying these details in her head and finally reminding herself that Mr. Robertson's affairs were really of no consequence to her. Right now, her only task was to enjoy the ball at hand.

In the far back corner of the room stood three gentlemen. Mr. Robertson swiftly navigated into this small circle, devoid for the moment of any females. One man, with jet-black hair and long features, was almost as tall as Mr. Robertson. He was introduced as Mr. Clayton. Another, introduced as Mr. Arnold, was very thin, shorter, and had a mop of curls on his head, which gave him a boyish look. The last was also very tall, just slightly shorter than Mr. Robertson. He had short blond hair and muscular, wide shoulders that complemented his defined jawline. His name was Mr. Oakley. The three of them were very jovial, making small jabs at each other and laughing about some inside joke. Christine was not sure how Mr. Robertson had procured such tall, handsome, and lively friends, but she was not about to complain about such connections. For a moment she forgot about Mr. Davenport entirely.

"These fine gentlemen are some colleagues of mine. Please ignore their light nature, for they can be quite well mannered when put up to it." Mr. Robertson smiled at the ladies.

"Come now," Mr. Oakley piped in. "We are not that bad! He gives us too much of a hard time. It has been a few months since we have had the pleasure of being together, and we are taking advantage of it by doing what we know best." Mr. Oakley hit Mr. Robertson on the shoulder and then nodded toward the young ladies. He smiled and apprised each one, but his gaze lingered when he came to Lizzy.

With a completely altered tone, Mr. Oakley continued, "It is so nice to meet all of you. Mr. Robertson spoke highly of your party, but I can assure you he did not speak highly enough." He finished the sentence with his eyes locked on Lizzy, who started to blush. Looking down shyly at the floor, she curtsied slightly.

For the rest of the evening, no lady wanted for a partner, each reticle keeping a ledger of dances, sure to be referenced during the next few days as the girls mulled over their new acquaintances. It had been more comfortable and more full of merriment than even Christine's most hopeful wish. She and Meg had danced each dance with a different gentleman, though their one disappointment was that Mr. Davenport and Mr. Grenville never showed their faces among the eligible young men. Mr. Oakley made the bold request to dance with Lizzy a second time, but she sadly declined, for her card was already full. Ivory danced once with Mr. Robertson, out of good form, but was very highly sought after by almost every other man in the room.

The ball ended just before four in the morning, each young lady more enthusiastic than tired of dancing. Lizzy was somewhere between ecstatic and delirious, and the attention from Mr. Oakley sent her into raptures above her already high expectations. The exhausted friends piled into Ivory's carriage, each girl becoming suddenly sleepy on the short ride back to Ivory's estate.

The young ladies finally reassembled for what they titled "breakfast" around noon, the air buzzing with recollections of the previous evening.

"The flowers were breathtaking!" Meg exclaimed. She had noticed the beautiful scenery more than any of the handsome men. Christine knew Meg thought of Mr. Grenville alone.

"And did you see how many couples danced?" Ivory added. "There must have been at least two or three score couples."

"Yes, quite impressive. London does not disappoint with its high circles," Christine acknowledged.

"I was rather impressed with Mr. Robertson's acquaintances, were you not?" Lizzy asked the group. She had confided to Christine the night before how taken she was with Mr. Oakley, though unsure of his true character. "For how can one discern such a thing at a ball?" she had exclaimed.

"Yes, I quite enjoyed seeing Mr. Robertson and his acquaintances last night," Christine answered, overcoming a yawn, and then added, "Although I do not think that Meg or I enjoyed the attention of any *particular* young man as much as you, Lizzy. In fact, it was clear that Mr. Oakley liked you from the very first moment he set eyes on you."

"It is true," Ivory smiled, putting her arm around Lizzy, "I have known Mr. Oakley for the past few months now, and while you were dancing with someone else, he asked me all about you. Seemed quite determined to ascertain particulars."

Lizzy grinned and blushed. Ivory then threw her hand to the side, and said, "And you all should know that I am completely through seeking any attentions from Mr. Robertson. But he is a pleasant sort of fellow, so I am glad we will continue on such amiable terms."

Christine thought back on Mr. Davenport's warning, relieved that she and Meg would not need to mention it now. Lizzy would want to see Mr. Oakley again, Christine knew, and although she herself did not find any of his friends as interesting as Mr. Davenport, Christine believed Mr. Robertson an invaluable resource to have in one's social circle. Nevertheless, they met him first through Ivory, and Christine did not want to abuse the relationship with Mr. Robertson just to make connections with his other acquaintances. Perhaps if he lived closer to Rothershire they might continue seeing each other more often, but for now the Harrison sisters would have to wait until they came to London again.

Perhaps through Mr. Robertson something might come of Mr. Oakley for Lizzy. Christine applauded herself again for her connection to Ivory and by extension, her ample social circles.

Mr. William Robertson

"It was the finest ball I have attended all Season, William. You missed a great deal," Henry said, walking into the firelit room and removing his outer coat and gloves.

William's eyes looked from Henry to Mr. Oakley, whose valet removed the last of Mr. Oakley's traveling clothes. William watched as Mr. Oakley nodded in agreement, his smile widening.

William shifted in his chair as he began, "And you, too, Oakley? Was it worth your time?"

"Indeed, I am afraid. I danced with some of the prettiest girls in all of London."

William looked down at his leg, which was propped up on a few pillows. "Well, it is rather convenient then that I was spared, on account of injury, from such an evening."

"Oh come, come, William," Henry began. "I do not want to hear of it any more. We are, after all, Oakley's cousins, and consequently there is no impropriety in going to such dances."

"Say what you want, Henry. But you know how I dislike the pretense of dancing with one above one's station." William smiled, good-natured but resolute in his opinion.

Mr. Oakley looked to support Henry. "It is no imposition at all. I fully intend to have you here as my guests and friends until I quit my stage as a bachelor—unless one of you marries before me, which, upon occurrence, you should forthwith take your leave."

Henry laughed heartily and continued, "Well, then we will be here a bit longer, because I have come to the sad conclusion that, though she is rich and beautiful, I cannot spend the rest of my life with Miss Ivory Rusket. We are too completely dissimilar. We would drive each other mad before a fortnight."

William folded his arms and stared at his brother, raising his eyebrows in amusement. "I have to say I am proud of you, Henry. It shows a great deal of forbearance of character to not win her over just because of her money."

Henry gave a wicked smile. "Do not be so quick, for I will find some other pretty and quite rich woman to marry, as long as I continue with Oakley's social schedule. You would do well to follow suit, for you could also use the money."

"I can assure you both, I do not plan on marrying at all—even if she has twenty thousand pounds—until I have made a way for myself."

Henry shook his head at his proud brother.

Mr. Oakley, completely unaffected, seemed to be daydreaming. "But Miss Rusket should still be an amiable acquaintance, to be sure, Henry. For I did think her friends the handsomest of the ladies you introduced us to. Would be impolitic to lose acquaintance with *those* new faces."

"I am sorry, cousin. All of that party, except Miss Rusket, will return to the north this week," Henry said, waving his hand. "But perhaps we shall see them again."

William closed his eyes, tired of such talk. He had heard those two speak of pretty ladies before. He had more important business matters to attend to. He did not have the heart just then to inform his brother of the two hundred pounds they had lost from an infested shipment of cloth. He had to make his business succeed, and dancing at a ball did not bring him any closer to accomplishing that.

CHAPTER 6

few months after Mr. Robertson's ball, Christine watched as the smiling, handsome Mr. Davenport sauntered up to Wellington Manor's garden entrance. He had been in and out of London for most of the summer, but seemed now to stay in Rothershire, making up for his absence by visiting quite often.

"Upon my word! I am sure I shot half a dozen more birds than you, Grenville!"

Christine, Lizzy, and Meg had just met them in their stroll from Allensby House to Wellington, feigning to stumble upon the gentlemen as their paths intersected. The men were the only ones who thought it was truly serendipitous, for the girls had expertly planned such a rendezvous.

"Hello ladies," Mr. Grenville said, noticing them first. "How do you do today? We have just been relieving your property of its fowls in residence."

His broad, burly form held up three slightly bloody, iridescent pheasants, and he smiled widely at Meg.

"Well I hope that you will put those birds into the hands of our cook and stay for dinner then," Christine replied coyly, directing her remarks toward Mr. Davenport, who was already staring in her direction. "I am sure my father wishes he were hunting with you both."

"We would have been delighted to have his company," Mr. Davenport said, continuing to gaze at Christine. In the past few weeks, he had begun to make it a habit of visiting—and staying for dinner—much to her pleasure.

"And Mr. Grenville, please invite your mother as well. My mother is in need of company with my father away on business."

"Naturally. We all will be delighted to dine with you once again."

A few hours later, the group gathered for a light dinner of an intimate party. Mrs. Grenville sat next to Mrs. Harrison, and the gentlemen sat next to their respective interests. Lizzy sat next to her sister, being in relatively good spirits despite having no one doting on her at this meal. The dinner was composed of several small courses, the bulk of the main fare being the delicious pheasants that the men had shot earlier that day. The food served to satiate the party's hunger and desire for company.

As Christine moved into the drawing room after the meal, Mr. Davenport seized the opportunity to have a more private tête-à-tête with her. He had become much more comfortable in the last few weeks, and tonight he seemed particularly talkative.

"Miss Harrison, I do not want to be too presumptuous, but what is it that has changed between us as of late? You seem so open, and frankly I am amazed I am able to spend so much time with you."

Christine looked across the room at the mantle for a moment. She thought of how just yesterday they had spent hours together walking the gardens, laughing, and discussing literature, their families, and their friends. Meetings of that sort had occurred at least twice a week for the last three weeks, and Christine's infatuation with Mr. Davenport grew steadily.

Knowing him well, she replied, "Ah, your speech conveys I have capitulated to you, Mr. Davenport. How are you so sure of yourself?"

She knew she sounded quite convincing, because for a moment Mr. Davenport's face filled with worry, turning pale, an emotion he usually did not allow others to perceive.

Christine's eyes teased with delight, and she allowed the silence only a moment longer. "Do not look so alarmed!" She then brushed his knee with her book. "I have been musing over the same point, and I believe I have come to a verdict."

Mr. Davenport's smile returned, his shoulders relaxed, and his eyes twinkled. "And what is that?"

"You and I are both so stubborn and headstrong in our views of the world. Neither wants to acquiesce to the other's opinion. But I think it was our time at Cassfield. You remember our conversation in the garden? Ever since then, I see you in a new light. I guess it caused me to hope a little. Do you not agree?"

She smiled at him openly, and his green eyes widened as they drew her in. He moved closer to her. "Yes, but I think it is you who has had the change of heart, Christine," he whispered softly, "for I have been convinced for quite some time."

A warm shiver ran down her spine and she started to blush. She suddenly became very conscious of her surroundings and her rising color. She breathed a sigh of relief as she realized everyone else was well engaged in their own employments.

Mr. Davenport struck a chord in Christine's heart, and she sat silent. Staring intently at the rug before her, feeling rather overcome, she finally summoned the courage to look up into his burning green eyes and say, "You have convinced *me* quite thoroughly, I am afraid."

Christine peered intently across the table. "Lizzy, you need to tell me every detail of what you desire. I will make sure it happens!"

Lizzy smiled back at her older sister. "Oh, Christine, I do not really care about the particulars. I am sure it will be brilliant!"

"But if you want it to be *perfect*, you need to plan!"

Lizzy had always been Christine's assistant when it came to planning things, and she had a habit of taking her opinions from her older sister rather than voicing her own. Today was no exception. Christine had been trying for the past half hour to extract the specifics of Lizzy's wishes for her seventeenth birthday ball.

"What will you wear, Lizzy? Mama will have a new dress made for you."

"Really? Did you have a dress you designed made for your birthday?" Lizzy's face lit up.

"You do not remember? The light pink—almost white—silk and organza dress!"

"Oh, I did not remember that it was made for your birthday. Let me think. I will need to tell Mama about the particulars, but how about something dark—perhaps blue?"

Meg looked up from her sketchbook toward Christine, who stated, "Usually the belle of the ball—in this case you, my dear Lizzy—wears something almost white. Although this party is not quite so high as a coming-out ball, I still think you should pick something very light colored. Most of the ladies will be wearing such dresses."

"I see," Lizzy said, finally sensing the grandeur. "I think I would like something cream then. And could it be covered in lace? Like the dress Ivory wore at Mr. Robertson's ball. Lace with flowers." She gestured to Meg, who immediately started sketching Lizzy's words, taking notes and outlining the described dress. Lizzy added to the picture, and Christine called a maid to ring Mrs. Harrison so they could tell her of the plans.

"These are wonderful ideas and starts, ladies," Mrs. Harrison stated as she perused the sketchbook. "But you should think about *who* is coming. Father and I of course have people we will invite, most of the important people from Rothershire and our parish, I would say, but it would be advantageous to you both to make sure your guest lists provide some entertainment and possibilities in the way of gentlemen. Leave the decorating and the food to me. I have thrown quite a few events in my day." She arched her eyebrows, turned her chin, and withdrew her index finger moving it side to side as she smiled. "Let me know who you would like present, and we will make sure proper and official invitations are sent."

That night as Christine and Lizzy lay in bed, Christine asked, "Have you been thinking of who you would like to invite to your ball?"

"I know I would like to invite the usual people in our circles. Meg, and of course Mr. Davenport"—her voice sounded as though she smiled knowingly—"and Mr. Grenville. I also think we should invite Ivory, although I am not sure she will be able to visit this time of year. Meg seemed to think Ivory's social schedule would not allow it, demanding as it is. I know Mother and Father will invite our other neighbors, although most of them do not have any eligible young men, but their daughters will enjoy it. We will need more men to equal out the women. Do you suppose Mr. Davenport has any friends he could invite?"

"Mr. Davenport did mention he has a cousin around his age, Carlisle by surname, I believe. He has told many stories of their adventures together as young boys."

"Invite him then! And I wish we could invite Mr. Robertson and his party . . ." Her speech quieted and she added, "I wish I could invite Mr. Oakley."

Christine smiled. For the first time in her life, Christine believed that Lizzy was beginning to move from a young girl to a young lady almost in love.

"I thought so," Christine said, nodding. "But I do not know how to contact him without seeming overly forward. I wish we lived closer to London. I think it might be a bit much to invite his party to come all the way to Rothershire for our small ball."

Lizzy nodded, her thin lips pressing together. Christine felt sure her sister thought of Mr. Oakley often.

Mr. Davenport came to call the next morning, requesting a walk through the hedgerows. He buzzed with excitement, walking briskly. He carried a true vivacity for life which was especially contagious when he was talking about something he cared about.

"You know," he began, "I think that Mr. Grenville would like to propose to Miss Allensby. He was asking me how long he has to wait before it is proper to ask." His eyes danced, and then he added mischievously, "But you probably should not tell her I shared this with you." His smile widened.

"Oh, your secret is safe with me. But what did you tell him?" Christine's excited dialogue often had a way of turning rather coquettish when under the clutches of Mr. Davenport.

"I told him to stop being a dolt and ask her. In my opinion, some people wait far too long before asking. If you know you want to marry that person, then you should ask."

Christine's mind started racing. She quickly turned to the garden roses next to her, feigning great interest in their blooms. Was this a hint that he would ask her to marry him soon? A not-so-subtle way of stating that he thought they had courted long enough? Or was this proof that he was not sure about her? That their attachment was not strong enough? Would it ever be? Christine knew that people often spoke of another's circumstance as a roundabout way to discuss their own situation. Her eyes narrowed as she pondered if this was the case.

"I am not so sure," she countered, her playful nature now absent. "I think sometimes it takes a good amount of time to know if true attachment exists."

He looked steadily at Christine, peering into her eyes as if trying to discern her thoughts. She gazed back and tried to discern his.

He seemed so conflicted. It was as though he wanted to show more but was guarded at the same time.

Twice Mr. Davenport began to speak but then stopped himself. Finally, after a few minutes, as the increasing silence grew more uncomfortable, Mr. Davenport burst forth once again, a hint of nerves in his voice as he stated, "I need to tell you . . ."—his voice hesitated a moment—"that I have an opportunity to seek a very promising venture that would improve my standing in town. It would require me to live in London for quite some time."

"Oh is that so? How exciting!" Christine paused a moment and then asked, "When would you move?"

"I would not need to move for at least six months."

Christine's shoulders relaxed a little, realizing he had not come that day to tell her of his immediate departure. Perhaps he wished for something more to happen between them in the next six months.

Mr. Davenport had a good-sized inheritance, but he was always seeking to further his holding and investments by engaging in more business dealings. Christine knew some of his monetary situation, but at this time he informed her about his duties while in London. He said he would be gathering information for many of the parliamentary men and compiling reports to better serve them in their duties. Christine tried to show interest, masking the indifference she felt about his future civic obligations. She did not care what he would do in London, as long as they would be married and there together. What other particulars really mattered?

She realized then that every meeting between them felt one step closer to engagement. Did Mr. Davenport feel this way? Christine wondered if he was truly interested in her or if he was just filling his time before he moved to London. Surely after his mention of Mr. Grenville's desire to propose to Meg, Mr. Davenport felt it was his time to do the same with Christine?

And then, as though he discerned the diatribe in her head, Mr. Davenport stated, "I hope by that time to have someone to take with me." He looked slowly at Christine with his convincing green eyes and half smile.

Christine colored deeply, and then a smile spread across her cheeks.

She vacillated in thought: Did he mean this as a proposal? What exactly did he have in mind for their future? Why did he not state it more directly? She always had faltered with the right thing to say in a critical moment, her emotions swiftly dominating her ability to respond gracefully. She did not want to assume too much. Mr. Davenport waited patiently during Christine's inner struggle. After a few moments, she still did not know how to respond. Finally, she lowered her chin and looked up at him, smiling.

"Mr. Davenport, I do love to hear you so animated about your future prospects. Thank you for sharing with me. We cannot lose you to London entirely."

As soon as she said it, she knew it was not enough. He had wanted more. Mr. Davenport smiled again, this time somewhere between infatuation and vexation. She felt his frustration at her overly proper words.

"And if I asked you to come with me, say as Mrs. Davenport, how would you answer to such a question?"

There. Finally, Mr. Davenport became clearer in his meaning.

"I would ask you to ask me the question directly, and of course, to speak with my father," she said with a coquettish smile, crossing her arms and shrugging her shoulders. She had finally regained herself.

"Well then," he said, "I suppose I have much official discussion to conduct before I plan to move." He sat back, smiling openly at

Christine. She waited for him to say more, but he remained quiet. She watched him then gaze across the green shrubs before him, and his eyes seemed to cloud a bit. He moved away and straightened, and then he said, "I must be going. I am sure we will talk of this more at a later time, when we can make it all much more official."

He stood and bowed low, meeting Christine's eyes for only a moment. He turned and walked briskly away, going straight to the groom house, and left on his horse. Christine watched his every move, surprised at his quick departure. He had mentioned marriage, but she knew in her heart that she could not count it as an official proposal yet. Something still seemed a bit uneasy between them.

CHAPTER 7

The town of Rothershire stood somewhere between a large city and a country town, a two days' journey north of London. Today's visit to town was to complete the accoutrements for Lizzy's ball. Christine needed gloves, Lizzy desired some new embellishments for her hair, and they of course brought Meg, who wanted a new spencer jacket after having saved her allowance for the last few months. They took the carriage, on account of the muddy lane, and the footman deposited them in the center of town.

The three happy purchasers traipsed into the dressmaker's shop to see the progress of Lizzy's gown and match her hair ribbons with the new garment. Christine picked out a pair of gloves made of silk, having lost one of her last good pair while staying at Ivory's house.

Looking into the dress shop display, Christine commented, "Meg! That jacket is quite perfect for you! The maroon velvet will be just the thing for this winter. And I love how the tailor crafted the sleeves. He knows all the newest fashions from London and France!"

At the mention of France, Christine watched Meg's eyes sparkle, knowing Meg thought about Mr. Grenville, whom she had just seen the night before.

As the group left the dressmaker, they turned to walk along the main street back to the carriage. As they approached, Christine noticed two striking men crossing the street. Dressed in a gentleman's coat, the blond man was slightly taller and much broader than his dark-haired companion.

How familiar the taller gentleman seems, thought Christine. The two men walked briskly, discussing something of great importance, judging by the fervent body language and hand motions involved. Christine then took Lizzy's wrist and would have pulled them into the gentlemen's path, but there was no need. The girls slowed as the men, oblivious, came closer and closer until finally the blond gentleman looked up just before walking directly into the ladies.

"Good day!" The taller blond man smiled cordially, breaking from his debate, and then his eyes grew large as he realized he knew the strangers before him. With his hands opening wide he bowed slightly, "It is truly a pleasure to run into you ladies!"

"And run into you we *shall* if you continue as you are!" Christine answered with a smile.

"How nice it is to see you again, Mr. Robertson," Lizzy said, with a bit more decorum than Christine had presently mustered. Remembering their manners finally, the three young women curtsied, and as they stood again, Christine noticed the dark-haired companion step out to the side.

"Allow me to introduce myself," the darker-haired man said, outstretching a palm. "My name is Mr. William Robertson."

He gazed at all three girls, straight faced but full of confidence. Christine looked at his extended hand and, after staring at it for a moment, realized she had no choice but to shake it. He had no gallantry about him, just a matter-of-fact demeanor. Surely he could have learned a little charm and decorum from his brother. Who did he think he was?

They were not well enough acquainted for a handshake. It seemed so low, without any sense of propriety. Did he not know that shaking hands with a lady—or three—whom one just met was rather untoward? Especially since Christine's new gloves remained in her satchel and not on her hands. Perhaps a handshake greeting prevailed in the Orient. *Although I doubt such a thing,* Christine surmised. Such a character she had never known upon a first meeting.

"I am sorry, ladies, excuse my manners," Mr. Henry Robertson finally said, hastily introducing them by name. Christine did not know if he was making up for his brother's unusual introduction or covering himself for forgetting to lead the formalities. "This is my brother. The one that caused me to leave Cassfield so abruptly while visiting you."

"Ah, this is the Cassfield family?" William said to Henry, and added, "I now realize the sacrifice it was for you to come take care of me. I am surprised you left such company for your poor brother."

He said it quite straight and serious, but Christine wondered if she saw a jest behind his eyes. This William Robertson seemed quite unlike his brother—straightforward, businesslike, with no charming words and gestures. His eyes, however, were quite engaging. They were handsomely cobalt, distracting Christine from analyzing his character any more. She blinked away from them after a moment, realizing that with such a serendipitous meeting, she must seize the occasion presented her.

The Robertsons were in Rothershire. This fact was all she needed to invite them to Lizzy's ball. She lifted her head and lowered her shoulders to appear as formal as possible. "I think I should take this opportunity to invite you both to the ball we are having next Friday. I realize it is short notice, but if you would still be in the north country, we would be delighted to have you in attendance." She directed most of this speech toward the smiling Henry, hardly knowing how to address his austere brother. "I know Mr. Harrison would love to see you again, Mr. Robertson."

She paused for a moment and then continued. "And might I ask, why *are* you in town?"

Henry cleared his throat and smiled. "When I met your family in Cassfield, I did not realize that your family's estate bordered Rothershire. You have one of the finest dressmakers in the country in this town, and we supply fabric to him from the Orient. William and I are here on business, and we are on our way to his shop this morning."

"We just came from there!" Lizzy interjected. "How exciting that we should cross paths. We love that dress shop. Their gowns are exceedingly fine."

"Yes, Lizzy is having a dress made," Christine continued, "because our ball is for her seventeenth birthday."

"Happy birthday, Miss Elizabeth!" Henry imbued in his warmest way. Then William, quite determined, snapped his pocket watch open and shut in a flash. This more severe brother turned to the ladies and said, "We must be going. A pleasure to meet you all. We will be sure to be in attendance at your ball."

William offered Christine his card and then gave a short nod to Henry, the two brothers continuing in the other direction, taking up their previous argument without missing a moment. With the touch of William's hand still lingering, Christine realized she had not finished her work with these unusual brothers. They were the one connection to that Mr. Oakley Lizzy had so enjoyed at the London ball. She might be able to convince the Robertsons to bring Mr. Oakley with them.

"Go back to my father's carriage, and keep Lizzy occupied," Christine whispered to Meg. Meg obeyed instantly, looping her arm through Lizzy's and directing her interest toward a shop ahead.

"Carpe diem!" Christine murmured to herself, acting immediately on the scheme that just entered her mind. Hurrying back to the two Mr. Robertsons, she slid three feet in front of them and then came to a dead stop. Noticing her immediately, hand held high in some explanation, William froze. Christine turned her head and looked swiftly at Henry, who seemed much less annoyed.

"Excuse me, gentlemen." She took a quick breath in and let it out in one moment, "Could you also extend an invitation to your friend Mr. Oakley as well? Although I assume he is in London? I know it would mean a great deal to Lizzy." She pursed her lips and added an innocent shrug, hoping to get her matchmaking message across.

Henry's mouth remained open slightly, having stopped mid-word in his argument when Christine intersected them. He tilted his head and raised his eyebrows—for he was as much the matchmaking type as was Christine—and grinned back. "Yes, I believe we can extend such an invitation. I shall write to him tonight and see if London might spare him for a weekend."

"Thank you!" Christine half-whispered as she curtsied, triumphant, and turned on her heels.

As she whipped around, she heard Henry say, "I am shocked, William, that you accepted their invitation so readily."

"I had no other choice, as of course we must consent when asked directly," William responded, devoid of emotion.

"And as you have no excuse with your leg any longer, stop being such a miser and wrap your mind around dancing."

Christine smiled, her pace quickening as she found her way back to Lizzy and Meg, who were waiting at her father's carriage. She feigned innocence to both Lizzy and Meg and said nothing.

Christine mused to herself on their ride home. Mr. Robertson was in town. They had met his brother. And Mr. Oakley might be coming to Lizzy's ball. *That* was quite a productive shopping trip.

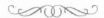

"Meg?" Christine asked as the two walked from Allensby House across the field to Wellington Estate a day later. "I think Mr. Grenville will propose soon. Do you not agree?" Nosiness and direct questions were becoming a strong point for Christine.

"I do, indeed," she said with a downward look and a shrug of the shoulders.

"Is something the matter?" Christine asked, surprised by her tone.

"I know this is completely wrong of me," she said, "but I am not sure I want to marry Mr. Grenville."

Christine almost stopped walking. "How long have you felt like this?"

Meg avoided a direct answer. "I do so enjoy his presence, but I am not sure we match very well. Besides . . ." she said, heaving a heavy sigh. "Besides." She stopped moving and ceased her speech abruptly.

Christine had been Meg's close confidant for years, but often Christine found it hard to really distinguish Meg's true feelings. Quite the quiet diplomat, Meg never wanted to offend or cause a stir. This was one of those moments, and Christine found herself wanting to raise her hands high and declare, "Out with it!" But alas, Meg stood silent, making a determined study of the rolling grass before her.

There must be some reason, thought Christine. Something had to have happened in her courtship with Mr. Grenville. They were perfect for each other in so many ways. Meg's sweet disposition, his ability to dote, not to mention they had similar incomes and family standings.

"Meg—Mr. Grenville worships the ground you walk on. He is romantic. He is chivalrous. He speaks *French*. He is well connected and benevolent and your families find each other *quite* agreeable. How does that not match?'"

When people were not well suited for each other, Christine found it obvious. For example, the ill-matched interchange of Mr. Robertson and Ivory: different family standing and status, social class, views on subjects, ability to see eye to eye, and a general lack of complementary components, to name a few.

But here, with Meg? Christine was quite taken aback.

"I just have other ideas . . . Besides . . ." Meg said, as she traced the lines on her skirt.

This time Christine could not let it go. "Besides *what*?"

"I think I am interested in someone else," she let out quietly.

Christine's mind quickly raced over the past few months. *Who else could she be referring to?*

"Meg, I am afraid I must speak my mind. First, it has seemed as though you love Mr. Grenville! Your very actions point to that conclusion. Have you been leading him on? Do you know if you do not continue now with Mr. Grenville, you may lose your chance with him forever? Are you willing to let that opportunity go?"

"I am not sure," she replied, "I am just so conflicted inside. My heart is saying one thing, and my mind is saying another. I cannot reconcile myself."

Christine took a deep breath and glimpsed, for the first time, into Meg's soul. This was a matter of great import that weighed deeply on her heart. Although sympathetic, Christine had never felt as Meg did. To have such a wonderful option in a mate and not accept it because one's heart was somewhere else seemed a burden almost too hard to bear. How was one supposed to resolve such a problem?

"I do not know how to put this to rights," Meg said. "The only thing I feel I can do is see if there is anything there between . . . him and me. Then perhaps I would know by comparison if I really should be with Mr. Grenville."

"Who is 'him'?" Christine asked.

Meg looked down at her skirts and tugged on the side seam of her dress. She pursed her lips slightly and took a nervous breath in. "His name is Mr. Carlisle," she replied.

Christine and Meg had just reached the drawing room of Wellington. Normally the two friends would have spent the remainder of the morning there, but Christine motioned up the stairs toward her room, knowing Meg would want more privacy for this conversation. Without speaking, Meg followed Christine. Meg sat down quickly on the chair near the window, and Christine curled up on the bed, focusing all her attention toward her melancholy friend.

"Tell me how this came to be," Christine said, ready to listen.

Looking down and fiddling once again with her hands, Meg began with a story from two years prior, when she went to stay with her grandmother to study art. She was quite skilled at anything artistic and had an aptitude for painting. Her grandmother had taken pity on her family's reduced circumstance and held great hopes for her granddaughter's future and marriage, which she thought would be greatly augmented by a summer refining her craft.

"My grandmother procured the finest tutors in all of London. I had great exposure to fine culture and circles, with many favorable experiences there. We would spend a few days a week in London, but once each week we would go into the outskirts of town and paint for hours. Some mornings I would attend lessons and then be free to set up my easel outside of a church or barn and paint the beauty of the scene. One Sunday, I was attending church with Grandmamma when he walked in." For a moment, Christine watched Meg's eyes close around a scene in her mind.

"He was attending the university to become a doctor. His end goal was to become a parish physician, which was entirely too lowly for Grandmamma's approval. She wanted only a titled man with an estate for me. I had never hoped for such fine associations through marriage, and his circumstances suited me just fine. She, however, did not want me to fall into the same downfall as my mother had with my father. I was young, and he was the kindest man I had ever known. Every moment in his company was a mix of pleasant friendship laced with a tinge of forbidden excitement. He was easy to talk to, and so amusing and dynamic. I began to serve at the almshouse and arrange times to meet with him there. Grandmamma would never allow him to call, though. No, he was never to step foot in her home."

With a blissful but somewhat guilty look in her eye, she continued in her reverie, "So, we never told Grandmamma, but once we met up when I was on an assignment painting a landscape. Then we began to see each other a few times a week. I never went to see just him, I will have you know, but we conveniently coordinated my painting sessions and his schedules. One of my instructors eventually told Grandmamma, and that was the end of our visits. After that I only saw him at church, and Grandmamma would not give me the chance to talk to him. My grandmamma played on my conscience and forbade me to ever meet Mr. Carlisle again. She convinced me to be more worried about my future and reputation. This is why I never told you about it. I was very young, and I treasured spending time with Mr. Carlisle. The attachment grew quickly, but the relationship was short-lived. My Grandmamma died the next year, and I never went there to visit again."

She then pulled out a creased piece of paper from within her dress pocket. Handing it to Christine, she said, "But he sent me this two weeks ago. I do not know how he found me."

Dearest Miss Allensby,

It has been two years this August since we have spoken or seen each other. I must tell you that I think of you often. I imagine you with your brush in your hand, head tilted to the side, deciding whether to outline the landscape or a nearby building. I see you speaking to me with your beautiful blue eyes and dark hair, telling me about your life, so freely, your face so becoming in the summer sun. I know this may sound strange, but I must know if you are married. If you are not currently engaged, it would be my honor to call on you in Rothershire. I have saved some of my earnings and the trip would be well worth my time and effort. Please let me know if you would like to see me again, for I unquestionably desire to see you once more.

Best,
Mr. George Carlisle

Christine's eyes raised and met Meg's, the romance clear through the words of the letter.

Meg took it and pressed it to her chest. "So, how shall I answer him? I cannot determine what to do. I have delayed my response . . . thus far."

Christine folded her hands in her lap and looked back at her dear friend, trying to formulate a suggestion, when Lizzy came bouncing into the room.

"Here you are! I was looking all over for you! I just finished with the dressmakers and Mama. We had the most delightful time in town, although we did not run into Mr. Robertson again."

"Oh, is that so!" Christine smiled, grateful for the provided change of subject. Christine usually fancied herself one to offer abundant advice, but this time she was at a loss.

"Yes," she continued. "And Mama and I just went over the guest list for the ball. Mr. Robertson and his brother will of course be coming—which adds to our number of gentlemen! The Skinners will be attending, although the Lambleys are away on some type of trip." She turned to Meg. "And of course, Mr. Grenville will be coming. And Mr. Davenport, Christine, and he said he will be bringing his cousin, a Mr. Carlisle, too. Truly delightful, is it not?" She walked to her dressing table and started removing her bonnet, gloves, and shawl.

Christine gulped back her gasp as she remembered suggesting that Mr. Davenport bring his cousin. Could it be the same Carlisle family?

Meg wrung her letter like a dish towel and looked furtively at Christine, who watched Meg's realization wash over her face. Mr. Carlisle would attend the Wellington ball. Her emotions vacillated like a wistful love story. First excitement, followed by nervousness.

Christine stood and walked to Meg's side, resting her hand on her shoulder. Quietly she whispered, "I think you should hold off writing a reply to your letter for a few days."

Meg shot Christine an alarmed glance, and the two did not talk about it more in front of Lizzy.

Before dinner, Meg and Christine found some time alone again.

"What should I do?" Meg asked quietly. "Should I not attend your ball?"

Christine thought that suggestion over for a moment and then answered, "You must come. Mr. Grenville will be present, and it will raise suspicion if you do not attend. But with them both there together—I do not know what to tell you."

Meg sighed and looked down at her half-boots, lost in thought.

Up until that point, Christine had always fantasized about having multiple suitors at her disposal, reveling in such an exhilarating prospect. What a foolish notion! Meg was about to walk into a dreaded curse taking place on a ball floor. For once Christine felt relieved to be in the crowd. This would be quite the drama played before their eyes, and Christine, as a spectator, feared for the exhibition at hand.

CHAPTER 8

The morning of the ball, Christine sat alone in their parlor, reviewing the names of the guest list one more time. A maid opened the door, and Mr. Davenport walked in, gallantly removing his hat. "Is there anything I can help you with, Miss Christine?" he whispered.

Her lips turned upward at him, and she basked in his use of her first name and said with as much feigned worry as she could muster, "Well, I *am* terribly worried no one will dance with me tonight. So, if you see that I am free, you might ask for my card?"

Mr. Davenport laughed and spun Christine around by her hand. "Undoubtedly! I think you might have your hands—or your arms—full this evening."

Mr. Davenport imitated an allemande as he crossed the room, when the door swung open and Mrs. Harrison entered. Mr. Davenport, also a favorite with Christine's mother, dropped his dance position and asked, "What can I do to help make this evening easier, Mrs. Harrison?"

"Oh nothing," she said as she picked up the list Christine had left on the side table. "Your presence, Mr. Davenport, will be enough!"

Mrs. Harrison shot a knowing smile of approval in Christine's direction. Christine blushed and tried to act employed by the intricate flower arrangement next to her.

The clock seemed paralyzed as the day went on. Everyone waited with excitement for the six o'clock hour to arrive. Perhaps the most amusing facet of the day was watching Lizzy anticipate this party held in her honor. Her countenance, infused with eagerness, glowed as she waited for her guests to arrive.

There were few occasions in his life when Mr. Harrison approved of sparing no expense, and this was one of them. Mrs. Harrison had employed every resource she desired, and the effect was breathtaking. The lawn glistened with torches lighting the way to the front antechamber. The entrance, lit up with candles, smelled of roses, and great bouquets of flowers came out of vases on every flat surface. Mrs. Harrison had made special arrangements for the servants from Cassfield to come up to Wellington Manor, with maids and waiters ready to receive and serve respectively. The main ballroom bustled with servants preparing the room for a dance. More flowers edged the walls on side tables, and navy drapes trimmed in silver flanked the windows. The main part of the room was left open, ready for willing dancers to take their positions. Tall silver candelabras brightened the room in between every window, the room feeling dazzling and silvery-white.

There were hired musicians, tuning their instruments, and Christine watched Mrs. Harrison, buzzing above all, whisk through the room with one last scrutinizing eye. Her mother found no complaint; indeed, she clasped her hands together and smiled. She then moved to her perch like a phoenix newly reborn at the zenith of day, standing triumphant near the entranceway to greet her guests. Mr. Harrison stood stalwart, smiling generously and discussing with Christine the menu he had provided for his guests. They stood in a line: Mr. Harrison, his wife, and then Lizzy, holding the position of honor at her special party, with Christine standing next to her.

The first to arrive was Mr. Davenport, with Mr. Grenville in tow. Surprisingly, Mr. Carlisle was not with his cousin.

"I trust Miss Allensby has not arrived yet?" Mr. Grenville spoke to Christine as Lizzy welcomed many more guests.

"Yes, you are correct, Mr. Grenville, but I am sure she will be arriving shortly. She is usually quite prompt."

Christine feigned a smile as she spoke, which was all she could muster. Christine dared not imagine what this evening might entail for him. Then a true smile washed across Christine's face as she turned to Mr. Davenport, momentarily taking his arm. "I cannot accompany you just yet. But I promise I will sneak away as soon as my parents and Lizzy find themselves employed with guests."

His green eyes smiled and he sent a sideways glance toward her as he said, "I am looking forward to keeping your card full tonight, Miss Christine."

Within the next half-hour, several families, about twenty in all, filtered their way into Wellington Manor. Finally, Meg arrived. Christine analyzed her friend's countenance, trying to gauge her feelings. She seemed cheerful, but slightly on edge. Meg pulled Christine aside and said, "Mr. Carlisle came to call this morning. I was thoroughly surprised. He told Mr. Davenport he was on business and said he would be coming on his own to the ball. Has he arrived yet?"

"No," Christine whispered. "So does Mr. Carlisle know about Mr. Grenville?"

"Only vaguely," Meg shifted her eyes.

"And the reverse?"

"No, certainly not."

Christine bit her lip. "I will be in the ballroom as soon as possible. You ought to go spend some time with Mr. Grenville before Mr. Carlisle arrives. Good luck!" Christine ushered her down the hall and then returned to her post.

Christine had envisioned just what Lizzy's face would look like when she recognized Mr. Oakley, if indeed he could come. Christine spotted him well before Lizzy, behind a few other guests. Mr. Henry Robertson entered first, with Mr. William Robertson behind, and last, hanging back a bit, Mr. Oakley.

Lizzy saw Henry Robertson first and greeted him warmly. She curtsied and as she looked up, beheld Mr. Oakley. Her face flushed and she smiled widely and unencumbered. She shot a quick glance sideways to Christine. Mr. Henry Robertson bowed to Mr. Harrison and said, "Mr. and Mrs. Harrison, allow me the pleasure of introducing my brother, Mr. William Robertson, and our esteemed cousin, Mr. Edmund Oakley."

"We are delighted," Mr. Harrison responded as Mrs. Harrison curtsied. Lizzy curtsied next, and Mr. Oakley held Lizzy's gloved hand

and kissed it, saying, "We are charmed to be invited to your ball, Miss Elizabeth."

"Thank you, Mr. Oakley. We as well are pleased you are in attendance," Lizzy breathed back. Her voice sounded sweet and cool, like a bird singing on a new spring morning. Christine observed Henry's face, basking in his matchmaking, which he so prided himself on, smiling and watching this interchange. She watched Lizzy's face too, until William turned to greet her.

"Hello, Miss Harrison. This is a splendid party," William stated. "But may I ask why do you wait here with your sister? Do you not wish to be mingling with all of your invited guests?"

He seemed to be challenging her. Did he think her a socialite who invited every group of gentlemen she saw walking down the street to her ball?

"I do intend to mingle with them all, Mr. Robertson," Christine said with feigned superiority. "But perhaps I will walk with you now into the ballroom, as most of the guests have arrived."

"Then why did you wait in this line?" William continued. Christine noticed his strong jaw and dark hair. He was much more handsome than his brother. And much more analytical.

"As a support to my sister," Christine said quickly, looking up at him and feeling rather intimidated by his intensity and confidence. She would not let him know she had waited to see Lizzy's face at the surprise of Mr. Oakley. He surely would not understand the joy of sisterly delight and would think it childish of her.

"I see," he said evenly.

As Christine accompanied the three gentlemen down the hall, Henry turned to Christine and said, "We wish to thank you for you invite, Miss Harrison."

"Of course, Mr. Robertson. And thank you for bringing *your* party," she returned with a smile.

Then William turned toward her again. "Miss Harrison, I wonder if I might have the pleasure of a dance this evening."

His blue eyes carried a certain strength and confidence. She stood surprised he asked so early, but his face showed he expected an affirmative response.

"Of course," Christine answered quickly, feeling once again nervous in his presence.

Christine's step quickened as she saw Mr. Davenport in his handsome black dinner jacket. He wore a white cravat, tied smartly, and his countenance was full of delight and approval as she made her way to his side. The Robertson brothers had already moved to the other side of the room before Mr. Davenport noticed them and were soon lost in the crowd.

Mr. Davenport stepped closer, overshadowing Christine. "You look absolutely marvelous tonight, Miss Harrison. That dress suits you very well. And I do like your hair." He exhaled pleasantly and smiled. "Might I fill out your card?"

Christine curtsied, holding her skirts out wide and turned her face to the side as her eyes danced. "Mr. Davenport. I will not dance more than two times with you this evening. You must allow me to mingle with other guests!"

"Ah, this coming from the lass who thought she would never be asked. Interesting." He tisked, and then added, "I see you already have one dance reserved, hmm?"

Christine thought she saw his eyes thin as he looked at the other name on her card. He looked up and scanned the room quickly. Did he disapprove of her dancing with someone else? Surely this was a ball, and he ought to expect her to dance several dances. Christine surmised then that Mr. Davenport disliked Henry's brother just as much as he disliked Henry.

Despite this quick change, his alacrity returned presently as he said, "I have taken all of my allowed spots, my dear."

His eyes danced as he gave a short bow and then turned to discuss something with Mr. Grenville. Mr. Grenville's eyes would not leave Meg, his husky form inching closer to her as Mr. Davenport spoke to him.

Christine, filled with confidence now that Mr. Davenport had given her such a welcome, walked toward Meg. Her excitement stopped short, however, as she saw Meg look over her shoulder to the entrance of the room.

A man of average height and build with tightly curled brown hair and a dimpled smile was staring at their small group. His head tilted slightly and he nodded a greeting at Meg with a reserved smile.

Christine heard Meg quickly catch her breath and watched as her eyes riveted on him. Meg edged along the outside of the room until she reached him. She curtsied, her long brown lashes looking up at him with wonder. He had a very pleasant look on his face, and she was beaming. They began discussing something, and both party's mannerisms spoke of missing one another. Christine weaved her way through the crowd in time to hear this part of the conversation.

"I was surprised to learn from my cousin that his best friend was courting a certain Miss Allensby. I could only assume he meant you. I do hope that tonight you will give me a chance to prove myself. I understand it might be an uncomfortable situation for you. But I ask only for a chance."

"I hardly know what to say, Mr. Carlisle. But I can accept one dance."

Christine had made her way almost to Meg, who welcomed her gratefully. "And please allow me to introduce you to Miss Harrison. This is her family's party, as I am sure you have gathered."

Christine bowed, and Mr. Carlisle replied, "Pleased to meet you, Miss Harrison. Might I also ask you for a dance?"

Christine consented, noticing the wise move by Mr. Carlisle to not monopolize Meg all night. He seemed like a cunning piece in this evening's chess game.

Not wanting to linger too long, Meg took Christine's arm and walked toward the entrance.

Christine watched as Lizzy finally strolled into the room, her eyes even larger than usual as she took in the scene. She seemed pleased, her gaze slowly washing from left to right.

Last to enter were Mr. and Mrs. Harrison, engaged with some newly arrived guests. The musicians tuned their instruments, and the first dance began. Mr. Davenport walked toward Christine with his long, confident strides. He took her by the hand, and, escorting her to the center of the room, stated, "I must tell you again how beautiful you look."

Christine smiled and blinked her eyes slowly. She stared back at him for a long moment as the introduction sounded in her ears. He wrapped his arms around her as they prepared to dance. As they started dancing across the room, she remembered Meg and asked, "Have you had an enjoyable time with your cousin?"

"I have not seen him much," he responded. "But I have come to understand that he once possessed a strong friendship with Miss Allensby?"

Christine remained silent for a moment, but her eyes betrayed her.

"I must ask, is it more than friendship? If so, I do not know who to stand behind—as it seems my best friend and cousin are both pursuing the same woman." He lifted Christine's arm as she spun gracefully.

"Does Mr. Grenville know of the danger?" Christine asked.

"I do not think so, and I am not going to be his informant."

"Nor I," she replied. His strong hands gripped her waist as they turned again. Christine continued, "We shall see how this plays out, but I for one am quite uneasy for Meg."

Christine watched across the room as Meg and Mr. Grenville danced happily, Mr. Grenville seeming oblivious to Mr. Carlisle's presence. Lizzy had started the ball with a dance from Mr. Henry Robertson, a perfect way to involve his party. As this dance ended, Christine made her way to Lizzy.

"My card is completely full!" Lizzy said quietly as she held up her reticle, glancing sideways at Christine. "Tonight is perfect! I just want to remember every part of the evening!"

"It truly is a delightful sight," Christine agreed. "Has the charming Mr. Oakley asked you for a dance?"

"Two!" she whispered back, all the while looking straight forward to survey the group, not wanting to give herself away.

"I would have guessed as much," Christine answered, her eyes twinkling with triumph.

The sun had set and the glow of candles made the room shimmer against the dark curtains. It felt magical to have her sister next to her, swelling with so much happiness. And then Lizzy looked Christine in the eyes and said, "Thank you for inviting him."

The musicians had stopped, and the couples throughout the room had dispersed to their own or new parties once again. Christine threaded her arm through Lizzy's as the pair walked across the room, relishing every moment.

A few minutes later the music began again, and the room swirled as partners took the floor. Mr. Oakley walked gracefully up to Lizzy and took her hand, while Mr. Carlisle had asked for Christine this dance. She saw his tightly curled head making his way through the crowd like a sheep emerging in long grass. Was he smarter than an average headstrong ram? This was Christine's chance to discern such things.

Christine and her partner hardly said anything as a quick allemande rattled off from the winds and strings. Then, his first gesture of friendship was simply thanking her for allowing him to come. *Polite, and well played*, thought Christine, *although he seems a bit insincere*. His face looked inviting, but the tone of voice contradicted his words. Surely he must know that she was somewhat privy to his situation. Seeking for more intimate information, Christine asked, "How long do you plan on staying to visit, Mr. Carlisle?"

"A few weeks, or longer if necessary," he replied. By the stern set of his jaw, Christine suspected he was not about to offer more information.

But after a few more refrains, Christine again ventured with her sweetest and most pleasant voice, "What brings you to Rothershire, besides this party? Do you have business with Mr. Davenport?"

His face hardened, and he focused his eyes on a far point across the room.

"I have a project I am working on," he answered curtly, Christine thinking him to be a rather curmudgeonly character. There was simply nothing warm about him at all. He made it seem that dancing with anyone but Meg was nothing but a burden. As the allemande finished, Christine was grateful that her next dance was with Mr. Henry Robertson.

Around nine o' clock, the party dined together. This commensal experience was more lavish than Christine could remember ever having at Wellington Manor. The food alone was a paragon of taste and variety. The dinner offered pork and beef, with seafood delivered fresh from Cassfield's shores. There were sweet meats and fresh fruit, with an array of cheese that would have impressed a traveling Frenchman, had there been any in attendance.

Christine positioned herself in between Mr. Davenport and Mr. Grenville during the meal. Mr. Grenville grew quieter, and Christine was beginning to sense something had changed. He spoke little—Meg sat on his other side, but their conversation was strained. Christine felt no lull, however, because Mr. Davenport happily made up the difference.

Just before the last course, Mr. Davenport turned to Christine. Her hand rested on the table, and his brushed against hers slightly, as though perhaps he meant to. Mr. Davenport faced her and said softly, "Christine, I will be gone within a few days on business. I did not realize I would have to leave this soon until today. I should only be gone a few weeks." His voice slowed and he continued, "When I return, I would love to discuss our future and speak to your father."

Christine looked around the room, and again Mr. Davenport had chosen a moment when the general buzz of people enshrouded their own intimate conversation. She put down her fork and folded her hands in her lap as she felt a flush go through her cheeks. She smiled and took a deep breath, and then turned to him.

"I would like that very much," she said, a wide smile across her lips as she peered into his eyes. Her hand anxiously reached for her fork again, causing her prawn to do a jig across her plate. She thought about her future, about Mr. Davenport, and about what he had just implied, unable to contain her excitement. Lizzy cleared her throat and looked at her, wordlessly reminding her sister to have better manners. Christine then found her napkin and endeavored to clear her mind and not completely give away her feelings for all to see. She turned once more to Mr. Davenport and smiled gently. She wished for a moment he would ask her father before he left to London, but said nothing to Mr. Davenport, knowing it must be his timing.

Looking down a few guests, Christine watched as Meg talked across the table to Mr. Carlisle, and from the look on Mr. Grenville's face, Christine guessed that he was beginning to ascertain a troublesome realization about his beloved Miss Allensby. Christine watched this scene for a moment and then turned away, afraid of adding even more tension.

Henry Robertson began lightly tapping his glass. He stood, and in his characteristic manner, he said, "I believe a toast is in order. I am sure you would all join with me in thanking Mr. Harrison for hosting us, and for Mrs. Harrison for orchestrating such an exquisite meal!" The tapping of crystal rang in agreement. Mr. Davenport shot a glance at Christine, seeming to ask why they still interacted with the Robertsons. Christine leaned over and said quietly, "They have great connections for our dear Lizzy, so we felt they ought to be invited." Mr. Davenport relaxed again in his chair, assenting to the toast.

It was not much later when Mr. Oakley stood and said, "My dear friend Mr. Robertson toasted to thank our hosts, and that was in great order. I now would like to toast to our Miss Elizabeth for her birthday. Would you all join me in wishing her a happy year to come?" Lizzy sat directly across from Christine at the table, beaming and nodding to all those on either side of her. Again the pleasant clinking of glasses sounded. Christine watched as understanding dawned across Mr. Davenport's face when he realized the connection she had implied.

Around eleven the guests returned to the ballroom. Christine had scarcely donned her gloves when Mr. William Robertson made his way to her side and said, "Miss Harrison, I do believe it is time for our dance?" He took her gloved hand and escorted her to the side of the ballroom, saying nothing else. Christine noticed Henry dancing with Meg, her pale plum dress swishing gracefully, and Mr. Oakley taking his second dance with Lizzy.

"This is quite a grand party, and a delicious meal," Mr. William Robertson began as his tall frame gave an opening bow.

"Thank you," Christine replied, "My parents quite enjoy hosting."

"I would dare say you enjoy hosting the parties yourself." He took her arm as they fell in rank, promenading in a circle with the other dancers.

"Why yes, I do, Mr. Robertson. How did you know?" His comment seemed rather personal, considering his customary lack of interest and dry tone toward her.

"I thought it might be the case, Miss Harrison," he continued, "The way you watch the guests, the way you take on the air of hosting. I feel as though you prefer being the hostess more than a guest?"

"That . . . is correct," Christine said slowly, surprised by his insight. A few moments of silence followed, a friendly silence, like a cloudy summer afternoon. One could feel the warmth but not see the sun. Not at all like the icy silence between Mr. Carlisle and her as they danced, she reflected.

The quadrille began to wane, but before it ended he continued, "Then as such a hostess, my brother and I have a proposition for you. Come find me again tonight and I will discuss with you our grand idea. I promise it to be advantageous to your party, as well as mine."

Christine curtsied slightly, nodding her head in agreement to his small monologue. His usual stern voice had something of intrigue and good humor, which surprised Christine. He bowed and led her to the side of the room, where Meg and Lizzy had also been deposited by their partners. Meg grabbed her friends' arms and whisked both Harrison sisters around the corner into the foyer.

Distress and desperation shown on Meg's face. It was as though she had just come off a wild horse galloping at midnight.

"I need to talk to both of you. I cannot handle this anymore. My heart is going to break, and moreover, I have two gentlemen who are fuming with rage, silently and decorously, whilst they uphold all graces requisite to a ball! Surely, I have never seen two men who are quite so close to coming undone!"

Lizzy, not knowing the backstory, and being thoroughly engaged in her own pursuits before this moment, replied, "Meg, what are you talking about? I have not noticed anyone who is out of sorts!"

Meg shot Christine a glance. Perhaps in Meg's haste whisking all her feminine resources around the corner, she had forgotten that Lizzy was privy to no such previous information.

"The time to notice is now upon us," Christine concluded quietly, assisting Meg in her explanation, "for Meg is almost engaged to Mr. Grenville, and her long-lost friend—and romantic interest, we should add—named Mr. Carlisle is currently also attending this ball. Conveniently, he was invited because we told Mr. Davenport to bring his cousin before we knew the ramifications and the relations associated there. He is indeed both her long-lost interest of two years past and Mr. Davenport's cousin. Such juxtaposed connections make for quite the hazardous evening sport."

"Christine! Please keep your voice down," Meg importuned, not fully appreciating the alacrity with which Christine recapped the situation.

Christine lowered her voice and asked seriously, "What would you like us to do? We are completely at your service." After a momentary pause, the sisters exchanged a glance as only sisters knew how.

Meg's countenance became more distressed, and she let out a sigh coupled with a shrug. "I need distractions. Lizzy, will you make sure you talk with Mr. Carlisle if I am engaged in conversing with Mr. Grenville? And Christine, I need you to keep Mr. Grenville interested in anything you can think of to keep his mind away from the situation."

The league of the beguiling females had commenced. The three nodded in quick agreement and hurried back into the ballroom, trying to feign innocence on all fronts.

Christine straightway went to Mr. Grenville's side, curtsied, and started talking to him as animatedly as she could. She tried to time her arrival perfectly, just before the next dance began.

"Do you have a partner you must be attending to?" Mr. Grenville asked, folding right in to Christine's plan.

"Oh no, I do not," she said sweetly.

"Well, by all means," Mr. Grenville said, coming out of his glare across the room, "I am sure I can oblige."

He extended his arm, and Christine slipped hers through the crook in his elbow. After Mr. Grenville's silence, Christine said, "Mr. Grenville, what a perfect moment to ask you my questions. What does Mr. Davenport think of me?" Mr. Grenville had been scouting over her shoulder for the past two minutes, no doubt looking for a curly-haired masculine target, and Christine thought this was a surefire way to distract Mr. Grenville, as she knew he cared much about his friend's situation.

He finally looked at Christine and answered, "Oh . . . right, um, Miss Harrison, he holds you in very high regard."

She smiled but was not content with this answer. "High regard? He respects me as a person, you mean. Oh *that* is quite encouraging."

Surely he has more to say than this, thought Christine. He should know he would not be let down so easily by a feminine conversationalist such as herself. "I must ask, has he mentioned anything else?"

The look Mr. Grenville shot back at her told her at once that he did not wish to be trifled with such matters. Trying to lessen the tension, Christine added, "Please keep this conversation in confidence?"

"Miss Harrison. I believe you can read the signs as well as I can. Mr. Davenport is *very* taken with you. But what becomes of it is his business, not mine. A man must let his friend pursue his own destiny, I daresay?"

"Yes, of course," she conceded. Christine pondered his answer for a moment but did not want to let any time lapse where he could ask about Meg.

"Mr. Davenport says you have a flourishing business prospect in London in the next few months, is that true? Please tell me more about it!" By the look on his face, Mr. Grenville seemed relieved to have something he enjoyed to talk about. He spent the rest of the dance, as well as the next several minutes afterward, speaking about the accounting portfolios of several of the wealthiest lords in London.

Christine held her breath as Meg made her way across the room. She gracefully entered their circle, and Mr. Grenville took her hand at the next dance, seeming to claim his prize for the entire room to see.

Having been discharged, momentarily, of her duty, Christine noticed Mr. William Robertson was not dancing. He gave a faint smile as she walked up to him and curtsied, and this time he bowed, and Christine could not help but wonder if perhaps his brother had informed him that shaking hands with a lady was all too informal. Instead, he extended his arm to escort her to the balcony. His manners tonight seemed to fit more in line with his brother's.

"It is quite warm. Would you care to join me for some fresh air?" William said. And then, with more candor, he added, "I thought this a great place to exchange confidences."

He looked at Christine, and for a brief moment she felt approval rather than intimidation. "You see," he continued, "my brother and

I plan on staying in town for at least another week, and we will have Mr. Oakley with us. I have been sent on errand from Henry, who is always dancing. He believes it would be advantageous if we planned a party next weekend with our two groups—in order to help our friend Mr. Oakley?"

Christine tilted her head, realizing this was all a scheme to help Mr. Oakley and Lizzy further their acquaintance.

"Why yes! I would find that quite agreeable, and I happen to know a certain sister who would most definitely approve." Christine gave a coy smile and continued, "What did you have in mind?"

"I thought since your cook is so accomplished—so my brother informs me, and I have witnessed tonight—and we have just returned from traveling, we might have a dinner with some rather exotic foods? If I could just send you with suggestions for your cook this next week, I am sure we could have it all arranged."

Christine briefly thought over his suggestion. She liked his proposal but thought it might need another element to make it more exciting. She always loved an excuse to dress in costume. William had been in the Orient for the last year, but did he know that costume parties were in now in vogue? She secretly relished the fact that she might convince such a serious person to consent to something so cheery as a costume party.

"I feel to liven the party, we should require our guests to dress in the costume of some foreign country, perhaps in your case where you have traveled." Christine grinned, making her wish known.

Christine watched as William furrowed then raised his eyebrows, trying to determine whether she was serious or not. Determining that she indeed was, he sighed and then pursed his lips. "If you say so, Miss Harrison. That *would* add an interesting element to the evening." He seemed unamused.

"I must be getting back to some of the other guests," Christine said, "but please inform Henry that we shall continue planning our mysterious soiree."

She turned and walked back into the warm ballroom. The night was beginning to close. Meg's situation had not improved. Christine watched her friend delicately balance most of her time with Mr. Grenville, while still interacting a bit with Mr. Carlisle.

Lizzy seemed to be getting along fantastically with Mr. Oakley. Christine could not be happier for her sister. And as for herself, Mr. Davenport had again suggested he wanted to speak to her father. Then she would be officially engaged. She sighed, thrilled at such a prospect. If only he did not have to leave on business so soon. She looked around, taking in the evening and giving a contented sigh when Mr. Davenport came to her side and robustly grasped her hand. "My last dance, my dear?" he murmured and escorted her to the floor.

CHAPTER 9

The sisters awoke the next morning talking of nothing but the ball. The aim of the menu and the flowers had been to impress without comparison, but it was the company that stood as the apogee of the evening.

"Christine! Did you know the interesting connection of Mr. Oakley to the Robertsons? In between our *two* dances," Lizzy breathed, "he told me of the whole matter."

"I know they are cousins, but do report, for perhaps you know more."

"Mr. Oakley's mother married exceedingly well to Mr. Oakley's father with eight thousand a year." She lowered her voice and continued, "And the young Mr. Oakley will have just as much. Though our Mr. Oakley did not directly state such a sum to me. He spoke very modestly. Ivory mentioned the amount to Meg back in London and she informed me of it last night."

Christine smiled and nodded in approval.

"But his mother's sister married Mr. Robertson's father making the Robertsons and Oakleys cousins! They hardly present themselves as such, rather as good friends. Mr. Lewis Robertson, although quite a gentleman, has the unfortunate fact of being Scottish, so it was quite a shock to Oakley's mother when her sister consented to marry a Scotsman."

"How does Mr. Oakley come to be on such amiable terms with his cousins, then?" Christine asked.

"The snub against them lasted only a few years, and then all was forgotten. Especially after Robertson's mother died. Mr. Lewis Robertson did all in his power to insist his sons stay in England and mingle with their older cousin. Seems he was not very proud of his Scottish line after all."

"How very interesting," Christine said, logging away such facts of their London friends. "Did he say how much the Robertsons have per annum?"

"Oh no, and I did not want to pry. I did not want him to think I cared only of that."

"Certainly," Christine smiled, "Although your Mr. Oakley having eight thousand pounds is nothing to scruple with. And they seem like gentlemen even if we do not know their income, especially as friends of Mr. Oakley. I daresay we should keep them as acquaintances for your sake, Lizzy."

Later that day, Christine walked to the Allensbys' to check on the after effects of the ball from Meg's viewpoint. Meg reported that the evening felt like living through a ball held in infernal fire and brimstone. The night had left her with two very belligerent and frustrated suitors on her hands. Her temperament and feelings were not much better.

Luckily, Mr. Grenville decided after the ball to travel with Mr. Davenport and "support him in his business endeavors." Mr. Grenville did not come to call again before leaving and this provided an opportunity for Mr. Carlisle to visit a few times at Allensby House. Mrs. Allensby made a point to let Meg do whatever she pleased when it came to finding a match, feeling the need to prove to the world that she was the antithesis of her own mother in this regard.

After a few instances of interacting with Mr. Carlisle, Christine felt a different perspective. Mr. Carlisle doted on her friend, to be sure, and admired every painting crafted by Meg's hand. Christine hated to admit it, but he had quite the refined eye for beauty and artistry, and Meg's abilities were not lost on him.

But his long speeches on the nuances of Meg's abilities grew tiresome, for he seemed that he could formulate no other words on any topic when in society. Unless, of course, he spoke of himself and his vast knowledge on every subject related to medicine. Christine knew more of his profession in three days' time than she had ever wanted to know.

Additionally, Christine believed the most agreeable solution would involve Meg and herself marrying best friends. Surely, one must occasionally stack the odds in one's own favor, and this was Christine's plan.

"Meg," Christine pleaded as they sat in Wellington's drawing room the next Tuesday, "Can you not see that Mr. Carlisle has little to offer you in the way of a future? It is so important to marry well. Mr. Grenville is a man of means, and he is so gallant and romantic! What more could you ask for?"

"I do not agree with your emphasis on status," Meg countered. "In fact, I detest that such a component should exist and weigh so heavily." And then she added, "I will do what I want regarding Mr. Carlisle."

Christine had never seen Meg be so outspoken and determined about anything in her life. This *was* the side of her mother manifesting itself, declaring she would marry whomever she chose. Christine sighed deeply and said, "I believe you will regret it." Disliking the tension, which was quite unusual for their friendship, Christine changed the subject.

"So the Robertsons, with Mr. Oakley, are coming to dine this Friday. You will attend, will you not?"

"Yes, I will," Meg answered, and then almost as a challenge, "And I will come alone, as I am sure you desire it so?"

"Well yes, that would be preferred, as there will already be quite a few gentlemen," Christine responded, trying for a light tone and failing.

Just then Lizzy entered the drawing room, with Mr. Oakley, followed by both Mr. Robertsons. Christine and Meg stood and extended a greeting, Christine feeling grateful new company would help dissipate her strained conversation with Meg. All but William sat down. He glanced toward the large windows and slightly nodded his head. Christine walked over to him, ready to exchange information while the others were employed in conversation.

"I have a list of the items your cook might attempt for Friday, if she has heard of such things," he said as he handed Christine a note.

Christine nodded, taken back once again by his direct and commanding manner. "I have quite a good relationship with our cook. She can make anything. My mother prides herself on employing the best cook in the county."

She felt delighted to have someone to host a party with, but was slightly astonished by William's businesslike approach to everything. Not knowing what else to talk about, Christine thought of the information from Lizzy a few days earlier and turned toward Henry. "Now you must tell us the truth about you brothers. I have been dying to know the whole of it. Who is older? Are you twins, as is the rumor?"

The room quieted, and suddenly everyone listened only to the discussion between Christine and William.

"Rumors, miss? Why yes, we are twins," William said first, before Henry could answer. He continued seriously, "But I do not like the sound of rumors surrounding our family. We have a clear conscious and a clear name, I promise."

So stoic and defensive, thought Christine. He *always* came off serious, but this had more heat and fervor than usual. She only asked them if they were twins.

"We quite enjoy the camaraderie of being twins, of both sharing the title of Mr. Robertson." Henry laughed, trying to lighten the tension. He tilted his head to the side and raised his hand. "Although I was born first. So you may call me the eldest Mr. Robertson if you wish to distinguish us." The happy eyes of Henry wrinkled as he chuckled.

"Well, then, the *eldest* Mr. Robertson," Christine continued to pry, "What will become of *your* inheritance? Shall you share with your brother?"

Henry smiled mischievously, "Yes, in that regard, William and I are equals. We plan on putting a wall directly down the middle of our grandfather's estate. My half and William's half. Unfortunately, being born seven minutes before William did not win me any kind of estate."

Christine shot a glance at Lizzy, wanting to know more of his true meaning. Henry noticed his humor fell on deaf ears and said, "I am not serious!" as he waved his hand. Lizzy laughed and Christine still looked puzzled, but William stared at Henry, seemingly discontent with his brother's summation.

Was he embarrassed by his brother's light take on everything? Or perhaps he wanted to hide something? William then clarified, his voice rising slightly, "As a matter of fact, what we do with our father's and grandfather's property is none of your concern. Our father has raised us to stand on our own two feet and make our way as our own men. Such lack of emphasis toward holdings and rank are *sure* to be appalling to you English gentry. In Scotland, and especially as Robertsons, we put importance on greater things. You should not be so worried about our estate, Miss Harrison."

Christine stared back at William and said nothing. How could he be so pointed and so deliberately rude? She had no reply for such a statement.

She moved away from William and came to sit next to Lizzy, thinking over what had just been said. It seemed so very odd: extremely defensive, excessively vague, and leaving them with no direct answer about their holdings and property—and yet defending their stance as well bred. Christine did not know what to make of it, but her excitement for their upcoming party diminished greatly at that moment.

Alas, she would not let proud, indignant William unravel her. She knew her social standing and genteel breeding to be just as it ought, and soon she knew she would find herself the perfect model of a well-married oldest daughter. Arrogant, outraged William wanted nothing of her family in his future, but she knew that to be his loss. But both she and William would continue, she trusted, to maintain the perfectly crafted guise of civility that their society had so artfully ingrained in them.

The air in the room felt stifled, at least to Christine, who could feel her burning cheeks start to subside. She sat a little taller, raising her gaze. William's eyes furrowed, as though he had much on his mind, looking across the room, his hand on the ledge of the mantle, his back almost facing everyone else.

It was all rather perplexing to Christine, who desired a clear-cut analysis of their fortune, and a sum total of just how many pounds they had per year. What Englishman—or Scotsman, she must include—could not rattle off their holdings in their sleep? Such facts played so eagerly on many gentlemen's tongues. Why could she not elicit it now from William? Surely these men must have much at their disposal. Could Mr. Oakley not state it? Or Henry?

But all stayed silent.

Christine thought then how she had heard no definite sum even gossiped by those of their acquaintance. Mr. Davenport held an important name and respectable fortune, which had been clearly stated since the beginning of their acquaintance—and he made it very clear that his investments continued to make him even more money. She found herself quite pleased that she had such a prospect nearly certain in her future, even if he had left for London again the night before. Christine had secured, excepting the formal engagement, a future social standing that would allow her all of the fine company, good name, and monetary backing she could hope for.

The Robertsons seemed unable to provide such for any young woman. She scoffed at the conceit and presumption William displayed.

Christine's mind clung to her future with Mr. Davenport as the room remained silent for a few more moments. The tension had gone on for so long that Mr. Oakley, Henry, and Lizzy then started their own conversation composed of much lighter tones.

Mr. Oakley began, "In other news, Henry and William seem to be familiar with your esteemed friend, Mr. Davenport."

Christine had witnessed no such interaction at the ball, but asked, "Indeed, you are?" She turned more toward Henry, trying to avoid William's gaze.

"Yes, we attended school in Manchester together, a few years ago," Henry offered, as Christine smiled with assurance.

"And were you much acquainted?" Christine desired to know what they thought of her revered Mr. Davenport.

Henry shook his head, and William, his tone now perfectly even, said, "We started out as friends but ended our time in differing social circles."

Indeed, thought Christine. Of course Mr. Davenport would naturally gravitate toward higher company. Mr. Davenport knew how to be well connected.

"Is that so? It is a shame you were not more acquainted," was all Christine dared to say.

William then paced across the room to the furthest spot from Christine. His gaze still met no one.

After another minute of silence, Lizzy looked plaintively at Mr. Oakley and stated, "Shall we go for a walk?"

Meg, Mr. Oakley, and both Mr. Robertsons immediately assented to the idea. Christine declined, stating, "I must take my leave, for I have a few things to attend to. We shall see you on Friday," she said quickly, with a hint of a curtsy toward the room.

Christine knew she needed to talk to Cook Cooper, but mostly wanted to avoid the insulting Mr. Robertson for the rest of the day.

As she descended into the kitchen, Christine instantly spotted Cook Cooper mending something at the great galley table.

"Good day, Cook. How are you? Do you have a moment?" Christine asked.

"Why of course, deary. I always have a moment for you," she answered.

With a slight sigh, Christine said, more indifferent than excited, "The Robertsons and our family were wanting to hold a dinner on Friday. Mr. Robertson has in his head that we should have some exotic dishes."

"Well, I am sure I am up to the task!" the kind cook responded.

Christine handed her the paper.

"Ah, food from the Orient? A French dish . . . and one of these is Scottish, I daresay! I like these visitors!" Christine remembered again how intelligent and well bred their cook was, Christine knowing she married below her station but had been brought up with an education. The cook's portly form moved toward the spice cupboard and threw it open.

"We shall have to conjure up quite a few more ingredients, but I'll do anything for these Scottish friends of yours."

Christine fought the urge to roll her eyes, thoroughly unamused by the abundance of Scottish countrymen camaraderie that was suddenly ubiquitous. Christine did *not* consider William her friend.

"So you can indeed cook these things?"

"Yes, miss," she said, winking confidently. Christine gave her a few more details and thanked her for her willingness, and then she walked the several stairs from the servant's quarters into her room.

Sitting now at her desk, Christine began to contemplate if she should write a letter to Mr. Davenport. He had left only one day before. Surely it was best to wait a little longer before sending anything. He would be returning sometime next week, and Christine did not want to appear precocious. He traveled to London quite often it seemed, but he always returned quickly to dote on her.

She would just have to endure some stubborn Scotsmen in the interim. What an abhorrent task that seemed to be, but alas, she could do it for her sister. Hopefully her great sacrifice would at least help Lizzy obtain a suitor, Christine mused. She put away her quill but could not repress the thoughts of Mr. Davenport from her heart, longing for his return.

MR. OLIVER DAVENPORT

The door to the inn swung open, and the warm light of candle and fire welcomed Mr. Davenport inside. Weary from a long day's ride, he was grateful for a prepared room and savory refreshment. He had just given instructions to the innkeeper concerning his horse when he saw a familiar face sitting at one of the tables. She had long, wavy brown hair, half pinned up, and a slightly olive complexion, which radiated beauty as she sat in a green gown. She appeared unaccompanied for a moment, her father apparently fetching more drinks. She was reading something when she raised her gaze, their eyes meeting. She closed her book slowly and walked over to Mr. Davenport's table. He stood and bowed slightly.

"I did not expect to see you here," he said.

"Nor I you," she shyly laughed back.

"I was riding to town for some business."

"And I was just returning from traveling with my father," she said, almost cutting him off. There was some familiarity in the air, laced with unidentified tension from the years apart.

"Do sit down." Mr. Davenport gestured to his table, not knowing what else to do with her presence weighing so heavily on his space—and his mind.

As she sat she said, "When I saw you last, we did not have the opportunity to exchange much conversation."

Mr. Davenport recalled her violet dress and bewitching words as she had emerged from the shadows. Here he could not make such a clear escape.

She continued, "How is your family? Are they in good health? It has been well over a year since we last really spoke to each other."

She carried herself and spoke as if she were a lady, but there she sat, unaccompanied like a peasant, in a dusty inn across from a gentleman. Her well-kept coiffure and elaborate gown seemed oddly out of place—not because it suited a woman of higher standing but because it made her seem like she was trying to be something she was not.

"I am very well, thank you," he lied, having been better before he saw her. "And my family is all in good health. And yours?"

"They are well, thank you." She had been tracing small circles on the table with her ungloved hand. She paused a moment and drew her dark eyes up slowly from the table to ensnare his. "I wonder if I might be so bold as to ask a rather personal question?"

Mr. Davenport was taken aback, and then he remembered she never minced words and answered quickly, "You may."

"Are you engaged to be married, Mr. Davenport?"

Mr. Davenport looked down swiftly, pondering for a moment. Such a bold question surely had implications. He had, over a year ago, spent much time with this woman. But that was when he was a more impulsive man. He was now planning on returning to Rothershire next week with the hope to propose to Christine officially, asking her father for her hand. Mr. Davenport had changed, looking to Christine as the prudent match to secure an illustrious future. However, his engagement was not official yet. So answering quietly, he said, "No, mademoiselle, I am not."

Her countenance shifted, her visage becoming more beautiful and more beguiling in a moment. She smiled, pleased with his answer. "Well then, sir, if it is not too bold, I would like to see you again when we are in London."

Should he have just lied to her? Would that have stopped her from locating him again in London? Mr. Davenport doubted it.

"I am afraid you will know where to find me," he answered, masking his worry with an elusive air. She stood to leave, and he felt a shiver run down his spine.

CHAPTER 10

The next Friday, Henry, Mr. Oakley, and a reluctant William waited in various styles of dress in the antechamber, handing their cards to the servant. "I cannot believe we consented to a costume party," William murmured under his breath.

"Do come in, our esteemed visitors!" Mrs. Harrison said as she welcomed them into the dining room. Mr. Oakley was quickly winning favor with Mrs. Harrison. He held a certain ease of understanding and conversation with Mr. and Mrs. Harrison. He seemed to feel confident in himself and always looked outward. If Christine were a betting woman, she would bet ten to one that her mother wanted him for her future son-in-law.

Christine appreciated Mr. Oakley's thoughtful character. He was well matched to Lizzy in that way, never wanting to harm a creature and often playing the role of peacemaker or pleaser. Christine had always admired Lizzy for her charismatic way of drawing people to her, herself not possessing the ability to always act so kindly.

Gratefully, Christine had not seen Mr. William Robertson since their awkward conversation earlier that week. But she tolerated him and his brother here now if for no other reason than to further the relationship between Mr. Oakley and Lizzy.

The group moved into the dining room. Mr. Harrison wore a red waistcoat of lighter linen than was customary for this time of year. He said he was to be imitating a sea captain in the Indies, which Christine did believe was his secret occupational ambition had he not been born into the role of an upper-class Englishman. Christine's mother wore a dress fashioned in the Parisian style, calling to her love of French design and culture. Having decided to represent the Italians, Christine wore a green, scarlet, and white dress, looking much like their flag, donning a black plume in her hair. Meg also had a French aura about her—something Mr. Grenville would have doted on had he been in attendance. Lizzy and Mr. Oakley must have coordinated, for both wore rather plain clothing, much like a peasant farmer from some colony. Henry wore an oriental suit with large billowing pants and a whimsically tied cummerbund, open shirted sans-cravat, representing his Asian style. William, unsurprisingly, wore a kilt with the appropriate accessories.

Cook Cooper had outdone herself once again. She had made haggis—customarily impossible to like, but somehow tasting quite savory. Even Henry and William asked to send their compliments on it. Her French dish of sautéed snails and oysters infused with garlic dissolved flavorfully in Christine's mouth. Perhaps the most exquisite dish of the night, however, was the rice and chicken dish. When Christine asked her later, Cook told her it was a yellow curry that she used, a spice that was hard to come by but made the most vibrant colors and flavors.

The table was arranged with Christine sitting between Henry and William, Meg and Lizzy across the table, and Mr. Oakley in between them. Mr. and Mrs. Harrison sat at the ends of the table, and the conversations were quite delightful. Mr. Oakley made many witty remarks, with Henry playing off all he said. William laughed along with them and added a few cunning comments here and there that Christine had no choice but to hear, even when they were lost on the whole of the party. She quelled her desire to laugh at these quips, on account of her general commitment to disapprove of him. Lizzy's countenance radiated happiness, her esteem and affection for Mr. Oakley deep. He seemed just as thrilled with her, and all in attendance did their part to further their relationship. Christine said nothing directly to William, and he also chose to speak to the whole rather than to her.

After dinner, they all moved to the drawing room. Christine wanted something to continue their time together, facilitating an opportunity for Lizzy and Mr. Oakley to have a more private conversation, and dared turning to William. "Perhaps you could tell us of your time in the Orient. Having been newly returned, I am sure you have many interesting things to speak of?"

He started a bit at such an amiable suggestion from Christine but answered, "Of course. I would be delighted."

Mr. William Robertson then began speaking of people in the Orient, of their hardworking efforts to provide for their families. He spoke of the harsh, hot conditions they worked under to produce things like spices and fabric that the British took for granted. He last spoke of his travels to Scotland, where he saw local poor farmers shearing, carding, and preparing wool. His eyes livened with his passion for his subject. He knew the people in each of these lands, and they were not just people he had worked with, but dear friends.

"And so, I must conclude my speaking of the incredible people I have come to know all throughout my travels. Many have different beliefs and cultures than we do, but their personalities and desires for life are not far different than ours."

His voice spoke firm and resolute. There was nothing romantic or whimsical in his recounts of his travels, just decided facts. Christine had to admit him well spoken and well traveled, if she could not claim him charming like Mr. Davenport. Still, the evening as a whole felt tolerably comfortable, and she began to realize their company would be to her—and Lizzy's—great advantage. On every subject but inheritance and money, William seemed a willing conversationalist. What other group of gentlemen could be so advantageous to her family to pass the time before Mr. Davenport returned?

It was in this state that she resolved to make some kind of amends with William. She admitted to herself that she had been too harsh a judge, and he had not forgotten. He had seemed cold to her ever since she questioned about his family and holdings, his eyes fixing a steady gaze across the room quite often throughout the night. Not once did he engage Christine in any direct conversation. She felt a bit intimidated by his indifferent presence, but she felt a little feminine charm and flirtation might be used to her advantage at such a time as this.

"Mr. Robertson," she said, addressing William with a broad smile and the most pleasant and inviting tone she had ever used toward him, "I have quite enjoyed your stories tonight. You are *most* welcome here at Wellington Manor any time you come back to Rothershire to visit. I hope any of your party would choose to call at Wellington."

She ended such a comment with a small curtsy and her full lashes employing themselves, seeking the confidence to look into his cool-blue eyes.

The pleasant manner he had worn minutes earlier while talking to Mr. Oakley had now vanished. His eyes shifted to the side and then shot in her direction. The stare lasted only a few seconds, but it spoke volumes of his dislike of her. He had not taken to a single word she had said.

"Thank you, Miss Harrison, I will make a note of that," he answered curtly, his steely-eyed stare returning. "Although I suspect you shall be employed with those you deem eligible of your rank. We are but poor Scotsmen." He turned and looked amiably at Mr. Oakley and Lizzy. His cold response permeated Christine's being.

"Yes, but I . . ." She trailed off, staring down at her feet. He had swiftly wounded Christine's pride, and nothing she would say could alter his feelings. She simply curtsied with her head bowed toward her chest and moved to the outside of the party.

It took Christine a few moments more to gain her composure, and when she dared look at him again, William seemed pleased with his commanding performance that evening. He looked quite determined that no speech from Christine would change his feelings toward her. She would choose to ignore him then, from now on, any time they were thrown together. If he had the audacity to ignore her and snub her, she would do just the same while remaining as polite as possible.

William was the first to head toward their carriage, giving a civil farewell to Mr. and Mrs. Harrison, a smile toward Lizzy, and glossing over the top of Christine's head as he collected Henry and Mr. Oakley. As soon as they left, Christine retreated, smoothing her skirts, finally unclenching her moist, balled-up fists, and withdrew angrily to her bedroom.

Mr. William Robertson

Upon returning to their rented apartment, William sank into the only armchair in the room. Mr. Oakley had rented a room next door and had already turned in for the night.

Henry smiled and said, "Splendid party! Capital food. What an incredible cook they keep. And I like those Harrison girls. They are quite charming."

"Save your breath," William said, standing and facing the fire. "You may say what you want concerning Oakley's Lizzy, but Miss Harrison is insufferable."

"Do you not think her pretty?"

"Oh, she is that, to be sure." He riffled a hand through his thick, chestnut-colored hair. "But her manners are insupportable. She treats us with disdain a few days ago, prying about our inheritance, and after we show we know a little something about the world, she grovels at our feet. As though she has all power because of her handsome face and can win any gentleman on a whim. I will not be part of such female games."

Henry laughed and rolled his eyes. "A bit harsh, brother," Henry chided, leaning against the mantle. "She has got to be one of the prettiest girls in this county, you could not find a more amiable family anywhere in London, and might I remind you, she has *fifteen* thousand pounds upon her marriage."

"Not that again," William said, pacing the room, his tall riding boots clicking across the floor. "You know I shall not marry—especially for money. That may be your solution, but it will *not* be mine."

Henry smiled and nodded. William knew his brother thought it a nice thing to marry a woman of fortune—as soon as a tolerable one came along.

"I do have to say I was quite impressed with your cordiality toward them all at Lizzy's ball. You even danced with both sisters." Henry prodded his brother, smirking as he said it. "I guess it did not last."

"The dancing was a strain, do not forget it," William said, finally stopping and bracing against the wall. "But I do wish to seem amiable for Oakley's account."

"Well then you might have been a little more relaxed toward Miss Harrison when she asked about the inheritance. Your disapproval was quite transparent. You have no obligation to explain any of it and could whisk over such details pleasantly, if you would choose to do so."

"And act against my principles? Certainly not." William looked at his brother. "I will not let a beautiful girl with a large fortune unravel my standards. She is far above our station, and her sister will be perfect for Oakley, but I do not pretend to make any acquaintance beyond furthering his chances. Miss Harrison would never want to associate with us if she knew. It is all a charade. Can you not see that? I may seem defensive, but I am a realist."

William collapsed in the chair, hands on his temples. His feeling of gravity toward their financial circumstance would always outweigh his brother's. William followed details, while his brother, although wonderfully hopeful and emotionally charged, sometimes overlooked blaring variance in circumstance—most often in his pursuit of women. William watched as Henry looked out the only window, opening it and letting in a crisp breeze.

Then suddenly Henry's head spun back toward William. This tall, blond brother finally became serious and walked toward William, grasping his brother's shoulder.

"We shall never agree on women," Henry concluded good-naturedly. "But on a more important note, I saw something unnerving on my way home from town today before dinner. I think I may have an idea of what happened with our shipment last month in London. The one the day of the Fowlers' ball."

William's countenance tightened, recalling how last month their shipment had gone awry, and they were still left without a clear explanation. He ordered as he normally did, procuring silk and other cloth to be delivered from Asia, scheduled to arrive by boat to London. The account he had received said the wooden casks that held the shipments were infested with diseased rats and consequently had to be discarded upon entry at the docks. And yet there was not even a trace of the containers or spoiled fabrics anywhere to be found. William had been searching every detail meticulously for weeks.

Henry continued, "The day of the Fowlers' ball, as you remember, you sent me to the docks on account of your leg. The port master said our shipment had not yet arrived."

"And then," William interjected, "later that day, I sent Oakley's man and received the news that the shipment had been infested and discarded." William's tone still rose to anger every time he thought about it.

Henry continued, "Yes, but what I did not tell you was that near the port master, I saw a large wagon. I thought nothing of it then— until I saw the same wagon in Rothershire earlier today."

Henry continued to describe a large wagon, driven by a swarthy, curly-haired sailor. On the side of the wagon was a crudely painted *B* in Gothic lettering. He had seen this wagon on the docks in London then and thought nothing of it until he saw it quite out of place in Rothershire earlier that day.

In London, he recounted, the driver was a beautiful dark-haired woman, wearing a large hat to mask her features. Henry, had he not examined the cart so closely, would have thought her a young lad. Today, however, the wagon was driven by a man who had similar dark hair and olive complexion.

"And it all started to make sense after I stopped by our dressmaker on the way home. She told me that she had found someone else who could sell her beautiful Asian silk at a cheaper price. I asked to see it, and it is the very same we ordered last month."

William's eyes narrowed as he began to understand the deception.

"So whoever drove that wagon intercepted and stole our ship-ment . . ." William fumed.

"And then sold it to our customers," Henry finished, dejected. "Something must be done."

"And something *shall* be done," William answered resolutely. "We shall prepare for them. Our next shipment has already shipped from Asia. I will be there to intercept it."

"When it arrives, I am coming with you," Henry answered.

Mr. Oliver Davenport

Miss Estelle Braxton came upon Oliver Davenport as he left his family's small apartment in London. How had she known he would be leaving that morning?

She caught him as he began to walk and said, "How fortuitous we should run into each other! I had just started this way. It is rather wonderful your family's apartment and my brother's house are so near each other."

She smiled up at him, a failed attempt at being demure. Her crimson skirt rustled as they walked. Then, without his invitation, she deliberately rested her arm on his. Her maid trailed far behind, almost disappearing in the hedges. Estelle walked closest to the riverbank, practically mincing as she went. She gingerly touched a curl now and then, and everything about her tried to ensnare Mr. Davenport.

A minute into their walk, she spoke again. "I was thinking, since you are *not* engaged, that we might see more of each other? Perhaps on purpose next time?"

"I probably should not, Miss Braxton. I have plans to return to Rothershire next week and well . . . propose."

He arrived at the office he had just set out toward. He pulled his arm away as she said quietly, "But perhaps you will want to reconsider?" She sidled closer. "Perhaps . . . there is another course you could take?" She smiled openly at him, her eyes trying to trap him.

"Miss Braxton. I mean you no ill will. But my mind is quite made up." Mr. Davenport brushed the edges of his jacket and started to move forward.

Miss Braxton then lifted a gloved hand and pressed her finger to his lips. In her most coquettish voice she whispered, "But I am the only one who knows of your little secret arrangement with my father. You would not want that coming out to everyone, would you?" She crossed her petite arms across herself, her eyes flashing.

He gawked and stumbled to the side. Then, catching himself, he stood motionless.

She lowered her voice and leaned slightly forward. "As your wife I would never tell." She smiled wickedly, gathered her skirts, and spun around to walk away.

Mr. Davenport remained frozen, paralyzed in body and speech. After a few moments, he finally righted himself, shaking his head and wringing his hands several times, and walked into the office before him.

That night, overcome with fear and dread, he wrote to Christine. Perhaps he would need a few weeks to sort this out. To reason with Miss Braxton. She could not really mean what she said. There must be some way to deter her from her resolve. He could not let himself dwell on it, for surely she could be reckoned with. But thoughts of Miss Braxton and her threats would not leave him.

CHAPTER 11

"Have we received any post?" Christine asked one of the servants impatiently at breakfast the next morning.

"No, miss, but I will let you know if any comes through."

Christine waited most of the day to no avail. Mr. Davenport should have returned that day, possibly the next, and thoughts of him consumed her. She scanned the windows and waited for any kind of note from him. She made special efforts in her dress and hair, adding a few more curls and her best day dress. By dinner, she heard nothing. Perhaps he would send a note or come to call tomorrow. The day dragged on to night, and she went to bed with much anticipation for what the next day might hold. When would he return?

In the morning, she dressed quickly and went down for breakfast. Still nothing arrived. She waited around the house all day, making three full loops of the garden, checking in with each round to see if any letters had come. Finally, just before dinner, she received a note.

Christine took the letter and found a solitary spot in the music room. The sun beat over her shoulder and christened the paper with its rays. It was not until she scrutinized the script on the outside of the letter that she realized what a messy pen it had been written with.

She opened the letter, and the contents within had no better penmanship. But it was Mr. Davenport's hand, she was sure, and it was brief, so it must be an invitation of some sort. She quickly read it.

Miss Harrison,

I am sorry to inform you that I will not be returning this week. Business has proved quite more complex than I feared. I do hope to return to you soon. A few more weeks in London should be all I require. I shall write again when I know more.

Sincerely,
Mr. Oliver Davenport

Christine knew dinner awaited her, but she could not move. She read the letter three more times through—it was so short and curt it did not take long—and she could not fathom it. After a frustrating fifteen minutes and several servants informing her that dinner was ready, she finally moved like a mirage to the dining room. It was not only that he would be gone longer—that she could bear. But his tone. His coarseness. Something had changed. Why did he not give her details of his trip? Or at least ask a question of what she had been doing during his absence?

Trying her best to keep her composure, she said little at dinner and ate even less. Lizzy and Mr. Oakley tried to engage her in conversation, but she was completely lost to herself. Christine went to her room as soon as the meal finished, only partially feigning an upset stomach. How she wished him back that week. Why was he staying, and why not give more details to ease her mind? His letter had been so concise—and so unfeeling.

Christine's only solace was Meg's invitation to spend the weekend at her house. Although the girls' families were the closest neighbors, any change from her dull setting came as a welcome respite. Lizzy also went with Christine to spend the day, and it proved to be quite the diversion, owing to the fact that Ivory was in town. Now Christine would be forced to act as if nothing happened and would not have to explain many of her own particulars because Ivory always possessed much to tell. It had been many months since Christine had seen her, and she had graciously taken a few days away from her busy social schedule to visit the country again. For once, Christine was grateful for any gossip or news from London.

"After the last ball of the season—the one we attended together— I spent some time in the lake country. Oh, it is ever so delightful. I cannot begin to describe the beautiful views, warm breezes, and sunshine. Then I came home to several months of my persistent parents discussing the future of their estate and how they would marry off 'their only daughter.' Sometimes I feel as though our family is more a business entity than a clan." She exhaled forcefully and continued, "Which reminds me, have you talked with your Scottish friends? I daresay Mr. Robertson and I have not been in the way of close conversation lately, but you all seemed to get along quite well at the ball last year."

"Yes, we ran into them in Rothershire when they came for business, and then Christine invited them to my ball," Lizzy began. "They shall be here for another week and then off to Scotland to visit their grandfather. My—I mean, Mr. Oakley will stay for a few weeks longer yet, though!"

"Mr. Oakley?" Ivory said, raising both eyebrows and teasing, "Of course! Do you *love* him?"

"Oh Ivory, you are always talking about love. I do not know! But I like him very much, and I hope it continues."

"And the Robertsons gone to Scotland, really? You know their grandfather is nearly famous there? At least that is the way Henry made it sound when we were . . . spending more time together . . . than at present . . ." She looked around the small parlor the girls employed, running her hand across her upholstered seat, showing her indifference.

"Really? You do not say," Christine said, in a mood to cast a bad light on anyone. "That is very interesting. Perhaps they pride themselves on their modesty. They would not talk of their inheritance to us last time we were together."

"Well if you are talking about William, I do not know. And come to think of it, Henry never discussed how much he receives a year. He just told me of his prodigious and generous grandfather."

Christine had heard so many stories of the Robertsons' background that she did not know what to believe. It was no matter, however, as

Christine was sure the next time she saw Henry or William, one or both of them would be nearly engaged to someone, ready to collect all of their inheritance money first.

There was more talk of gentlemen—Mr. Oakley, Mr. Grenville, and Mr. Carlisle, Ivory's several suitors—and Christine had heard plenty. She did not want to stay around long enough for others to pester her about Mr. Davenport. And with each conversation about another's interest, Christine's longing for Mr. Davenport grew deeper.

She finally excused herself and walked to the hill between Wellington Manor and Allensby House. She walked for an hour at least, trying to clear her head concerning Mr. Davenport but thinking of little else.

Christine's absence was the least of anyone's worries. She returned just before dinner. Miss Rusket informed her in a whisper that Mr. Carlisle had been peacocking around for a half hour before dinner, vying for attention.

Christine watchd as Meg tried to balance his personality and Miss Rusket's together. He had called at such a time that Mrs. Allensby felt obligated to invite him to dine. Mr. Grenville was still on business with Mr. Davenport and had also not returned. Apparently Mr. Grenville had chosen to stay with his best friend, and Mr. Davenport did not care to come back to his cousin. Who Meg had chosen was yet to be determined; however, after this dinner with Mr. Carlisle, Christine would have chosen Mr. Grenville's company over the cousin's too.

The small dining room had light-blue walls, the paper slightly faded, but the Allensbys presented the best dinnerware in an attempt to please everyone. The close seating arrangements made confidences nearly impossible, and heat of the discussion made the room even warmer.

"Do you not see, Mr. Carlisle," Ivory said as she passed the potatoes, "that she was totally in the right to act that way?" She had been telling a long story about one of her London friends' illnesses a few months ago and the methods her friend had used to try and regain her health.

"Yes, I see that you might think it should be resolved that way, but it is more likely that she had limited knowledge on the subject."

Ivory pursed her lips and did not answer, but the look on her face shone with contempt.

"When I received my schooling," Mr. Carlisle relentlessly continued, "we understood *that* practice to be something of an old-fashioned solution. So many people, even in your circles, Miss Rusket, do not understand anything about how to stay healthy. Wives' tales and witchcraft, I say."

Miss Rusket rolled her eyes, and neither party did much to hide their disdain for each other.

Later in the evening, Mr. Carlisle started off the conversation with, "In my professional experience," and then proceeded to explain how the Harrisons' way of keeping staff would only create problems and possibly sickness. He would interject at any moment where it might fit the conversation, even if it corresponded only slightly.

Although Christine found him slightly rude and self-promoting, Ivory and Mr. Carlisle especially clashed.

"Can you not see that he is abrasive and insensitive?" Miss Rusket confided to Christine in a whisper as they walked into the small dining room.

"It does seem that way," Christine consented, thinking of earlier in the evening when she had overheard Mr. Carlisle's own rant about Ivory to Meg.

"How can she act so haphazardly in her dealings?" Mr. Carlisle had hissed. "I have heard her brag about her interactions with young men, and I cannot believe it. It is appalling, truly."

"Perhaps you do not understand her," Meg had whispered, never faulting anyone.

"Oh dearest," he had said, brushing her chin, "*you* do not understand. But I cannot fault you, for you cannot choose your relations."

Christine knew the summations of both Mr. Carlisle and Miss Rusket were partially erroneous, founded in half-truths that were expanded out of proportion. Mr. Carlisle was one of the most black-and-white, cut-and-dry characters there were. And Ivory did entertain many suitors, and she enjoyed the chase of such men, was a desirable catch, and did not want to settle down. But her true indecisiveness, which Mr. Carlisle had no knowledge of, came from a combination of not knowing what her heart and mind were saying coupled with agitation from her parents continually setting up matches and perfect candidates to augment the family tree.

Meg, however, almost always failed to identify Mr. Carlisle's less desirable qualities. She had been smitten many years ago, and his actions now were shrouded by her girlish perception of him.

Thankfully, Mrs. Allensby had also invited Lizzy and Mr. Oakley to dinner, and they saved the conversation more than once, keeping the tension at bay. Mr. Oakley had the gift of asking different people pertinent questions, which steered the conversation in light avenues rather than rocky paths. "And tell me about your practice," he would ask, and after Mr. Carlisle had promoted himself, Mr. Oakley would graciously say, "And Mr. Allensby, how is business in town?" One could only praise Mr. Oakley for his command of conversation. Christine could not be happier for Lizzy, if indeed his affections did turn to a proposal for her sister.

The evening was trying on Christine's nerves, especially with Mr. Carlisle's ever-present babble. Christine and Ivory turned in to bed early, with Meg and Lizzy entertaining their men much later than Christine or Ivory were wont to stay. Ivory continued to chat about all of her comings and goings in London—no doubt grateful to be out of Mr. Carlisle's scrutinizing eye and runaway mouth. Ivory successfully took Christine's mind off of Mr. Davenport for a few moments, for which Christine was grateful. Christine tried to pry slightly about his whereabouts, and although Ivory knew almost all of the London gossip, Mr. Davenport's status had evaded her. She did tell Christine of a few interested suitors, who she was not sure would last, if her parents had anything to say about it.

"I think I can stay for perhaps one more week, possibly two at the most. Then I must travel back to town," Ivory said, "for spring is here, and with Parliament fully in session, London is teeming with excitement. But perhaps in the interim I will come to Wellington. I need some space from Mr. Carlisle."

"You are of course welcome. And when you go away we shall indeed miss you. I do love our foursome, you know," Christine said gratefully. The ache from the delay of a gentleman was always lessened with a few female acquaintances and their ever-continuous prattle.

CHAPTER 12

"May I ask you your opinion?" Lizzy asked her sister a few days later. Christine had been daydreaming, wanting more than anything for Mr. Davenport to return to her. She longed to spend an evening with him, waiting as he talked with her father, and listening to him ask her the one question she wanted to hear. She ought to be engaged before Lizzy, and Mr. Davenport's return would secure that desire. But she had received no more post from him, and the silence was driving her mad.

"I have determined," Lizzy continued, "though I think I shall have Father extend the invitation, to have one final dinner with Mr. Oakley and the Robertsons before they leave Rothershire. Surely it must be easier to extend an invite to Mr. Oakley with the Robertsons still in town? I am vastly afraid of only asking Mr. Oakley too soon in our acquaintance."

Christine agreed, knowing it to be a wise scheme by her sister. "Since Miss Rusket is here with us, perhaps you might suggest inviting Meg and Mr. Carlisle as well," Christine added.

"Yes, of course. A large group would be just the thing."

And so the guise of civility reigned supreme all day. Or at least it ruled Christine, who spent most of the morning reminding herself of the need to be kind and unpretentious in an effort to change William Robertson's opinion of her.

Finally, at half past seven, the butler greeted the Robertson brothers and Mr. Oakley, showing them into the drawing room, its intricate wallpaper and ample candlelight welcoming them once again to

Wellington Estate. Christine and Lizzy stood ready to greet them, and Mr. and Mrs. Harrison stood also already assembled. Christine wondered if her patterned muslin gown would blend in to the soft green tapestries hanging on the wall behind her, for at this moment she wished to be part of the backdrop only. She resolved then for silence to be her mode for the evening. Henry, dressed in a dark-brown coat, sent a smile in her direction, but William, in a crisp navy jacket and matching pants, seemed quite aloof, not quite meeting her gaze.

Let Lizzy shine, and say nothing offensive or provoking to anyone, Christine reminded herself.

"I know a gentleman often arrives hungry at a dinner invitation, so we shall not wait!" Mrs. Harrison proclaimed, her usual self duly concerned with the stomachs of her guests—especially the young male ones. With a wave of the hand, she turned, and all followed Mr. and Mrs. Harrison through to the dining room.

That invitation took the sharp edge off of what could have been a strained encounter, and Christine heaved a sigh of relief at their initial meeting. *Perhaps a Scotsman does not hold on to one's existing opinion of others,* thought Christine doubtfully. But as soon as William entered the dining room, Christine sensed an affable demeanor. The cordiality from all sides was palpable, and Christine believed that he had sworn to be on his best behavior too. Henry seemed to keep a close eye on his brother, and perhaps it was him who told William to act more pleasant, for he smiled quite often that evening. Apparently, William *did* know how to disguise his disdain and disgust in outward graciousness. Christine was mildly surprised, considering his ardent exclamations at their meeting the last time. But she almost gave him credit that he did indeed possess the skill of flawless manners, a talent all young men, especially of any consequence, should master. Christine followed her own admonition and spoke much less than usual. During dinner she observed a great deal more than she was wont to do, and for the first time felt that there stood great reward in listening and watching.

The young men carried most of the conversation, Mr. Oakley staving off Mr. Carlisle as often as possible and asking Henry and William several questions to keep them engaged.

As the night moved on, Christine felt that Henry and William were quite at ease at the Harrisons' table—or so she let herself believe. William seemed completely genuine in his compliments: highlighting Mr. Oakley's good qualities, complimenting Christine's parents, and even condescending to speak occasionally to Christine. Either he spoke as he really felt or he was an able and well-practiced charlatan.

"Miss Harrison," William said after the men had come through to the drawing room, "I hear from my brother you are quite proficient at the piano."

He offered this statement as either a challenge or a compliment— Christine was not sure which. By his calm tone this statement could have been either.

Hesitating, she said, "Why thank you, but I play mostly to accompany Lizzy's excellent singing voice."

"On the contrary," Henry chimed in, his ever-present smile on his lips, "I remember you playing a few solos for us at Cassfield. I am very fond of Mozart and his many sonatas."

"You have an excellent memory," Christine said.

Mr. Carlisle then came to their group and pulled Henry away, saying, "Now tell me what your opinion is on the recent tax change in Parliament."

Henry nodded and began talking with Mr. Carlisle. William, to Christine's surprise, continued the conversation immediately. "I as well love Mozart, Miss Harrison." William finally consented to meet Christine's eyes for a moment.

She felt his gaze weighing her. Not knowing what else to speak of, she said, "Which of his pieces is your favorite?"

"That would be his Sonata in C. My mother used to play that song when I was young."

"I see," Christine began as she watched his face reminisce about his family. She continued, "I had the great delight of learning that piece years ago. But I have not practiced it in quite some time." And then, wanting the focus away from herself, she dared, "May I ask about your parents—are they still alive?" Her hands stiffened for a moment, nervous to ask too personal a question of him.

His intense blue eyes focused across the room to a bookshelf and then came back to Christine's. He inhaled slowly.

"No, my mother died when I was nine, from a chronic condition that finally took her life. My father passed away two years ago just after returning from England." His tone bore off steadily, but Christine could tell it was hard for him to speak of his parents—especially his father.

"I am sorry to hear that," she replied. "But I am sure they were the best sort of people."

"Yes, indeed they were." He exhaled quickly, as though shedding that memory once more. "Thank you, Miss Harrison."

He then stood and walked away, seeming agitated once again. The green and gold chair he had just employed now looked starkly empty, and Christine found herself alone in the corner of the room nearest the piano. She had not meant to pry, but had genuinely wanted to know more of his family. She was sure, by his hasty removal across the room, that he had thought her impertinent yet again. He seemed absolved of his duty to be cordial, having said enough, and remembered the distance he preferred to keep between them. His amiable demeanor was nothing more than a game.

Christine watched as William walked to the side of Mr. Carlisle, whose long explanation to Henry seemed still in full force. Christine saw William, with all the ease of a skilled conversationalist, relieve Henry from his tedious conversation with Mr. Carlisle. William seemed, when removed from her presence, full of easy dialogue and high spirits.

She sighed to herself, recalling that Mr. Davenport would be back soon, and she would be free and comfortable once again. *Terribly comfortable*, she mused, *and perhaps engaged*. She tried to forget the concise letter he had sent.

Oakley spent most the evening with Lizzy in what seemed an intimate conversation. He held a book in his hand, and several times they appeared to discuss some passage or another. How well suited they looked, completely involved and content in one another's countenance.

Finally, after all guests had gone home, the two sisters lay tucked in their beds, sharing their large suite as they always did, talking by candlelight.

"Mr. Oakley says he wishes to stay in Rothershire longer and call quite often in these next few weeks! Do you think that a good sign?" Lizzy's eyes shifted from side to side as she smiled at Christine.

"Good sign? Oh Lizzy, he is quite in love with you. I am no prophet, but you shall be engaged before a fortnight, I believe."

Now, if I only had an engagement to report myself, Christine thought, hoping to be engaged as the eldest sister, especially before her younger sister would entertain a proposal. She troubled over the fact that Mr. Davenport still had not returned, and she nestled deeper into her bed, trying to ward off any doubtful thought of his intentions toward her.

MR. OLIVER DAVENPORT

Miss Estelle Braxton found Mr. Davenport two weeks later at his same small apartment in London. She had attempted to visit him twice the week before, but they had only talked a few minutes each time before Mr. Davenport declared he must be off. Today she arrived at the door in an emerald gown, her hair wisped up in a braided bun, her maid in tow. She arrived with more determination, having learned from one of his servants that he possessed no immediate business. She was altogether a beautiful siren, ready and waiting to call her sailor to his dreaded fate.

"Mr. Davenport," she began as soon as she was in the drawing room, "I was hoping I could suggest a walk with you? I thought perhaps you had ruminated on our earlier conversation?" She always acted a bit too forward. It could not have been clearer that she came that day with an agenda. She was absolutely stunning—a perfect figure—all the grace of a baroness coupled with the allure of a fairytale sorceress.

Mr. Davenport knew he must give in sooner or later and therefore acquiesced to the walk. She laced her thin arm through his, and they headed out behind the house to a long strip of grass that led to the mooring docks.

They strolled for several minutes, first in silence, and then exchanged some small talk. It became silent again, and the heaviness of what she wanted weighed on Mr. Davenport. He knew it was only a matter of time before this beguiling Miss Braxton would unveil her design. For weeks he had avoided her, but she persisted. As their walk continued, Mr. Davenport noticed that Miss Braxton's maid had seemed again to vanish. He also noticed Miss Braxton had removed her gloves, now twirling them aimlessly in one hand. Mr. Davenport acquiesced to her ungloved arm on his, and she relaxed into him as they walked. She was aware the power of her touch, and he wondered if she could sense his weakening with every stride.

Her aim and desire tore at him, and finally he decided to ask.

"I cannot help but think, Miss Braxton, that you have something to say to me. I do think you will be more at ease if you express yourself."

"How well you know me, Mr. Davenport," she said with a laugh, raising her hand, again putting on airs. "I would think it rather obvious."

For a moment, Mr. Davenport pulled himself away from his walking partner. He stopped moving and turned to face her directly.

"I am afraid, miss, that I do not wish to give any encouragement. You prey upon my eligible status, but I have volunteered no reassurance in that direction."

"That is right," she breathed back as she came closer to whisper at his throat, "I want to know if you feel anything between us again."

Mr. Davenport moved down the lane, in part to distance her tempting and sweet-smelling body slightly farther away from his and remember his plan to marry Miss Harrison. They continued to walk quietly for another minute as he gathered his thoughts. They were approaching a large group of trees at the water's edge. Mr. Davenport led them to the edge of the trees, leaning his hand against one thick brown trunk. He attempted a resolute gaze across the water, watching the boats come into harbor for a moment. Finally he drew back toward Miss Braxton and then answered, "If you are wanting to know of my affections toward you," he gulped sheepishly, "I have been otherwise involved this past year, as I said before."

He wondered if his tone sounded convincing. If he could not convey his resolve to her, how could he keep it himself? He attempted to stand straighter, and she walked nearer to him, forcing him into the thicket of trees.

She stood silently for a few moments in the flickering, half-shaded light filtering through the trees. Her steady, eerie silence wore him down further, and she crossed her arms and asked, "But there is no official engagement, Mr. Davenport? You said so yourself."

"Yes, that is correct, but we are nigh coming to such an agreement in a week or two, I believe. It is all but expected, all but formally said. I cannot—should not—break my understanding with Miss Harrison."

Her eyes turned cold and narrowed. This Miss Braxton knew what she wanted, and she would do anything to get it.

"And you think that even an official engagement would stop me from asking this of you?"

Mr. Davenport knew then that she had started devising a plan from the moment she saw him at the inn.

Her tone changed to a hissing, scalding whisper. She would not move as slowly now. "I think you must change your intentions," she said. "I believe I have a much better option for you." She stepped back, more completely secluded in the trees. Mr. Davenport followed her, leaning his defeated shoulders against one of the trunks.

Mr. Davenport thought back on the past few years, when he had started to participate in business trading internationally. He had found loopholes in the system and had made friends with some of the most dissolute shoremen London had to offer. He had enlisted the help of Miss Braxton's brother and father, who were experts at trading on the black market and smuggling goods in and out of port. They had also helped forge and file reports of the missing goods to the opposing party. Mr. Davenport had never been caught, and it made him handsome amounts of money, which he now smartly invested. This had been wrong, dishonest, he knew, but the monetary reward propelled him further into the business. And, he admitted to himself then, more entrenched with the Braxtons. And now he became more entangled with their daughter.

Fear dawned across Mr. Davenport's face, but it would be nothing to the shame and compromise he would feel after she fully explained herself. As she drew nearer, she began laying her terms before him.

"This is my proposition," Miss Braxton began again, coming in close enough to clutch his arm in hers. She was half seducing and half demanding as she continued her speech.

"I know the whereabouts of your last three shipping and receiving accounts, which, might I add, made you quite a profit. If I tell those parties of your deceit, you will be ruined forever." She sighed, narrowing her eyes at him. She then softened her tone and whispered, "I, however, do not wish to turn you in to anyone. I have wanted, all my life, to have a respectable fortune *and* a respectable name, as the latter is hard to come by in my family. If we marry, I will gain a better name, you and I will share your fortune, and nothing will be lost."

She then reached up and caressed his cheek with her soft fingers. Even quieter she added, "And it helps that we have such a romantic past. I have always loved you."

She raised her hand and ran it through his hair, her dark-brown eyes locking with his jade ones. His countenance filled with rage and feverish worry. She had loved him, of that he was certain. He thought a few years ago that perhaps he loved her back. But this was blackmail.

Her dark eyes tracked his every movement although he tried to look away. Angry, his gaze narrowed as he studied the ground. But as he processed all she said, his eyes opened wide and filled with worry, coming back to hers.

What was he to do? If anyone found out about his dealings, he would ruined forever, becoming lower than a hired servant. He knew she was serious about her threat. She could, and would, undoubtedly turn him in if he did not agree.

She came closer and laid her head on his chest. She would stop at nothing. She would not leave until she had an answer.

But what about Christine? He wanted to marry her. His affections had transferred to her over the last year. Their marriage would complete his perfect name and standing. He could continue trips to London, securing his shipments. She would never know. Not even Grenville knew.

And Christine's fortune and name coupled with his increasing holdings would secure them in the highest of circles in all of England. No one had yet questioned his ability to increase his estate. All had gone according to plan. He had smiled and danced his way into Christine's heart, he was sure. But he had never quite committed to her. Why had he not asked her earlier?

It did not matter now.

Now he must preserve himself above all else.

The dark part of him—which had been whittled down by Miss Braxton's increasing closeness—won over that moment.

He had to acquiesce. He thought at first it was because of Estelle. But deep inside he knew it was because of himself.

He could play this part just as he had played in Rothershire.

Mr. Davenport swallowed and tugged on his coat. He stepped away from the tree and came closer to Miss Braxton again.

"I understand all you have said perfectly, Miss Braxton."

He said it slowly, one last time weighing his options, trying to stifle the voice inside that told him this was completely wrong. He felt a surge of terrible emotion and in that moment gave in to the darkness.

He slowly grasped her shoulder and pulled her in, a flood of memories coming back from their carefree past. She had, in her evil persuasion, combined attraction with ultimatum in the scariest form of alliance. And he would surrender to such threats to his status. He closed his eyes and swallowed.

Her arm now in his, they walked a few paces deeper into the trees, secluding them from any onlookers. Estelle sent Mr. Davenport several glances, coming closer each time as they came to the shadiest spot.

"We are quite alone," Miss Braxton said with suggestion in her voice. His eyes met hers, and he committed to his course.

"Miss Braxton," he said, pulling her close, "I agree to your proposal." His arm circled around her delicate waist. "Will you marry me?" he whispered. He tilted his head downward, and she answered with a long kiss, which he did not refuse.

CHAPTER 13

A few days after the Robertsons came to visit, Mr. Grenville returned to Rothershire—alone. He requested a private meeting with Christine, who agreed heartily, hoping she would learn something of Mr. Davenport in the course of their conversation.

"We are quite by ourselves, are we not?" Mr. Grenville asked as soon as he sat in Christine's parlor.

"Yes, of course Mr. Grenville. Do tell me why you have come."

"I should think you would know—to ask about dear Miss Allensby, of course. I must know how she fares and how involved she is with that Mr. Carlisle."

Christine's heart fell a moment, wishing he came to report news of Mr. Davenport. Mustering a smile, she began, "She still sees quite a bit of Mr. Carlisle. He has come to several dinners and calls on her a few times a week."

Mr. Grenville swatted his hand across his thigh and drew his face tight. "Just when I finally thought I found someone again . . ." he mumbled to himself.

Christine leaned forward, her face sympathetic. "Between you and me, sir, I think she ought to choose you."

Mr. Grenville offered a sad smile. Christine wondered how soon she could ask about Mr. Davenport without seeming unfeeling when the door behind her swung on its hinge.

"I thought I heard your voice!" The commanding sound of Miss Rusket rang through the room. "If you are here to ask about Miss Allensby, Mr. Grenville," she said, sidling up to him on the same blue chaise, "my dearest cousin is completely wrong about even *entertaining* the idea of Mr. Carlisle. In my opinion, it has gone on far too long."

Mr. Grenville shot Christine a look, and she returned it with a shrug.

"Miss Rusket, I did not expect you downstairs this early," Christine said, trying to explain why they were no longer alone.

"Yes, well, Mr. Grenville," Ivory said, turning toward him, "I have even chosen to spend a few days here at Wellington rather than submit myself to any more meetings with Mr. Carlisle than I must endure. But alas, Miss Allensby will not listen to me! I have told her several times, in no uncertain terms, that I think him inferior in every way. But I guess she will do what she pleases."

Mr. Grenville shook his head, and then stood to take his leave. Christine wanted him to stay so they could speak of what he knew concerning Mr. Davenport, but with Ivory now present, Christine did not wish to have too candid a conversation.

"I must be off, ladies," he said with a curt bow. He spun on his heels and was outside within a half minute. Christine had no chance to even mention anything.

Ivory stayed one day longer and then declared she must return again to London. The day after that, Meg wished to walk into town with Mr. Carlisle, and Meg implored Christine to accompany them.

Christine agreed to the role of chaperone, which, she thought, was becoming her most frequent and useful employment. Today, she found herself especially willing so something else would occupy her mind other than when Mr. Davenport would return. She walked behind the pair, but close enough to hear Mr. Carlisle say, in a hushed whisper, "Surely you see the error of their ways, for they are ignorant of what is right. Your father and mother's opinion of me is too harsh."

Meg meekly wrinkled the folds of her dress, nodding slightly. It was only from years of experience with Meg that Christine noticed the hint of pink rising in her cheeks. For Meg's mother to speak against Mr. Carlisle, she must really disapprove.

"And your friends," he whispered, thinking he was quiet enough, "they are too prejudiced. I am an honest man, and I wish someone would enumerate my good qualities now and again."

"Indeed, Mr. Carlisle," Meg began shyly, with a glint of fire behind her eyes. "You do have many great qualities. That is not the issue I wish to discuss." Seeming to gather her courage, she proclaimed boldly, "I just wish you would be kinder. I feel you have dealt with my family and friends rather harshly."

"On the contrary, Miss Allensby,"—the indignation heightened in his voice—"your Miss Rusket was downright rude, Miss Harrison does nothing but glare at me, and the scoffs and comments I have taken from Miss Elizabeth have been insufferable."

Christine, feeling awkward, tried to slow her pace to give them room to continue their argument. She watched Meg's color deepen to a darker shade of red. That comment seemed to be the last straw. Luckily they were almost to town so Christine feigned interest in the dressmaker's shop as Meg prepared her response. Christine did admit that Ivory definitely possessed the tendency to speak her mind, and she herself was not always gracious, but Lizzy never, ever acted badly toward people. And Meg knew it.

"Do not speak of my friends that way. Lizzy is the kindest creature I know, indeed my kindest friend, and I have *never* heard her speak ill of anyone, let alone you." She turned her shoulder and walked quickly to join Christine. But before she was too far away, she faced Mr. Carlisle again, with glinting eyes. "You have imagined such things in your mind. I have tried to look past your differences with my family and friends for long enough. But I cannot overlook them any longer. What you have said may be your own interpretation, but I can see clearly for myself now that you are a rude, unfeeling man who cares about himself more than any others around him. I am sorry, but I cannot tolerate your nefarious character anymore. Please do not call again."

Meg came into the dress shop trembling, and Christine nodded, having heard the entire interaction. Christine took Meg by the arm and smiled. Meg shook her head and continued to stare in Mr. Carlisle's general direction.

"It must feel nice to have that decision made," Christine said after a moment, and Meg laughed nervously. Christine embraced her. Meg's speech amazed Christine, and Christine admired her for finally speaking her mind. Then, noticing Meg's distress, Christine tried to change the subject to what lace trimmings she could buy to dress up a few old gowns that needed mending.

"This would complement the green rather nicely, do you agree?" Christine said, turning Meg away from the window.

"Yes, quite."

"Right, then," Christine said. "How else shall I spend my allowance this week?" They laughed, and Christine hoped that shopping for dresses might make Meg forget her troubles with men. After a few minutes, Meg seemed a bit less flustered and purchased a few ribbons and some cake for the two of them to share.

The rest of the afternoon held no mention of Mr. Carlisle. Nor did the girls speak of him for a long while. Their walk to town started with a party of three, but their return thankfully lacked one component.

CHAPTER 14

The Harrison sisters took tea in the sunshine a week later, the weather hinting of spring. They sat on the same balcony on which Christine had talked with Mr. Robertson during the ball, the same one Mr. Davenport had pulled her from for their last dance together. The large, shuttered, floor-to-ceiling doors remained open, letting in the pleasant air.

Surely this will be the week Mr. Davenport returns home, thought Christine.

A maid knocked lightly, delivering post arrived from London, holding out two letters on the tray. Christine snatched them quickly, both addressed to her, imagining they both came from Mr. Davenport. Perhaps his first had been misdirected.

"Shall I leave you?" Lizzy said, looking at Christine.

"No, please stay. It is a letter from Mr. Davenport," Christine said, and then she slowly lifted the other as her brow furrowed. "And another from . . . Ivory."

Her hands shook a little. She would read Mr. Davenport's first.

Miss Harrison,

I regret to inform you that I will not be returning north to Rothershire anytime soon. I have decided to make London my new home. I have appreciated our long friendship, and wish you best of luck in your endeavors. Please give my regards to your family as well.

Best,
Mr. Oliver Davenport

Christine fell back into her chair and dropped the letter. She clamped her eyes shut and thrust her chin toward the floor. Her hands rose to her temples, and she began to cry. Lizzy came to her side immediately, putting her arm around Christine's shoulder.

"You may read it," Christine said to Lizzy in between sobs. Lizzy quietly lifted the letter from the ground. Christine continued to weep, completely in shock.

Lizzy read the letter and said nothing. She gently stroked Christine's back. After several minutes, Christine burst out, "How could he? I was so sure we would be engaged. And this . . . this letter? I do not understand. Oh, why?" Christine oscillated between anger and complete devastation.

Christine continued to sob as Lizzy tried to comfort her. Christine was too busy crying to notice when Lizzy finally pick up the unread letter on the table from Ivory.

"Perhaps this letter from Ivory will cheer you up? Her letters are so diverting."

The last thing Christine wanted was to read a letter from Ivory, probably singing her successes with who knew how many suitors. But Lizzy looked at her so plaintively, Christine finally agreed. "Only if you read it aloud," she said to Lizzy. "I cannot see anything at present."

Lizzy opened the seal and read.

Christine,

I felt compelled to write to you concerning Mr. Davenport, whom you spoke of briefly during my last visit. Since returning to London, I have learned of Mr. Davenport's current status. I do not wish to add to your grief, if you have heard already, but I thought it important you know the truth as soon as possible.

I have long been slight acquaintances with a certain Miss Braxton. She comes from quite a large sum of money, but her family came into it rather unscrupulously. (It is rumored her father has traded with some smugglers for many years). Suffice it to say, she is wealthy and thus attends many of the same parties I attend. I have it on good authority, from one of my closest acquaintances here, that Miss Braxton has had the desire for years to marry someone with good name and breeding to "officially" allow her into higher circles.

According to my friend, Miss Braxton has known Mr. Davenport for quite some time, and a few years ago, mutual interest existed between them. He had not contacted her for a long while—I can only presume his intentions were true and honorably set on making a match with you—until he came back to London a few weeks ago. He had many affairs to set in order, and one of these affairs seems to be marrying Miss Braxton. He must be very eager, for in three weeks' time, they shall be married.

I am sorry to report such unfortunate news, but I thought it might help you avoid any uncomfortable situation, if perhaps you crossed paths. I love you dearly, and such a volatile man is not worthy of your affections.

Sincerely,
Miss Ivory Rusket

Christine gripped the edge of her chair and stood slowly, moving silently like a ghost, and walked listlessly inside to the drawing room. She fell into the closest sofa, crumpling into a pile across it. Tears streamed from her cheeks. Such a report after his horrible note was too much.

He is to be married? Christine was sure Mr. Davenport would propose to her, and in less than three months since his mention of his intentions he would marry someone else?

"Perhaps Ivory was wrong, or misinformed, or confused on particulars . . ." Christine let out, tears still coming down her face. Lizzy smiled softly and Christine wished in her heart it might be true.

But the sinking feeling in the pit of Christine's stomach reminded her that Ivory was almost always well informed, and she had never known her to have her gossip incorrect. It must be the truth.

Lizzy raised her hand, gently stroking Christine's hair for a few minutes.

"Christine, may I help you to your room?" Lizzy asked quietly.

Christine's tears had subsided, and she wiped her cheeks as she swallowed. "No, thank you, I think some fresh air and solitude will do me the most good."

Lizzy waited by the door for a moment, until Christine sat up and smoothed her skirts.

Finally, Christine rose, determined to walk until she sorted this out in her mind. She knew this might be an ill-suited plan, for it would take several days of walking if she were truly to clear her mind. She had been holding on to the hope that although he was not returning at present, he would soon come back and all would be clear, that of course he cared about her despite his absence, and extending his trip had to do with business alone. That they truly loved each other and he would come again to her and ask her father for her hand. His character had stood still gallant in her mind. She had thought, until that morning, that his love remained constant.

But the one indisputable way to prove that he had never loved her—that it was all a lie—was to marry someone else. And this was his course of action. So swiftly, so assuredly.

Christine wandered up and down the hills behind Wellington Estate, not venturing into town, and not going into the Allensbys' property, for fear of running into anyone. She wanted space, she wanted solitude, and she wanted to make sense of how she was now officially alone, with no prospect of a future. How could he marry so quickly? Was nothing he had said, nothing he had done of any meaning? Her mind raced through past experiences and conversations. He had seemed unsure a few times, but she had passed them off as normal steps toward an engagement, not to him thinking about another woman. And how could he change his mind so suddenly? Perhaps Miss Braxton lived always in his thoughts, competing with Christine on every account.

For hours she reworked conversations in her head and reenvisioned scenes, trying to find what she had missed. What clues had he given? How could she have avoided this? What would people think of her? What would she tell those around her? She felt a great relief that she did not have to explain it to Ivory, at least.

The sun began to set over the rolling green hills, and she still could not make sense of his actions or words. She tried to force herself to push out thoughts of Mr. Davenport, but they kept creeping back to no avail. She crawled into bed early, having no appetite for supper. It took Christine hours to fall asleep, tortured over past conversations, cursing her forthrightness, and feeling ashamed for putting her true feelings out when they would just be bashed into pieces. It was well into the early morning when she fell into a defeated, tear-stained slumber.

CHAPTER 15

Mr. Oakley became the saving grace of Wellington Estate and the Harrisons. He seemed to be the only gentleman the ladies could keep. Meg and Christine had driven away the rest; Christine doubted Mr. Carlisle would make another appearance in the town of Rothershire any time soon after such an exposé, and any gentleman who came in contact with Christine seemed to leave rather abruptly, desiring someone else.

Christine spoke to no one, went nowhere, and lost most of her appetite for weeks. Life felt dull. She saw the world as only gray, and her complexion, usually so warm and clear, began to match her worldview.

After three weeks of sullen, empty days, Christine acknowledged that Mr. Davenport's wedding day passed. Then Christine sank to her fullest low. She did not leave her room and refused contact with anyone. She lay around sulking, lamenting the fact that Mr. Davenport chose to be without her.

The more Christine retreated, the more Lizzy felt it her duty to rescue Christine. Continuing in such a way would lead to Christine's ruin. A week and a half after Mr. Davenport's marriage, Lizzy shook Christine awake and said, "You ought to dress quickly, for Mr. Oakley and I have quite the enjoyable day planned ahead, and you must come with us."

As Christine gained awareness of the morning, she remembered the horror of Mr. Davenport's situation just as she did every morning as she awoke. Had it not been for the overly excited look on Lizzy's face, she would have remained in bed much longer. Christine looked up and saw her maid, obviously summoned by Lizzy. It was all Christine could do to pull on her dress, have her maid attend her hair, and go down to breakfast. Christine said not a word, her gloom chilling the room. Despite her foul disposition, Christine knew she had nothing better to do that day, and she surely needed something to remove herself from thinking of Mr. Davenport at every moment. She turned to Lizzy and said dryly, "Where will we be going?"

Her cheery face beamed. "Just wait and see." She was always good at making a situation seem light and positive. Lizzy's plan was advantageous for all parties—it seemed Christine was their chaperone for the day and they were her diversion.

The party rode for about an hour and a half and came to a large cliff. The horses and coachman stopped. Christine had passed this cliff several times on the way to Cassfield, but they had never stopped there before. Large austere drops stood in front of them, with grassy meadows at the bottom. Mr. Oakley pulled out a picnic box from under the seat of their carriage. Lizzy had thought of everything. She brought all of Christine's favorites: crackers with Brie, fresh fruit, and some tarts to finish it off. Eating one's sorrows away and filling one's heart with tarts was not beneath Christine, and Lizzy knew it.

They spent the afternoon exploring the cliffs and caves. The new terrain took Christine's mind away from her circumstance. She could not believe that such a place existed so close to Wellington. Why had she never ventured here before? What a beautiful day trip this made. The small ferny grottos and large stone outcroppings occupied most of her time and energy, filling her mind with new pictures instead of living in old ones.

Something about nature always drew out Christine's philosophic side. Here she was, wallowing in self-pity and gloom, and there, not a half day's drive away from her, stood some of the most beautiful landscapes she had ever beheld. It was true she knew of them but had never explored this wonderful place.

What facets of her life stood about her just as these cliffs and peaks? How much of life's goodness and wonder resided within her reach?

How long had she been blinded by the thought of income, prestige, and high standing and overlooked the beautiful surroundings before her eyes—the friendships, relationships, and interactions that she could partake of, if she was willing to look beyond herself?

Christine's mind expanded more that day than it had in the last year. Life contained so much goodness that she had never experienced.

She leaned her back against a mossy rise of stone, looking out over a precipice. For the first time in a long while, she desired to change.

Christine stayed there some time, until Lizzy and Mr. Oakley came upon her from their own path. The rest of the day they walked together, pointing out the great vistas and beautiful foliage all around them.

After spending the day with Lizzy and Mr. Oakley, Christine hoped for their marriage even more. She noticed the way they interacted with each other and admired the way they chose to serve her. Indeed, she forgot about Mr. Davenport a few times that day—at least for a few moments at a time. The shock of the situation began to settle, and the reality of Mr. Davenport's marriage began to turn into a dull ache rather than the overwhelming pain from before.

She thought about the superficial relationship Mr. Davenport and she had entertained. It was not like what she saw now from Lizzy and Mr. Oakley. They truly loved each other. There was nothing of pretense: no emphasis on social standing, money, or superior remarks. It was not a game or a charade. Both cared more about the other than themselves.

Had she married Mr. Davenport, this would not have been the case. Someday the perfect pair they made would fade and wither into nothing more than a mutually beneficial alliance. To be subjected to such a state for the rest of her life would have been just punishment indeed for her selfish pursuits. But by God's grace, and Mr. Davenport's deception, she had been spared such a fate.

She was, indeed, saved—dejected, sullen, and fragmented, yet her heart had not truly broken. Her pride stood wounded. But her heart, she realized, had never been his.

She smelled the mossy clean breeze as it washed over her and saw the crisp cobalt sky shine overhead. Christine closed her eyes, imagining that if she worked hard enough she could become different, improved.

As the days passed on, Christine still sometimes thought of Mr. Davenport moving through life, blissfully happy with a girl he was madly in love with. Christine felt she moved nowhere, her small sphere standing still. This dull, basic existence continued each day with almost no variance. Every now and again she would close her eyes and transport herself to the cliffs and peaks she had seen with Lizzy. For moments at a time, she remembered her feelings, her desire to learn and move on.

Most days, however, she felt little improvement.

Amidst such doldrums, Christine had to admit that Meg and Lizzy made progress with their respective gentleman situations. Lizzy would almost certainly be receiving a proposal from Mr. Oakley within the month, although Christine anticipated such happiness for her sister at any minute due to the strength of their mutual affection. Meg had absolutely no interest or contact with Mr. Carlisle—his courting had run its course like a strong fever, which now left no trace. Lizzie and Christine exchanged sisterly confidence that Mr. Grenville ought to try his hand once again to marry Meg, for they guessed their friend would probably acquiesce happily.

Christine began to reconcile herself to years without prospects. Among their friends and acquaintances, she perhaps could eventually find someone to marry, but she did not want just a "someone." No one for miles and days could tempt her, and she wanted only the company of her sister and Meg. She knew that a life unmarried would suit her better than a life married to someone whom she did not really love.

There was the slight hope of continuing a friendship with the Robertson brothers, but she had not heard or seen them in connection with Mr. Oakley for a month. Gone to Scotland, and then to London—probably to stay, Christine assumed. They had no reason to return to Rothershire, let alone call at Wellington. William had shown his indifference all too clearly, refusing Christine's invitations to Wellington Estate completely.

The next two weeks were quiet at Wellington Manor. Christine became quite proficient at many piano pieces and consumed almost all—excepting the business ledgers—of what her father's library had to offer. With Mr. Oakley having an annual meeting with his steward in London, not a single male visitor came to call. All of this confirmed to Christine that she would probably be quite old before she married. Or she would just be quite old and unmarried.

But Christine and Lizzy still frequently visited Meg. It seemed all of Rothershire knew Mr. Carlisle was gone forever. Christine assumed such rampant gossip traveled through the Allensby servants, a few of which were known to have quite a loose tongue. Even Christine's maid had asked her if "her dear friend Miss Allensby would be seeing Mr. Grenville again," to which Christine answered she did not know. "But did you hear about Miss Allensby?" Christine had asked. "Oh, miss, well people do talk . . ." her maid had replied.

So it was a great thrill, but not a great surprise when the next morning Meg's maid came through the door of the Allensbys' parlor. Christine and Lizzy sat across from Meg in the small room, all three perched comfortably in the closest of the mauve-covered chairs to exchange confidences.

The maid stood taller, sweeping her hand in a gesture toward the door, and said, "Miss Allensby, quite *sorry* to interrupt"—an impish grin crossed the servant's face—"but Mr. Grenville is here to see you. Shall I let him in?"

Meg's eyes opened wide. Christine looked at Lizzy, and both stood quickly.

"Forgive me, Meg," Christine said, smiling wickedly, "but I think Lizzy and I need a bit of fresh air at the moment."

Lizzy nodded with a full smile. The sisters bustled through the door, skillfully leaving it open just a few inches to hear all of the conversation from afar. The girls knew Meg would not care if they listened, and in fact she expected such a practice from her friends. It was one of those unwritten female rules.

"Miss Allensby," they heard the sure voice of Mr. Grenville say as they sat on the stairs outside the room, "how do you do?" Christine heard a rustle as he lowered his hat and exhaled. "You are looking well." Although Christine could not see it, she imagined Meg's soft pale skin flushing ever so becomingly.

"I am well, thank you. Do have a seat. My mother is . . . out right now, but I would be pleased to have you stay." She was trying to explain away why she was in the drawing room by herself. It was then that Lizzy and Christine stole a glance at each other with high eyebrows and large smiles from behind the door. *This is the moment,* their sisterly confidence seemed to say.

"You may not have heard," he said, "but Mr. Davenport and his cousin have both moved back to London." *Wanting to establish his place,* thought Christine. His cousin. Right, let us not reference the enemy's name. How Christine wished he had also not mentioned the name of Davenport.

"Yes, I am thankfully aware of such things. It seems the women of Rothershire did a fine job of running *that* family out." Meg gave a nervous laugh. "But I think those gentlemen will prefer the society in London," Meg added with an air of indifference.

Christine knew both herself and Meg were truly grateful those men were gone, though she knew she thought about Mr. Davenport far more than Meg even remembered her moments with Mr. Carlisle. Mr. Carlisle was easily forgotten. Mr. Davenport could almost never escape Christine's mind.

A silence passed between Meg and Mr. Grenville. Christine imagined Mr. Grenville looking deep into Meg's eyes and summoning courage.

"Then I would like to ask if I might come to call more often?" he finally spoke.

There was a slight pause, which Christine could only guess was a wide smile bestowed on Mr. Grenville by Meg. Christine could then hear the relief in Meg's voice. "Of course, Mr. Grenville, I would like that very much."

It sounded then as if Mr. Grenville moved, his boots brushing the floor.

"And it is perhaps too early, but I fear I cannot contain myself, you having received me with so much encouragement. Miss Allensby— Meg, darling—would you consent to be mine and marry me?"

Christine heard an audible gasp and the rustling of a skirt coupled with a few steps. Then a very pleased, "Yes," came from Meg.

Christine looked at Lizzy, whose mouth had dropped into a small *o*. Neither sister expected such a meeting, or they might have not dared to listen in. Christine gently closed the door, determining to stay outside until Meg came out and told of the good news.

Christine heard Mr. Grenville speak again, muffled through the door. "Of course I shall go directly to your father and ask his consent, if you feel it agreeable between us."

"Yes, of course," Meg said again, the smile almost audible.

Christine thought she heard a silence again fill the room, and after a few minutes a pair of boots traipsed across the floor toward the front entryway.

Within moments, Meg flew through the door, hugging both sisters at the same time. "He came back!" she cried. "He came back!" Her cheeks could almost not contain her smile. Meg had finally realized whom she did indeed love. She paused for a moment. Christine took her squarely by the shoulders and said, laughing, "And I think you made sure that he will stay this time!"

There must have been a conjugal fever running through the air of Rothershire, for not three days after Meg's engagement, Christine received a post, written in a masculine hand.

Miss Harrison,

I shall return to Rothershire next week. Could you meet me in the town square next Tuesday at noon with your beautiful sister in tow? It is my wish to provide quite the surprise that day. I shall bring Mr. Robertson and hope you two would serve as chaperones as we picnic that afternoon. I trust you will keep all a secret.

Until then,
Mr. Edmund Oakley

CHAPTER 16

*B*ut if you wanted a new pair of slippers, why did you not come with us yesterday?" Lizzy queried, naively going along with Christine's story. The sisters walked arm and arm down the road, past hills filled with newly sprouted flowers. Christine smiled to herself, knowing that gullibility was often one of Lizzy's greatest virtues, and this moment was no exception.

"My head was hurting yesterday," Christine feigned as she stopped to point out one of the wildflowers. "But I really do need a new pair of slippers."

In truth, this stood as one of Christine's first outings to town since she learned of Mr. Davenport, and she went now only on account of her sister. It felt wonderful to be in the fresh air, clean and new from the light rain the day before.

"I love going to town," Lizzy said as she checked her handbag and placed her arm again through Christine's. "And the weather is so nice today. *What* a beautiful sky."

"Yes, it is lovely."

The road changed from packed earth to cobblestones as they reached the edge of Rothershire. "Oh, let us stop here and ask the price of pork," Christine said, needing to stall for a few minutes. "Cook Cooper wanted me to see if it was a good value."

"Why did she not send a servant?" asked Lizzy.

"Normally she would, but you know she and I are quite comfortable, and I spoke with her just yesterday when I delivered mother's weekly list. I told it would be no inconvenience."

They looked around for a few minutes, Christine asking a few questions while Lizzy gazed out the window. After leaving the butcher's, Christine directed Lizzy toward the town square.

Christine acted quite consumed with finding the perfect pair of shoes, walking into a nearby shop, when Lizzy spotted a tall young man giving her a wave and a slight bow.

"Christine! Mr. Oakley is here! I did not know he was in town! We must go talk to him at once."

Christine almost fell to the ground as Lizzy wrenched her sister out of the shop and ran over to him. Behind him was an even taller man with wavy blond hair. Christine's heart fell for just a moment, surprised she felt disappointed that it was not William standing there.

Christine smiled and greeted Henry as an old friend, curtsying briefly. Henry returned a matchmaker's smile as his eyes rolled toward the happy reunited couple. Lizzy and Mr. Oakley were already in their own world, busily talking of their "chance" meeting.

"Hello, Mr. Robertson. It is a pleasure to see you again," Christine said, once Lizzy and Mr. Oakley pulled ahead.

"And you as well, Miss Harrison. I am glad we can facilitate such a meeting." His eyes had their customary humor behind them, for he dearly loved to scheme. He gestured to follow Mr. Oakley and Lizzy, who were already walking away toward Mr. Oakley's carriage for the picnic.

The coach carried the foursome away for a half-hour until they came to a beautiful field of flowers and green grasses. The gentlemen laid out a blanket, and Mr. Oakley unloaded their lunch. The rest of the afternoon passed peacefully. Christine talked almost exclusively to Mr. Robertson as Lizzy and Mr. Oakley held their own intimate conversation. When the lovers were not conversing, their eyes conveyed tender looks back and forth, having a dialogue all on their own. The discourse between Christine and Henry flowed naturally, as he always knew what to talk of to make others easy.

"We spent a few weeks in Scotland with my grandfather. William persuaded me to go. And then we have taken up residence in London again with Oakley."

Always London . . . thought Christine.

"And does your brother come with you now to Rothershire?" Christine asked, trying to sound indifferent.

"Certainly not. He is much too busy worrying about our textile business. I am, as you know, involved in it as well. Unlike William, however, I find ample time to enjoy myself."

"Are you implying your brother does not enjoy himself? Surely he must be privileged to the same sort of life you live?"

Christine longed to know who these brothers *really* were.

"We gain a good many pleasures from our cousin, Mr. Oakley. I find myself always willing to do his bidding, as I am in his debt. It is, however, a mutually beneficial situation, I assure you. Look— here I am, serving as his illustrious chaperone! But yes, in speaking of William, he is much more serious than I."

Christine could not help but ask more questions in this regard. "More serious? Oh, but I thought you the *model* of gravity." She smiled and continued, "How would you say he is different than your odious person?"

Henry chuckled. "He works a good deal more, I must admit. He concerns himself about every particular that I cannot seem to worry about. And of course, we think *very* differently in regard to the females around us."

"Is that so?" Christine asked, piqued. "What do you think of them, Mr. Robertson?"

"That is just it! I think of them, a vast deal. I would not be opposed to marrying some fine lady of class and fortune."

"And your brother?" Christine could not help but pry.

"Exactly contrary! He does not think of them. He is determined not to marry and thinks only of our business and the comfort of our grandfather—nothing of his own happiness. But perhaps I say too much of his notions."

Christine's questioning stopped. She tipped her head to the side, pondering for a moment. "I cannot say if this retelling of his charac- ter is a virtue or a vice," she said slowly, "but we cannot fault him for caring so much about your grandfather."

Henry turned grave, very unlike his usual person. It was as if something else hid behind his words, but only he knew the meaning.

His altered visage did not last long, as Henry then changed the subject and began a long speech on the perfection between Mr. Oakley and Lizzy. Christine agreed in every regard, while her thoughts drifted frequently toward Henry's brother.

As the foursome returned to Wellington Estate, Mr. Oakley asked if Lizzy would like to take a turn around the gardens. This was Christine's cue to leave, and she dismissed herself from Mr. Robertson, who took a carriage back to town.

The evening passed, both Mr. Oakley and Lizzy arriving together at supper. Christine did not know what intimate conversation transpired in the garden, but before the evening expired, Christine had an engaged sister and a future brother-in-law, and Lizzy wore a sparkling opal ring couched in gold on her finger as a token of Mr. Oakley's regard for her.

A few days later, Christine set off toward Allensby House to call on Meg. The air was warm, and the sun shone over the green hills. Everything seemed fully in bloom, and Christine felt more like herself than she had in many weeks. As she walked, she unfolded her most recent post from Ivory.

My dearest Christine,

I could tell you much of London, but I do not have time to write of every particular from each of the many balls I have attended. At least three times a week, I dine at a friend's house, and at least once a week attend a fine ball at someone's estate of varying importance. I know you might be wondering, as you hinted in your last letter, but no particular young man has yet won my fancy for more than a few weeks at a time. They all seem much too interested in my inheritance, and half of them are not even handsome.

I did attend one ball a few weeks ago where I saw Mr. Davenport and his new bride for a moment, though I fear they may have left early when they learned I was in attendance. Mr. Davenport and his wife seemed quite miserable anyway. The person hosting the ball was one of my least-connected acquaintances, and I daresay it was a dreadful party altogether.

I have heard my cousin and your sister have both been making great strides toward favorable matches. How tiresome that must be for you to be among those lovebirds all the time! What would you say to coming to stay with me in London for a bit? Surely your family can spare you, and I would love some company! I am sure being introduced to new gentlemen would not be disagreeable to yourself. There are many young men here you would find quite charming. Plus, with you as my guest, my mother might not have time to ask me about each suitor after every event. Write to me quickly. I could receive you as early as next week.

Sincerely,
Miss Ivory Rusket

Christine mused over such a letter. Over the past months, Ivory had proven herself quite the true friend, especially after the kind and delicate way she reported on Mr. Davenport. And now to think of Christine and invite her to London? Christine would write back as soon as she returned home. Anything seemed enough of a diversion, but London, with Ivory as her guide and the scores of new people she might meet? Christine could think of nothing better. But what if she were to somehow run into Mr. Davenport? She dreaded ever seeing him again. But the distraction and company Ivory would provide soon won out in Christine's mind. She would go and start enjoying life once more.

Christine looked up, finding herself at the end of the long gravel walkway of Allensby House. She tucked the letter inside her spencer jacket and knocked on the front door. As soon as Christine was let into the drawing room, Meg burst inside and said, "Have you come to inquire about Mr. Grenville and our engagement?"

Christine began to exude the best-friend-tell-all persona that every girl is wont to have as an audience. "Yes, of course! Tell me every detail—spare nothing."

"Things are really going well. But unfortunately, he travels to Paris next week. How I shall miss him so," Meg said. "He comes to call a few times per week, when his schedule allows. And Mama has extended a perpetual dinner invitation to him. As for me, I find our relationship completely altered. At least on my part, I daresay. For I believe he is the same doting, charming Mr. Grenville we all knew, but I find him so much more dashing and enthralling than before. I am quite taken, Christine."

"What has made the difference?" Christine asked as she settled deeper into her chair.

"I believe it is my perspective. I see what he is and what he can become. He has always been so good and genuine. He is steady and kind, and he has in every way won me over."

Christine watched Meg sigh contentedly and touch one of the pink pearl earrings she had started to wear again.

As Christine looked out the window to the back of Allensby House, she mused on the happenings in Meg's life over the past several months. Perhaps Meg's time with Mr. Carlisle had been worth it, although it ended painfully. Meg now knew how to understand the true character of a person. A skill, Christine reflected, in which she herself had no prowess.

Perhaps I shall be able to practice such things in London.

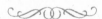

The next morning, Christine finished her crust of bread and hurried downstairs to the kitchen. She had her usual long list of requests from her mother for the next week's dinners. They were to have Mr. Oakley every day, and Mrs. Harrison felt the need to make each meal exquisite.

Acting as liaison to Cook Cooper had been Christine's assigned job for the past three years. Every Monday morning, her mother would deliver a list to her and say, "You must learn how to be mistress of a great household someday."

Someday indeed, Christine thought to herself that morning. She might never become the mistress of anywhere.

Christine pulled herself from complaints as soon as she stepped into the kitchen.

Today Cook looked different.

The great galley stood at a lull in between meals. The kitchen servants had gone to assist in other tasks, and Cook sat by herself at the large, rough-hewn wood table, peering over a letter. She seemed more subdued than usual, and as she looked up at Christine's face, she wiped the back of her hand quickly across her cheeks, willfully holding back tears. Christine stopped short in the doorway. It was not like Cook to be undone in such a way.

"Cook Cooper, whatever is the matter?"

"It is of no consequence." Cook said, trying to cover the letter with her hand. "Did ye have a request, deary?"

"I have my mother's usual list." She handed the note to Cook, but Christine, worried and curious, pressed further. "But may I ask what your letter says?"

Cook Cooper lowered her head and looked deep into the paper before her. She seemed to deliberate on her course of action for a moment, sighing heavily. She then pursed her lips and nodded to herself, taking Christine's arm and leading her into the dish room, closing the door behind her so no one could hear.

"I do not know if I should be tellin' ye, miss, but ye asked. I have thought of tellin' someone, but I didn't know who. Mrs. Harrison cannot help me for she would be starting something of a precedent. And none of these here servants can be trusted to keep a tight tongue, not to mention I do not think any a one of them would have power to help."

She stammered for a minute and then spoke in a rush, "My dearest and only Kathryn—from my first husband—has fallen into some mighty trouble. See, I done everything I can to raise her smart and good. She is a teacher and a tutor now by trade, for my first husband and I insisted we raise her right. My second husband was a bit more low-brow, but alas, that does not matter here. Her employer let her go a few months ago because she caught my Kathryn being coerced by a man against her will, and the lady of the house thought Kathryn to blame. She has been living off her savings for a few months and did not want to trouble me but writes now saying she has no money left. This same man who made her lose her tutor position recently offered her a job to be his housemaid, and she said she 'as decided to take it, for she has no other options. She wrote me all about it here," she said, pointing to a beautifully written letter. "She said he has been trying to convince her to be his mistress, and she has been refusing, but needs to keep her job in order to have enough to eat. She wants to come to me, but he keeps close hold on her. I am afraid of what he will do to her, miss. The letter was dated two weeks ago, but I think it was misdirected. I fear what has happened by now. But I know if I leave here, it will raise suspicion and could put me job at stake. Further, I don't know if I have any power among him, as he is from a higher circle than a cook, and I have no way to help her. Can ye help me?"

Christine's eyebrows furrowed. *How could this be?* she thought to herself. *How could someone be so reduced and so destitute?* But what could she do? She sat thinking for a few moments and then said slowly, "There may be some way I could help, as I travel to London this week with my father. May I take that letter with me?" She looked into Cook's blue eyes now welling with tears.

"How will you find her, miss? Look at the return address. It is so damaged, I cannot make it out."

Christine took the letter, noting the smudged return. Christine did not know what she would do, but she said, "I promise I will help your daughter."

Slowly and thankfully, Cook Cooper handed Christine the letter, rising from the table toward a large bubbling pot. They said no more, and Christine's mind started racing. How could she help? She had almost nothing to go on. She walked slowly upstairs, scanning the contents once again.

I must prepare for my trip to London to visit Ivory. And now, she thought, *to find this Kathryn.*

CHAPTER 17

few days later, Christine hurried down the main staircase to travel with her father to London. As she turned the corner, she passed Mr. Oakley in the foyer waiting for Lizzy to come down. She curtsied briefly and hurried by, thinking only of Cook Cooper. Mr. Oakley gave her a concerned look. Always observant, he asked, "Are you feeling well, Christine?"

She smiled and clasped her hands as her eyes shifted around the room. Christine had always had a problem with overactive body language, which told too much, and she did no credit to her manners here once again.

"I am quite all right, just eager to be off."

"Yes, you have a long distance ahead of you," Mr. Oakley said. Christine knew it would take two days to travel from Rothershire to London. A few seconds of silence then ensued, until Mr. Oakley said, "Christine, I realize you are quite busy, but I feel as though I must take this time to mention an important matter."

"Oh, of course," Christine said, trying to act calm. "Please go on. I hope it is of a pleasant nature."

"It could be, in a manner of speaking. But I fear Miss Allensby will find it a great surprise. Mr. Grenville possesses a great part of his past that he has not shared with Meg."

Christine shot him a furtive glance, not at all expecting any news of Mr. Grenville at this moment and confused why Mr. Oakley would be reporting on that man's dealings.

"I had no idea. What kind of secret?" Christine said. "And, may I ask, what causes you to know the affairs of Mr. Grenville?"

"He mentioned something to me a few weeks ago, when you ladies were sharing confidences while strolling around the gardens. It just slipped out, and then he warily said that I must not mention it to Lizzy or Meg and that it was well in his past. I guess he did not think I would mention it to you."

"Go on." The knot in Christine's stomach tightened.

He crossed his arms and then uncrossed them, pacing a moment. He opened his mouth to continue, when Christine's maid entered through the door. Mr. Oakley looked relieved and heaved a great sigh. "I . . . am not quite at liberty to say," he finally blurted out, looking purposefully at Christine's maid.

"Mr. Oakley!" Christine said, coming closer toward him, fully perplexed. She dropped her voice to a whisper, "You cannot stop there. You must tell me."

Mr. Oakley shook his head and clenched his jaw. "No, no—Miss Allensby must be the first to know. But I thought I would tell you so that you could perhaps prompt her to ask Mr. Grenville about why he must go to France next week. I cannot believe he has not told her yet of his reason. In my opinion, she deserves to understand."

What could he possibly be alluding to? And such a time-sensitive request! Christine's mind reeled. And now she was to leave town, without time to talk to Meg in person.

"I appreciate you speaking with me," Christine answered, thoughts flying across her mind. What could Mr. Grenville's trip to France mean?

Mr. Oakley straightened himself as he looked up and saw Lizzy descending the stairs. "I am glad to have that burden lifted," he said quietly toward Christine. Christine gawked at him. This was all he would say?

Christine's maid came back to her again and said, "Begging you pardon, miss, but they are waiting for us at the carriage."

Christine nodded and gathered her skirts around her, looking again at Mr. Oakley. "Thank you." Christine curtsied, full of wonder and suspicion. *What a strange conversation*, she thought. Christine knew she must talk to Meg. She would write as soon as she could.

Christine entered her father's carriage and they drove away from Rothershire and toward London, traveling near the peaks and cliffs she visited with Lizzy. Christine asked her father if they might stretch their legs a moment, for she dearly wished to behold the scene one more time. She would not let opportunities pass her any longer.

Mr. Harrison acquiesced readily, and the two exited the carriage. Christine breathed deeply, circling her arms around herself. As she stood among those high, stalwart cliffs, she formed a resolution. Their presence spoke to Christine once more, reminding her that she could change. She could be more steadfast in her desires. She determined then to look outward, toward others, and stop caring about herself and her status in life. She affirmed that day that she did not need high connections to validate her existence. She did not need a man to establish or promote her social standing. And perhaps most importantly, Christine resolved to never again let these base motives stand in her way of real and lasting relationships with the people around her.

And as for love and marriage? She would only allow herself to care for another wholly and completely based on character and not position or wealth. That was true, lasting love, if she could but find it.

Christine took one last look at her surroundings and remembered she must make it to London in haste. She hurried back inside the carriage, and they did not stop except for when they reached the inn that night. The next day Mr. Harrison would deposit her at Ivory's and then be off for his most important week of the year settling his accounts, and Christine could start to look for Kathryn. How she would find her, Christine still did not know.

The next morning, as they reentered the coach, Mr. Harrison said, "I am sorry I will not be able to spend much time with you and Miss Rusket, Christine."

"Do not worry, Father, I understand. It is not your obligation to visit with the Ruskets. You have much to attend to! It will just be a nice diversion to stay with Ivory, it really was so thoughtful of her to invite me for a visit. I will be plenty busy with her and her multitudinous social engagements," Christine said, knowing that she might be employed in a different sort of way than her father thought.

Christine longed to tell him of her quest but knew he would forbid her from taking any action. He would deem it much too dangerous for his daughter.

Christine acknowledged to herself that there could be some danger involved, if the man who employed Kathryn was truly as vile as he seemed from the letter. Would he resort to violence? Coercion? But Christine knew she had to find Kathryn, after promising Cook, no matter the risk that would befall her.

Late in the evening, the carriage pulled up to the Rusket mansion, Molliard Place, their path opening to a stone archway. Christine and Mr. Harrison came inside the massive wooden door and through to the marble antechamber while two servants unloaded Christine's bags quickly. Christine remembered the great white hall with baby-blue curtains she had seen last summer as they prepared for Mr. Robertson's aunt's ball. The warm setting sun shone through, but the coldness of the house still permeated the walls. A coldness, Christine acknowledged, which came less from the marble stone and more from the stoic interactions of the Rusket family.

Lord and Lady Molliard greeted Mr. Harrison with civil decorum, and he said goodbye to Christine, assuring her he would be back in one week's time. Christine kissed him goodbye and wished him luck with his accounting. He bowed to the rest of the party and exited.

Miss Rusket greeted Christine warmly as her parents gave subdued nods in Christine's direction. Christine quickly washed up and changed her gown and then came down in her best dress to dine in a late supper with Ivory as well as Lord and Lady Molliard. It was quite the formidable dinner party, and Christine did not offer much to the already sparse conversation. Christine thought then of the diplomatic but distant relationship Ivory entertained with her parents. Lord and Lady Molliard's desire for Ivory to make a perfect match clearly showed, and Christine felt glad that, most nights, she and Ivory would dine out at one of Ivory's engagements.

As soon as was appropriate, Ivory excused herself and Christine to check the status of Christine's things and settle in for the evening.

Christine had been debating just how much detail she wanted to divulge about her plan, and she decided she had better wait until morning to give any incriminating particulars.

The next morning, the girls awoke and dressed to go out, taking a late breakfast in the breakfast room, its striped wallpaper greeting them cheerfully. Attempting to enlist Ivory as little as would be absolutely necessary, Christine asked her willing friend to take her carriage around London and see part of the city she had never seen before.

"Of course! You ought to come to London a great deal more, you know!" Ivory commented, duly willing to oblige and having a carriage at her disposal each morning anyway.

Christine smiled, pleased at how easily her plan began.

The girls started in the normal boroughs and drove most of the morning, Ivory pointing out all of her friends' large manors. That night they were to attend a dinner at the home of one of Ivory's male interests, so they returned in the afternoon to prepare. By the time they came back to Molliard Place, Ivory became suspicious of Christine's several questions. As they walked into the drawing room Ivory asked, "Why were you asking so much about those small low-class areas we kept passing?"

Christine's shocked look all but betrayed her plan. Should she divulge her design? She quickly analyzed the benefits and negatives. It would prove helpful to have an accomplice, but Christine did not want Ivory to stop her from finding Kathryn.

"If you must know," Christine began, "I am looking for someone."

"Why did you not say so in the first place? I am sure I could help you find whomever it is you are looking for! I know where *all* the prominent families live."

"That is just it. This woman is *not* of a prominent family. She has no family . . . in London, you see. I only know the general area where she lives. It is among the lowest of the gentry."

"Oh." Ivory's tone changed. "Who are you looking for, then? And why?"

Christine fiddled with her hands, still unsure of how many details she should offer. "If I tell you, you must promise me you will not stop me from finding her. I will understand if you do not want to help me any further, but I cannot alter my plans. I must assist her, for I promised someone I would."

Ivory scrutinized Christine's face for a moment, which returned a serious expression. "You can tell me," Ivory said gently. "I will keep your secret safe."

Christine pursed her lips and looked even more intently at her friend. Ivory crossed her arms and nodded slightly. Ivory could and would keep her secret. They walked to the corner of the room and huddled together, and Christine lowered her voice. "Her name is Kathryn. She is the daughter of Wellington's cook, who asked me to find her. She has fallen into a situation with a dissolute man and must not continue with him or she will be ruined."

"Your cook, Cooper right? She has a daughter?" And then just as alarmed, Ivory asked, "You have a friendship . . . with your cook?"

"Never mind the friendship, Ivory! Some of us are not *so* high and mighty that yes, we talk to our servants! This girl is in need of our help."

"I see. You must find Kathryn Cooper then?"

"Yes. We need to find Kathryn, Mrs. Cooper's daughter. Although I do not believe Cooper to be the girl's surname." Christine unfolded the letter Kathryn had written to her mother and pointed to the end. "She signed it here. The return has been badly sullied. But she works as a maid prese—"

Ivory's gasp curtailed Christine's speech immediately and her eyes widened, filling with disbelief and worry. She grabbed the letter from Christine's hands. "I would know that handwriting anywhere. Miss Kathryn O'Rourke was my personal tutor for four years."

CHAPTER 18

Thre was no keeping Ivory out of Christine's scheme now.

"Let me read it," Ivory said, pouring over the contents several times. Christine watched as Ivory's eyebrows furrowed. "I do not understand," Ivory said finally, holding her face in her hands. "Miss O'Rourke is not a maid. She is a very well-educated teacher."

"You are sure it is the same person, Ivory?"

"Yes, quite. I watched her handwriting for years. Remember at Cassfield I told you my mother dismissed her. Although I had no idea she was related to your cook all this time!"

"And have you heard from her since she was dismissed?" Christine probed.

"No, come to think of it, I wrote her one letter, but I had never heard back from her—which, by the way, is terribly unlike her. She is so good and sweet, I cannot believe this is happening to her." The initial shock had now subsided as Ivory's sadness took over.

Ivory began telling Christine of her relationship with Miss O'Rourke, starting four years ago and leading up to last year. It appeared they were much more than teacher and pupil; in fact, Miss O'Rourke had been the kindest mentor she had ever known. Ivory felt more love from her than from either of her parents.

"And then one day, she just left," Ivory said, looking down at her hands. "She did not even say goodbye to me. Mother told me what I have told you. I mourned her leaving for days on end. I had been spending time with that wretched Mr. Braxton, and he had just informed me that he did not wish to court me any longer, just the day after Miss

O'Rourke left. He simply left a letter. My whole world had been shattered within two days' time. I felt so crestfallen to lose Miss O'Rourke and so embarrassed that a man who was hardly a gentleman could refuse to pursue me."

"Wait," Christine said, narrowing her eyes, "Was this the man who broke your heart just before you met Mr. Robertson? The one you wrote to Lizzy and me about?"

"Yes, I am afraid so," she said looking to the floor. "I am ashamed I fell for him. I was *humiliated* that I was once connected with him, so I never mentioned his name to you. And I deliberately left out the connection to his sister's name when writing about Mr. Davenport."

Christine's head felt dizzy, trying to connect the details. "So his name is Braxton? And he has a sister? The very one you wrote to me about—who married Mr. Davenport?"

"Oh yes, that is the one," she said, defeated. "Quite a family, I have to say. Cheats and liars, the whole of them. But we are not talking about the Braxtons. I do not want to even *think* about them. We need to find Miss O'Rourke."

"Yes, you are right," Christine said, leading Ivory to the closest couch. They sat down, still huddled together as they continued to discuss. "We must get to the bottom of this right now. I think it might help my understanding. What happened to Mr. Braxton after he stopped courting you? Who did he pursue next? Is he married now?"

Ivory looked away and sighed. "I lost track of him for some while—I guess I should truthfully say that I ignored anything about him. Last I heard, he coerced some poor girl with no fortune to become his wife or mistress or something. When I heard that, I could finally let his vile character go. I could not believe he would fall so low. I was so grateful I did not make a match with him. No one hears from him these days. He does not come to any parties or gatherings. He is an outcast—officially now, although before it was implied based on his inferior birth and questionable employment— from anyone of status. His sister and Mr. Davenport occasionally make an appearance, keeping up their pretense of gentility. They live in a shanty of a great house on the edge of anywhere respectable in town. But no one can really tolerate their company."

The tightness in the air was palpable as Christine and Ivory realized the connections before them. It all seemed too coincidental. Ivory knew Miss O'Rourke and Mr. Braxton. They both left her life around the same time. Miss O'Rourke had been found with a man in her quarters, and the story of Mr. Braxton's life and where he now was sounded too similar to what Kathryn had described in her letter.

"Do you know where Mr. and Mrs. Davenport live?" Christine asked after a few moments of contemplative silence.

"I have been there once, I think, when Mr. Braxton used to live there," Ivory said, looking down.

"Perhaps that is where Kathryn works as their maid. We must go there tomorrow," Christine resolved.

"Yes, I think I remember the area, and I would know the house if I saw it again," Ivory said quietly, still quite in shock.

At that moment, Christine and Ivory saw the hem of Lady Molliard's gown encroach into the doorway of the drawing room.

"Hello, mother," Ivory said without emotion.

"Oh hello, dear," Lady Molliard replied. "Should you not prepare for your dinner tonight?"

"Oh, yes of course," Ivory said, standing.

Christine hoped Lady Molliard had heard nothing of their secrets.

Christine and Ivory hastily excused themselves to their rooms to freshen up before they went out, but truly they needed to gain composure and absorb what had been said. Ivory did not speak as they ascended the stairs. Christine could hear her start sobbing as the door closed.

The two young ladies emerged an hour later, perfectly plaited and poised, to travel to dinner. Although Christine still had much on her mind, Ivory's friends and their dinner did not disappoint, with a Mr. Ternbridge hosting them. He seemed to be in the running for Ivory's current favorite and, as Ivory had promised Christine, had a handsome friend as well. That Mr. McMilne made even Christine laugh more than once throughout the evening, and for a few moments he distracted her thoughts from finding Kathryn.

Ivory excused herself and Christine fairly early that night, and as the girls rode home, they knew without speaking what must be done tomorrow.

She had four days left in London. Tomorrow they would continue the pursuit and somehow bring back Kathryn.

The next day was spent entirely in Ivory's carriage. Ivory quickly lied to Lady Molliard that they were off to visit Mr. Ternbridge, amply exaggerating the fact that she was furthering her male prospects.

Christine knew that Ivory understood exactly what had happened—that her own teacher was also involved with her own previous suitor—but Ivory handled the situation with a level of grace that spoke to her true character.

After breakfast, the girls went out to the carriage house, where a spry groom waited to assist them. He hastily mounted the riding box, and Ivory ordered him to drive toward one of her friends' estates. But then, when the girls were a few blocks away from Ivory's manor, Christine motioned to the driver to stop. She needed to have a conversation with Ivory's servant that she was sure Ivory was not comfortable having.

"Excuse me," Christine started as she opened the door of the carriage and curved her head outside, "today will be a bit unusual. I need you to keep what I tell you just between the three of us."

He looked through the window at Ivory and then nodded, duly intrigued.

"I am here to find a servant who belongs to my household. Her mother works for me and I need to locate her daughter. We believe we know the general area where she is employed, but it may take some time to find the exact house."

The groom nodded and tightened his lips.

"This is where we need your skill. We must drive until we find her. Her situation is somewhat precarious, and at times we may need to stay hidden until just the right moment. We will tap on the wall when we want you to drive or follow someone. Do you think that we will be able to communicate that way?"

"Yes, of course, miss." He paused a moment, rubbing his shaggy red hair and then continued. "If you want me to stop, tap twice. If you want me to go, tap once. And if you want me to follow, tap three times quickly and I will follow whoever I see a-movin'." His tone turned more excited toward the end of this speech, and Christine smiled, guessing that today held more adventure than an entire six months of his usual occupation. Extracting the letter from her purse, Christine showed him the smudged address. Miss Rusket then spoke to him, directing him to the general area.

"One last thing," Christine said as she closed the door, "You must keep us safe. I do not want damage of this carriage on my hands."

Christine meant this statement more lightly than he took it, his freckled face turning to pale ash. He was invested in this cause and his carriage, and they started off to the borough he believed those streets to be in.

Christine pulled herself inside and turned back toward Ivory, smoothing her hair. "Does Mr. Braxton have some type of employment?" Christine asked, seeing Ivory's shock, trying to seem like a conversation of that manner with a groom was completely routine.

Ivory smiled at her unconventional friend. "I believe he deals with the port. Perhaps shipments of some sort? He was very vague with me about his dealings. Although . . . rumors abound about what he does. He acts like a gentleman, though."

"No doubt he was vague because what he does is illegal," Christine said under her breath. The depth of this man's debauchery knew no bounds.

Their groom headed toward the ports, so Ivory's information must have been correct. The houses became smaller and more ramshackle, attempting the look of grandeur but falling short. They were large, to be sure, all two or three stories tall. Yet paint flaked from the sides of houses. Some doors hung askew, with several windows so cloudy they seemed uninhabited. Then the driver continued further toward the docks, and Christine saw many ragged urchins, unkempt women, and dirty-faced men walking through the alleyways. Christine had never seen such a place in her life, and the raw earthiness of the scene took her aback.

"This is futile. How will we ever find them?" Christine asked Ivory as they passed docks. "Surely it must be back a few blocks?"

"Yes, I believe you are right. I never would have traveled to this part of town."

Christine motioned the driver to stop and peered just two inches out her window.

"Please take us back toward those houses a few blocks to the west. The tall ones, with the peeling paint. We want to go up and down each street there."

Ivory nodded at all Christine said, and the groom found a place for the carriage to turn around. After two blocks, Ivory's gaze became more intense as she studied each home they passed.

Christine sat lost deep in thought, when she felt Ivory stiffen, her eyes jutting to the left. Christine spun her head around.

"See that man and woman over there?" Ivory said, barely pointing to a dark-haired woman and a tall man, going behind what looked to be a cobbler's shop a hundred feet away. She need not say anything else. Even without knowing the woman, the man's sure gait was unmistakable to Christine. They had found Mr. and Mrs. Davenport. Not quite Mr. Braxton, but perhaps he was close.

Christine swallowed hard, pushing down the rush of emotions that erupted from somewhere within her. She gripped the edge of her seat cushion, her whole body tensing.

You have to put this aside, Christine, she thought to herself. *This is your chance to find Kathryn.* She took several deep breaths. Ivory had cast off her personal feelings to help Kathryn, and so must she. It took everything within her to let go of her past with Mr. Davenport. Part of her wanted to stop the coach and rush up to him and let him know that she was there. The other part of her wanted to hide, to retreat, knowing he had found someone and left her alone. Christine said a silent prayer for the pain and anger to dissipate. She could and would champion her feelings. She gathered herself to her purpose and reached for Ivory. "We must follow them." She rapped on the roof three times, and the groomsman increased his speed, turning the corner to not lose sight of the couple.

Ivory grasped Christine's hand, pressing it with great feeling.

Mr. Davenport and his new bride had no idea the young ladies were anywhere near. Another carriage had just passed, but Christine and Ivory had gained enough speed to now see their faces clearly. The couple laughed, Mr. Davenport clearly inebriated, as they disappeared around another corner. The girls watched them both enter a wagon with a *B* painted on the edge. The young ladies continued to follow Mr. Davenport until Christine tapped the roof twice and the groom stopped. Ivory and Christine watched with guarded eyes from their carriage. Mr. Davenport stepped out of his wagon, walked into a business, and then returned ten minutes later, leaving the wagon there. Then a much finer carriage pulled up to the business and, after he and his wife entered, drove to a more pleasant part of town. Tapping three times, the girls' carriage now followed the Davenports to the nicer area of the borough, where Mr. and Mrs. Davenport exited.

"This is it! I remember the blue trim on the front," Ivory said in a whisper.

Christine's gaze looked intently at Ivory. "Are you sure?"

Ivory nodded slowly. "So what shall we do now?"

"I think we must wait until Mr. and Mrs. Davenport leave. Then perhaps we could sneak in through the servants' quarters and speak with Kathryn."

"But what if Braxton is home?" Ivory asked.

"That is true," Christine said, as she knit her brow. "Perhaps we should watch the house for some time."

It was just past noon, and the girls decided to watch for at least an hour or two. There was little movement of the house, excepting a maid leaving from around the back, which confirmed the servants' entrance to Christine and Lizzy. The young ladies watched an hour longer, during which Mrs. Davenport exited the house, a large man's coat covering her as she entered a carriage, Mr. Davenport following behind her.

The girls had no way of knowing if Kathryn was somewhere inside, or if Braxton could be in the house at that moment. But Christine knew at least the Davenports were absent, and this might be their best chance to act.

"Stand at the ready," Christine told the groom as the girls slinked along the side wall toward the servant's entrance. "We could return at any moment."

Mr. William Robertson

William Robertson lay prostrate on the ground of the shipping yard next to his brother and Mr. Oakley, all three covered by a pile of planks.

William lifted his head slightly and pointed toward a man driving a large wagon which had just pulled up to the street behind them that led from the docks into town. "I know that must be him! It is indeed the same marking you described?"

"Aye, brother, the very same," Henry replied quietly, pointing at a painted *B* in the corner. The brothers and Mr. Oakley had been there for most of the morning, waiting for their fabric shipment to arrive via cargo boat. At fifteen minutes to three, the expected vessel docked, tied up, and its driver lowered the offloading ramp. Seeing this as his cue, William, dressed as a longshoreman, jumped up from his covert spot and scurried across the dock to make sure it was indeed their shipment. He knew he had to move fast, before the real longshoremen came to unload the cargo.

William jumped over the mooring cleat and headed toward the large crates, prying the first open a bit. Inside shone beautiful crimson silk. He twisted the fabric in between his fingers and looked at the slightly variegated pattern.

"It is our stock, for sure," he said under his breath. "Ordered just two months ago."

Satisfied, he then tried to weave through the boxes back to where Henry and Mr. Oakley lay hiding. Having verified the shipment, they needed only to watch who took it and follow behind them on horseback.

Just then, however, the actual longshoremen arrived to take the goods. William dashed behind the stack of crates, but it was too late.

"What are you doin' 'ere?" a round, burly man bellowed.

Caught, and trying to play the part, William stammered, "I was sent here to unload these 'ere crates. They send you too?"

"You scrawny mutt, how did they ever let you get a job?" the big man said, and William noticed two other thick men behind him. All three began walking toward William, arms folded across their chests.

"We hain't 'bout to let another man get our pay, y'see, so you best be going." The men closed in on William, coming close enough that he could smell their stench.

"Or we could make him do our work for us," another one of the men said. "I'll sit back and supervise the likes of ya." William observed the scabbed-over knuckle he was pounding into a fist as he said it, and no one argued with him.

Just then a gapped-toothed foreman came up to the four of them.

"You boys ready to work?" he asked gruffly.

"Yes sir," the biggest man said, puffing himself up.

"And I don't recognize you," the foreman said, pointing to William with a dirty fingernail.

William watched as the foreman muttered something under his breath and pulled out his flask to take another guzzle. William noticed the way the foreman shifted his eyes to the side, but the three longshoremen did not seem concerned. William thought then that although this foreman was in the beginnings of a drunken stupor, he might have still registered that something was awry, perhaps not as daft as he looked.

"Now you listen to me, chaps," the foreman bellowed when he finished swallowing. "No matter what happens, you make sure that the man with the large wagon gets his goods." He pointed over his shoulder to the curly-haired man sitting in the box of the wagon painted with the *B* on the side. The foreman continued, "He will be transporting them to a shop in the next town tomorrow."

Immediately, the three burly longshoremen started loading the crates, pushing William along in front of them. William tried to make eye contact across the dock with Henry and Mr. Oakley, who still remained hidden, but unable to communicate with them, William determined to continue to play along as he unloaded the crates down the dock.

As they finished loading the last crate, William startled as he looked up and saw a tall, well-dressed man walking briskly toward the wagon. William knew in an instant that it was Mr. Davenport. He seemed alert, unlike the curly-haired driver, and seemed to be the brains of the operation. Could it really be him? William thought of the Mr. Davenport he knew in school, remembering the way he coerced colleagues to get what he wanted. He doubted it was a personality trait he had outgrown, and as he considered it, it must have been how he had convinced Christine Harrison to be interested in him a few months ago.

But this was a new facet of his deceit. William shot a look toward Henry and Oakley, wondering if they noticed Mr. Davenport as well. If Mr. Davenport saw William, all would be lost. Looking around him, William realized it would be too suspicious to run across the dock. He had no hat and no coat, no way to cover himself as Mr. Davenport came closer. Having loaded the last crate, William decided he had no choice but jump in the back of the wagon and wedge himself in between the cargo until Mr. Davenport passed.

The three other longshoremen had already returned to the foreman, looking for payment, purposefully grabbing their coin before William joined them. William heard them as they walked off, joking about how they scared the poor scrawny mutt out of his share.

Thirty seconds later, Mr. Davenport grasped the front of the wagon and mounted the box, and he began explaining something quietly to the driver. The wagon immediately started rumbling toward the foreman. The driver paused for a brief moment as the foreman said, "Mr. Braxton, sir, sumthin' seems a bit off. One of the longshoremen today I didn't hire. I ain't the smartest of the lot, but yer'd have to be mad to not notice that somethin' was fishy among those longshoremen."

"What makes you think that, Scab?" Mr. Braxton scoffed.

"Didn't ya see the one of 'em? He was much too clean, 'an too sober. Not like most of 'em I hire. I think they be up to sumthin', though he didn't come back fer payment so maybe they scared 'im off," Scab the gap-toothed foreman replied.

"Never bother, Scabby. To you, everyone's cleaner and more sober," Mr. Davenport chortled, waiving his hand nonchalantly and clapping Scab on the back. "I have just given instruction to Braxton here, and now I have a rendezvous with that tavern. Would you want to join me there to talk about our next deal?"

Scab nodded vigorously. Mr. Davenport jumped down from the wagon, and he and Scab crossed to the tavern. William watched through the slats in the wagon as the man named Mr. Braxton slowly chewed his tobacco, trying to rouse himself from his drunken stupor, and gave one long spit before he turned the wagon around.

All this time, William dared not move. As the wagon moved away from the docks, William observed Henry and Oakley pull themselves out of hiding and walk slowly toward the horses they had tethered near the tavern a few hundred feet away, watching for Mr. Davenport.

The wagon picked up speed, traveling quickly away from the docks. The driver named Braxton turned several times, and William hoped that Henry and Oakley had made it to their horses fast enough to follow them. William watched through the slats as the wagon wound through several more streets, moving far away from any sort of shipping and receiving area and well into the slums of London.

William started to worry more with every turn, knowing nothing had gone as planned. They were all to follow the wagon on horse, see where they deposited the shipment, and then go to the local magistrate and explain the fraud, possibly leaving one of them to keep watch. But now William lay in between the crates, completely at the mercy of this Mr. Braxton. *When it does not go to our tailor, we can catch them red-handed*, thought William. But he knew this mode of uncovering the smugglers to be much more dangerous than he had anticipated. He did not know how to escape without discovery.

William felt the pistol still lodged in his pocket. He thanked himself for making sure to carry one that day. How would he escape without Braxton noticing? He had never drawn a gun on a man, and he wondered just what he might have to do to defend himself if Henry and Oakley took too long. Would they be able to find him? What if they were delayed at the dock?

But then the wagon turned before William expected, having traveled no more than a few blocks further into some more developed houses. The houses looked as though each might have been grand but now stood a shadow of someone's money fallen from grace. Next to one particular house, they approached a small, dark alleyway. The wagon slowed into the tight easement, fitting snugly between two long townhouse rows.

This was the destination? Should he try to exit the wagon? Could he run the other way without Braxton noticing? Or should he stay put for a moment longer?

Before William had a chance to reposition himself, Mr. Braxton lit from the wagon box, striding pompously to the back of the cart. William pressed himself against the wooden crates, holding his breath, bracing for eminent discovery.

And then, through the slits in the wood, William noticed two well-off and out-of-place young women in his periphery. They carried a shabbily dressed servant between them, held in their arms, dragging her away out the servant door of the large blue town house next to them. It was a scene entirely otherworldly for such a place as this. But the woman in the middle fit this part of town, or looked even more destitute, seeming dejected, with dirty, unkempt hair falling across her ashen face. As he continued to watch the young ladies, he realized the woman in the middle had a bruised and emaciated body covered with a threadbare gown, which hung off of one of her shoulders.

Remembering his precarious state, William clutched his pistol on his waistband and expected the worst kind of confrontation from his driver. Braxton's calloused and strong hands clutched the wagon flap and raised it halfway, no longer holding in the wooden box hiding William. One more move from Braxton and William would lay visible. But then Braxton suddenly froze.

Mr. Braxton's eyes shot back to the open door. The women were far away now, trying to turn the corner out of the alley, but not entirely out of earshot as he yelled, "Get back here, you disgraceful tramp, good for nothing! You belong to me." The wagon flap clattered closed again and he started charging after the women, into the dark alley, at a dead run.

William had little time to think. He must allow the women to be attacked or risk his own discovery. Instinct trusted that no matter what Braxton was doing, he must be in the wrong. The emaciated lass looked over her shoulder and then tripped. The two young ladies continued to drag her as best they could, barely picking up speed and still struggling. Braxton would overtake them in a matter of seconds.

William pushed out of the wagon and began to run after Braxton. He grasped his pistol, lifting his weapon, and shot intentionally to the left, just beyond the women and Braxton, shattering debris off the side of a row house. Braxton turned around and stopped dead, looking square into the eyes of William, not one hundred feet from him. He drew his pistol quickly and, without wasting a second, fired directly at William. The bullet lodged deep into William's left shoulder, knocking him to the side. *Thank goodness he was drunk,* William thought wryly as the pain struck and he fell to the ground.

Mr. Braxton turned to run again, seemingly unfazed by his brutal action. William gathered everything he had in him and stood, shooting his last bullet, this time not as a warning but as the only way he could think to stop this incensed man, aiming at Braxton's left leg. William seldom missed, and this was no exception. Braxton stopped and twisted in pain, his face livid that his first attempt had not been enough. Deliberate and furious, Braxton limped toward William. He lifted his pistol once again, hefted his weight onto his right leg, and steadied himself. William, seeing that Braxton would not stop, moved swiftly toward his opponent with a force beyond himself. In one motion, William seized Braxton around his husky trunk and threw him to the ground as Braxton's aimed pistol discharged in the air. William, with his only good arm, swung the butt of his gun around and knocked Braxton on the side of his head. Oozing, sanguine blood dripped from the cuts on Braxton's forehead, and he fell unconscious.

William stood slowly, blinking and wincing, the sun becoming brighter and brighter. Was Braxton dead? And the women—where were they now?

William slowly teetered back toward the wagon, looking to see if he should follow them. This had not been his design—he had not planned on confronting Braxton, especially alone. He just wanted to track the shipment. And that poor woman and the ladies saving her . . .

William turned and staggered toward the wagon box, losing blood rapidly, his mind turning white. He was all alone and far too close to Mr. Braxton, if he came to.

And then there was silence.

CHAPTER 19

The sound of a gunshot rang in Christine's ears. She and Ivory pushed forward, supporting Kathryn between them. Kathryn's matted brown hair brushed their shoulders, and her bruised face grimaced in pain and fear, tears streaking down her dirty face.

"Hurry, HURRY!" Christine whispered to Ivory. "Ignore the man! Kathryn, you must help us if you can." Christine and Ivory glanced over their shoulders as Kathryn took a long look behind them. Christine caught a glimpse of the fear in Kathryn's eyes, and then Kathryn fell limp in their arms.

Suddenly they heard another gunshot ricochet through the air. Ivory let out a gasp and increased her pace. Ivory, despite her layered skirt, ran faster than any female Christine had ever known. Adrenaline coursed through Christine veins, and they ran harder, trying to pull Kathryn along, pressing forward as best they could.

How far is the carriage? Christine's mind screamed as they finally turned the corner of the alley. The footman had heard the gunshots and had started moving the coach toward the entrance. He jumped from his post and whisked Kathryn out of their arms and up into the squabs. Christine followed Ivory into the carriage and shut the door tightly behind them. The groom swung into his seat and began driving at bolt-breaking speed past the alley and back roads, toward Ivory's estate.

For several moments, Christine's brain and body moved at the same pace of the carriage. The full ramification and import of what had just occurred did not register. It was several minutes before Ivory's breathing calmed and Christine gained some composure.

"At least she finally consented to come with us," Christine ventured, looking carefully out the carriage window and finally gaining her self-possession. "How long should it take her to wake?"

Christine met Ivory's eyes, which still seemed filled with worry. Kathryn's limp body lay in the carriage, her head resting on Christine's lap, eyes closed with mouth slightly opened. Her breathing was slow and steady, but the poor, sullied girl did not wake.

Christine recalled the scene they had just endured, putting together the full danger she had exposed them to. They had entered the servants' quarters not one hour earlier and were warily directed upstairs, where they found Kathryn slumped over on an armchair in one of the back bedrooms with large bruises on her arms and face from the latest beating. Mr. Braxton had stayed with the Davenports for the past few weeks, and when Kathryn had entered his room to stock the firewood, he again pressed her to stay with him. She resisted his advances, and she explained to Christine and Ivory that though she had been planning to escape, she had not yet saved enough money to make the journey to her mother. Mr. Braxton had threatened Kathryn that if she ever tried to leave, he would find and harm Miss Rusket in retaliation. Kathryn had not known what to do, and that morning as she resisted, Braxton's temper flared worse than ever before.

Now Kathryn was not much better—quite unconscious—but at least they saw her thin frame begin to stir beneath her threadbare servant dress.

Kathryn had told them wearily of her circumstances that afternoon, and the young ladies—especially Ivory—convinced her that she must leave, that Braxton could do nothing to harm her and that Kathryn deserved to be free of such imprisonment. Kathryn had been so weak she could hardly walk. Braxton had just finished this morning telling her that she was nothing, did nothing, and could become nothing.

Christine realized then, as Kathryn had indicated in her letter, that the poor girl really did not believe she could elevate to any greater status than what she had resigned herself to with Braxton.

Christine knew removing Kathryn was the only solution—and luckily Ivory was able to remind her of her past and coax her out of her circumstances.

The carriage slowed to a much steadier pace—for surely the groom knew that a raging carriage through inner London would raise suspicion—and Kathryn began to revive, her blue eyes fluttering open at last. They were her only attribute that hinted of beauty as she lay there. She pushed her hair out of her face and sat up slowly, clinging to the edge of the carriage seat for balance. She then gazed across the coach at Ivory.

"Where is he?" she said, nervously pulling at her skirt. "Has he gone? Is he following us?" Her voice was hoarse and hushed.

"Miss O'Rourke," Ivory began, laying her hand over Kathryn's, "he is gone. He cannot harm you, he will not hurt me, and I daresay you will never see him again." Ivory smiled at Christine and then back at Kathryn, exhaling slowly. "Now listen carefully, as I must explain the next part of our journey."

Kathryn O'Rourke started crying quietly as Ivory began to speak. The shock and relief she felt at once overcame her.

"I imagine my mother," Ivory said, "does not particularly want you in our household again. I have spoken to the servants"—Christine looked aghast at Ivory to think of her speaking to the servants—"and we will hide you in their quarters. They knew you were dismissed without cause and have agreed to stay silent. My maid will attend to you tonight. You are to stay in her chamber and not leave. You will be returning with Miss Harrison here and her father in a few days. Do you understand?"

Kathryn O'Rourke's face filled with gratitude and disbelief.

"Miss Rusket I . . . I cannot thank you enough," she said, bowing her head.

"And I promise to take you to your mother," Christine added, smiling at Kathryn.

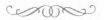

Mr. Henry Robertson

Henry and Mr. Oakley mounted their horses and took off in the direction of the wagon. But the wagon had gained speed and turned a few times, and Henry and Oakley were unsure of its movements.

As they rode, questions filled Henry's mind. *What if they could not find William? Was he still hiding? Which way had the wagon gone?*

Catching a trail of dust, Henry yelled to Oakley, "Follow me this way—I think I see something!"

They continued out of the dilapidated apartments, coming to the edge of some old townhouses. Just as the dust started to settle, Henry heard a few gunshots and turned to follow, Oakley coming up behind him. Henry pulled swiftly on the reins of his dark-brown horse, its black mane flipping recklessly. As he turned another corner, he spied a large house with peeling blue paint. They would have charged past, but Mr. Oakley pointed to a small alleyway behind it, with a stopped wagon.

From what Henry could see, the wagon held no driver. They charged into the alley, both dismounting their horses, as they hurriedly inched to the side of the wagon. There, draped eerily across the bench, lay William, his arm twisted in an unnatural, disconnected way. His shoulder was bleeding, making his entire shirt scarlet. Henry ripped off the edge of his shirt sleeve and made a tourniquet for William's collarbone. He wrapped it under William's arm and tied on top of his shoulder, carefully removing any bullet shards that he could see. The bone protruded through the broken flesh, and Henry did the best he could to cover the wound with his cloth.

Henry heard someone move and looked to see the driver of the wagon writhing on the ground as he regained consciousness. "What shall we do with him?" Henry breathed ominously at Oakley. "Shall I dispatch him?"

"Forget about him!" Oakley replied, securing William in the wagon. "We must go now!" Mr. Oakley gestured over his shoulder as another wagon came tearing down the street toward the alleyway.

Henry left the driver writhing and climbed into the wagon box, abandoning their horses. Henry knew there was no other way to escape with William. Taking the reins, he charged out of the alley toward the street. Oakley jumped in the back and pushed a few crates off the edge, trying to block the other wagon's path.

Henry looked over his shoulder, realizing the wagon coming down the street held Mr. Davenport and the foreman from the dock. Davenport must have recognized Henry as they mounted their horses and decided to follow them. Henry's heart sunk as he realized there was no way to outrun the other wagon. Theirs weighed more, carrying the heavy bolt boxes, and their only hope was to gain enough of a head start to impede Mr. Davenport and the foreman for as long as possible. They had to make it to Oakley's house so they could call a physician and save William's life. The shipment did not matter.

Henry glanced over his shoulder again as he saw the driver—Mr. Braxton he thought his name was—coming to in a rage with a vengeance to rival it. Braxton motioned to Scab, and the wagon stopped only briefly to pull Braxton inside as he yelled in pain. Having been blocked by the crates, they made a tight turn in the small alley and circumvented the house, chasing the Robertsons.

"Follow them," Henry heard Braxton fulminate against Davenport. "We shall kill them and retake the rest of the shipment." Oakley, in his haste, had only dislodged two crates, and four still remained in the back of the wagon.

The two wagons raced through the streets of London, much like a fox chasing a hound, Henry continuously throwing glances over his shoulder and Oakley apprising him of the shortening distance between their wagon and Mr. Davenport's. Henry could hear the crack of a whip behind him as their wagon quickened.

"He just pulled a pistol from the gun box," Oakley yelled to Henry. No sooner had he said it than a bullet whizzed to their left.

Henry looked over his shoulder to see the wounded but incensed Braxton opening fire on them, narrowly missing Oakley as they swerved onto a more open street.

Oakley, still in the back of the wagon, heaved out another crate toward Braxton and Davenport's wagon. Davenport swerved skillfully, the streets widening as the houses became more robust. Henry turned once more to see Mr. Davenport grasping Braxton's barrel. Henry could hear the fear in Davenport's voice as he yelled, "Hold your fire, you idiot! We cannot risk being found among these great houses. There will be too many witnesses."

"He has lowered his gun," Oakley said to Henry again, "but he is gaining on us!"

Henry lunged forward, trying to pick up speed. Oakley pushed out another crate, and Davenport veered left as it crashed to the ground.

Davenport's wagon closed in with only a hundred feet behind them as Henry finally spotted Oakley's large gated house two blocks away.

Braxton apparently gave no heed to Davenport—Henry heard another gunshot, this time close enough to send his ears ringing. The sound echoed off of the houses around them, and Henry could hear Davenport yell once more at Braxton.

Davenport could not have spoken too soon. There, Lord Ruggleston, the local magistrate, stood in front of his manor calling his horse. He lived only a block from Oakley and had come outside upon hearing gunshot.

Henry pulled past the sweep gate, jerking to a halt. As gravel sprayed the ground, Henry watched Davenport's wagon shutter to a stop as he jumped from the side. Scab, seeing his friend's action, attempted the same, but trailed much slower. Braxton, unable to move quickly, sat still and bleeding, discharging one more shot, shattering the box of Henry's wagon as he jumped out.

Henry rushed to the shattered side of the wagon bed as he saw Mr. Davenport roll across the street onto his feet. Scanning the large gate of a house next to him, Mr. Davenport bolted between the two thickest areas of shrubbery and did not stop running. Lord Ruggleston, just beginning to grasp the scene before him, focused on Scab and Braxton and their wagon and did not track Davenport's exit.

Do I follow Davenport? Henry wondered. Looking down at William, gray as the moon, his shirt soaked in blood, the only thing to do was secure medical attention. Having reached Oakley's front gate, Henry scooped his brother into his arms and ran inside.

"You there, call a physician directly," Henry yelled to the butler. "And you come with me," he said to a servant. "Bring me hot water and some linen."

Mr. Oakley trailed behind Henry and bellowed more orders to a servant as Henry scaled the stairs.

"I will see to everything William needs," Oakley said as he bounded the steps in twos and took William out of Henry's arms. "Lord Ruggleston is demanding you report to him immediately to assist in apprehension and questioning."

Henry gave a painful glance to his brother and then to Oakley. "You must let nothing happen to him."

"You have my word," said Mr. Oakley.

Henry turned and raced down the stairs, rushing out the front doors once again.

After several hours, Lord Ruggleston finally excused Henry from his questioning. It had been an arduous evening, and Henry wanted nothing more than to return to William. Mr. Davenport had made a clean break away, but Braxton and Scab had been caught and delivered to the courthouse. Braxton now lay detained and unconscious, close to bleeding to death, his thigh still oozing despite the bandage. Scab fumed, handcuffed in the cell downstairs. For the time being the case was not yet resolved, but it would hold for the night, and more investigation was needed to charge the men for everything they were guilty of. Henry mounted the horse he had borrowed from Lord Ruggleston and galloped home.

As he walked past Oakley's butler and up to the room that held William, Oakley came out and took Henry by the shoulders. Oakley met Henry's eyes but said nothing and sank into the armchair outside the room.

Henry went in and turned to the physician, whom Oakley's family had trusted for years. Henry saw that William's collarbone had been carefully reset, and his shoulder now carried several clean bandages.

"He has lost a great deal of blood. But he has only a slight fever, and I have stopped the wound from bleeding. I cannot tell yet if he will be able to use his left arm again, but there is a good chance he will live, if infection does not set in. It is a miracle he is still alive. Good thinking of you to stop the bleeding. Otherwise he would already be dead." The doctor paused, blowing out a large breath. "The only thing left to do is wait. He should turn within a day or so. If he does not revive by that time, I am afraid the infection will have taken over."

Henry shook the doctor's hand and gave him a solemn look of thanks. The doctor simply nodded and left quietly.

Through the night, Henry and Oakley sat in the room with William, hoping that the fever would break and he would recover. For a full day, William neither spoke nor moved due to the loss of blood. Henry spent most of that day pacing at the foot of William's bed. Oakley took to sitting quietly near William and left the room only once to briefly dispatch a short note to Lizzy, informing her he would not arrive at Rothershire for a few more days.

MR. WILLIAM ROBERTSON

The following morning, William gained enough strength to open his eyes and also take some warm broth. By the evening, he finally found strength to speak and relayed the details of Mr. Braxton's abrupt stop and the altercation that ensued. William could not thank his friends and his God enough for the way in which he was watched over. He had no movement in his arm and only a little feeling in his fingers, but he lived.

Over the next few days, the scenes of the dock replayed constantly in William's mind, and Henry and Oakley informed William of all that had happened while he was unconscious. Every spare minute, he thought about the details, trying to piece together each particular of the events from a few days ago.

On the third day around noon, William, Henry, and Oakley sat again discussing the course of events that befell them in the days previous. William was sitting up in his bed for the first time, a fresh shirt draped loosely over him.

"Oakley, I am sure I have told you, but I cannot remember what is in my head and what is not. Did I mention I saw two upper-class women dragging the destitute woman away? Why would such women escape with a servant through the back door? What were their connections?" William attempted to shift his bandaged arm and winced.

Oakley stood and looked across the room, hands clasped behind his back. "You did mention that yesterday. Another question I have thought: what were two upperclass young ladies doing in that part of town without a chaperone?"

"I do believe the woman they had with them was in dire straits. I hope they made it out successfully." William said as he attempted to shake his head slowly. "How I wish I knew the end to their story. Whatever became of them?" he said quietly as he stared out the window.

"Yes, it is all very puzzling," Mr. Oakley said. "It all seems so out of place and dangerous." The three sat there for a few minutes, and then Mr. Oakley spoke of their next few days. "I am supposed to leave as soon as I can to rendezvous with my dear Lizzy. Her parents are throwing us an engagement party, so I must return to Wellington Estate. I was *supposed* to leave yesterday, however involving myself with the likes of you two again causes me now to be rather behind." Oakley grasped Henry by the shoulder.

Henry lowered his head and responded with his hearty laugh, his great frame bouncing, holding his face in his hands. "I am sorry William and I dragged you into this, Oakley," Henry said.

William just smiled and tried to curtail his laugh, his wound smarting with every movement.

"I would not have wanted it any other way, and you know it," Oakley replied. "But perhaps you two adventure seekers should come with me to Wellington Estate before I make my way to Cassfield for the wedding in a few weeks. The Harrisons would not mind, and I could keep better eye on the both of you. We can arrange William so he is comfortable in the carriage. Surely there is nothing there that can harm either of you."

"Aye," William said quietly, "I think Henry and I would enjoy such a respite in Rothershire. Let us leave on the day after tomorrow. I will be well enough off by then."

As the day went on, William could not reconcile all of the feelings he had at the prospect of visiting Wellington Estate again. Could he admit to himself that perhaps Rothershire held some interest beyond recovering from his wound and checking on his textile business? Now that he knew who had exploited his business—and his actions had put an end to such dealings, could he think of other matters? Did the Harrison house—a handsome lady in particular—hold some other compelling reason to assent to traveling to Rothershire?

Chapter 20

*T*wo days after they rescued Kathryn, Mr. Harrison returned to collect Christine. She waited outside on the lush grounds of the Ruskets' manor, taking in all of the beautiful flowers and climbing ivy that surrounded the large alabaster house, pacing nervously as she anticipated her father's reaction to the whole event. Christine made sure she intercepted her father before he entered the Ruskets' home and asked him to take a turn around the garden. There she explained to him what had transpired, and asked if perhaps Wellington had room for another servant or if he knew of a governess position of some kind in Rothershire.

"My dearest Christine," Mr. Harrison said, hands wide and open, "how could you take such danger upon yourself? Surely you understand what harm you all could have found yourselves in!" He smiled softly and crossed his arms. "But I do have to say I admire your concern for Kathryn. It was quite noble of you. And since none of you are hurt, I shall not hold such a valiant act against you."

Mr. Harrison then cocked his head to the side and lifted his index finger in the air. "I believe your brother is beginning to need a governess for his two sons, come to think of it. Surely his eldest does, as rambunctious as he is! We shall see them in the next few weeks, and perhaps arrangements could be made. Until then, she may help out her mother in the kitchen, as we will have quite a few guests coming for the wedding."

After a quick exchange of thanks, Mr. Harrison and Christine paid their leave to Ivory and Lord and Lady Molliard and entered the carriage, Kathryn already hiding inside, having entered in the groom house from the servants' quarters.

"Thank you for taking me to Rothershire, Mr. Harrison," Kathryn said as they drove away.

"Of course. You shall be reunited with your mother soon," Mr. Harrison said nodding kindly in her direction.

"Thank you ever so much, sir," Kathryn said again, saying nothing else during the ride and sometimes dozing, but most often looking out the window. Her frame was still weak, and it would be some time before she would return to full health.

Mr. Harrison, on the contrary, seemed in the mood to talk, and after a minute of silence, he turned to Christine. "Did you have the opportunity of making any connections while in town?" he asked.

"Only a few, Father. But I did meet some of Ivory's acquaintances. She has a close relationship with a Mr. Ternbridge—I believe you know his father—and his friend Mr. McMilne might come through Rothershire in a few weeks. I told him perhaps you could write to him that you would be delighted to receive him at a dinner."

"Splendid, my dear girl. I will do just the thing. Remind me to take his card from you later." He smiled and rubbed his hands together. "And what of Miss Rusket's other connections—the Robertson brothers, for example?"

"Oh yes, well, we did not have the pleasure of seeing William or Henry, although I believe they were in town. Mr. Oakley was also in town, but I only saw him briefly one night, and there were so many people there we hardly spoke."

Mr. Harrison's brow furrowed a bit. "How strange. I would have thought them all to be at your same gatherings. Mr. Oakley is to return to Wellington very shortly. It is a pity you did not see the Robertsons either."

"Indeed, Father." Christine smiled to herself. "They are very good sort of gentlemen. I wish we had the opportunity of seeing more of them. I have felt for a long while that we ought to keep our acquaintance with them."

She then fell silent, musing over her feelings toward the Robertsons, her mind dwelling on William for a moment. She felt safe here in the carriage with only her father really listening or understanding, for Kathryn did not know who they spoke of. Her father would never tell anyone of her feelings. Perhaps her father wished Christine to see more of the Robertsons too.

It was then that Christine reflected on how much her feelings had changed since entering London a week ago. Just a few days prior, she had seen Mr. Davenport with his charming wife. Mr. Davenport had seemed happy, yet altered, now fallen from a higher state of being. And then, thinking of what her father said, Christine realized she wished quite strongly to see the Robertsons again—especially William. *But why?* she thought. He had been *quite* insufferable to her at their costume party, although quite articulate. But the last time they were together, when they discussed his mother and father, he had seemed so amiable—and genuinely so. And there was something in the way he looked at her. She need not remember his beautiful eyes and striking face without recalling him one of the handsomest men she had ever been acquainted with. But perhaps the most compelling aspect was the way he conducted himself—caring, perceptive, and smart. Not as gallant and flirtatious as some men she knew—but so much more real.

Christine sighed as she looked out the window. The streets had slowly changed from large gated estates and ornate places of business to smaller apartments and cottages. The sun shone promisingly, welcoming her home. The country lay before her, neat and orderly, open and beautiful, beginning to bloom. Her mind cleared like the landscape, and she realized that she could leave Mr. Davenport—with all of his attendant baggage—behind in London.

How fortunate I did not end up with such a man, she thought. He never truly loved her. Christine shuddered at the thought of being tied to him for life. She quelled the part of her that still missed him, her heart telling her she had been rescued from a terrifying fate. When would she have realized that he did not love her from the start, perhaps not even for a moment? He only loved her for her money and good standing. She hated to admit it, but she had been drawn to him for those same reasons. She stood no better than him.

And then her thoughts faltered at the next question bubbling in her mind.

Did she possess the ability to truly love? She read of love often in books, and she thought her infatuation with Mr. Davenport *was* love, but now she knew it was no such thing. Was she capable of such a feeling? Of caring more for another than for herself?

Love was not meant to be egotistical; instead it was the embodiment of unselfishness. She knew true love meant caring about others, concentrating effort in another's behalf.

She wanted someone she could give everything to. She wanted someone she could share all the joys of life with. Real joys like having children and meaningful relationships, not just money and status and holdings. Someone who cared more about her needs than his. And someone whom she cared about more than herself. That would be true happiness, true love. She sighed inwardly, thinking just how far her relationship with Mr. Davenport behaved from such a sentiment.

Could she ever find such a love?

CHAPTER 21

Christine returned home, and Lizzy received Mr. Oakley's letter a few days later, causing her nothing but worries and conjectures. Christine had tried to console Lizzy assuring her several times that day that all was well. It was not until Christine read the letter that she understood Lizzy's concern. What exactly had happened to Mr. Robertson?

"I heard nothing of his injury while staying with Ivory," Christine told Lizzy the next day. "Although I do not know how much I would have heard, for the first few days were spent helping Kathryn, as you know, and neither Mr. Oakley nor the Robertsons were present at the dinners I attended. I did see Mr. Oakley briefly early in the week there, at the home of a mutual acquaintance, but I hope he does not fault me for not coming to call more often while I was in London." Christine looked at her sister, whose worry had driven her into a cold, and she sniffled through Christine's entire retelling.

"We were quite busy, as you know, finding Kathryn, and we had to keep up Ivory's rigorous social calendar every evening. Can you believe Ivory has three different men interested in her currently? All three were at the same ball, and we had dinner with two of them. It is masterful and fearful to watch her at a dance. One of them has a friend whom I interacted with a fair amount, and I daresay he is quite charming."

Lizzy's eyes brightened at the change of subject. "Well that is rather fortunate! Ivory does always have *so* many connections. What is his name?"

"Mr. McMilne. I do not know if I would have been so interested had I seen him only once. But after a dinner, the ball, and when he and Mr. Ternbridge came to call on our last day, we saw a fair amount of each other."

"Ah I see! Mr. Ternbridge is one of Ivory's beaus?" Lizzy smiled.

"Yes, indeed. Perhaps the foremost contender at present. And Mr. McMilne said he was on his way to tour the north country and would be in Rothershire within the week. He said he shall be here in two days, and father has invited him to dine with us."

The conversation then turned to Kathryn, Christine giving Lizzy even more details. Kathryn was adapting splendidly for one with so much sorrow and distress in her past. Her mother accepted her with open arms. Christine admired Cook Cooper's forgiving nature, issuing no judgmental remarks and not feeling threatened that her daughter's misfortunes had hurt her family name.

The Harrison family was scheduled to journey to Cassfield within the next week and stay there until the wedding a few weeks after. And hopefully, after Cassfield, Kathryn would go to live in Christine's brother's household as the family's governess.

The next morning, after breakfast, Christine donned her riding clothes and had her maid hurriedly fix her hair in a simple low bun. She had decided to go through the edge of town and then visit Allensby House to meet up with Meg. Christine had much to say, for Meg would want to know all about Ivory and the men they had danced and dined with. Christine had invited Lizzy to come, but she declined, going up to the northeast wing to be on active scout duty, looking for any sign of Mr. Oakley's return.

Christine relished the thought of a long ride, for there was no sign of rain anywhere in the sky. She rode through the fields of Wellington all the way to the edge of town before she planned to turn around and finish at Allensby House. The sun radiated off the newly blossomed bushes and shrubs, a breeze rustling through the trees and making them sway back and forth. She decided riding into town might provide more added diversion, and just as she turned into the first street, she spotted Miss O'Rourke, who was running an errand for Cook Cooper.

Christine slowed her horse as she heard, "Hello, Miss Harrison," from Kathryn as she curtsied lightly. Christine stopped her horse and smiled in response. Christine could not help but notice how altered Kathryn was from a few days before. She was looking so improved—healthy skin with bruises fading, well-kempt hair—but most of all her countenance glowed with confidence and freedom she did not before possess.

"I wonder if you might direct me to the butcher's shop? It is only my second time in town, and I am a bit turned around," Kathryn said.

"Oh yes, my pleasure. Let me see. It is down that street, on the right." Christine gestured the way and watched Kathryn until she found it. She was about to turn her horse toward Allensby House when she suddenly looked up and saw a young man in the distance. He was tall and thin, well dressed, and, from what she could tell, very handsome. He wore a brown suit coat with a crisp white shirt underneath and lighter brown pants. A new gentleman in town intrigued her. He crossed directly in front of Christine's path, not fifteen feet ahead.

He turned his face a bit toward her, and Christine, realizing who it was, called out without thinking, "Hello there, Mr. Robertson!"

His head whipped sideways and he looked Christine square in the eye. She would not have forgotten that gaze if she had not beheld it for ten years. William Robertson came close to her cream horse as she pulled on the reigns.

"It is a pleasure to see you," she found herself saying. "I did not expect you in Rothershire. But you are looking well."

I should not have said so much. Too complimentary, she thought instantly. She recalled how often he had seemed put off by her.

But he bowed his respectfully. "Why thank you," he replied, smiling. "This is the only coat that can cover my bandaged arm."

Christine cocked her head, looking at his left arm wound tightly, which she had not noticed until he turned.

"Oh, that is right! I am very sorry to hear of your misfortune. Lizzy informed me that you had been injured. How is your arm? And may I ask what happened?"

Rambling, Christine. She pursed her lips shut.

"It was nothing of consequence," he said nonchalantly. Christine noticed he seemed a little less annoyed than he usually did when talking to her. Her eyes widened, after processing such a comment, for she did not believe that it was nothing. He laughed lightly and his eyes creased, narrowing mischievously just as they did when he had told Christine of his great plan for a dinner party a few months ago.

"I can see you do not believe my response. But I shall ask you a question instead."

Christine stared, surprised but pleased. "Go on, Mr. Robertson." Christine smiled eagerly.

"I happen to know that Edmund and Lizzy plan on a robust game of croquet tomorrow, which I fully intend to be a part of. I am sure we could use another player. Would you care to join us? Perhaps I shall explain myself then."

Christine shifted on her horse, willing herself to control the smile that overtook her mouth.

"Oh, yes, I would be happy to oblige," Christine said as she nodded her head and tried to think of something else engaging to say. This William was quite a different one than Christine was accustomed to. He seemed as eager to see her as she was to see him, which Christine found odd, considering his past coldness. But no matter the reason, Christine wanted to spend time with him. Something about him compelled her to want to know him more. His lighthearted invitation, his voice, even his stance drew her to him.

Christine realized the silence that hung between them and looked away from William.

He suddenly seemed to remember an urgent matter of business, clicking his heels together as he prepared to turn. He gave a quick bow. "I must be off," he said as his right arm placed his hat again on his head. "But shall I expect to see you tomorrow at noon?"

"Yes, at noon." Christine nodded, as she watched him walk away briskly. She had probably kept him from something important. She had no idea why he had come to town with Edmund. She had not her wits about her enough to ask him more in the course of their conversation.

Christine sighed to herself, her shoulders relaxing into contentment, not quite turning her horse until Mr. Robertson walked down another road out of sight. She gathered her reins triumphantly and rode to Allensby House with a pace she scarcely recognized, thinking only of her excitement for tomorrow. As she pulled up to Meg's front gates, her smile still had not left her lips.

"How do wedding preparations come along, Meg?" Christine asked as soon as she entered the drawing room at Allensby House. Meg sat embroidering a small, delicate piece of lace. "Is it all as you like?" Christine thought that perhaps by asking, she might learn if Meg knew Mr. Grenville's secret.

"Yes, it is. I feel quite prepared, excepting this lace veil." She brandished her needle toward Christine for a moment. "Truly, the wedding has been the only thing to occupy my mind or Mama's for weeks. Although I do worry about the finances of the thing. Mama and Papa do not have much to spare, so this is rather hard for them. Nevertheless, I am sure it will be splendid! Yet we have not set an official date. Mr. Grenville wants it to be the perfect time."

Meg did not seem as though anything had changed between herself and Mr. Grenville. She took hold of Christine's hands and smiled. "And how do you fair, dear Christine? Anything new to report?"

"Oh, not much I suppose," Christine answered, holding back her excitement about the meeting she just had. "One of Ivory's acquaintances I met in London will be passing through town tomorrow, and he shall dine with us." But as Christine thought of William, she realized she felt less excited about her new gentleman from London.

"Also," Christine added, trying to keep her tone even, "Mr. Robertson—William Robertson that is—was just in town, and he will be coming to Wellington tomorrow."

Meg glanced at Christine and turned her head sideways for a moment. "With whom does he visit?"

"With dear Mr. Oakley, naturally. We are to play croquet together."

"Ah, that explains things. Of course Lizzy wishes for your company. That is just right. I am sure Mr. Robertson feels he owes his time to Mr. Oakley for what he did for him."

She seemed very dismissive and vague about Mr. Robertson, and Christine thought perhaps Meg knew more than she was letting on.

"What do you mean, Meg? What did Mr. Oakley do for him?"

"Oh, I thought you might have heard by Mr. Oakley. Mr. Oakley saved William's life a few days ago in an accident. Although I heard from my maid that Mr. Oakley is just arriving in town today." Meg did always have the latest gossip, for her maid had quite the loose tongue.

Christine watched as Meg began picking at her lace again, stating, "What I mean is William is indebted to Mr. Oakley and therefore feels he must spend time doing as he wishes. Otherwise I am sure the Robertsons would stay in London."

"But perhaps he is here on business," Christine said, deflating a little.

"Perhaps. On any account, do not waste your time with him. I heard Mr. Oakley telling Lizzy that Mr. William Robertson never wishes to marry."

For a moment, Christine cursed the fact that her friend always seemed to know everything before she did. She sighed quietly to herself and responded to Meg, "Indeed, I am sure you are right, for Henry said the same thing of his brother. How very strange that he should not wish to secure someone in marriage."

"Yes, especially as it seems they currently rely on Mr. Oakley for much of their privileges. Seems it would be worthwhile to marry someone of your status, Christine."

Meg even seemed to know of the rumors that surrounded the Robertson's background. How Christine wished that she herself had more knowledge of who these brothers truly were.

Christine folded her hands in her lap, much more subdued than when she first entered the drawing room. "I can assure you that neither brother has ever given any hint of interest toward me. Henry would not dare after spending time with Ivory—it is too much in conflict of interests, not to mention we could never take each other seriously. He is too flippant and jovial. I am much too intense for him. And as we said of William, he is only cordial when we are thrown together. I know he has no desire to pursue any sort of lasting attachment."

Christine realized she gave this speech more to herself than Meg, whose absent look seemed to have already returned to daydreaming about Mr. Grenville.

Meg simply sighed. "Oh, but I do wish you the same happiness someday I am experiencing! How I love my Mr. Grenville! He has plenty of money for both of us! And he keeps telling me that we must travel to Paris on our honeymoon! Just think of what I could paint there. That will be just the thing! Although I do not know if painting will be the order of the day . . ." She shot a nervous grin toward Christine. "But by the by, he does say that we must wait a few more months. It is no matter; I will wait however long it takes. I do love him so, Christine."

Just then, Meg's mother entered the drawing room and took up the conversation with the two girls. Christine did wish to ask Meg if she had received the letter she wrote from London and had asked Mr. Grenville of the secret Mr. Oakley had referred to, but Christine feared that it might best be asked without her mother present. If Meg had learned of Mr. Grenville's secret, she did not seem at all dismayed about it, or its effect toward their impending marriage.

With the addition of Mrs. Allensby, Christine felt happy to shift the conversation to Meg. Christine did not stay as long as she had planned, for Mrs. Allensby seemed determined to stay the whole of the evening. Christine also felt quite tired and put out, unable to wrap her mind around her feelings for William and his situation. She felt sheepish for her flirtatious greeting earlier that day, knowing now that he was indeed only in town on account of Mr. Oakley.

And with so many voices speaking of his indifference, she knew this meant she would never have the opportunity of forming any lasting acquaintance with Mr. Robertson. And yet how close such a relationship had seemed earlier that day.

She left while it was still light outside, this time taking the long way home, meandering through the hills and fields that separated Wellington from Allensby House. These old familiar woods were Christine's sanctuary. Just like the tides that washed the shores of Cassfield, the leaves wafted in the wind, reminding her that their change was forever steady. Nature sometimes seemed to vacillate, and yet it had its own sort of consistency.

Now Christine desired to change as well, coupled with a new determination to develop genuine kindness and temperance. But even if she could change, she knew there was no way to prove this alteration to William. He would blow by, much like the breeze that chilled her as she rode home. But she would change, soften, and cool off for the sake of becoming better.

It was suppertime when Christine returned. Lizzy greeted her as though she had missed nothing, saying, "Did I not tell you that Edmund would arrive today?" Lizzy weaved her arm through Mr. Oakley's and looked up at him, beaming. "And you ought to know that we shall see William tomorrow. Although he and Henry are staying in town for the next few nights. Mr. Oakley says they chose an inn to facilitate the ease of their business."

And that speech validated Christine's suspicions, confirming all Meg had reported earlier that day. They wanted nothing to do with her or Wellington Manor. Hiding her emotions as best she could, Christine made the requisite pleasantries to Lizzy and Mr. Oakley, ate a small meal, and then excused herself forthwith to bed. It would be a few hours before sleep would overtake Christine's active mind. At least she would soon be escaping to Cassfield, where she could put all this—and William—behind her.

CHAPTER 22

Mr. William Robertson arrived at Wellington Estate promptly at noon. Christine and Lizzy greeted him in the entryway while Mr. Oakley busily attended to all supplies. The foursome loaded into the carriage, William first offering Christine his good arm.

"Why thank you, Mr. Robertson," Christine said with a large smile. She had actually been nothing *but* smiles since William came to Wellington that morning, despite the nagging reminder of his indifference that lingered in the back of her mind.

"'Tis the best I can do at present," he said, shrugging. He seemed quiet, but Christine noticed his eyes following her every move.

Mr. Oakley then stopped to have a quick exchange with Lizzy before helping her into the carriage.

Situating herself against the squabs, Christine looked down at her skirt, smoothing it carefully on her lap. She had chosen a gown that she deemed a bit more elegant than a picnic necessitated, but she chose it knowing that the dark-blue hue and the long intricate sleeves complemented her figure. She had also attended to her hair more precisely that morning and felt that no matter William's feelings toward her, she would feel confident presenting herself the best she could.

Mr. Oakley and William entered the carriage, both smiling pleasantly at the sisters as the coach rambled to one of Wellington's back hills. Christine felt nerves run through her, the proximity of Mr. Robertson turning her thoughts in every direction. To distract herself, she kept gazing out the window, watching the ominous, rolling clouds in an attempt to avoid staring at William too often. The men unloaded the supplies, and Mr. Oakley dismissed the carriage, instructing the groom to return in two hours, as Mr. Robertson started placing the wickets.

"A light rain, I see," Mr. Oakley said as a few drops fell on him. He withdrew a *T*-shaped item from the bag. "Perhaps it will pass quickly. I see a small strip of sunlight peering through those clouds over yonder." He then turned and explained what he held was called a mallet, instructing the sisters on how to use it.

Christine had noticed the sky growing exceedingly dark that morning, but she would not allow herself to believe it could rain. She had hoped nothing would spoil their outing. But the party had not even made it through the first wicket when the rain started falling at a much steadier pace.

Lizzy, cupping a few drops in her hand, leaned a little on Mr. Oakley's arm and whispered something to him. He nodded back at her, putting his arm around her shoulders.

"Perhaps it is best that we walk back to Wellington and find some sort of indoor sport," he said. "Lizzy has just come out of a cold, and I would hate for her to turn for the worse again."

Christine, crestfallen, nodded and made her way closer to the first wicket.

William, however, seemed quite unaffected by the moisture. He stood a little taller and did not budge. "I agree that Miss Elizabeth must be taken home. We cannot risk her cold returning. You two go on ahead, and Miss Harrison and I shall collect the game and then start walking that way as well." Christine could see Wellington in the distance and convinced herself they would be just behind her sister and since the house stood in view, it would be permissible for her and William to be without a chaperone for a few minutes.

William looked up at the sky, then at Christine, who smiled in consent politely, and finally at Mr. Oakley. "I believe it to be just what we call a Scotch mist and will soon pass. A little rain has never deterred me from enjoying an afternoon out of doors. Let us save your new game, Oakley, for another day, and we shall join you soon."

Mr. Oakley gave a slight bow and offered his arm to Lizzy, and they hurried down the hill, trying to stay under as many trees as possible as they walked toward Wellington.

"We shall be just behind you," Christine called after them.

William put on his black hat with a look of confidence and rested his palm on his mallet. *He does not seem too eager to be heading back*, thought Christine. She took a short breath and clasped her hands, feeling nervous but slightly excited as she found herself alone with Mr. Robertson.

William looked slowly up at the gray-blue sky. "Do you think it shall stop, Miss Harrison? Or should we return with haste?" He then looked intently at her eyes with more weight than the question warranted. Christine felt the thick folds of her long-sleeved blue dress. It was only a *bit* more than a drizzle, and she *had* felt quite healthy—and the fresh air seemed rather pleasant to her. Besides, her bonnet needed repinning anyway if it did take some rain. But putting aside all logical thinking, Christine knew her heart longed to be near William, regardless of the weather. She would have trudged through several inches of mud if it meant more time with him.

Mr. Robertson seemed to use her pause to his advantage. "Miss Harrison, you seem dressed rather warmly." He gestured at her long sleeves. "Would you not appreciate these hills for a bit?"

Christine hugged her arms around herself and smiled. "I suppose, Mr. Robertson, when you put it that way, I am enjoying the fresh air this afternoon."

He smiled broadly and started to slowly collect each wicket. "Perhaps our walk back can be somewhat leisurely."

"Perhaps," she said with a smile, but she turned her head so he would miss her blush.

Somehow, Christine stood alone with Mr. William Robertson on Wellington's rambling knolls. She was not sure this would be an entirely comfortable afternoon, but part of her thrilled to be with him. She immediately felt the same intimidating aura she so often felt in his presence. Some feeling composed of wanting to know him better mixed with a formidable allure, which led her to not know what to say in his presence. She did not know how to start the conversation, and Christine convinced herself that he would not feel the need to say much more than the common pleasantries, or possibly remark on the well-matched union of Lizzy and Edmund.

She picked up the few mallets and walked them over to William, stuffing them inside the bag as he helped her open it with his only good arm.

"Thank you, Miss Harrison. I am sure I can gather wickets. Perhaps you should wait under that tree while I finish things." He gestured toward a beautiful beech tree, its large boughs creating an almost dry canopy underneath.

"Are you sure, Mr. Robertson?" Christine looked at his injured arm.

"It is really no problem." He nodded back quite confidently. Christine did not know if he meant the wickets or his arm posed no problem. Either way, she gave in to his request, feeling tongue-tied.

As she removed herself from William's immediate presence, she regained some clarity of mind. How *had* he been injured? She knew no more details than Lizzy's letter, and her curiosity and concern to understand exactly what happened burned within her. Just as she began to formulate a question, she remembered William's aversion to answering personal details. William had always answered so curtly to any question relating to himself, and to ask him now could risk furthering his belief of nosy superiority and create an uncomfortable walk back to Wellington.

As she thought more, she looked around her, touching the short, soft grass covering the dry ground. There must be some unobtrusive way to ask him to explain.

William, having finished the wickets, then came close to her. The spot granted a beautiful view of the hills in the distance and even a few buildings from town could be seen. From here one could also spot Wellington Estate, Allensby House, and beyond.

As Christine leaned her back against the tree, she became aware of the silence between them, stealing a glance at William, seeing again his strong jaw, thick brown hair, and clear, cobalt-blue eyes. She had not expected him to sit and make himself comfortable, but he seemed content to rest a moment. Christine admitted that he truly was a handsome figure, although she would not allow herself to stare at his face quite as long as she would have preferred.

He turned his head to the side, taking in the view for a moment. Christine looked again, wanting to speak to him, but after a minute he looked back, catching the end of her gaze. She shifted away quickly, afraid of the blush that crept across her cheeks.

She felt her resolution for silence steadily wane, her desire to speak with him trumping all other logic. She thought she ought to stay away from the subject of his arm, and so she began with a roundabout way of getting to the same place.

"Mr. Robertson," she said, "I understand from my sister that you were in London this past week with Mr. Oakley. But Miss Rusket and I did not see you at the same event Mr. Oakley attended. Why did you not join him?"

Mr. Robertson eyes widened and he seemed slightly alarmed by the directness of the question. He then squared his good shoulder and said, "I . . . sometimes do not feel the desire to socialize in the same high circles as others."

"I see," Christine answered, perplexed. "But I recall you being a rather willing and skilled dancer at Lizzy's ball."

He looked away and then said, "I have been brought up in such circumstances that I must know of such things." After he said it, though, Christine watched his eyes, which had seemed so resolute, now recall something. His mouth turned upward. And he shifted closer to her, and the movement sent pain to his face.

"Oh, but of course!" Christine said as she gestured toward his bandage. "Perhaps your inability to dance made it so you would decline this one time?"

William squirmed a little. "Um . . . yes, in this particular instance, my arm did make me quite unfit for . . . well, anything."

He was not fully explaining himself. But at least he did not seem agitated about her questions. This speech confused Christine, for despite his vague answer, his voice carried a clear, strong tone, his manner of speaking relaxed and confident once again.

"But tell me, Miss Harrison, what all were you doing in London?" One of William's best skills seemed to be deflecting attention from himself.

Christine sat taller, trying to rest herself against the tree trunk, attempting to appear easy. "Oh, visiting Miss Rusket of course. I accompanied my father there, and while he took care of business I took the opportunity of participating in Miss Rusket's dizzying social schedule."

He looked more intently at Christine, as though he could see through this answer. As though he suspected more. Had he heard something of her dealings in London? Had Mr. Oakley explained what happened with Kathryn? Christine tried everything she could to keep her involvement a secret, for the sake of Kathryn's well-being.

Or did William think her capable of only furthering connections with men of high society? Of becoming as much a flirt as Ivory?

Christine debated what else she should say. She did not wish to draw any more notice to herself, especially to one who deflected his attentions so well. She pushed the pleats of her dress underneath her anxiously. Christine wanted to avoid telling of her role in saving Kathryn, not wishing to a cast a servant in a bad light. And she did not wish to appear proud or grand, for that had never impressed this man, and she knew it. And most of all, he would most likely think her impertinent and a fool for participating in such a dangerous task. Such a scheme would surely seem haphazard to him. Folding her arms across herself, Christine thought of an escape.

"Mr. Robertson, I daresay you have not yet told me what *you* were doing in London. I can assure you, yours is a much more interesting story. You promised you would tell me what happened to your arm— and what happened in London. Please," Christine said, gesturing her hand forward, "the floor is yours."

He smiled his straight, closed-mouth smile and tilted his head slightly. He had been caught.

"I knew you hold me to my word eventually." He sighed and his face drew into a wry smile as he rubbed his bandaged shoulder.

"As you know, I receive shipments every so often in London, which are then distributed to the proper merchants. We have had some trouble lately with the fabric distribution. To ensure no further issues, Henry, Oakley, and I followed the delivery of the last shipment. There I encountered a rather unfortunate situation, which left me with this wound."

He leaned back on his right arm, looking at the small stream babbling beside him. He spoke as though it were nothing. This retelling told her not much more than Oakley's letter to Lizzy. Christine knew she saw more behind his eyes that he had not told. She longed to understand the truth, marveling that he seemed quite at ease and so confident. She loved the quiet self-assurance he wore like an outer jacket.

If only she could feel so easy in his presence.

He then leaned slightly toward her, scanning her eyes. It was as though he suspected something.

"But tell me, Miss Harrison, surely you did more than *just* attend balls and dinners in London with Miss Rusket?"

Why did he feel the need to ask again? Christine shifted slightly, wanting to keep the rest a secret. Her eyes avoided his gaze. She had always been a terrible liar, her body language usually betraying her.

Mr. Robertson perceived the slight change. Somehow, he knew there was more.

He seemed to understand her. She marveled that their conversation had become so pointed and personal, yet it had no sense of pretense. Even his voice rang with openness in what seemed a covert conversation. His tone felt familiar to Christine. She stared at him. What did he know? He sat calmly, waiting for her to answer.

In that moment, she felt she could tell him all her secrets and they would be safe in his keeping. He smiled at her, his eyes twinkling, and Christine's ability to resist quickly faded. Taking a deep breath, she gave in and said, "I guess if you must know, that is not *all* I did in London." She gathered courage. "The daughter of our cook needed some help, and I went there to ensure her safe return home." Trying to make light of such an explanation was like trying to cover the sun with one's shawl.

"I see," he responded, and Christine could not tell what he thought of her answer, or if he wanted more details, but she took this brief pause as an opportunity to shift the focus.

"Now," Christine said authoritatively, "what sort of *misfortune* did you encounter amid your shipment? Did you fall from a horse? I do not fully understand how your arm could be in such a state."

William sat up, brushing his good arm across his thigh, and chuckled to himself. "Yes, I suppose I did not explain everything," he replied. "And perhaps you deserve more details in that regard."

Deserve more details? She puzzled and leaned a bit forward, confused at what she had done to *now* earn his explanation, but pleased he would say something—anything.

"It started many months ago when Henry and I realized one of our shipments was missing." He began telling Christine the details of his business. He told her Henry was the first to recognize it, and they had then determined to hold some way to catch the smugglers in the act.

"So we went to the docks to check on our shipment and watch from a hidden post what would happen to our goods," he said, shaking his head and then looking over at Christine. His face was probing hers, watching for something. Christine did not understand why he looked at her that way but wanted to be a part of whatever he said anyway.

"Through some unfortunate circumstances, I had to hide myself in the wagon carrying the shipment, which then traveled to where the thieves wanted to deposit the goods. But the wagon stopped before I had time to get away." His gaze met hers once more.

She sat, silent, and pulled her legs up around her, hugging them.

"So, holding on to my pistol, I lay next to the crates of fabric and expected the worst kind of confrontation upon my discovery by the driver. And that was when, through the slats of the wagon, I saw two beautiful, well-dressed, and quite out-of-place women dragging some sorry girl through the alley. Unfortunately, my driver noticed them too and took after them in a sprint."

With that, Christine dropped her head in her hands, his story sounding familiar, the realization of what he said truly dawning on her. *Could it be?*

She began to cry softly.

William stopped talking and looked gently at Christine. She looked up at him through wet eyes and then held her head in her hands once again.

William wrung his hands, trying to catch her gaze. "Are you unwell, Miss Harrison? Are you cold or ill? Should I stop? Perhaps we should return to Wellington straightaway." He started to stand.

It was just like to him to assume bad health rather than overwhelming emotions. Surely this was every man's conclusion to such a feminine display of feeling.

She motioned to him that she was not ill, and he sat back down. After a moment, Christine looked up and stared directly into his eyes.

"You stopped him, did you not? *You* were the man who chased after him?"

"Aye," he said quietly, and he drew himself back.

Christine noticed how close he had moved toward her. "And your arm . . ."

"In all that happened, a bullet hit my arm and I went unconscious because of loss of blood. Luckily Oakley and Henry followed after the wagon and found me before it was too—before I lost too much blood."

And then he was silent, and Christine wept quietly, unable to speak. There was a tangible feeling in the air, but only the faint sound of water flowing carried their thoughts.

"You saved my life," Christine finally whispered, staring at the green grass in front of her. "And Ivory's life, and most definitely Kathryn's, for I know he would have beat her to death after seeing that she was trying to escape."

Christine was overwhelmed with gratitude for what he had done. Tears continued to fall down her warm cheeks. Finally, she looked up at him, and he just smiled a soft, wide smile.

"Thank you," Christine said finally, her voice full of appreciation. "How shall I ever thank you enough?"

"I require no thanks, Miss Harrison. I cannot tell you how many times I have relived that scene, longing to know what became of the women. And then I heard from Oakley about Kathryn among your servants and thought just maybe this might have some connection. I am gratified by your confirmation. Now I know the happy ending to this scene that has haunted me as of late."

His mouth turned upward as he looked at her. "I know what you did to change that young woman's life. It was an act truly compassionate and courageous. You sacrificed much for her."

Christine said nothing and tried smoothing her skirts, her hair, and her tear-stained face, feeling more disheveled internally than externally. After a long moment, all she could manage was, "She deserved some help, poor girl."

Silence then returned. Christine's heart overflowed with desire to know this man and truly be close to him—forever. He had risked his life doing what was right and had saved her. His goodness knew no bounds, and she longed to spend more time with him. But she reminded herself that he came here only to find answers. He had no interest in courting her, or anyone for that matter. William was not—and never would be—hers.

Feeling the weight of the silence between them, Christine tried to change subjects, for she feared how intently she looked at him and how close she had moved toward him. She pushed back, not yet in control of the many emotions that consumed her. She thought to try and start a conversation, but nothing lighthearted came to mind. She looked around, noticing the rain had stopped.

"Shall we walk home?" William said, standing and extending a hand down toward her. "Are you well enough, Miss Harrison?"

Christine felt a calm fall over her body. Filled with gratitude, she took his hand briefly and stood. He lent Christine his handkerchief as she tried to brush the tears from her face. After she deemed herself presentable, she smiled meekly at him and took his proffered arm, which he held outstretched, ready to escort her.

They walked back to Wellington in almost complete silence. Christine looked up gratefully into William's face a few times, and each time he glanced down at her with a soft smile. Christine felt his tall frame next to her and acknowledged once again the sacrifice he had made for her. Happiness spread throughout her being, and she felt so completely whole. The wet hem of her skirt and tear-stained bodice of her dress held no chill against a heart so warm.

As Christine and William entered the drawing room of Wellington Estate half an hour later, Mr. Oakley called out, "Did you have an enjoyable walk, despite the rain?" Until that moment, Christine had not realized how wet she looked. They had stayed under the beech tree for most of their time away, but her dress had still managed to become somewhat damp. Christine quickly removed her bonnet and tried to brush herself off.

Lizzy sat near Mr. Oakley, holding a fresh cup of tea with a blanket wrapped around her. *If only Edmund he knew what had transpired between them that afternoon,* thought Christine. The rain had been the least of their focus.

"Yes quite, although I am sure your afternoon with Miss Lizzy was just as enjoyable, having the house to yourself." Christine smiled back, teasing him and her sister. Mr. Robertson was very quiet and somewhat distant, and Christine guessed it was because he had found out what he wanted. He grew more formal and intimidating once again.

"I fear it is late enough that I must be going," William said, seeming a bit agitated. He excused himself to call a carriage.

What had changed between them? Everything had seemed so cordial until they returned to Wellington.

"Will you not stay for dinner as well?" Lizzy said to William as he turned to leave. He looked at Christine and then back to Lizzy, seeming to weigh the question for a moment. "Mr. Oakley is staying," Lizzy continued, "and Christine has a friend from London visiting as well." At that moment, Christine thought how she wished Mr. McMilne had chosen any other evening to dine with them.

Mr. Robertson looked steadily across the room, his jaw clenched. "I thank you for the offer, but it is best that I get going," he said with a smile that seemed to mask something.

As she watched him disappear out the door, Christine's shoulders fell, matching her countenance. She turned slowly as she and Lizzy ascended the stairs to dress for the evening.

Once upstairs, Lizzy asked, "Christine, would you ever consider William if he were to court you? I know Edmund says William declares he will not marry, but he seemed a bit more amiable today. Not as he was leaving, I guess, but during croquet . . ."

Christine shook her head and cut off her sister. "I do not think he would ever connect himself with me, Lizzy dear. William asked me to come because Mr. Oakley needed another person to play that game. I have heard of his determination to involve no one in any sort of lasting engagement from several sources, including his brother. They have made it too clear."

Lizzy knit her brow and pushed her lips to the side for a moment. "Well, I daresay I must believe you if *that* is your source. I was hoping William was interested in you. It would be so enjoyable to marry cousins, would it not?"

"Yes, of course, Lizzy." Christine said, grasping her sister's hands. "Perhaps we better start exploring Mr. Oakley's other connections," she replied, smiling as heartily as she could muster.

MR. WILLIAM ROBERTSON

Two Years Previous

The letter in William's hand held several sheets, the first looking like an explanation, the rest seemingly full of many tables and figures. He rubbed his hand over the wax seal Henry had just broken, looking once again at his brother. The two of them had already experienced one of the most emotionally grueling days of their lives saying goodbye to their father.

Now William feared greater tragedy might lie within the contents of the pages before him. He heaved a great sigh, sinking further into the wooden chair in his family's study. He looked once more at Henry who gripped the arms of his chair in anticipation, and began to read aloud.

Dear Henry and William,

I write to you both this letter to be opened on your twenty-fourth birthday. I am proud to call you my sons.
We have always made it a point that our family is distinctly

different from others, hoping that you both will learn to be independent and hard workers. But what this truly means I would like to explain here. You know, all too well, how I have stressed that your income and living will not come from family assets. I tried to instill in you both that this was for your best interest to encourage you to become the best men you could be so that you learn the principles of hard work and thrift. I have seen you adopt these values over the years. I have been impressed with the development of your shipping business, and I give you my blessing. I only wish I could help to fund such a venture. Alas, there is no money with which to do so. This was not some guise to make you work harder for the living; rather, I now include the sad tale of how our family has all but lost our estate.

Growing up among the gentry of Scotland, and knowing your lineage comes from gentlemanly stock, you are right to assume your place among your peers. But I fear the sad truth is this: there is no living—there is no inheritance I will be able to give you. Almost all of the holdings and land is gone, and we are lucky to still have claim on our house. You must make a way for yourself. You have been given the blessing of good breeding, education, and manners, but the estate that once belonged to my grandfather is no longer in existence.

Why is this the case, you may ask? You know that it could have been passed from father to son easily in our family and not entailed elsewhere. Alas, I have enclosed the original document with this letter. Your grandfather entered into an agreement many years ago with another gentleman who lived near us. As you can see by the enclosed ledger and contract, slowly over the years our property and estate have been whittled away to this man. Now, his family sees no fraud in this, although we know it to be such. However, this is a legally binding document, and I fear by the time either of you marry and have children, you will have nothing to live on besides what you make for yourselves in your shipping business. I am terribly sorry. I have tried to reverse the agreement between our families, but it cannot be done. Our pride in standing behind what is legal has stopped your grandfather and me from any retribution or challenge. We must simply live with the consequences. I expect both of you will take this blow in stride and continue in your current plan.

I wish you both all the luck and blessings I can offer as a father.

Take courage,
Lewis M. Robertson

Henry grasped the ledgers and pored over them. As he finished looking at each page, he handed them to William, who patiently waited and scanned each document before him.

After several minutes of William studying the tiny scrawled columns and numbers, Henry let out, "I do not understand." He waved the accompanying legal document toward his brother for the third time. "It makes no sense."

"Yes, we see that *now*," William explained patiently. "But they did what they thought best at the time."

"Why did Father never speak to us of this?" Henry asked, his voice rising.

"He wanted to fix it himself. Had the flock increased . . . none of this would have happened. But there were too many years, with too much cold and too many sicknesses . . ." William trailed off.

His brother calmed down, relaxing in his seat, and nodded in agreement.

The legal document outlined the agreement between their grandfather and the Stewarts, the neighboring gentleman's family in Scotland. There had been a time years ago when the Robertsons' holdings threatened total loss due to some incurred debt over the years. Too many of William's family members had unwisely spent money or invested in bad ways, and the estate was all but ruined. That is when their grandfather implored Lord Stewart for help.

The contract read, "The sum of 12,000 pounds given immediately, to be repaid thereafter, over the next twenty years, 800 pounds per annum, the excess counting as the interest."

William grieved as he reread the next line, "And if the 800 pounds per annum is not collected, all land and holdings equal to such amount will be forfeit to Lord Galliard Stewart of Darfries Estate in addition to, but not in lieu of, said payment."

That was it. The line that ruined their family forever. Little by little, they had not been able to repay what they owed. Next to each year, their father outlined the sad circumstances that often precluded them from paying the interest. According to the record, just two years after the agreement, an epidemic worked its way through the flocks of Scotland, killing almost all of sheep raised on the Robertsons' land.

Their fields the next year froze, and fourteen of the next eighteen years had not been profitable enough to repay the debt. Portions of their land were claimed by the Stewarts, until it almost all belonged to them.

William and Henry's father had said nothing, and most still believed they owned much property. But the agreement stood, and Mr. Lewis Robertson gave all proceeds to the Stewarts year after year. Such open avowal to the community never happened and would surely make Lord Stewart seem an unjust friend and neighbor, and so the agreement remained hidden, the Robertsons becoming indentured slaves to their once friend. The more land that had to be entailed away, the less they could meet their debts.

William watched his brother as his temperament vacillated. Henry's calm began to wane once again, and he reached for the worn-out document with its tattered and torn edges. Henry looked at William with a wild, livid stare, amplified in his already sorrowful state. Those lines had been read many times, by several of the Robertson men, and now William and Henry analyzed them as well. They noticed annotations in the margin, as if someone were writing a legal case against the claims, but it was to no avail. The document read clearly—each year over the last twenty years a certain percentage left the Robertsons and entered the Stewart's holdings.

"This cannot be right!" Henry slammed his fist on the desk, his voice rising. "And all those years I thought that our Stewart neighbors Grandpa talked about were close friends or distant cousins! I want to challenge this. It would never stand in a court of law."

William said nothing and calmly took a deep breath again. He studied the documents, analyzing each word and sentence, looking for some kind of detail or loophole. After several minutes of searching, he found nothing. "Henry, there is nothing to be done. Did you read this last paragraph? It is the final word on the matter. It cannot be reversed. And furthermore, there is an extra clause that says that land held by Lord Stewart for longer than ten years will remain his permanently. So most of the property is set permanently to Lord Stewart—even if we were able to find something now in this contract."

Henry seized the paper from William's hand and paced back and forth, reading the last paragraph. William sat silent, looking at the floor, waiting for Henry to become calm again. It took Henry some minutes before he settled and then reconciled himself to the fate that lay before him.

"Perhaps you are right, brother. We had better hope our shipping company turns into something worthwhile." He smiled half-heartedly and left the room. It was obvious he was still very distraught about his father's death, and this news had left him even more undone.

William clenched his fists on the great study desk before him. Both brothers were still mourning their father's death, and now this knowledge increased their sorrow. Surely, Henry and William had always surmised that when they married or reached a certain age, they would perhaps receive some kind of inheritance, though money was scarcely talked of in their family. But there was nothing. But it was more than the money—the pride of the family had been desecrated.

The shock settled on William, knowing now why he had always felt that it was up to himself to make his way in the world. As he sat and contemplated his future, he was glad to know the truth behind his family and resolved more firmly that money would not be his only pursuit or desire. The fact was that his father and grandfather were great men, of sound understanding and knowledge, and did not let a change in their finances ruin them. Some men would have become slanderers of the other family, but not his father and grandfather. This was the example William had to live up to. The family integrity must still be upheld.

He would do everything in his power to reestablish his family. His business would gain success and his surplus would go to Scotland, until all debt and interest was paid, and perhaps, with some artful negotiating, the Stewarts would at least allow him to purchase back some of their family's holdings.

William promised himself he would not rest until all was set to right. Nothing and no one would stand in his way.

CHAPTER 23

*C*hristine stood at her washbasin and wrung her hands, threading her fingers through a few soft curls. Although her dinner the night before with Mr. McMilne had been quite pleasant and her family enjoyed him immensely, she thought nothing of him now. Only thoughts of William bombarded her mind that morning, and she longed to be free of them.

If she had but acted less self-important last year, maybe he would have courted her. But even then he seemed—regardless of her actions—resolved in his course to remain mere acquaintances. Had his interest ever been strong enough to court her? But she had behaved so poorly and let Mr. Davenport consume her every moment. Since then she had changed, she had grown. She was different now. But did William even perceive that? They had not been much together, and perhaps he never cared for her.

But what made him hold to his course to pursue no one? Where did that determination come from? She knew in her case he had now learned what he wanted to know about Mr. Braxton and Kathryn and stood appeased.

But how Christine wished for just one more chance. He had saved her life—he had stolen her heart—and yet he would move on and forget all about her. She would always feel gratitude for what he did, but she knew she felt more. She admired him—his steadiness, his kindness, his strength of character.

A voice from downstairs then pulled Christine from her reflections.

"Christine, dear, are you ready?" her father called from the front stairs. She heard other voices and realized Kathryn and Edmund—for he was now to become her brother—had already assembled.

"Yes father," she called back, eagerly descending the stairs. She smiled at Kathryn, who, with an additional maid, would travel with them from Wellington to Cassfield Manor to assist in the kitchen. Christine had been pondering in her room for hours, keen to travel, hoping that her removal to Cassfield could distract her from thinking about William. Leaving Rothershire would be the only way to be free of him.

"Hello, Edmund," she said as she finished the last of the stairs, "Are you ready to be going?"

"Yes quite, dear sister, though I wish Miss Lizzy was joining us today." He smiled, his eyes looking a bit lovesick as he spoke.

"Ah, you shall have her all to yourself in due time. For now, you must be patient." She tapped a finger at him. "You know she must stay with my mother one day more to make sure all is in order."

He clapped his hands and nodded toward her, knowing this to be the case.

Her father then exclaimed, "I have quite the surprise for you both." He smiled widely.

Christine looked over her shoulder and noticed the extra coach ordered behind them.

"Do tell us, Mr. Harrison!" Edmund encouraged, indulging his soon-to-be-father-in-law.

Mr. Harrison paused a moment, quite pleased with himself. He rubbed his hands together, and then finally said, "I ran into Henry and William Robertson yesterday in town, and I invited them to come early to Cassfield and stay until the wedding."

Christine's stomach tightened. She shot her gaze to the ground, trying to hide her anguish. "And they accepted, Father?" she asked, avoiding eye-contact.

"Why yes, how could they resist?" Mr. Harrison said, proud of his invitation.

"What a splendid addition, I thought it not my place to invite them myself, but I am glad to have their company!" Edmund said.

Christine rubbed her hands together and remained silent. She finally felt master of herself enough to raise her eyes. She followed Edmund over the threshold and into the front park. She waited on edge for a few minutes until a carriage came through the sweep gate, depositing the Robertsons.

"Good day, gentlemen," Christine said evenly. She reminded herself to avoid staring at William.

They both bowed and Christine thought she saw William's eyes linger a moment. Why did he have to come now to Cassfield? Why did he not come just the day or two before the wedding, like most of the other guests? Her father's generous offer had once again allowed the Robertsons at Cassfield without her consent. The next two weeks would hardly hold a reprieve for her soul.

The gentlemen shuffled a few pieces of luggage to the servants as Mr. Harrison asked, "Shall we be off, then?" He mounted his black steed and waited. Christine hurried to the first carriage, her maid trailing and Mr. Oakley seeing it his duty to accompany them. Kathryn and the additional scullery maid found themselves assigned to the Robertson brothers.

As she tucked herself into the corner of the carriage, Christine tried hard to not process what the Robertsons' coming—William's coming—would mean for her. Of course she wanted to spend time with him, but every minute she did attached her more to a man who would not attach himself to any young woman. She folded her arms and sighed, focusing on the quiet journey before her, knowing that this day's ride would be the last uncomplicated moments she would have for the next few weeks.

Mr. Sebastian Grenville

Five Years Previous

"Now, Sebastian," Mrs. Grenville reminded him, "do not lose your head in this adventure. Your uncle is a wise man, and you would do well to learn from him. Not only from his business skills but from his level of *decorum*."

Sebastian himself thought it high time to be leaving his mother's clutches and could not wait to arrive in Paris. An excited nineteen-year-old, he felt he was ready to see the world and desired thence to proceed in taking it over in some fashion. Little did he know exactly how much his life was about to change.

His uncle was a man who, although not as well connected as the Grenvilles, had made his fortune and name through trading between France and England. He had learned what goods were more inexpensive in France and used that to his advantage to sell in England and vice versa. Sebastian was to learn his accounting and practices as an apprentice of sorts, now that he had finished his schooling.

"Right this way," his uncle said to him his first day in the city. "As I see it, there is no time to delay." Sebastian had just finished settling into his room that morning and had made sure he reported to his uncle's office before nine o'clock in the morning.

"Here is my ledger. Now, if you will follow along with me in the left column, you will see the listed commodity. Then, in the right corresponding column, you will see the listed price. I have one column for English price and one column for French price. Your task will be to figure out the differential in price for each item over the last twelve months. Now, this will require you to take into account the currency fluctuation and also the way each item has changed per unit with each purchase . . ."

Uncle George, as Sebastian called him, continued at such a dizzying pace that by the end of day, Sebastian felt quite overworked and underqualified. This kind of rigid expectation would prove to be beneficial to Sebastian in the long term, but for now he just felt as though his head were swimming.

After one week of this abuse, Sebastian began to gain an understanding of his uncle's business. It was then that his uncle came and asked him how his French fared.

"It is somewhat developed," he responded, not knowing if this would add to his litany of tasks or relieve him of some. "I studied it in school, but my practical application has not been as strong."

"I see," Uncle George said, stroking his thick black mustache. "I have an assignment for you, then. Every Saturday, Sunday, and evening is to be spent among the people of Paris. Start talking to everyone. Talk to my servants, talk to the baker on the street corner, talk to the cobbler down the road. I want you proficient in dialogue before you leave here."

"Yes, uncle," Sebastian responded, relieved. Uncle George left the room, and Sebastian sat a little taller in his chair. Tomorrow was Saturday, and he would be able to spend it as he wished.

Sebastian Grenville had planned on staying with Uncle George for six months. At the end of his first month, however, he began to think he might live in Paris indefinitely. It was his sixth "free day," as he called it, when he met her. He went into the bakery with the object of buying some bread and making an acquaintance there, as his uncle had suggested. As he came out of the door with his baguette under his arm, he bumped into a slender, petite woman with dark eyes and loose curls.

In broken French, he stammered, "Excuse me, madam."

She curtsied and did not seem at all flustered, and she replied in the sweetest French he had ever heard, "It is mademoiselle, sir."

"Beg your pardon," he continued.

"It is nothing," she responded, in a heavily accented English, and then, like a true Parisian coquette, she said, "Will you walk me home?"

From the moment he saw her, he was taken by her. He was young and easily persuaded, not having much interaction with the opposite sex heretofore. Fortunately, she was only a flirtatious young woman who knew a foreigner when she saw one and was nothing any more dangerous.

As he walked her home, he became more enamored by her easy speech and beautiful figure alongside his. Knowing where she lived proved quite dangerous for him, as he could not help but walk past her house every evening when he finished balancing his uncle's ledger.

For several days he did not see her again, and he did not dare to call at her small flat. However, after two weeks of frequenting the bakery, he saw her once again as she intercepted him at the door. This time as he walked her home, he could not help but ask for a planned meeting. By the end of that week, they had scheduled some sort of rendezvous nearly every evening. Mr. Grenville's French was indeed improving, at least to be able to communicate sweet sayings to her, although his business vocabulary did not increase with such alacrity. He justified such a relationship by making sure she would speak only French with him, which satisfied his conscience a very little.

"How are you liking your time here?" his uncle asked after two months of work. "Do you think you will stay your full six months? You are beginning to lighten my load a considerable amount." Such a comment should have been taken as quite the compliment, coming from his austere uncle, but Sebastian's mind was already somewhere else.

"Yes, sir," Sebastian replied. "I plan to stay at least six months. Perhaps longer, if I can be of service to you."

"Liking it here that much, eh?" he said, nudging his nephew with his elbow. "Paris does have a charm, so they say."

"That is just it, Uncle," he said stammering a bit, "I have decided I want to marry. I met a young woman at the baker's shop a few weeks ago, and I cannot get her off my mind. I love her, Uncle." He had been reluctantly trying to determine how best to go about informing his uncle, and since this opportunity had smoothly presented itself, he decided to use it to his advantage. His uncle, however, looked unimpressed.

Uncle George had been a bachelor his entire life, and his face went suddenly stone cold. If one asked him why he was a bachelor, he could give one of several reasons why he had chosen such a lifestyle. He had been thwarted early in life by a woman whom he almost married—just as he was to propose, she jilted him for a childhood sweetheart. And then there had been the many short-term, unsteady relationships of flighty Parisian charmers. Now he lived without much diversion of that kind in his life, turning more to the gluttony Paris could provide rather than the romance it sometimes afforded. This kind of whimsical decision was unacceptable to him. He had mentioned many of these facts off-hand to Sebastian in their time together, and now Sebastian could see the affect of such an opinion.

"I forbid you to marry. I do not approve of the institution, and you have known this woman for only a few weeks. This is absurd. If you do marry her, you shall lose your position here."

That night, Sebastian did not leave his room to court his sweet Parisian mademoiselle. He simply wrote her a note and left it outside her door the next morning.

I will not be able to meet with you again for quite some time. My uncle has forbidden it. I am so sorry.

> *Yours truly,*
> *Sebastian*

Sebastian managed to stay away for three days, until the pain of not spending time with her ached too much. He would not heed his uncle's council. He did not care much for his apprenticeship anyhow.

That night, he went and waited at her door until she came home. She seemed to have experienced as much agony as he had and accepted him back completely. True to form, she held him close in an embrace that betrayed the social customs he came from. This gypsy-like girl had bewitched him completely.

"Elope with me?" he whispered in her ear that evening.

"Oui," was her reply.

CHAPTER 24

*C*hristine descended to breakfast two days after arriving at Cassfield to see the room full of the young people of the party. The day before, the men had all gone fishing with Mr. Harrison, much to Christine's peace of mind. But today she sought some way to avoid William again.

Kathryn had just delivered breakfast from the kitchen and stood for a moment near the tray of food, exchanging a pleasant good morning with the Robertsons. They seemed quite at ease with each other, apparently well acquainted in the carriage ride from Rothershire to Cassfield.

Lizzy had just arrived the night before and was speaking with Edmund, discussing the day ahead, when Kathryn had made her way discreetly to another tray of biscuits, looking as though she felt a bit out of place among the gentry of the house. Christine hurried to her, taking her arm and turning toward a corner.

"Kathryn," Christine began quietly, "What are your plans for today? I am in need of diversion, and I have chosen you as my companion."

"I believe I must help my mother," Kathryn said quietly.

"Well, I have spoken with my mother and she has agreed to let you have a free day before you assist your mother and then start work as a governess. I was hoping you might join me today in town."

"How kind," she said. "I am honored." She smiled softly toward Christine.

Christine sighed, feeling glad to have a companion in Kathryn and to be free of the gentlemen of the party.

And with that, Christine and Kathryn left the others and started on their way. As Christine exited the room, she glanced over her shoulder, noticing no one had acknowledged their leaving.

Broughington Lake was beautiful this time of year, and the winds were especially high that day. The sea breeze smell permeated the air, and as they walked, the winds rustled Christine and Kathryn's skirts.

"I have no previous plans or designs," Christine stated as they started along the sea wall, "mostly I want to walk around town and see what is new from last year—peruse the shops."

"That all sounds lovely. Everything is new for me," Kathryn responded.

The stroll into town took half an hour by way of the sea wall, until they made their way into quaint streets lined with small businesses and fisheries.

Christine asked Kathryn about her mother, about Ivory, and about starting as a governess soon. Kathryn could not be more grateful—or more different from a few weeks prior. Finally, after an hour together, Christine could not help but ask, "Kathryn, have either of the Robertsons asked you about the Braxtons?"

"No, miss," she said, her speech stepping into one of a servant for a moment at the mention of her previously reduced circumstances. "What do you mean?" Kathryn's eyes dimmed slightly, remembering her past few months.

Christine continued, "You see, Kathryn, I have just recently learned more to our story." Christine brushed a blowing curl from her eyes. She inhaled slowly, thinking once again of William's service. "I have learned that Mr. Robertson—William Robertson, that is—is the man who fought off Mr. Braxton when we rescued you. Do you remember that someone chased after Mr. Braxton? William, Henry, and Mr. Oakley were trying to intercept a stolen shipment and were the ones who found Mr. Braxton and his group in their deceit. I believe it is because of the Robertsons that Mr. Braxton is now facing criminal charges."

Kathryn's eyes broadened, and she grasped Christine's arm slowly. The two young women stopped walking for a moment.

"Then he is who I must thank. For I know you did much, Miss Harrison, but without Mr. Robertson, I would most certainly . . . have been beaten to death." She shuddered a little as she said this and looked out across the ocean at the crashing waves pummeling the sand.

"Yes, it is quite remarkable what he did for us. I think of it often. I am still amazed how our timing overlapped that day. I believe it to be more than chance."

"A miracle," Kathryn said softly. "Truly a miracle."

The rest of the day held a reverenced air, but as they visited the shops together the young ladies enjoyed themselves fully. There were a few new businesses in Broughington Lake—a confectionery, a shop that sold sea curios, and a dress shop with new owners.

Just as Kathryn and Christine turned to leave the dress shop, the Robertson brothers walked through the door.

"Why hello, Miss Harrison and Miss O'Rourke," William said with a polite smile. The girls curtsied but said nothing. William walked past them briskly to the storeowner.

Henry stayed near them and leaned in conspiratorially. "Do you like what you see here? William has it in his mind that we ought to become this shop's fabric supplier. He is *always* on business, you know."

Yes I know, thought Christine. Perhaps *that* was why the Robertsons consented to come to Cassfield so early—or William at least.

Christine watched William head toward the back of the store, browsing fabrics, and Christine thought it just as well. She had come to town for the express purpose of avoiding him.

She glanced in his direction and turned to Henry, trying to sound pleasant. "It is rather clever of you both. William seems *quite* busy. How fortunate you came early to Cassfield to secure even more business connections." She wondered if her indifferent air hinted of agitation. "I hope you find it all to your liking."

Christine nodded toward Kathryn, and the two turned to leave. They had not walked more than a few feet when William shot his head up and said quickly, "You are returning so soon? Surely you might both stay while we finish here and then accompany us on our walk back?"

She had been trying to avoid him, and now he asked her to stay? She was sure her mind would go blank in his presence, feeling awkward and confused once again.

Kathryn looked hopefully at Christine, who could think of no valid reason to refuse them. William continued to gaze steadily at them.

"Of . . . course," Christine said slowly, "what an amiable suggestion. We shall continue to browse."

Kathryn smiled, seeming pleased that her friend wished to stay. Henry walked over to William, and together they approached the storeowner, a young man himself with a measuring tape draped over his shoulders. William presented his card and began talking, when the shop owner peered over his half-rimmed spectacles at Christine. She had been staring, watching William's every movement, and abruptly turned to feign interest in a pelisse that hung in the window.

After a few minutes, the brothers completed their conversation, and the party left the shop.

Henry came first to Christine's left, and William came around to Kathryn's right. As they walked toward Cassfield Manor, William leaned his head forward to address Christine. "Miss Harrison, what did you and Miss O'Rourke do in town this morning? We were wondering what happened to you after breakfast."

Christine's face immediately turned toward William. He *had* noticed their absence. And now she had to have some way to account for leaving without an invitation to the whole party to join her. "Oh, I was just showing Kathryn around. She has never been here before, and she begins her work as governess soon. I thought we might be seeing some shops you would have already seen. Therefore, we took a private tour this morning."

Kathryn nodded emphatically, and then to Christine's surprise, William asked, "And how did you find Broughington Lake's shops, Miss O'Rourke?"

She acted particularly more shy than normal, knowing now what William had done for her. She paused briefly, lowered her head, and said, "It is one of the most beautiful places I have ever seen. This part of the kingdom is mesmerizing. The entire town feels like a breath of fresh air."

For all of the setbacks and disadvantages life circumstances had given her, Kathryn was extremely well spoken and articulate.

"I am so glad to hear that," William said.

MISS KATHRYN O'ROURKE

As they approached Cassfield Manor, William lagged behind the party, and Henry, still escorting Christine, asked her about what she had read since they had last discussed literature.

Kathryn, therefore, found herself alone in William's presence for the first time in her life. She had known him only a few days, but now with the knowledge of his deliverance of her, she could not help but shy away. The memories of her past month conjured by Christine's earlier conversation only made Mr. Robertson's presence more foreboding. She had her guard up—humbled, inferior, and quiet. Knowing he had saved her life from that wretched Mr. Braxton, she could not ever repay him or feel to stand as his equal.

"Miss O'Rourke?" William said quietly as Christine and Henry entered the back doors of Cassfield. "May I detain you for a moment?"

They stood near the large stone steps that led from the sea wall up to the patio of Cassfield. A small hill of silt and long grass stood between them and the great latticed windows of the house.

"Oh . . . yes, sir," she said, like a servant, and a little like she was expecting it.

He kindly extended his arm, and said, "Perhaps we could sit by these stones for a moment."

She, feeling even more confused and shy, begrudgingly slipped her arm into his as they walked down the beach a few paces. Massive gray-black stones dotted the barrier between the ocean and the start of Cassfield's property. Kathryn chose a flat one a few feet away and sat quietly as William remained standing.

"Miss O'Rourke, I have been meaning to ask you a few questions when the opportunity presented itself," William started, "and it will not take long."

She looked down, studying her hands in her lap. He waited for an answer.

After a moment, she looked up and smiled faintly. She tried to discreetly wipe a tear off her cheek as she lifted her head.

"You, sir, may ask whatever questions you may like. In fact, Miss Harrison warned me you may request an inquiry. I *am* quite out of sorts today. . . but that is because I just learned it was you who saved my life when Miss Rusket and Miss Harrison came to rescue me." She wiped away another silent tear and continued. "I do not know how to thank you. Indeed, I never shall be able to repay you."

William's lips parted, and he nodded in sympathy. He crossed his arms and looked at her. "Do not feel uneasy. It was imperative that I take action. It was the right thing to do in that moment, and I thank God that you and the other ladies' lives were spared."

She sighed quietly and lowered her head again.

"Miss O'Rourke," he continued kindly, "please do not let this fact change the way you interact with anyone here, least of all me. You and I are nothing less than equals."

She nodded slightly and he began, "First, can you verify that Mr. Braxton, his father, and Mr. Davenport were all in business together?"

She whispered a quick "yes," and William queried on. "And their business consists of smuggling and stealing merchandise from various companies?"

"Yes," she answered again. She then gained courage. "And although they thought me to be rather dim-witted, I can tell you each of the items they smuggled. They either sought redress from one of the parties illegally, or as in your case, they took the goods directly and sold them." She watched as William's eyes looked over the ocean, processing all she said.

"And can I ask you to explain their business dealings and your former relationship with them in a letter? We need more evidence against their case. The London officials need to be completely sure. I have already told them of your connection, and they have assured me that you will not be harmed or accused in any way."

Kathryn stood and turned her back to William. Although completely safe now, remembering her former life filled her with a fear she almost could not tame. Brushing her hand gently over the tall grassy hill, she said, "I will write such a letter straightaway. And if a verbal testimony is requisite, I would be willing to give one. But . . ." Her beautiful eyes met his. "You can guarantee my complete protection?"

"I promise no harm will come to you," William answered, and she knew his word was his bond.

"Miss O'Rourke," he began again, "I have one question left."

She hoped the worst was now over, and she felt a tangible burden begin to lift. She turned back toward him and sat again on the stone. "Very well, but may I first ask a question of you, sir?"

He seemed slightly surprised but quickly changed his countenance to veil his worry. This was a question she had been longing to know the answer to, ever since their carriage ride.

"Where is your family from?"

"The south, miss. Dumfrieshire, to be exact."

Kathryn turned slightly away but smiled as her eyes beamed. "You mean the south of Scotland, correct?"

"Yes, Miss O'Rourke, that is right. My mother met my father there, and my grandfather still lives in Dumfrieshire."

It was just as she had suspected. William's brow puzzled for a moment, but he quickly hid his emotion from Kathryn. He glanced around. Then, even though no one else stood near, he said quietly, "My last question, miss, has to do with the Harrisons. You mentioned Miss Harrison told you about my involvement with the Braxtons. Do you know how Miss Harrison truly feels about my brother and me?"

Kathryn looked a little dumbfounded at William. What was he getting at? What did he suspect Christine of? All she could do was to answer truthfully the facts she did know. "Mr. Robertson, I am afraid I do not know the meaning of your question. All I can tell you is that she spoke very highly of you when she told me the details of our rescue. And from the first time I met her, she has said nothing but what a good family you come from. More than this I do not know."

He asked no more questions. She stood, and he escorted her back to the steps. He then excused himself, and Kathryn watched as he walked through the hills headed down toward the shore.

She climbed the steps and then turned directly to her mother's quarters downstairs. She had much to report and to explain—Cook Cooper wanted answers.

Later that evening, as Kathryn delivered the second course, she noticed William come in late at dinner. Kathryn watched him as he took his place next to Mrs. Harrison, giving some small explanation for his delay. It was not until that night in the drawing room, when she came to collect the tea, that Kathryn noticed William's every action as Christine played a song on the piano.

Although William sat near Henry and Lizzy in the drawing room, he had positioned himself in direct sight of the piano. Christine then played a rather lively Mozart sonata perfectly articulated in every note, as though she had practiced it much. Kathryn noticed William— seemingly rapt by the tune—gaze at Christine. For one brief second, she saw Christine's and William's eyes meet.

As Kathryn turned to leave, she saw William sitting so distracted by the song that Mr. Oakley had to ask him his question three times before he received an answer.

Cook Cooper

"Now you listen here," Cook Cooper said in her thick brogue. "This is an express. I need it taken straightaway to the address. It has to get aboard the next direct coach, y'see?"

The slight gentleman nodded his head profusely and then mounted his even slighter horse. Cook Cooper wondered if such a beast stood trustworthy enough to ride, let alone carry express mail across the country. Shaking her head, she turned back to the kitchen to watch a few pots of stew simmer.

"I shall never forgive myself if this does not make amends," she muttered, quietly enough that none of the other servants could hear. She knew it could take several days to make its way into the owner's hand.

"And what shall he say?" she muttered again, seeming to have a conversation with the bubbling carrots below her. She often spoke to her food this way, as it was always her constant companion. Her carrots, however, stayed silent.

"I always had a good feeling about them," she said definitively.

Chapter 25

Christine awoke to a loud knock. The sun shone through the window, and Christine realized it was already midmorning. The sound woke Lizzy, too, who had stayed up later conversing with Edmund. The sisters looked at each other sleepily, and Christine hurried to the door. A maid in a blue dress curtsied quickly and said, "I am rather sorry to wake you, miss, but you have company downstairs in the breakfast room. What shall I tell them?"

Christine did not know who would be visiting, and especially calling before noon.

"Go tell them we will be down shortly, and then come help us dress!" Christine answered frantically. Lizzy and Christine threw on their freshest dresses and the maid helped each sister put her hair up in tidy buns. Within twenty minutes, both girls stood presentable and headed downstairs swiftly.

The girls came into the breakfast room, where a familiar blonde girl with her hair perfectly plaited and wearing a light pink dress had her back to them, chatting very closely with another turned head possessing dark, thick curls. Sitting across the table from her was a man, turned sideways, laughing and making some kind of joke to Edmund as he munched on a biscuit. He locked eyes with the sisters and stood to bow to both Lizzy and Christine. This is when the visiting young women recognized the Harrisons' presence and turned around, coming toward them in two bounds.

"Ivory—Meg!" Lizzy and Christine exclaimed in unison. Christine hugged Ivory as Lizzy embraced Meg.

"Why did the maid not tell us it was you? Surely she knew it was you!" Christine said.

"We wanted it to be a surprise!" Ivory smiled. "We knew you would not have expected us yet, but Mr. Ternbridge and I," she said, gesturing toward him, "came from London through Rothershire to collect Meg and thought coming a few days early to Cassfield would be just the thing!"

Christine felt momentary surprise at Ivory's scheming and unplanned arrival and then recalled whom she was dealing with. It was a good thing Mr. Harrison had so many guest rooms at Cassfield, for Ivory would do just as she pleased.

Christine turned and curtsied. "Welcome, Mr. Ternbridge. It is a pleasure to see you again. This is my sister, Miss Elizabeth."

Lizzy curtsied and then stole a smile at Ivory. *And now I shall have another distraction from William,* thought Christine. Ivory's timing always seemed impeccable and a bit presumptuous, but Christine did not mind.

"And of course, the four of us ladies must spend the morning together, to reminisce on old times! I am sure we all need some female time." Ivory smiled to everyone in the room, and Christine nodded.

Henry and William then entered the breakfast room, noticing a new man among them.

Ivory quickly went over to her beau and said, "This, gentlemen, is Mr. Ternbridge. I will be spending the morning with the ladies, so would you mind keeping him engaged? We will be back in time to dress for dinner."

"We are going fishing this morning and will surely bring Mr. Ternbridge along!" Edmund said, nodding.

Mr. Ternbridge seemed quite at ease with his newfound friends, or at least he seemed to have the pretense of such feelings. Ivory, in true fashion, had a way to demand and command the attention of whatever suitor she was with. Lizzy found it possible to be spared this one morning from Edmund, and Meg tucked her arm into Christine's as the old party made their way to the shores of Cassfield, much altered from their time there a year ago, having many more secret affairs to discuss.

"And is Kathryn in the kitchen?" Ivory asked Christine.

"Yes, she is helping her mother here until after the wedding."

"I know she is a servant, but I thought, just for today . . ." Ivory began.

Christine smiled wide. "You wish to mingle with the servants, Miss Rusket?" Christine teased. "How far you have come." Christine upturned her chin and continued her ruse. "I like this change. I think she might be spared from the kitchen one more day, since you wish to see her so." Christine clasped Ivory's hand, feeling a deep love for her friend.

Christine sent a note to the kitchen, and within a half hour, Kathryn joined them in her nicest dress. Ivory engulfed her in a hug the moment she saw her, the two acting as old friends immediately.

Then, as the girls walked out to the water's edge, Ivory wasted no time opening her floodgate of emotions.

"Ladies! I just do not know what to do! I had spent so much time with Mr. Ternbridge at his estate and was becoming so confused, I just needed to come talk to you about it so I would know what course to pursue." She looked first at Kathryn and then at the others.

"My parents, as you know, were just as critical of Mr. Ternbridge as any gentleman I have ever entertained. But during his stay in London, I daresay he won my parents over. They are quite fine with him now—and his twelve thousand a year—which was, to be truthful, the selling point for them."

"However, now *I* am not sure I like him all that much, but he is so very persuasive and would marry me this instant if he were to have his wish. And I cannot decide if I could pass on such a marvelous opportunity. Though he holds no title, his great uncle is an earl or something of rank, and his family comes from enormous wealth. Plus he is rather attractive, sometimes, I believe. And therefore," she said, "I often think I love him and other times think he would drive me mad, despite twelve thousand a year."

They all paused for a moment, and then Lizzy said, "Ivory, sometimes it is hard to know one's feelings. But sometimes one must continue to move forward. And you sounded as though you were not quite sure if he is handsome enough for you. Perhaps that can grow over time?"

"Yes, perhaps, Lizzy. You always understand me so well."

Christine turned her head toward her friend and gave a smile.

"My one advice to you is this, Ivory," Christine offered hesitantly, feeling least qualified to assert her knowledge of men. "Many men have loved you for your money or your beauty or your connections to Parliament. If this man loves you just for being you, I believe he should be the one you choose."

For a moment Ivory looked out at the sea and said nothing. Christine saw Ivory's eyes realize that she knew Mr. Ternbridge did truly love her. Christine wondered if Ivory felt the same way.

The girls kept walking, and Christine was silent for a few moments, mulling over a different question in her mind.

Meg, looking a bit agitated, then began speaking. "I am so glad we are here together again. I have much to tell you all."

Christine watched Ivory glance narrowly at Meg, as though she wondered why she had not been apprised of any interesting news on their trip from Rothershire to Cassfield.

"What I have to say is"—Meg heaved a quick breath and spoke quickly—"there have been a few surprising facts I have learned about Mr. Grenville, although we shall still be married this summer."

Christine, Lizzy, and Ivory, with Kathryn at her side, all stopped walking for a moment, Ivory's mouth opening indignantly.

"Is everything agreeable between you both?" Lizzy asked, eyebrows raised. Christine, less surprised, waited to hear what great secret Mr. Grenville had been keeping all this time.

"Yes, quite, although it has a longer explanation than I deem you could even imagine."

"We would love all the details," Christine urged as she started walking again, preparing for a long story. Ivory leaned closer, not wanting to miss anything. And then Meg began her extensive discourse.

She started by relating all of the reasons she felt so much in love with Mr. Grenville and admired his noble character. She then began an explanation of a part of his past that he had not shared with her until recently. He thought he need not ever mention it and declared how passionately he loved Meg, and he had promised her that his past would have no bearing on their current relationship or future marriage.

All of this was the case, however, until his last trip to France on business. There he had learned of one part of his story that would change his life forever.

"And so, you see, he thought that it was all a part of his past. He loved her, indeed, enough to elope with her. When they returned from their elopement, his uncle found out and disowned him. He would not let Mr. Grenville work with him any longer. So Mr. Grenville struggled for money, to even have enough for him and his new wife to live on, and decided he must come back to England to make enough money to provide for her.

"His family had no idea, but he became a factory worker in southern England, and lived on almost nothing in order to send all he had back to her. He scraped by for a few months, working all day and most nights until he had finally earned enough to have her join him. It had been seven months since they had last seen each other. When he sent for her with money for her passage, he received a letter from her parents saying that she had died a few weeks prior." Meg's sad eyes looked into Christine's. "He never saw her again." Meg paused and took a deep breath before continuing.

"After hearing such news, he finally returned to Rothershire. For years he mourned her loss, silently, not really telling the full truth to his parents. No one believed he was actually married to her—they all supposed her to be some French mistress that they should conceal to keep the family name untarnished. And even if they were married—which thing his mother declared to be quite impossible—she was so much below their social standing it would still remain a grievous blemish to their name.

"His uncle refused to speak of the matter, not even disclosing the few details he actually knew. Even on Mr. Grenville's wife's side, her prideful parents hated the foreign man who stole their daughter, claiming he caused her death. They would not give any details of how she died and said that he should never contact them again."

Christine remembered then how Mr. Grenville had traveled to France to learn from his uncle and "attended university," as Mrs. Grenville had called it. Now Christine knew what really transpired during his two years when no one saw him.

Meg continued, "So Grenville continued with his questions and grief these past years. He said it was not until our time at Cassfield a year ago that his heart began to open. He said that I brought new breath and joy into his life that had been missing since his wife's death. He was finally able stop thinking about the past and move out of his gloom to something new. This time, he was determined to make a match that would last, one that he could provide for, and make sure he would never have to leave.

"About a month ago, you will recall, he stated he needed to go to France 'on business.' But what he did not tell me is that his wife's parents had, after all this time, finally reached out to him. They requested that he come see them as soon as he could. And that is when everything changed."

Christine listened carefully, her countenance filling with worry because Meg was such a kind, forgiving person. *Perhaps*, thought Christine, *Mr. Grenville had some secret that should not be easily overlooked when deciding on a husband.* Meg then withdrew a letter from her dress pocket and looked meaningfully at Christine. "I had the thought that I should ask Mr. Grenville about his past, so I wrote to him during his last trip to France." She continued to stare at Christine. "And he wrote me this letter in return. As soon as he arrived in Rothershire, he came to me and we discussed it fully. I shall read you his words here."

Meg started mid-letter, *"There I was, unsure of why I was there or how I should act. I knocked with much trepidation on the front door of their dilapidated little shanty. Although they were very poor before, their family had fallen into even greater ruin.*

"When the door opened, there stood her father, dressed in rags, bent over and coughing a great spell. He ushered me in, and I could see that he was a changed man. Humbled, he asked me to sit down. His wife lay on a makeshift bed near his chair, and she seemed almost too sickly to be conscious.

"'My dear boy,' the father began, 'How we have abused you and neglected you these many years. I am so sorry and must ask for forgiveness from you.'

"I simply nodded, and I forgave them. The father continued, 'When our sweet daughter left us to marry you, we were heartbroken. And then when she came back and told us you left, we felt even more hate. In fact, we told her that she must not write to you of the state she was in. The night before she died, she told us all of the details and the truth of your marriage and your happy, although meager, life together. We had assumed you had stolen her away without any thought of marrying her or coming back to her.'

"The father paused for a moment, and the change in his voice was notable. 'What she did not tell you is that she was pregnant. We urged her to not tell you, sure you would abandon her if you knew and so she kept it a secret. We feared you might never return and did not want any disappointment to harm the baby. But the baby came early, and she died giving birth. We decided we must tell you she passed away but raise the child on our own. The baby was the only piece of her we had left, and we wanted more than anything to forget about you and remember her. And . . . therefore, we never told you about her—your—son.'

"At that moment, my dearest Meg, I saw a small urchin of a boy with a dirty, curly mop of hair come out from around the back room. The boy looked to be about four or five and had the eyes of his mother. The father continued, 'So we kept the boy to ourselves and have been raising him these past years. We decided to name him Jacques, as was his mother's wish. But now my wife has contracted a disease, and I think I have part of it too, and I am afraid we shall die and he will become an orphan. The doctor said we have an infection that does not leave easily, especially from the old. We have asked you here to tell you that you have a son, and to ask you to take him as your own.'

"Meg, darling, what was I to do? This changed everything.

"But I turned to the little boy and said in French, 'Hello there, Jacques, I am your papa. I loved your mama very much. Will you come see me?' Slowly the fledgling lad walked to me and warily sat on my knee.

"After a few moments, I turned to Jacques's grandfather and said, 'I have a few affairs to attend to in England to prepare a home for him. Perhaps the boy can come with me and stay at my sister's house until I have made all necessary arrangements through my solicitor? I swear I will *care for him always. Does this proposition suit you? I shall also leave five-hundred francs to help make your life as comfortable as possible.'*

"*The father agreed to my suggestions, and I stayed for a little while longer, talking with the family and coming to know my son. I will return to Rothershire within a fortnight, and Jacques will stay with my sister until I can fully explain all of this to you and my mother.*"

Meg looked up, not finishing the letter. She held the paper close to her chest. "The rest is quite personal. He is so kind and thoughtful, expressing that he understands if I wish to call off the engagement. Can you imagine the worry and conjectures that filled his mind?"

Meg looked at Lizzy, Christine, and Ivory with her large, beautiful blue eyes and fair skin. She was near to tears.

"Yes, of course it is a surprise to him," Christine began, taking Meg's hands in her own, "but how do you fare, Meg?"

She took a deep breath and looked away from her friends. "It has been hard for me to learn that he loved another—that he was married—and that he had a past I never knew about."

She turned back toward them and then continued, "We all know Mr. Grenville to be such an upright, good sort of man. I indeed could not have been more shocked. But the more I thought on his story, the more I saw that every aspect continued to support his true character. I did not reply to his letter, for I knew it would not reach him before he left."

For a moment, Christine witnessed much pain cross her friend's face. Meg then inhaled deeply and, smiling, continued, "For some reason, when he described little Jacques, I knew that he needed a mother. I am meant to raise him. I am sure this will cause some confusion to my family and friends, and some people who think too highly of themselves will say that my little boy has a tarnished past. But I feel that Mr. Grenville has done nothing wrong, and in fact, taking the boy in is the only right thing to do."

"And so," Meg said as she clasped Lizzy's hands, "Mr. Grenville brought the boy to his sister's and came straight to Rothershire to talk with me. I told him I still love him and all should continue as planned. He also broke the news to his stubborn mother. He shall return from his sister's with Jacques within the week."

"Will they be here for the wedding?" Christine's smile showed her approval.

"Yes, they shall," Meg said, and her grin seemed to reach across the sands.

The girls walked further down the shore, Lizzy suggesting they meet up with the fishermen finally. She seemed the only one free of secrets. Christine and the others walked quietly, reflecting, no doubt, on all the interesting truths behind the gentlemen they interacted with in the last year. Mr. Oakley had nothing to hide, nothing questionable. But Kathryn owned an unfortunate past with Mr. Braxton, they had at once all questioned Henry Robertson, Mr. Davenport had been a complete disgrace, William was the mysterious gunman who saved their lives, and now Mr. Grenville had added a child to Meg's life.

After a few minutes, Ivory began again telling more details about Mr. Ternbridge. Kathryn then gave some counsel to Ivory. Lizzy and Meg listened intently, but Christine had other ideas occupying her mind. She remembered the questions concerning Mr. Henry Robertson over a year ago. Mr. Davenport had been the informant, so she had long dispelled the belief that it could be something of import, but now she began to wonder anew. There were too many well-kept secrets, and she realized then that she did not have all the answers to Henry and William's inheritance.

The only time Christine had tried to learn of their status, William dismissed her quickly, and she would not try her hand at asking again. She remembered William speaking of his parents, but only briefly. Henry generally never spoke of the subject, and because the Robertsons were from outside Rothershire, none of Christine's acquaintances knew of their income or estate. They spoke and carried themselves as gentlemen and appeared as gentlemen. But just how much lay in store for them?

The Harrisons had never been to the Robertson estate—for it was somewhere in Scotland, Christine surmised—and no invitation to dine with them had ever been extended from the Robertson family.

The Robertsons had some family in London with a reputation, for they had attended that ball, surely from Mr. Oakley's side of the family, but Christine knew nothing else of their background. Christine and Lizzy, and Meg and Ivory for that matter, had always dismissed their family and connections, knowing them as well-bred and consequently well-moneyed Scotsmen. Mr. Oakley offered little information of his cousin's background but constantly treated them as equal in rank and standing.

What would become of Henry—and William—when they married? They seemed men of means and status, coupled with quite developed business acumen. Christine admitted then that she wished to know because, despite her last few days of trying to avoid him, she cared about William. Her feelings for him would not go away. She longed to know who he truly was.

Like an answer to her questions, several meters off stood four gentlemen, some of them exceeding handsome—with overcoats missing, trousers rolled up, and boots cast aside, almost knee deep in the cold water. A few feet up from them stood some large rocks with a basket lying on the sand at their base. The girls made their way to this part of the beach, and as they walked, Christine heard Edmund say, "Oh, that is quite impressive, William. I daresay that is your third fish, is it not?"

William had his vest and cravat removed, shirt slightly open with his sleeves folded up, and wielded a slippery, verdant fish about the size of his forearm into a basket to the left of Edmund. His brown hair was blowing a little in the breeze, and his eyes matched the water he was standing in. Christine noticed how strong he looked, his trim frame full of agility as he disposed of his catch.

He smiled at Edmund and said, "Aye! But you, Oakley, have already four!" Mr. Oakley shrugged and chuckled as the other men laughed, and it was Henry that first noticed the ladies approaching.

"Good day, ladies!" he said as he waved his hand toward them. "Come see what these gentlemen have caught! Although I have not contributed much." His great laughter filled the air.

The young women stayed near the water's edge and inspected the basket that sat on the sand.

"Four of those belong to Oakley," Henry said, "William three, Ternbridge one very small specimen, and I unfortunately stand at zero."

The men continued to fish, but Christine thought she noticed a few proud smiles, especially from Mr. Oakley and William.

Edmund spoke next, "Miss Rusket! You should be very proud of your Mr. Ternbridge here. He has never fished before. And already he has caught more than Henry."

"Which is not hard to accomplish," William retorted, slapping his brother's back as everyone laughed.

Christine curtsied and spoke to the group. "You all look quite busy." She raised her hand up the beach. "Perhaps we shall make ourselves comfortable among those rocks and grass until you have finished and watch your sport for a moment."

"Splendid!" Edmund replied, who had nearly caught another as he said it. The young women settled comfortably, enjoying the cool breeze from the ocean coupled with an occasional spray from a wave. After a few more minutes and only one more very small fish, which Henry finally caught, the men came out of the water, collected their things, and joined them.

"I suppose we should call it a day, now that Henry's caught *something*," Mr. Oakley bellowed loud enough so that the ladies could hear. He brushed himself off, and the rest of the gentlemen came out the water, putting on their shoes and jackets once again.

"What do you think of our fishing, ladies?" Mr. Oakley queried as he tied his cravat and walked toward them.

"You have all done splendidly," Lizzy said, bestowing her warmest smile.

"Yes, we have!" Mr. Oakley replied. "I think I shall give our catch to the cook for our dinner tonight, and we men are in need of some washing up before we gather again!" He threw the basket of fish under his arm, smiling wildly. The ladies of the party stood and brushed the sand from their skirts, preparing to follow the gentlemen.

The group began walking back, Lizzy and Edmund taking up the front, Lizzy inviting Meg to come on Edmund's other side. Christine was glad for the position they chose, for the smell of the fish would be blowing up wind. Henry extended an arm to Kathryn next, and they started walking together. Mr. Ternbridge offered his arm to Ivory, yet she quickly declined on account of his current perspiration and uncleanliness, but still consented to walk next to him. This left William to Christine. She pressed her lips together, feeling a bit of nervous excitement fill her being. What was it about the proximity of his presence that affected her so much? William walked confidently and steady, his shoulders relaxed, his face smiling. Being outdoors seemed to invigorate his spirit, and this was Christine's favorite version of him.

Christine's heart stirred as they walked, although she knew he felt it his duty to walk by her side as they were the last two of the party. Because she had been somewhat avoiding him for the last few days, Christine did not know what to say to begin conversation. The only thing she could think of was his conversation with Kathryn.

"Kathryn mentioned briefly to me that you asked her to testify against the Braxtons."

He looked slightly alarmed, as though he wondered what else she knew, but then said steadily, "Yes, I think she is the best inside witness and voice in the entire matter."

"I think it was wise that you asked her. I hope you did not find it impertinent that I told her of your involvement in the rescue." She looked down, awaiting his reply.

"Quite the contrary, Miss Harrison. I am grateful she had some inkling before I spoke with her, for it was hard for her to discuss such things. I believe her testimony and facts will be just what the magistrate needs to see the Braxtons safely charged and detained."

Christine gave a small smile, relieved and grateful that they had something to talk about between them. The wind gusted, throwing hair across her face, and Christine looked over her shoulder to the left.

As she brushed her curls aside, she felt William study her countenance. Christine then realized the silence between them, knowing it was her turn to speak. She felt the warmth of the sun on her skin, wondering if some of the heat came from her nearness to William and his current gaze at her. She shifted her eyes to the large, steel-colored rocks and driftwood logs that formed a small alcove. She felt his eyes follow hers.

"This is my favorite spot along the shore," she whispered.

"It is beautiful," he replied, seeming to capture it in his mind.

And then he smiled at her and offered his arm as they walked over a few craggy patches. As her bare arm rested on his, she felt a pulsing thrill through her spine. She felt William step closer as they walked, their eyes meeting. For a moment, they both stopped moving. Christine remembered their afternoon in the rain at Wellington Estate. His eyes studied hers heavily, just as they had then. William said nothing, his head tilted, ocean-blue eyes searching. She kept his gaze as long as she could and then looked away. The moment now gone, he looked toward the water and cleared his throat. His arm continued to steady hers as he escorted her over the sand until returning to the outer gate of Cassfield. Her joy of being near him increased with every step. As they ascended the gray slate stairs, she realized with a smile that some of the nervousness had dissipated. She could not say how or when, but she knew she loved being close to him.

COOK COOPER

A week passed, and Cook Cooper, having just gone into town to order the meat for the wedding, now tumbled out of her carriage. She waddled her wide hips down to the servants' quarters and kitchen. There, standing at attention, were three new kitchen hands to help with the week's festivities. She thought nothing of the express post she had sent several days before.

"You, what is your name? Rowan? Right. Now, have you ever made a meat pie, girl? And you," she said, squinting at a gangly, greasy-haired young man, "have you a good arm for chopping? I am going to need you preparing most of the vegetables. That means washing—scrubbing, more the like—and chopping, lots o' it. This next week must be perfect. Our reputation is on the line. An' I am the best cook in this county, and Mrs. Harrison knows it. So you best not disappoint me, ye hear?"

The poor new helpers were maybe fifteen years old, and each looked frightened by Cook Cooper's large presence and demanding orders. She turned to the last one, still young but quite portly, and said roughly, "An' I have not forgotten you, sonny. Now I am going to expect you to do most of the heavy liftin' and prepping, ye see? There are tables to set, meat to bring in, cauldrons to move, and the like. Do not forget your place."

He nodded rather emphatically and then gestured his hand up slowly. "Beggin' your pardon, missus," he stammered, "but just before you let in, a post a came fer ya." He slowly brandished a tattered letter, sealed and addressed to her.

She quickly snatched the communication from his hand and for a minute appeared slightly flustered. Noticing her new charges pick up on the change, she clicked her heels together as though about to salute and said, "Now be about your duties. I will have no lollygaggers around this kitchen." She threw her hand emphatically toward the ceiling and waited until the three new workers were fully engrossed in some kind of useful employment. She then turned about herself and made her way into her room. Settling rather roughly on top of her bed, she broke the wax seal and began reading the letter.

CHAPTER 26

Meg and Ivory had arrived a week before Lizzy's wedding was to take place. A few other guests trickled in a day or two before the wedding, including Mr. Grenville. During that week, the friends had spent much time together, enjoying the full light of spring days with long walks along the beach, afternoons comprising refreshing drinks and ices provided by Cook, and evenings of music and elevated conversation.

"My dear friends," Mr. Grenville said upon his arrival to all of the party, "allow me to introduce my son, Jacques." He smiled proudly down at the curly-haired blond boy at his side. "I shall share the story of how this came to be this evening after dinner, but I wanted to present him to you now." Mr. Grenville stood tall, his hands holding on to the boy's shoulders.

"G-llad to m-ake your 'quaintance," little Jacques let out in broken English as he shook Edmund's, Henry's, and William's hands.

The young ladies curtsied toward him, and then Mr. Grenville turned and said in French, "Jacques, I would especially like you to meet my dear Miss Allensby, who shall be your new mama. Shall we go for a walk with her?"

Little Jacques nodded, and the three took their leave. After that, if not at Meg's side, Jacques could be found with Christine's nephew Gavin and his younger brother, the three boys managing to become quite dirty and mischievous in no time.

Kathryn spent almost all of her time in the kitchen helping her mother. She would occasionally exchange a nod or a few sentences with Ivory and Christine if she was serving food, but she never wished to seem impertinent, and she kept to the servants almost exclusively. Christine noticed that Kathryn seemed prettier and more confident each day.

But two days before the wedding, Christine noticed Kathryn lingering a moment after breakfast, until she walked toward the servants' quarters as William descended to eat. Out of the corner of her eye, Christine saw them meet in the hallway and heard only, "Begging your pardon, Mr. Robertson, but I wondered if I might . . ." and then the two stepped to the side and Christine could no longer make out what they were saying.

Filled with interest, Christine wondered what was spoken of as William entered not two minutes later, looking flustered. But Christine caught his eye, and he attempted to hide his emotions with a cheery, "How do you do this morning, Miss Harrison?" He nodded his head curtly and turned to the rest of the party, seeking out Henry in particular.

Christine thought maybe Kathryn had some other piece of evidence to disclose to William. She tried to dismiss their meeting as nothing.

Later, Christine went on Mrs. Harrison's errand to make sure all food was procured and high quality. Nothing could be amiss for her mother's party, and Mrs. Harrison sent Christine to check on the status of the kitchen. Christine lifted her skirts and scurried downstairs, fulfilling her mother's orders as she heard the bellowing voice of Cook, ordering her troops hither and thither, making sure this was the feast of the decade.

A myriad of savory smells saturated Christine's nose. Her eyes scanned the room, impressed by the aromatic chaos. Cook Cooper spoke again, and Christine directed her question toward her. "Cook, Mrs. Harrison has asked that I check on the status of the meats. Did it all arrive as planned?"

"Good gracious, miss, who do ye think I am? Of course it is all here, or I would have someone's head faster than Mrs. Harrison would be a-knowin' about it!"

"And . . ." Christine added quickly, "she wanted to make sure you have prepared some extra place settings in case more guests arrive? She has a great fear of running out of food."

"Have we ever run out of food, Miss?"

Christine gave a conciliatory smile, placing her hands on her hips.

Cook spoke again. "No, we haven't, and this will be no exception. Now are ye done with yer pesterin'? I have the greatest feast since King Arthur and his mighty company to prepare." She waved her hand at Christine.

"Just promised my mother I would check," Christine said with a slight smile, trying to hide her amusement.

Cook harrumphed. "Miss, tell your mother she 'as nothing to worry about."

"Yes, Cook," Christine said as she started to leave.

Just then a footman came down the stairs, whispering, "Mr. Robertson is come back from his ride, Cook, if you are still wantin' to talk with him."

Christine cocked her head suspiciously, wanting to ask Cook what business she could possibly have with those brothers.

Cook suddenly seemed in quite a hurry. "Is that all you were needing, Miss Harrison?" She attempted to sidle her large frame past Christine.

"Yes, quite, thank you," replied Christine, hurrying up the stairs ahead of the cook. Unable to hide her curiosity, Christine added, "In fact, Mrs. Harrison also asked that I confirm the carriage orders for the next few days." She walked quickly, reaching the carriage house much faster than Cook.

Christine saw William immediately, still holding the reins of his horse, talking in a hushed voice to Kathryn. Christine's eyes widened, becoming more surprised and suspicious at another covert conversation between Kathryn and William. What could they possibly be talking of? And to step over such societal boundaries—speaking in secret with expressed guests of Christine's family?

Christine strode forward, curiosity getting the better of her. She knew she would not have been so intrigued had it not concerned William.

"Hello!" Christine called out in the direction of Kathryn and William, louder than necessary, trying to break them from their intimate conversation. William and Kathryn stopped talking immediately, and Christine looked back and forth between the two. William seemed visibly vexed at their run-in with Christine, shifting his weight and eyes nervously, but Kathryn stood still and calm and smiled widely.

"Have you by chance seen the groom, Mr. Robertson?" Christine knew she had completely disrupted their conversation but tried to act as matter-of-fact as possible.

"Uh . . . no," William said. "Which is why I am still holding my horse here. They say he shall be back soon."

"Right," Christine answered, crossing her arms and peering at him. "I need to check the status of tomorrow's carriages." She stopped not three feet from him, and waited silently, holding her stance. Kathryn did not move but sent an eager and happy smile to her mother.

Cook Cooper, having now reached the group, looked them all over and wiped her hands on her apron. "Beautiful day, I say," she said, seeming unfazed. She spread her feet and widened her posture, hemming and hawing in Christine's direction.

Surely they must understand how untoward this meeting is, thought Christine. But the silence grew awkward, with no one offering any more conversation and Christine knew *she* was the one everyone else wished would leave. Christine finally exhaled, frustrated, feeling perplexed and unwelcome. She retreated over her heels backward, grumbling, "I see I have no business here at present, as the groom is still away." She turned and strained her voice. "So I feel I must leave you to your own conversation."

Christine hurried off toward Cassfield, curving around the park so that she could steal one more glance over her shoulder. The group had begun talking as soon as she was out of earshot. She saw William's head nodding to Cook's animated gestures and Kathryn still looking at William with smiling eyes. Christine felt her face flush and wondered if the man she was in love with loved her friend instead.

Christine quickly entered the house, bustling past servants preparing the rooms for Lizzy's wedding tomorrow, reminding herself that the music room held the best view of the carriage house. As she reached the window, Cook Cooper could be seen waddling back toward the servants' entrance. The conversation seemed to have ended. She watched Kathryn curtsy and William nod, handing something to Kathryn and turn toward Cassfield.

What could this possibly mean? Had Christine missed the growing attachment between the two of them? Perhaps they had been exchanging letters then and the day before. Kathryn did have refined manners and superior intellect, and William never seemed to care very much about station or one's past.

Christine's mind reeled, and she felt miserable and jealous that someone could, in fact, win William's heart. She gripped the windowsill, leaning against the corner. She continued to sulk a moment when she heard footsteps ascending the stairs. She rushed quickly to the piano, fearful someone would find her pining.

Christine began a furiously fast Mozart toccata, executing it with less than her usual finesse. Not more than one minute into her song, someone almost passed the music room and then turned and entered. From her periphery, she saw a male—tall, with dark-brown hair.

Christine's heart raced. She looked up from the keys and saw William standing before her yet again. What did he think of her display of emotions just minutes ago outside? Could he hear the anxiety and frustration she felt in the notes of her song? She closed her eyes for a moment and then stopped playing. As her hands bounced from the keys, she stood and faced William.

His hands hung to his sides as his gaze rested on the wall behind her. "Miss Harrison. I beg your pardon. The groom has returned, if you are still needing his services."

What was that tone in his voice? Agitation? Obligation? Guiltiness?

William clasped his hands behind his back and walked a few paces closer.

"Thank you," Christine said, trying to add ease to her tone. But she did not want to leave now—it had been an excuse anyway, and here stood William before her. She remained next to the piano and said, "I think I shall have to look for him later. But I trust you had a pleasant ride?"

"Yes, quite," he said, furrowing his brow but offering no more details. She tilted her head, waiting for more of an explanation, but William stood silent. She had just caught him in a clandestine meeting with servants, and he made no reference at all. Driven by his deliberate lack of conversation, she let her mouth get the better of her.

"You do not often feel the need for elaboration, do you?" Christine challenged, with only a hint of a smile. She had him as a captive audience. He could not avoid her now.

"I beg your pardon, Miss Harrison, what do you mean?" he asked, still gazing behind her. His tone was even and calm.

"I just thought you might have some reason for your meeting with Cook and Kathryn . . ." Christine thought also of the day before at breakfast but did not mention *that* conversation. Christine shifted a bit closer to him and crossed her arms.

He turned away from the window and glanced down at the piano. His eyes smiled for a moment, as though he were amused. And then his smile fell into a pensive stare. "Have you taken a keen interest in my affairs as of late?" William returned.

Now he had caught her. Christine pressed her hands on to the lid of the piano, feeling flustered and embarrassed. "Well, yes. I mean . . . no. I just thought such a meeting seemed unusual. Is there anything the matter?"

How did he always have the upper hand in circumstances like these? Just like when he told of saving them in London, he seemed to always know more than Christine.

William smiled and said with a kind but sad look, "You of all people, Miss Harrison, need not worry yourself with my affairs." He exhaled slowly. "But I thank you for your genuine concern." His face filled with a steady steel-gray resolution she had seen before. He looked down and moved to go.

Her of *all* people? What a thing to say. Fire and indignation buoyed within Christine. She had avoided him long enough, ignored seeking to know the real William long enough. She would wait no longer.

She bit her lip and exhaled quickly. "I beg your pardon, Mr. Robertson, but I do not understand you. I must know why you insist on such secret concision. Surely we are good enough acquaintances for you to share some details of your life."

It felt like a weight off her back. No amount of frustration could quell her true feelings for him. She did not know how to tell him she cared. But she could tell him that he could at least trust her. His words would be safe with her.

William crossed his arms, his tight, thin smile crossing his lips before he let out a slow breath. "I have many reasons for modesty, Miss Harrison, which I shall not enumerate now. But I feel it might be best to express that my temperament does not lend itself to great expositions of feeling."

Even with her invitation, he stayed guarded. Christine's eyes lowered to the floor. "And so you would say that you feel deeply about very little?" she said quietly.

Through her periphery she could feel his eyes staring at her. He took two quick strides toward her, resting his hand on the piano.

"On the contrary, Miss Harrison. I feel quite deeply about many things, but one must know me to understand how they manifest."

Christine gathered her skirts in her hands and curtsied slowly. In her heart, she admitted defeat.

She turned and brushed past him. "Then how I wish I knew you better," Christine said under her breath, walking away quickly, not quite sure William had heard her.

CHAPTER 27

The next morning Christine woke before sunrise, unable to sleep any longer. She recalled images of Kathryn and William together, but she tried to focus on the happy events of the day ahead. She set off toward the shore, grateful for a few moments alone to clear her mind before the excitement of Lizzy's wedding ensued. She did not want any of her wayward thoughts disrupting the celebration.

What a different feeling Cassfield held this year. Lizzy was about to be married and Meg not far behind. Even Ivory had a man seriously courting her. And perhaps William was already courting Kathryn.

But Christine stood alone.

And yet, she thought, *better to be alone than ill-matched in marriage.* She reflected on Mr. Davenport and how different she had been a year ago. Selfish, self-important, and much too worried about what others thought.

But she had Mr. Davenport's cruel turn of events to thank for acquainting her to whom she had become. She still had far to go to be as selfless as she should be—as selfless as people like Meg—but she resolved to try.

Christine came close enough to the water's edge to see each soft wave lap over the sand below her. How she loved these tides, with their never-ending change. It taught her that she could be different, be better, and wash up anew just as they did each day.

She walked further, spotting her favorite alcove with its rambling rocks and driftwood. As she approached it, she noticed a tall figure behind her leaving Cassfield, beginning on her same path toward the sand. He moved quickly, it seemed, though still far away. Christine thought the only one to fit such a silhouette would be Mr. Oakley, perhaps coming for his last moment alone before making his vows.

She turned and walked on, giving him his own privacy. She listened to the gulls voice their morning cries and the waves fall rhythmically, noticing how calm the water seemed before sunrise. A few moments later, she felt someone close behind her.

And then she heard his voice.

"Miss Harrison, I am glad to have found you here."

Christine turned quickly, and there stood William. He was dressed in his navy suit, looking rather dapper, with a clean white shirt and matching cravat. He wore russet-colored pants with tall polished boots, prepared to walk. He appeared completely ready for the wedding, even though the sun had not yet risen. As she looked up, he gallantly swept his hand down around his waist and bowed.

Glancing down at her simple cream linen day dress, she brushed her skirt and her hair. Christine knew she needed much attention from her maid before the wedding.

"I am very sorry to have taken you off guard," he began, sounding concerned that he might have flustered her. "But might I have a word with you here, now? It is quite lovely outside, and I have much to say." He seemed as happy and free as when he had been fishing on those same shores a few days before. His face held a smile, his eyes seeking hers.

Christine stifled a nervous laugh in her hand. The man who the day before had offered her no explanation of anything had much to say? Surely he did not mean it. She continued to look at William, his perfect dark hair framing his face, a hopeful grin creasing one side of his mouth. Christine staggered back slightly, the hem of her dress becoming soaked with salt water. She tried to gather her wits and gave a small curtsy.

Christine wrinkled her brow and said amused, "Do go on, Mr. Robertson."

He took a deep breath. "I woke early, unable to sleep. I was dressing when I saw from my window who I thought to be you crossing toward the shore, and I could not help walking to find you. I have come to ascertain a few details. Please, would you do me the honor of accompanying me?

"Yes," Christine said with a nod, intrigued. What was he up to? Perhaps he needed more background information on the Braxtons for his case. This had been the one subject he had given details on. But why now, alone, and so early?

Seeming to sense her queries, he continued, "I sometimes have trouble sleeping, and last night and this morning were no small exception." He walked closer toward Christine's favorite alcove, and she remembered that she had pointed this spot out to him a few days ago. He gestured for her to sit on a smooth rock. He brushed his hand over his hair. "I fear many of my thoughts included you, so I wanted to talk with you, alone, before the wedding."

His thoughts included *her*? She really should be returning to help Lizzy soon. Part of her, however, wanted William to stay all morning in the warming sun and talk of everything.

She stroked her disheveled curls once more. She looked at him intently, waiting for him to begin. What was that look on his face? Confidence? Determination? Hope?

William's gaze fixed across the horizon. For one who professed he had so much to say, he took his time to begin. She realized that this was a version of him she had not seen before. He seemed to be having a conversation with himself, perhaps one he had many times. The moment felt eternal before he looked back at her.

He finally smiled and came even closer, so that his pants brushed Christine's skirt as he took a seat directly across from her.

"Miss Harrison, I feel the need to apologize for my formal and concise manner toward you. I realize, especially after our conversation yesterday, how odd my behavior must seem. Today I hope to cast away any confusion and wish to speak openly with you."

Christine's eyes widened and she filled with nerves. *What could he possibly say?* "Shall we go inside and discuss more of the Braxton's case with Mr. Oakley and your brother? We could even invite Kathryn to come give us details," Christine said, gesturing toward Cassfield. *He will surely want to include Kathryn*, Christine thought.

Christine looked up at his gray-blue eyes, themselves an ocean of thought at that moment.

His handsome face was turned toward hers, his head angled down, his mouth a firm, sure line.

Christine's heart echoed the sound of the waves behind her. What was he doing sitting here with her? What did this look like for the two of them to be together? Did William not understand the possible impropriety? Especially for a man who had no intentions of marry-ing—at least not her. And most of all, did he not understand how much Christine enjoyed seeing him at this moment?

She left her reverie and spoke with clarity. "I think I must be going back, for Lizzy will surely need my assistance at any moment. Please excuse me." She stood and began treading up the hill toward Cassfield.

He stood and turned his square shoulders directly at her, his intent face willing her back, "There is no reason for me to keep up such pre-tense," he said, "I have decided to give it up. Miss Harrison—Christine. Will you please allow me to speak freely with you?" His voice carried over the waves, his eyes following her every movement. "And will you please stop suggesting ways to end our walk? I will not leave until I have said my part."

Christine stood still for a moment and then stepped back down the hill slowly until she was again at his side. His eyes creased a little, filled with longing, seeming to petition her.

What did he wish to say? He had used her name. And nothing in his countenance spoke of disapproval—if anything, it looked quite the contrary. She glanced up as courageously as she could muster. He towered across from her, his piercing eyes bewitching her, her frame small and feminine compared to his tall one. His angled jaw clenched.

And then he smiled, openly. His head tilted to the side and his eyebrows raised, seeming to plead his case.

His honest and open look had a strong effect on Christine. He extended his arm deliberately, and Christine paused for a moment, smiling back at him. She acquiesced and placed her arm on his, this time feeling him pull her closer. She felt her skin against his warm body and could smell his clean scent. How wonderful it felt to be so near him. Christine realized then that she no longer felt nervous. Something about his presence completely calmed her.

He cleared his throat, and the pair walked in silence a few paces more. They came back to her favorite spot, a few of the rocks now casting a shadow as the sun crept over the horizon. There he gestured for Christine to sit once more, as he stood more composed.

"Miss Harrison, I have long felt uneasy about my future. As you well know, I have been quite involved with my family and my business. It has been my intention to postpone marriage until I could . . . until I . . ."

He stopped for a moment. "There is much to explain, but this I know. Ever since I realized you were the one to rescue Kathryn, I have not been able to put you from my mind. When you and I serendipitously ran into each other in Rothershire—I could not help myself and asked you to spend the afternoon with me. I wanted answers, but I also needed to know if I could possibly share a future with you. I learned a great deal about your rescue that next day during the rain, but I was still confused as to your feelings toward me. And now, even among friends here, I did not know of your regard. Every moment I watch you, I want more to be with you. I even asked Miss O'Rourke of your regard for me, but she did not know."

Christine's face shot up, far too speechless to respond. She studied his countenance without inhibition as he continued. He ran his hand through his hair again and looked directly at her.

"I must tell you the worst of it. I declared I would not marry two years ago. That is when I learned that my family has all but lost their entire fortune and estate. Our debt so great, we have almost nothing left. I know what you must think of me, masquerading as a gentleman when I am nothing but a pauper. I am often ashamed of myself but could not resist your company. Oakley has let us stay with him, and Henry does not seem to mind living this life, but it is all a lie.

"I promised myself that I would never marry until I could rectify the situation by my own labors. I wish to make enough money to reestablish our holdings. But this could take years. Thus, I am so invested in my work."

He breathed a deep sigh and continued, "I would never, ever want you or anyone thinking that I wished to marry to alleviate my debt. For that reason, I could never let myself care about you. My pride declared I could never have you—even though I think you perfect."

Christine's cheeks burned as she looked at him, clinging to every word of his continuing speech.

"And the more time I spent near you, the more agonizing this all became. I stand here with feelings which want to leap out of my heart. I know now that I cared for you all along, ever since we danced at Lizzy's ball. Then there was your rescue of Kathryn, which spoke of your true character. And finally, last week when I heard you play Mozart, the piece you knew was my favorite, I thought to myself, *I think I love her.*"

Christine's heart caught in her chest. Did he mean what he said? He thought he *loved* her?

"But I stand at a precipice this morning. As soon as the wedding concludes, Henry and I must journey to Scotland. There are many particulars, but I shall just say it is to face the man to whom we owe our debt." He heaved a large sigh. "Christine—I simply cannot ignore my feelings any longer. I have absolutely nothing to recommend myself besides my person. I love you and wish you to be mine forever."

Christine took a few deep breaths, clasping her hands together, processing all he had just said, and remained silent. He thought he loved her. But he would leave as soon as the wedding concluded. What exactly did he have in mind for his future? And what was *her* heart telling her at that moment?

She watched William's eyes fill with worry as she did not respond. His uneasiness grew as the silence lengthened, and he folded his arms across his chest as he said, "I realize I am not the most eloquent of men. I do not flatter and compliment as well as others. Charm has never been my strong suit. But who I love, I love deeply. You have won me in every way and I will be fiercely loyal to you, dear Christine—if you will have me. I love every part about you—your eyes, your smile, the way you care for others." He drew nearer and pushed a lock of hair from Christine's eyes, adding slowly, "And your curls," he smiled ruefully—"and your kindness."

Christine's eyes locked with his for a moment. She felt all of his goodness in his gaze.

He looked down and shook his head. "But of course it is quite possible you do not love me back. Or if you did ever feel any regard for me, it has most likely vanished, now that you know who I really am. It could take years for me to earn enough money to marry you, but there is not a man alive who will work harder than I will to provide for you and secure your affections."

He paced away from her, clasping his hands behind his back.

Christine's thoughts and feelings swirled around her, and she looked to the ocean, trying to collect herself, clenching her skirt in her hands. She could not deny that she loved him. But admitting it and becoming vulnerable filled her with fear. With no inheritance or holdings to recommend him, her life would be so altered should she choose to connect herself with him. And would she disappoint her family with such a match? What would they think of their eldest daughter marrying in such a way?

And had he just declared he would *not* marry her until he secured his future? What did he mean?

If she were truly bold, she would tell him she loved him back. But the fear of this ending like Mr. Davenport came back to her mind. Would it become an attachment that might lead to years of confusion and never quite to marriage? She closed her eyes, trying to search her own heart.

When she opened them, she saw William turn and look at her once more.

Christine stood.

All of the good she knew of this man came surging into her heart, filling her with peace and hope. He was honest and upright. He held to his principles. He had absolutely no guile, never wanting to promote himself for any kind of gain. Everything he did—from his family, to his business, to rescuing Kathryn, even trying to ignore his love for herself—had been for the benefit of others. Never had he acted in his own self-interest. And now he had been bold enough to declare his love for her.

Her eyes connected with William's in a silent moment, a new set of feelings coursing through her. She realized she had a choice to make. She could either let her old fears haunt her—and stop her. Or she could move forward, choosing to hope, believing that her future would work. And with this hope, commit to herself and William that this love could be theirs forever.

She did not know what her future would look like, but she felt confident in his love.

She could trust William.

"Mr. Robertson, I . . ." Her voice faltered for a moment. She stepped closer to him. She loved him—that she knew. Suddenly something welled within her and buoyed her courage enough to say what she felt in her heart.

She took a deep breath and fixed her gaze on him.

"William—I thought I could never have a chance to come to know you. I thought you had given me up for a conceited, self-important girl you would not deign to waste your time on. But how many times I have wished for a second chance." She paused, exhaling as a smile spread over her countenance. Then her eyes opened wider as her tone softened and she added much more slowly, "You have found purchase on my soul."

She turned toward the ocean, gathering the last bit of courage. She looked back at him, her smile the most confident it had ever been.

"William, I love you."

For a moment he said nothing, keeping his gaze on her. He just moved a bit closer and closed his warm, large hands around Christine's, drawing her near, looking over her toward the ocean, his head resting on top of her hair. The air held this new, pleasant silence for what felt like a long time.

CHAPTER 28

They basked in the sound of the waves and each other's company for a few minutes, as the sun grew stronger, until Christine could not help but address the subject again.

"William," she said, smiling, relishing his name, "surely you cannot scruple against my fifteen thousand pounds now? That must be enough to pay off your debts."

He put his arms around her for the first time as she lifted her chin to meet his gaze.

"My dear, I cannot live with myself if I use your money in such a way. We shall just have to wait to declare our affections."

"But I do not mind in the least," Christine pleaded. "The money would be ours, not only mine."

"My mind is quite made up, my dear. I promised myself, and I cannot stop now."

Christine pulled away slightly. "But . . ." she said, watching him shake his head, his eyes unwavering. She looked down, her heart sinking. This meant that he still was not hers. "Then what do you propose?" she asked quietly, a sad coldness entering her voice.

"I do not know at present." William gave a tense sigh, Christine watching his body go rigid. "I wish to marry you just as soon as we are able. Would you be willing, my dear, to go forward with that understanding between us both? I do not wish to hold you to an official secret engagement, for I do not abide such deceit, nor would I want to inflict such a mark upon your character." His eyes looked across the sea, his heart seeming far away for a moment.

Her shoulders crumbled in a long sigh, the ecstasy she felt minutes before deflating measurably.

"I believe I understand, Mr. Robertson. There is no engagement between us." She stepped away. She tried to stifle a tear as she turned her back to him.

"I think it best," William said, a heaviness in his voice. Christine felt him turn away, as though he knew the pain of his words. "I do wish to make all known as soon as I return from Scotland. I shall then speak with your father in private, informing him of my plans to continue my business until I can provide for you and reverse my debts, and we shall stay close acquaintances until I can ask for an official engagement and marriage."

He turned and looked into her eyes, deeper than he ever had before, and Christine felt maybe he understood her concern and hurt. "But never doubt, my dear Christine, how much I love you. With every part of my soul, I declare it."

He embraced her once again, but she withdrew quickly and started to walk toward the manor.

Christine, a few paces ahead of William, looked toward Cassfield and heard someone calling.

"Christine?" Meg came down the stone steps in search of her friend. She had been sent to fetch her, for Christine was needed—or at least her abilities were—at that very minute. Christine had not planned on staying at the ocean's edge for so long and was already hurrying up to the house. Mr. Robertson held back a little more at the sight of Meg.

"Oh, I am sorry. I did not expect to see you here, Mr. Robertson," Meg said as she flashed a wickedly suspicious glance toward Christine. "Your mother requests your presence immediately. She is in the drawing room."

"Of course. I shall go to her at once."

"Yes," William said, "And I will go too, to be at your—or your mother's—complete disposal."

They hurried inside, Mr. Robertson following directly behind Christine.

"Mother!" Christine said as she entered the drawing room. "I am so sorry for the delay. You see, Mr. Robertson has dressed early this morning and is ready . . . to help with anything that you need. I caught him outside Cassfield, and he declared he must be of service." Christine shot a tepid smile in his direction that only he could see.

"Yes, to be sure!" he said, a bit flummoxed. "What can I do for you, Mrs. Harrison?"

"How very kind of you to ask," She looked surprised but then set him to work overseeing the servant's outdoor preparations for the wedding.

Outside, the gardener and his other assistants began setting up places for the guests to congregate, and Christine was ever so glad that Meg was the only person to see her so close to William, and not several of the servants. Christine then went to Lizzy, to help her prepare, as was her mother's wish.

Lizzy sat at her dressing table, a maid gently unwrapping a few curls, and together the maid and Christine finished Lizzy's hair and her dress. Lizzy shone, absolutely stunning, with attention to every detail. Her silky blonde tresses seemed to sparkle, accented with ribbons, flowers, and pearls. The entirety of her dress was covered in delicate lace, which complemented her form beautifully. The sisters took breakfast in their room that morning, not wanting to jeopardize Lizzy's good luck. And then, an hour and a half later, the maid helped Christine finally attend to her own appearance.

The wedding was to take place on the lawn behind Cassfield Manor. As Christine filed into the front where Mr. Oakley's parents stood, she saw Henry with William by his side. Henry smiled at Christine, with more sanction than usual, and William's face was nothing but adoration and approval. She glanced at her rose-colored organza dress made for this occasion and silently thanked her maid for her more tamed locks. Christine hoped that although she spent most of the morning helping Lizzy, her appearance might impress William a little more than at their earlier meeting. She tried in that moment to focus on the wedding instead of the declarations from William—still unsure of what their future would hold together.

The clergyman pronounced a beautiful speech, and music started afterward, beginning an afternoon of festivities. Christine realized then that William no longer wore any bandage and now seemed eager and willing to dance, as though he could not help himself.

William had just finished the first dance with Christine when she looked over his shoulder and spotted Cook Cooper charging toward her.

What on earth is Cook doing coming now to the party? thought Christine. Cook looked sheepishly at Christine but continued on her course. As soon as William eyed the cook, he walked to the edge of the dancers, Christine still on his arm. He saw Cook placing her hands on her large hips emphatically.

"Beggin' your pardon, Mr. Robertson," Cook whispered, "but I have just received a letter, and Lord Stewart's health is failing even more. I think you and Henry ought to set off directly."

William's tall head bent toward her, surprised. "You declare we should leave *right* now?"

Standing a bit wider, the determined cook retorted, "Begging your pardon, but the sooner the better, sir. No time to waste. Ye shall not reach tomorrow's coach if you do not leave soon."

Christine puzzled as she looked at William's face. He was not in the habit of following orders and seeing him stop and take Cook's commands so obediently confused Christine.

"I am afraid, my dear, that I must leave straight away," William said in a low whisper, and he bowed toward her. He walked to Henry and the two spoke briefly before Henry headed back to the manor as William made his way to the horses.

"What was that about?" Mr. Grenville asked, walking toward Christine. He must have seen the whole exchange.

"Those Scottish brothers always have some task to attend to!" Christine laughed back, trying to smooth over the confusion she felt. "And Cook Cooper—she never lacked for gusto, to be sure!"

Henry and William had already disappeared and came out a few minutes later.

William strode over the grass toward the party and found Christine immediately. "Miss Harrison," William said formally, "will you accompany me to say my goodbyes and well-wishes to the happy couple?" He was already steering Christine in that direction and then lowered his voice. "There is so much more to explain but know that Henry and I shall be gone for at least a fortnight. I will explicate all when I return, for even now I am not sure of all the particulars. Cook demands we travel now, as she is a relation of those to whom we owe our debt. When I return," he said, even more hushed, "I will speak to your father." He was at once serious yet content. Christine did not know what to make of it. She did not feel the same, still quite confused and uncertain. Here stood the man she just learned loved her, leaving before she could even talk with him.

Still jumbled, Christine simply nodded her head, "Yes, I shall look forward to your return."

Reaching Lizzy and Edmund, William took Edmund by the hand and looked Lizzy in the eye. "My warmest wishes for you both. You are some of the best people I know, and I wish you every happiness. Henry and I must leave, but I am sure we will see much of each other in the future." He had a twinkle in his eye, and the new Mr. and Mrs. Oakley nodded. Christine wondered if Edmund might know of William's true feelings.

Christine and William began walking toward the house as William increased his pace. He pressed Christine's hand gently for a brief moment and looked over his shoulder. He then pulled a small envelope out of his coat pocket. "Take this," he said, handing it to Christine. "I think you shall understand much upon reading it. Perhaps I shall not have so many secrets now." He gave a wry smile.

Christine took the letter and tucked it into her dress. Christine tried to memorize his gaze as William's eyes shone toward her, and Christine felt secure in his love for a moment.

"I shall return to you as soon as I can," he whispered, and he walked briskly to the front gate. Henry stood waiting for him, carrying a small bag of their things, with their horses ready. Christine hardly had time to breathe.

Waving, she exclaimed, "Goodbye!" and the two brothers thundered eastward down the road.

MR. WILLIAM ROBERTSON

Henry threw the reins to William. Simultaneously, they mounted their horses and began riding at a break-neck speed. Their journey would take them several days. A day to reach the mail coach, another to travel through the lake district, and from there another day or two to reach their destination. They rode all afternoon and into the evening, stopping at a dingy inn to rest their horses and stay the night. Their plan was to ride to Kendal and from there catch the coach that would drive night and day.

"And you think this to be a positive meeting? He could not dare to exact more from us, could he?" Henry asked William as they settled.

"I spoke to Cook yesterday, and she said that it could change the course of our lives forever. Cook sounded so urgent—hopeful, but unsure as well—that I could not argue with her, but I pray for the best. I do not know how this will end." William cast a tired look toward his brother.

Henry sighed, rubbing his temples until a sly grin crossed his face. "On another note, I noticed you left our room quite early this morning." He smiled. "You seemed on *quite* better terms with Miss Harrison at the wedding." He threw up his feet on the small table in triumph.

William rubbed his hands together and sat a bit taller in his wooden chair across from Henry. "You have found me out, brother. I have, as I believe you have witnessed, long held interest for Miss Harrison," William glowed with pride and contentment. "She knows of my feelings for her as of this morning, but we are not yet engaged. Please say nothing to anyone yet."

"I knew you would win her . . . eventually," Henry teased, in true brotherly fashion. Henry threw his hand against William's head as William pushed him away with a laugh.

CHAPTER 29

That night, after the party had quieted, Christine retired to her room, without Lizzy, alone for the first time. Before extinguishing her candle, she finally opened the letter from William earlier that day.

Mr. William Robertson,

I hope this letter finds you in the best of health and spirits. Lest it seem untoward that I have written, I have learned of your whereabouts through my granddaughter, Mrs. Cooper, who has met your acquaintance. After corresponding with her, I cannot thank you enough for all you have done for my family and her daughter. Words cannot do justice for your part in Kathryn's rescue.

I am sure it came as a surprise that a cook and a governess could be so entirely connected to the Stewart name, but it is true. I should have stopped my son from disowning Mrs. Cooper so many years ago. I now find myself full of regret for the way in which I distanced myself from my posterity.

Having been apprised by Mrs. Cooper, I know that you know the full details concerning property dealings between our two families. I wish to discuss this matter with you and your brother at your earliest convenience. As my health is failing, I urge you to come quickly to my estate in Dumfrieshire. I shall explain all then.

Sincerely,
Lord Galliard Stewart

Christine sat up in her bed. She read the letter again. She understood that William traveled somewhere to meet with a man to whom his family owed great debts. But that this man—Lord Stewart—was the grandfather of Cook Cooper and the great-grandfather of Kathryn? Could it be true? The cook they had known their whole life—and the young woman she had rescued—could they actually come from a wealthy lord in Scotland? Separated by status, fallen rank, and pride. This must be the truth.

Suddenly, Christine understood the secret moments and hushed meetings between Cook, Kathryn, and William. No wonder Kathryn seemed so unconcerned and confident around him. And Christine finally understood why William had not explained his meeting with Cook and Kathryn. Over the last week, Cook and Kathryn must have informed William of such connections and delivered the correspondence from Lord Stewart.

So William traveled now to meet with Cook Cooper's grandfather. What exactly would happen between Henry and William and Lord Stewart? What would be said? What would be expected or exacted? Should she fear for William? The man she loved had saved Kathryn's life but lost his entire fortune to her great-grandfather. Christine marveled, not knowing what to think about such interconnected circumstances.

Mr. William Robertson

It had been five years since Henry or William had set foot on the Stewart Estate. Now as they approached its outer fields, the stone house stood like a castle set upon dilapidated peat. This mossy, gray-green mansion was something they would often pass by, in the distance, when playing as young boys. But the stories of the ghosts that possessed the house usually kept them away. William remembered once at an Easter Sunday service seeing a gray-haired old man in one of the front pews. He had asked his father who he was, and his father answered that he was the man who lived in "the great stone mansion on the hill." It was Lord Stewart, the great-grandfather of the family, his father continued to explain, and he was not to be bothered by anyone. But William could not help but stare at him throughout the service, and he distinctly remembered the scowl the old man bestowed upon him when their eyes met.

Now the house was inhabited by his son—who William surmised might look just as old as that man in the church by now. This was Cook's grandfather, Kathryn's great-grandfather whom she had never met. Cook Cooper's father had disowned her all those years ago when she married so beneath her station to a poor farmer in their town.

Henry bellowed to the coachman to stop. They would walk to the immense front doors, and the driver would wait outside until they sent him further instructions. William and Henry had no idea how long they might be inside. Expecting a recalcitrant old man upon entering, William smoothed his thick sable hair as Henry tightened his cravat. Swallowing hard, William knocked on the great mahogany door that towered over them.

A butler in crisp green plaid livery answered.

"We were sent here to see Lord Stewart," William said, offering his card.

The butler raised one white wiry eyebrow almost off his forehead and said with a thick brogue, "And who sent you?"

"Lord Stewart himself, via communication with Mrs. Cooper from Rothershire and her daughter, Kathryn O'Rourke."

The butler's countenance changed, and he clipped his shoes together quickly. "Right this way, gentlemen." He gestured for them to come inside.

William shot a glance of trepidation over his shoulder at Henry, and they continued through the murky, dimly lit hallway and up a spiral staircase. This mansion had once been a place of grandeur, no doubt. But now it seemed worn out, with not enough love or life to keep it going. The wall hangings spoke of an earlier splendor, the intricate tapestries now dust-laden, hanging heavily from windows and walls. Some of the candelabras lacked a light, leaving the halls feeling dark and forgotten. The few servants they saw looked tied to duty, but they had no one really to wait upon.

Finally they came to the corner of the third floor, where the doors to a large suite were barely opened. The butler rapped the door and then said, "Your grace, I believe the young men you sent for are here at last."

The butler drew the curtains so a little more light entered the room. There, engulfed in a plush, wing-backed armchair, sat a withered, cantankerous-looking man. Upon seeing Henry and William, however, the man's face softened and he smiled. For a moment, William thought he could see who this man once was, someone everyone enjoyed spending time with.

"Gentlemen! How you resemble your grandfather—and great-grandfather as well! Please have a seat." There was a long gold bench covered in scarlet paisley across from the armchair, and Henry and William quickly settled not five feet away from this man and his formidable gaze.

"I have not much strength left in me, so I will get right down to it," he began in a thick brogue. "As I am sure you have surmised from your grandfather and father, many years ago my father and your grandfather made an agreement of land. Although extremely advantageous to the family Stewart, it was rather less so to the Robertson clan. At first I reveled in the opulence such an agreement afforded our family. But over the last twenty years, as my family left me through death or estrangement, I felt guilty for the way I treated your family. Then my granddaughter finally reached out to me and told me of what you had done for my great-granddaughter, Kathryn. My saucy granddaughter scolded me in that letter and said that I must make it right with your family. I had not talked to . . . to Mrs. Cooper, as you call her . . . for twenty years, but she had the audacity to put me in my place. And I daresay she was right." He sighed deeply, a sigh full of regret and anguish. Then he looked up again. "Which one of you is William?"

Henry turned his head, and William briefly nodded. "It is I, sir," William said quietly.

The old man coughed, covering his mouth with a silky hand-kerchief. "I cannot thank you enough, young man, for saving my great-granddaughter's life. When I learned of it, I was so utterly and completely grateful, I did not know what to say. I know you did not know then that Kathryn was my great-granddaughter, but I feel I must repay you in some way. And then when I learned that it was the same

Robertsons whom we had done business with so long ago, my con-science haunted me. Mrs. Cooper's letter was the last straw, and here I am, requesting your presence."

He coughed thickly again and pulled a stack of papers from a drawer next to him. Swallowing hard, he continued.

"My only son passed away seven years ago. My only granddaugh-ter, as you know, is Mrs. Cooper, and she is not allowed under law to hold this property, nor would she want it. This place was never fit for her. I have much money saved, which I have allocated for her and Kathryn. As it stands, they shall live royally forevermore. Since I came to this conclusion, I have been working with my solicitor, and through some reversal of contract, and by some old-fashioned Scottish intimi-dation and bribery, I have had them write this estate into the hands of Mr. William Robertson. I have also entailed some of my other proper-ties in England to you, Henry. What do you say to that, gentlemen?"

William and Henry both wore a quizzical look as the gravity of Lord Stewart's speech settled upon them. They sat silent for a moment, William's eyes going wide. Finally, William cleared his throat.

"Sir, I think this is quite a generous offering to a person you have never before met," William stated slowly.

Lord Stewart did not speak but looked solemnly from William to Henry and back to William. It felt as though he were judging their souls, seeing if they did indeed measure up to the standard he had set for them. After several moments, Lord Stewart continued, "On the contrary, this is a just reward for your noble deeds, and moreover, I must make things right once again between our two families. I owe it to your grandfather and father."

"This is very kind of you, sir," Henry said. Lord Stewart then straightened his back as he shifted in the wing-backed chair.

He gestured to the two brothers. "Come here, and read these with me."

William pulled a chair near him, followed by Henry. The three men then dutifully went through each page, one by one, each reading and signing where it was necessary. The more they sat together, the more talkative Lord Stewart became, but his coughing increased.

"Sir," William said, "perhaps we should return tomorrow and resume this paperwork? I fear that such rigorous attention to detail may be a strain to your health."

Lord Stewart pursed his lips downward, looking surprised. He checked his pocket watch. "I was unaware of the hour! Now that you mention it, I am rather spent. But could you return tomorrow, around midday?"

William looked at Henry and then nodded. "Of course, sir."

"And you are both welcome to stay here tonight. I always have my servants keep a few guest rooms at the ready."

"That is very kind of you, sir. But with your permission, Henry and I would like to return to our own home and inform our grandfather of this . . . change of contract."

Lord Stewart sat back in his chair, folding his hands across his belly. "You must report to me what your grandfather says. If only I could see the look on his face." He smiled, chuckling to himself.

The next morning, William and Henry came again promptly at noon. The curtains were drawn open and sunlight shone through the windows. Lord Stewart wore a crisp new shirt and ornate jacket, and he seemed to sit four inches taller in his chair.

"Gentlemen, good day. Last night I had the best sleep I have had in years. I feel like a new person."

William and Henry smiled, sitting to continue looking through the documents. After another hour, Lord Stewart stopped and said, "You know, I feel I am improving in health by the minute. My conscience feels so light that my body has been liberated. Do you think, if I continue to improve the next few days, that I could return to Rothershire with you both? I long to see Mrs. Cooper again and lay eyes on my great-granddaughter for the first time."

William nodded, smiling. "Yes, of course. We are at your service. Staying a few days until your health improves would be no problem at all." He thought then of Christine, as he had so many times since leaving her side. He wished he would not have to endure so many days apart, and hoped she thought of him in his absence.

Four days and several meetings later—for Lord Stewart wanted to know everything about the Robertsons, the lives of Mrs. Cooper and Kathryn, and even meet with William's grandfather—the three men began their return to Wellington.

CHAPTER 30

$\mathcal{I}$t had been two weeks since Christine had seen William, with no post in the interim. Her family had left Cassfield and returned to Wellington, and her days had almost returned to normal. Yet every bit of her heart and mind was altered, and she stood trapped in a life that looked the same by every outward appearance.

She thought nearly every hour about William. She replayed the scene on Cassfield's shores over and over, rehearsing every part of their conversation to herself. What started out as curiosity soon turned to worry. The connection between Kathryn, Cook, and William's family astounded her. Three times Christine had found some excuse to go to the kitchen.

"I do not know much," Cook responded the first time.

"I fear, my dear, I am not at liberty to say," she answered Christine the second time.

The third time, Christine opened her mouth to speak, and Cook Cooper simply waved her wooden spoon and said, "Yer wasting your time, my dear."

Now a few days later, Christine's back rested against the warm bark of an oak tree, as she attempted to read *Lyrical Ballads* by Wordsworth, finding herself retracing several passages without much comprehension. Mid-stanza, over the babbling of the river next her, she heard the crunching of grass. It sounded as though something or someone was coming quickly in her direction.

She turned, holding her place in her book. Her hand suddenly dropped her literature to the ground as she beheld the most handsome vision of a man she could have expected just stepping off his horse. She stood slowly, as if in a daze. Then, in a few bounds he reached her side.

Finally William had returned to her. He was smiling broadly, barely able to keep his excitement within himself. When he reached her, he picked up Christine by the waist and spun her around once. Christine's eyes filled with surprise as her heart filled with joy, and William put her down abruptly.

"I am sorry, my dear. I could not contain myself. I believe we are alone, are we not? Lizzy told me the direction you walked," he said as he smoothed his hair and his suit coat.

"Yes, we are quite alone, but I was not expecting such an excited reunion! I have thought about you every day but was unsure of *your* feelings and actions. So please, tell me what has merited such enthusiasm!" Christine smiled up at him, not more than six inches from his face. She had never before seen or felt such an unrestrained display of emotion from William.

He smiled, tilting his head to the side, remaining close to her face. "Christine, I wish you would never doubt my affection for you again. Not a day has gone by when I have not thought of you and envisioned the moment I could see you again." He swallowed, pulling on his cravat. "For in our time apart I have come upon some wonderful circumstances."

"Whatever do you mean?" she responded, standing still for a moment, her eyes widening and her mind reveling in delight. First he had returned to her, and now what news did he have to report?

Seemingly unable to contain himself, William took Christine's hand in his arm and escorted her to a patch of grass by the river as they sat close to one another. She watched him begin to explain his time in Scotland, as she gazed unrestrained at his perfect countenance. Full of energy, William proceeded to tell her every detail of Lord Stewart and his estate. She often asked him questions, concentrating on even the smallest aspects of his story.

They had only been apart for two weeks, but it had felt like an eternity. Now their conversation progressed as though they had known each other for years. Christine felt her heart beating quickly as she soaked up his every smile, clung to his every word as he explained all.

Could she really be his?

After nearly an hour of retelling, William turned to Christine, and asked, "And so, what do you say to such a story?"

She smiled unencumbered, looking across the stream, then meeting his eyes again. She came closer as she viewed him wait anxiously for a reply. Christine wished to tell him every racing thought of her heart, thrilling that they could now be married. What words could she find that could adequately express the feelings welling inside of her? Nothing could do justice to her thoughts. It was not the estate and the land which filled her with happiness—it was that now she would never have to be parted from William. She would have to wait no longer.

William could finally be called her own.

"William," she said, feeling her excitement roll from her lips as she used his first name, "I am so very glad you have reconciled your debts and regained your estate." She reached up and brushed his hair, smiling as she memorized his cobalt-blue eyes, "I daresay you are noble enough to merit such a turn of events in your life."

He offered a thin smile and lifted his hand, cradling her face. He exhaled and bent his head down, as though to kiss her.

She looked down and then lifted her head, wearing a wry smile. "Oh, and one more thing," she watched his eyes open, quite taken from the moment. "The estate is all very well, Mr. Robertson, but you should know that I loved you just the same when you were a poor, struggling businessman. I believe you warned me once to not concern myself with your Robertson estate." Her eyes danced as she felt his arm around her. "To use your own words, I *think* I still love you."

William was quiet for just a moment. A genuine smile spread across his face as he looked at Christine with his most loving and tender eyes, slipping his other arm around her waist.

"Well I *know* I love you," he responded.

William continued to hold her close, tilting her chin toward him. "And how right you are, my dear. Our focus will never be on the money or the estate." He suddenly stepped back and folded his arms across his chest. "But I *would* like to tell your father, so that I may officially extend an engagement. Would you allow me?"

Christine nodded eagerly, keeping her gaze in his. He grasped her by the hands and knelt down.

"My dearest, kindest Christine, will you marry me and be mine forever?"

"Yes," she whispered.

She smiled at him, expecting tears from herself, but none came. Indescribable happiness encompassed every part of her as she looked into his deep-blue eyes.

He stood and pulled her in and lifted her chin as he had done just moments earlier. This time his head bowed, and tilted, coming toward her gently until her lips met his perfect mouth.

Christine had never before felt so completely whole. Nothing could describe the sheer joy and pleasure she felt at that moment.

The pair stood there holding each other for quite some time, until they noticed how low the sun had fallen in the sky. William then took Christine by the hand and led her back over the grass-covered hills to Wellington Estate, seeking Mr. Harrison directly.

The explanation took over an hour after dinner, Christine assuming William spared no detail in relaying the particulars to Mr. Harrison. After exchanging words, it was agreed upon that the marriage would take place on mid-summer's day.

Christine met Lord Stewart that night and found him to be a most agreeable old man, apparently much altered from his previous state in Scotland. A permanent suite was made for him at Wellington until he could obtain all of his possessions and move into one of the houses he owned in London. He reunited and rekindled the relationship with Mrs. Cooper that day and met his great-granddaughter within the next week, summoned permanently from her governess post.

Kathryn would now move to London and live with Lord Stewart, able to live as a woman of status instead of a governess or tutor. Although reluctant to leave the Harrisons, Mrs. Cooper gave up her post as cook to live with and take care of Lord Stewart.

Mr. Henry Robertson continued his robust social schedule, using his new property in town to facilitate mixing with as many ladies as possible at each ball, not yet securing any lasting connection. Meg was married a week before Christine, Mr. Grenville setting everything in order quickly. Mr. and Mrs. Grenville and Jacques would be but a day away from town, and Christine promised to visit them often. Miss Ivory Rusket still had Mr. Ternbridge at her side, though Ivory seemed determined to wait a few months more before truly determining her feelings toward her suitor.

The Harrison family had decided to hold Christine's wedding at Cassfield Manor. The night before their wedding, Christine and William sat on the balcony overlooking the shore. The air turned crisp, and William led Christine inside to her door, carrying a candle. It would be their last sleep ever apart.

He kissed her hand softly and said, "I cannot wait until I do not have to bid you good-night each evening."

She looked deeply into his eyes, their blue hue washing over her like a wave. Cassfield's tide had brought him to her. But unlike a tide, constantly changing, this steady gaze was now hers forever.

He smiled ruefully and touched one of her curls. His eyes wrinkled, teasing her. "I *think* I love you, Christine."

Such a sentiment was so like him, reminding her of the first time he declared his love to her. His eyes turned serious and deep as he drew her close. It was the way he looked at her then that meant more than any words could ever convey.

"And I *know* I love you," she replied as she fell into his embrace, confident that this selfless man, who always put others' needs above his own, was her match, and they had chosen each other forever.

ACKNOWLEDGMENTS

I suspect that most authors' book-writing journey starts with a love of reading. For me, that love was fostered from a very young age by my mother, Robin Rowley. I also am grateful to her being my literal in-house editor for most of the past twenty-five years. And thanks to my dad, Paul Rowley, who always supported me in everything I ever tried.

I must also thank Ms. Guanell, whose daily writing journal hooked me on imagining stories; Mrs. Landry, who taught me how to write creatively; and Ms. Creaser, for teaching me how to write quickly and write clearly. I wouldn't have known how to develop my craft without my writing group—MeLisa, Bekah, Jen, and Mara. Thanks for your cheerleading, expertise, support, and mentoring. I'm also grateful to my friends (you know who you are) whose personalities inspired aspects of some of my characters. A big thank you to many other friends and family members who read through drafts of my manuscript and edited with skill and honesty.

I'm deeply grateful for my husband, Daniel, who championed my writing and supported my creative outlet for the experience it provided me. And for reading, critiquing, and editing in a genre that is far from his favorite! I'm grateful to my sweet children for their love of good stories which helped me be more passionate about the written word. I'll always be appreciative as well for their silent support, sleeping soundly during many naps and nights.

I'm also extremely thankful to God for giving us all the ability to create. I feel He inspired me to write again and helped me find a way to tell my story.

ABOUT THE AUTHOR

From writing an award-winning tale about a dragon in third grade to regency romance written as an adult, Sarah McConkie has always had a passion for creating captivating stories. After graduating with a Bachelor's of Music from Brigham Young University, Sarah continued to endure years of singledom, looking for romance, and started a master's degree in literacy. While pursuing her master's, she finally found her true love and became a wife and eventually a mother. Using her years of experience in the single realm, a robust knowledge of regency classics, and a love of all things old-fashioned and proper, Sarah wrote her debut novel, *Love and Secrets at Cassfield Manor*. She now lives with her own Mr. Right and her three children and believes providing stimulating and moral stories promotes literacy in a world that needs more readers.

Scan to visit

sarahlmcconkie.com